don't tempt me

LORI FOSTER

don't tempt me

HQN™

ISBN-13: 978-0-373-80285-2

Don't Tempt Me

www.HQNBooks.com

Printed in U.S.A.

To Steven Hogel,
one of the funniest, sweetest, most caring and all around awesome people I know.
Thank you for everything you do, and for keeping things interesting.
I love you bunches and bunches!

1

DRIVING THE RENTED moving van was a heck of a lot harder than Honor Brown had counted on. Not since high school had she driven a stick shift. More than ten years later, she'd clearly lost the gift. Wincing as she ground the gears, she ignored her friend Lexie, who rode shotgun and was having a grand time at her expense.

After they bounced over yet another pothole, Lexie groaned. "I feel like we're killing this truck."

Maybe because they were.

While staring out the window to check out the new neighborhood, Lexie propped her naked feet on the dash and balanced a frosty can of cola on her midriff. "There are a lot of trees."

"I know. And they're so big."

"Throwing shade everywhere." She turned toward Honor. "You realize most of these houses look like a flashback to the sixties."

"It's the landscaping." And the cracked sidewalks and, yes, all those mature trees. "I'll have to redo my entire yard." Wrinkling her nose, she added, "It's mostly overgrown and pretty... messy." A grave understatement. The little patch of lawn in front of the house she'd bought held only weeds and dead bushes and debris. But who cared? She could buy shrubs someday, put in some flowers, maybe a bird fountain, too.

The backyard was bigger, she reminded herself. Though just as messy, it supposedly led to a wonderful creek. There were beautiful trees that were strong and healthy and only needed to be trimmed.

The most important thing was that she'd be on her own, and closer to her grandfather's facility. Since she visited him once a day, sometimes more often, the convenience would be a godsend.

"How is your grandfather?"

Bless Lexie for always reading her so easily. Honor showed her gratitude with a quick smile, but the smile was sad at best. "Every time I see him, he's a little worse. I just need to make sure he stays as comfortable as possible."

Lexie put a hand on her shoulder to show her commiseration. "I don't suppose the angry mob is helping much?"

Angry mob was one of Lexie's many derogatory terms for Honor's relatives. Given the general attitude of her two aunts, her cousin and sometimes her great-aunt, she wasn't far off the mark. "They're all busy, and upset with things, and—"

"You're a good person, Honor. You know that, right?"

And that was her code for *bullshit*. Honor sighed. "I try, but I swear, sometimes my patience isn't what it should be."

"Your patience is exceptional. They're just evil."

"Old," Honor corrected.

"*Hon-or,*" Lexie drawled in that chiding way she had that drew out the syllables of her name. "Stop defending them."

Was that what she'd been doing? Maybe. Mostly just to keep the peace, though. This was a momentous day and she wanted it to stay happy and upbeat, not get dragged down with worries and animosity.

They turned the corner on the quaint, older street and Honor could finally see the beautiful, wonderful, life-altering home she'd purchased thanks to the Ashwood, Ohio, Chamber of Commerce's new mission—to rehab the town of Clearbrook through initiatives around marketing, business attraction and retention efforts.

Supposedly they'd run off the crime element, cleaned up the streets and, luckily for her, offered special financing on run-down houses with the agreement that the owners would improve the property in a timely manner. She could hardly wait to get started.

Funds would now be limited for a while, but a lot of what needed to be done required time and energy more than cash. Somehow, in the middle of the craziness called her life, she'd manage to find some of both.

"Dear God," Lexie muttered, losing her amusement. Her feet dropped to the floor and she leaned forward as far as the seat belt would let her. "Please tell me that's not it."

"It is," Honor confirmed with pride. Sure, it was a little rough, the lawn overgrown, the landscaping obliterated. But now it was *hers*. Lexie might not see the possibilities—but Honor most definitely did. "All it needs is some TLC and love."

"Or maybe a…demolition?"

"Don't be dramatic." With a frown, Honor added, "I wanted you to be happy for me."

"I know, and I am. I just don't see why you always want to do things the hard way." Going quiet, Lexie drew in a breath and straightened her shoulders. "I'll help. With everything. No, don't argue. I can't claim I'm strong and I'll admit I've never remodeled anything. Honestly I've never held a hammer. But I'm here for you."

"Between dating and working and shopping, you mean?" Honor loved Lexie like a sister, but their social calendars, as well as their motivations, were as different as night and day.

As they neared the house, three men stepped out from the garage next door. They'd obviously been working. One held a motor of some sort while the other gestured toward it. The tallest nodded as he cleaned his hands on a towel.

"Oh, hey." Lexie perked up. "What's this? Man candy? Very *sexy* man candy." She rounded on Honor. "You've been holding out!"

Repeatedly glancing at them, Honor shook her head. Nope, no holding out. This was the first time she'd laid eyes on the men. Fact—because if she'd seen them, she sure as heck would have remembered.

"Oh, please, please, please," Lexie whispered. "Let them be single."

The guys looked up as the truck drew nearer.

Wiggling her fingers in a wave and grinning hugely, Lexie said, "Okay, so maybe Clearbrook has some appeal after all."

Flustered with all three men staring at her, Honor accidentally ran over the curb as she maneuvered the truck to the front of her house. Worse, she hit a garbage can and it clattered to the street with nerve-wracking noise.

"Oh, crap." The truck stopped with bone-jarring impact, and she sat there, stock-still, embarrassed and hoping beyond hope that the men went about their business and ignored her.

"Good going on killing the trash can," Lexie said with enthusiasm. "That got their attention."

"I don't want their attention," Honor groaned.

Laughing at her, Lexie said, "Relax. They were already looking."

What a way to make a first impression. Casting a glare at her friend, Honor said, "Shush it. And for heaven's sake, stop staring!"

"Too late." Lexie quickly fluffed her short pale blond hair and adjusted the V-neck of her shirt, tugging it a tad lower. "They're coming this way."

"Oh God." After a deep breath, Honor put the truck in Park, turned it off, and—okay, she needed one more breath. "Roll up your window. Pretend you don't see them. Maybe if we rush into the house real fast, they'll leave us alo—"

"Hello."

Cringing, Honor glanced toward Lexie—and found all three men peering into the truck at them. They were each so tall they had to duck down to see in. One guy wore a T-shirt, one a polo, and the other wore no shirt at all.

Combined they gave the impression of masculine curiosity, dark hair and beard shadow. Two of them grinned, and those grins had definite impact.

But the intense expression on the shirtless one about stole Honor's breath.

She blinked and stared, blinked and stared. Repeat.

The youngest of the three, the one in a T-shirt, laughed. "Busted. No sneaking off now."

"Colt," the unsmiling man said in a low, deep voice that teased over her nerve endings and made her heart race. "Pick up the can and spilled garbage, will you?"

Colt grinned. "Yes, sir." And off he went—with Lexie craning her neck to track him.

The smiling guy propped a shoulder against the side of the window frame and crossed his arms over his chest. With a warning in his tone, said, "He's seventeen."

"Who?" Lexie asked.

"My son." He nodded toward Colt. "Just so you know."

Jaw dropping, Lexie took another look. "No way. Does Clearbrook have testosterone in the water or something? He looks at least twenty-one."

Shrugging a thick shoulder, the guy said, "True enough."

Heat shot into Honor's cheeks. This situation just kept getting worse and worse. Not only had she taken out their can and been overheard conspiring to avoid them, but now Lexie gawked at an underage kid, never mind that the "kid" *did* look a whole lot older.

"As his dad," the man continued, "it keeps me on my toes."

"You sure you're his dad?" Lexie looked back and forth between both men. "Because he looks more like—"

"My brother," he interrupted. "I know. Jason got Dad's eyes, and so did Colt."

Brothers? Honor took another look—and caught Shirtless looking back. She swallowed.

"Bet your dad's a stud, too, huh?"

"Lexie!"

After winking at Honor, Colt's father met Lexie's gaze. "We all inherited his features."

True, Honor thought. Though the one talking appeared just under six feet, and Colt had to be at least six-three, they shared similar features and overall coloring. Only the eye color was different, with the father's eyes pale blue instead of the rich dark brown of his son and brother. The shape was the same though, and they each had ridiculously long, dreamy black lashes.

Without really thinking about it, Honor said, "You don't look old enough to be his dad."

He shrugged. "I was just out of high school. Call it a youthful indiscretion that I've never regretted."

Honor smiled, enjoying his pride in Colt—until she realized that his brother's eyes had narrowed, not with menace, but with new awareness as he stared at her mouth.

She couldn't recall the last time a man had looked at her like that. Might've been, oh…never.

It unnerved her and she started to squirm in her seat. These days she appeared more haggard than usual. Because of the move, she hadn't bothered with any makeup, not that she ever wore that much anyway. But she'd also stuck her hair in a sloppy ponytail, pulled on one of her oldest T-shirts and stepped into the jeans with holes in the knees. Lack of sleep and an overly busy schedule kept dark circles under her eyes.

She tried to concentrate on Colt's father, but couldn't. She glanced at his brother again, and her gaze got caught in his.

LORI FOSTER

Something, challenge or maybe interest, kicked up the corner of his mouth in a nearly indiscernible way. But she saw it.

Shoot, she *felt* it.

Breathless, Honor forced herself to look at Colt's dad. "So, um, you have a beautiful home. I noticed it when I was here before with my Realtor."

Snorting as if that was somehow ridiculous, he said, "It's not mine. Jason owns it."

"Do tell," Lexie said.

"I'm Hogan Guthrie. Jason is my overly serious brother."

Hogan the blue-eyed dad, Colt the mature-looking son and Jason…the far-too-hot shirtless hunk. As she committed the names to memory, Honor glanced at each of them, but repeatedly got drawn back to Jason.

The sun highlighted the cut of his cheekbones, the straight line of his nose and across those sleek, hard shoulders. Why didn't he put on a shirt? She couldn't quite keep her gaze from his chest, noting he had just the right amount of dark chest hair going from one well-defined pec to the other, then bisecting his body downward…

It wouldn't kill the man to pull up his well-worn jeans, either. Being healthy and female and, okay, more than a little sex starved, she automatically tracked the treasure trail leading down his abdomen to inside those low-slung jeans…

"Hogan and Colt live here, too," Jason said while silently accepting her scrutiny.

Busted again. She cleared her throat and got her eyes to focus back on his face. "I see." To Hogan, she asked, "You and your wife are in the neighborhood?"

Pushing away from the truck, Hogan said, "Colt's mother is gone."

That left her floundering. Did he mean…*dead*? Should she give condolences?

Or maybe he meant she'd moved away.

"For now," Hogan continued, "we live with Jason."

Oh. *With* him. In the same house.

All three of them—*right next door to her.*

Saving her from the awkward silence, Lexie took over. "I'm Lexie Perkins, and the new homeowner here is Honor Brown." Then to Jason, she added, "You're going to make her faint if you don't let up."

"Lexie!" Horrified, Honor felt so much heat in her face it nearly singed her. She'd gag her friend if she didn't stop with the outrageous behavior.

Jason cocked a brow but didn't look away.

Opening her door and getting out, Honor circled the back of the big truck instead of the front, because it gave her a few seconds more to compose herself.

Her neighbor's house was to her right, twice the size of the one she'd just bought and with a well-trimmed yard, a big front porch and a massive garage in the back. Through open barn doors she saw a lot of tools and some sort of workbench.

Their driveways ran alongside each other, hers to the right of her house, his to the left of his, with only about fifteen feet separating them. His was concrete, hers gravel. His led to the garage and hers led to…weeds and refuse.

He must hate having such a disreputable mess next to his very nice home. She'd have her work cut out for her, but she decided she'd make repairs to the outside first.

Knowing she'd stalled too long, Honor emerged to the other side of the truck where both men and Lexie chatted about something.

With his attention finally off her, Honor felt free to look him over in more detail. While Hogan and Colt both had their dark hair neatly trimmed, Jason's was a little too long and unruly, the wavy ends flipping in all directions as if he'd combed it only with fingers, and not any time recently. Pronounced beard shadow made her think he hadn't shaved for a few days. When he smiled at something Lexie said, his teeth looked incredibly white against his tanned face. Little lines fanned out from the corners of his eyes.

He wasn't muscle bound like a bodybuilder, but strength showed in his wide shoulders, furry chest and flat abdomen. He was a little sweaty, and so attractive she felt warmer just looking at him.

She hadn't been following the conversation, so it took her off guard when they all turned to her.

"I'm so sorry about your can," Honor blurted.

He stared down at her, first at her eyes, then at her mouth. "It survived."

Getting closer to the men emphasized the differences in their sizes. At five-six, Honor was a whole lot shorter than all of them. "I can buy you a new one." Although, truth be told, she was pretty tapped at the moment. Hopefully he wouldn't want it replaced today.

"It's a decade old and has been beat up before."

"Then I should at least help Colt pick up—"

"He's done," Hogan told her. "Now he's just texting friends."

"Girlfriends, I bet," Lexie said.

But Hogan shook his head. "He misses our old neighborhood. He hasn't quite settled in here yet."

Honor looked and sure enough, Colt stood beside the can, his thumbs working over a cell phone.

Jason held out a hand. "So we're neighbors?"

Her toes curled in her shoes and her pulse fluttered. Trying to hide her reaction at the prospect of touching him, she smiled. "Seems so."

His large, work-rough hand took her much smaller one, and she froze.

Good grief, you'd think I'd never been touched before.

With her voice too high, Honor asked, "Will I be meeting your wife?"

"Not married." He released her slowly. "You?"

"We're both single," Lexie offered fast.

Jason glanced at the truck with yet another frown. "You're both moving in?"

"Just me." New enthusiasm bubbled up. And her palm still tingled from his touch. "Lexie insisted on coming along to help with the heavy things."

Dubious, both he and Hogan glanced at Lexie.

"I'm having second thoughts," Lexie said. "I mean…is that place habitable?"

"I'd say no," Jason answered, his fingers rubbing the whiskers on his jaw. "But here you are." He stepped around Honor and opened the back of the truck to see her small sofa and chairs, little dinette set, bedroom furniture, plants and a whole lot of boxes.

Behind him, Hogan laughed. "So you two were going to unload all this?"

Lexie elbowed her way past him. "Why not? We got it in there."

A partial truth. She and Lexie had loaded all the boxes, but her old roommates had supplied their boyfriends to get the heavier stuff inside. They'd tired of her constant late-night runs and were probably happy to see her go. Lending a hand only helped speed up the process.

"No way," Colt said as he rejoined them. "You're both so little."

"I have a furniture dolly." Honor pointed at the folding metal moving contraption in the corner of the truck that she had hoped would make it easier to get everything unloaded. "The truck rental place recommended it, and it really did come in handy." When moving the boxes.

Hands on his hips, Jason studied everything. "The dolly won't help you with a couch."

"We could do it," Colt said.

Incredibly he sounded hopeful. But Honor had just met them all. No way could she ask for their help and she didn't want Colt putting his uncle on the spot. "It's fine, really." Having no real idea, she swore, "We can get it all, no problem."

Ignoring her protests, Jason squinted from the sun and asked Colt, "You didn't make plans?"

"With who? I don't know anyone here."

Honor felt for the young man. She'd been uprooted once herself, and it had sucked. "How long have you lived here?"

"About a month." He held his arms out wide. "But the only people around are ancient."

"You'll meet younger people when school starts." Hogan viewed the contents of the truck with a critical eye. "We were supposed to be helping your uncle with that—"

Jason cut him off, saying, "I need to buy a new part anyway." His gaze went from the truck to the front of her house. "Before we can get started, though, we need to clear a path."

"No, really," Honor tried again, horrified by the idea of imposing on them. "I don't need—"

"The mower won't make it." Colt gave her yard quick scrutiny. "But I could break out the Bush Hog."

Hogan agreed. "Wouldn't take too long to clear the front. The back would be a job, though."

"Save it for another day," Jason said. "I doubt that back door opens anyway."

As the three men talked about a game plan, Honor turned to stare helplessly at Lexie.

Her friend thrust a fist in the air. "Take-charge men," she whispered. "Lucky you."

"I can't—"

"Yes," Lexie insisted. "You can."

Overwhelmed, Honor shook her head and, raising her voice to be heard, addressed the men. "Really, this is *not* necessary."

"We don't mind," Colt told her, and he headed off for the garage.

Apparently to get the Bush Hog...whatever that was.

"Got a key?" Hogan rubbed his hands together. "Let's see what we're dealing with."

Lexie leaned in close to whisper, "One step at a time, remember? Trust me on this."

Honor wanted to resist. First impressions mattered, and theirs would be that she couldn't handle her own move. They were strangers, and they owed her nothing.

But Lexie was excited for the help, and Colt seemed so anxious to dig in. But Jason... Her gaze skipped to him and she found his expression now masked, impossible to read.

His words, though, were pretty plain.

He held out a hand, palm up, for the key. "The sooner we get started, the sooner we can be done."

Within an hour they had the front yard cleared, with a path created in the backyard so she could at least get to her driveway. Not that it would matter if he couldn't get that warped door repaired, but she'd been resistant enough that he didn't want to push things. Honor Brown already looked plenty confused by their willingness to pitch in.

Confused, and somehow worried.

Colt could work on the rest of the yard later. Once the worst of it was thinned out, she might be able to keep it in shape with a regular mower.

Only he hadn't seen one in her truck.

Everything else had been in there, though. Furniture, clothes, dishware and a few decorations.

She was average height for a woman, slight of build, but she worked tirelessly beside them, insisting on carrying in boxes that strained her shoulders despite the fact that he, Hogan or Colt could have carried three without a problem.

Curious behavior.

The mid-June day was sunny and hot and as they worked, sweat beaded on her smooth cheeks, and little wisps of her honey-blond hair clung to her temples and the nape of her neck.

He couldn't help noticing that on her, the overheated look was sexy as hell. He wasn't a man obsessed with sex 24/7, but seeing her now, all warm and dewy, especially with the satisfied way she smiled while working...well, hell, he was only human and he couldn't help that his thoughts veered to carnal activities—the best way he knew to work up a sweat.

In many ways, Honor Brown seemed naive and innocent. But there was something about her determination that obliterated that impression. He had the feeling that when necessary, she could hold her own. For sure whenever one of them tried to relieve her of a load, her big brown eyes turned defiant.

That, too, was somehow a turn-on.

Her slightly taller, blonder, much bolder friend, Lexie, showed she had more sense by staying inside and unpacking what they carried in.

It surprised Jason when he saw the inside of the place. It was still a pit, but a much cleaner pit than the last time he'd seen it a few months ago. Cobwebs, dead bugs, broken furniture and dirt were now gone. Apparently Honor had been over one day last week to scrub it out. How he'd missed her, he had no idea. Must've been when he and Colt had gone off fishing, and Hogan was meeting with his lawyer.

By dinnertime they had everything unloaded and most of the big items reassembled and situated, including mismatched bedroom pieces, a stack washer and dryer and shelving in the small living room.

Her couch, which had been the first thing put in the truck so was the last thing out, still had a secondhand sale tag on it. So she'd bought used furniture? Didn't matter to him—except that she was clearly stretching her budget, and given the costs inherent in buying a rehab house, that didn't bode well for anyone.

The fact that she was so attractive didn't help much, either.

As he and Hogan moved the couch in front of a clean but curtainless window, Jason looked to the kitchen, where he could just see Honor on tiptoe unloading a variety of dishes into a cabinet. Her profile was even more mouthwatering than the head-on view.

Snug, faded jeans hugged a perfectly plump ass. Her stretched-out posture showed the rise of her breasts and the dip of her waist. With every movement she made, her ponytail bounced.

Honor Brown was petite without being skinny, stacked without being flagrant about it and a true natural beauty, though she seemed unaware. Her tawny-blond hair almost exactly matched her golden-brown eyes, eyes shades lighter than his. Eyes that drew him in, especially when she looked at him with a mix of curiosity and awareness.

Several times he'd seen her yawn, but not once had she slowed down. The way she moved, how she blushed...her smile. He liked it all. He liked her. Too much.

She definitely shouldn't be here.

She must have felt him looking—*again*—because she went still, then glanced his way. For a second their gazes held before, once more, she looked him over. And damn, he liked that, too. The girl had a hungry way of devouring him with those whiskey-colored eyes.

Hogan stepped between them as he set out a lamp, unwrapped a decorative dish and tossed a throw pillow onto the couch.

That broke the spell. "Oh, you don't have to do that." Setting aside a plate and hurrying into her small living room, Honor said, "Just leave everything and I'll arrange it later."

"We're here," Hogan told her, carrying a box of books to a squat bookcase. "Might as well get it set up where you want it."

Fluttering around, fretting, she said, "Oh, but...you guys have already done so much and it's getting late and honestly I can get this all done myself, so—"

"I'm only here temporarily," Hogan explained. "But for now, we're neighbors. Besides, we didn't have anything else to do today."

"And I brought food," Colt said as he walked back in the front door with two boxes of pizza and a twelve-pack of Coke.

Honor's shoulders slumped. "I've worked you all through dinnertime."

That made Colt laugh. "Pretty sure we insisted."

"They did." Eyeing the pizzas with greed, Lexie said, "Those are mighty big pies."

"Yes, ma'am. Enough for all of us."

"You're a good boy, Colt."

The banter between Lexie and Colt only seemed to rattle Honor more. She made a beeline for her purse on the kitchen table. "I'll pay you for it. How much—"

"No," Jason said before Colt or Hogan could speak. The firm refusal stopped her in her tracks.

Softening things, his brother explained, "Jason gets a deal because the pizza girl is hung up on him."

Honor swiveled around and stared. "Pizza girl?"

"True story," Colt said. "But I'd call her a woman, not a girl."

"Only because she's too old for you." Hogan said to the ladies, "She's early twenties, and real cute."

Jason rolled his eyes. The pizza girl—emphasis on *girl*—was pretty enough, but he wasn't interested. She might be too old for Colt, but she was definitely too young for him. "Everyone's hungry, so let's eat."

Honor looked around her house. "It was super nice of you to go get food—"

"Because I'm *starved*," Lexie said.

"—but there's nowhere here to sit, much less eat."

Colt hitched his chin toward the back of the house. "I cleared a path for you over to our backyard. We have a picnic table. Let's go there."

She stared at Colt, wanting to refuse but unsure how to deny a seventeen-year-old boy. Using her wrist to brush bangs out of her eyes, she waffled. "But—"

"No buts," Hogan told her. "You don't want to be unneighborly, do you?"

Jason didn't mind Colt urging her, but what was Hogan's endgame? "You guys go on. Get out some paper plates and stuff. I'll help her finish in the kitchen and we'll be right over."

After a long speculative look, Hogan's mouth lifted in a sly grin. "Sure." Then to Lexie, "You coming?"

Lexie looked to Honor. "Do you mind? Or was there something else I could do?"

Immediately Honor shooed her away. "Go, sit. I'll only be five minutes." Unfortunately, the second the others were gone, she tried to shoo him away, too. "Really, Jason, I've got it. There isn't that much more to do."

Jason took in all the still-full boxes, the stacked kitchen, and shook his head. "Looks like a lot to me."

"Everything I need right away is unpacked. I'll get my bed together and then do the rest of it little by little. I promise, it won't be a problem."

He studied her and saw her cheeks go warm again. The woman blushed far too easily. Walking past her without a word, he entered the kitchen and picked up where she'd left off.

And he didn't have to go on tiptoe to do it.

From behind him, she said low, "This is ridiculous."

"What's that?" He didn't pause in unloading plates to the bottom shelf where she could better reach them, and putting serving bowls and platters toward the top.

"I don't even know you people."

Over his shoulder, he took in her disgruntled and confused expression. "Around here, neighbors help neighbors. When Sullivan Dean moved in across the street, we did the same thing. Few months ago Nathan Hawley moved in on the other side of me, and we lent a hand." He shrugged, broke down the now empty box and put it on the stack of cardboard by the back door.

"I haven't met them yet."

"You will." And though it shouldn't, that bothered him. Both Sullivan and Nathan were single. Neither seemed to be on the prowl, but with a lady like Honor, who knew? "Clearbrook has a lot of community stuff. Volleyball, barbecues, that sort of thing. You'll meet everyone in no time."

Edging back into the kitchen but keeping some distance between them, she started folding dishrags into a drawer. "You've had a lot of people moving in?"

"Houses around here stayed empty until the city decided to revamp things."

"Are you new to the neighborhood?"

"Grew up here, actually." He found another empty box, and another after that, breaking each one down so the cardboard made a nice flat stack. "The house used to be our dad's. When the area deteriorated, he saw no reason to keep maintaining the property. About eight years ago he decided he'd enjoy Florida, so I bought it from him."

"Wow. You must've been pretty young."

"Twenty-four. Old enough to know what I wanted." He'd always loved the house and the memories that came with it. Before his mom died, it was a home. After that...both his dad and the house fell apart. "It needed some work, so I got a good deal, and Dad got the cash he needed to relocate." These days, his father rarely visited any memories that reminded him of his deceased wife—including his sons and grandson.

"Win-win," Honor said.

"Right." Leaning back on the counter, he watched her close one drawer, then begin filling another with place mats, oven mitts and such. "So...no man in your life to help you get moved in?" Her friend Lexie had already announced neither of them was married, but a woman Honor's age, looking the way she looked, surely had a guy or two hanging around.

As if the question threw her, she paused, searched for what to say and in the end just shook her head.

Unbelievable. Was that a recent occurrence? A divorce, or a breakup of another kind? Or maybe she was more like the other blonde, Lexie, than he'd first thought. "What about a brother? Your dad?"

She concentrated on the drawer. "No."

That didn't feel right. "No one but your friend Lexie?"

Her face flushed, but this time it was with uncertainty. "Why do you ask?"

She thought he was being nosy. Or maybe she thought he was hitting on her.

The truth was probably a mix of both. "You being here alone...it's not a great idea."

Like a challenge, she said, "I already had new locks put on the doors."

His mouth quirked, but he didn't want her to think he was laughing at her, so he tipped up his chin, scratched the beard stubble underneath and decided on a few facts. "Last week, two blocks from here, some punks broke into an older man's house. Beat him up, robbed him. Less than a month before that a woman got jumped in her own front yard, middle of the day. Luckily Nathan was around and he stopped them before she was seriously hurt."

"Nathan, your neighbor?"

That was the part she found interesting? "Yeah, he's the sheriff." Continuing, he told her, "In the past two months people around here have had their cars jacked, been robbed, assaulted—"

"Your neighbor—*our* neighbor—is the sheriff?"

Jason stared at her. "You're not listening to the important part."

She waved a hand. "I get it. There are still some criminal activities. But the area is on the upswing, right? They're fixing up the park, new businesses are moving in and they're even going to reopen the old neighborhood pool—"

"Which is right across from a cemetery."

That slowed her down, but only for a heartbeat. "That's just because the cemetery expanded, right? And now it'd be too expensive to move the pool. I'm sure it won't bother most people. Definitely won't bother me."

She'd done her research. Or maybe Realtors had their pitches down. "The key point here is that it's a work in progress. They're still fixing up the park, too many businesses are pending and the pool probably won't be ready until mid-July, if then." He took a step closer. "Right now, this week, the area is not safe for a woman alone."

Agitated, she glared at him. "So I should what? Not stay in my own house? My *first* house? Should I put it right back on the market? Lose the opportunity of a lifetime?" She took a step closer, too. "Rhetorical questions, because I can assure you, I'm here to stay."

Jason stared at her earnest face, taking in each appealing feature. On top of soulful eyes, a lush mouth and a fine body, she had guts. And damn it, he liked that, too. "Get a dog. And a shotgun." He reached into his back pocket, pulled out his wallet, then found a business card. "And if anything spooks you, anything at all, call."

"I'm not helpless. I can take care of myself."

She said that so defiantly that he almost smiled. "Sure. But if you just need a hand with something, any heavy lifting, we're right next door."

"Muscle for hire?"

The smile cracked, and from that came a laugh. "You do seem to pick and choose what you hear and don't hear."

She looked at his mouth, and sighed. "I heard all of it. I'll consider the dog once I have the yard ready. I don't know enough about guns to get one."

"I imagine Nathan could teach you."

"Three guys right next door, and a sheriff next door to them. How much safer could it get?"

She was cute when she teased. Maybe he should tell her about Sullivan across the street. Talk about a badass…but no. He wasn't going to do Sullivan's work for him.

"The other side of your property butts up to woods. No lights. Wild animals."

She scoffed. "Wild animals, huh?"

"Middle of the night, when you hear noises you don't recognize, or maybe even gunfire nearby, no one is going to seem close enough."

"Now you're just trying to scare me."

True. She needed to stay alert. Because he watched her, he could almost see her thinking as she put the business card on the refrigerator with a flower-shaped magnet. She turned pensive, too quiet.

"I mean it," he said, drawing her out again. "If you need anything—"

"No." All too serious, she laced her fingers together and looked up at him. "You're really nice. I mean…*really* nice. All of you are. And I appreciate it. What we got done today would have taken me at least a week on my own. I'd been hopeful of just getting unloaded and getting my bed together so I'd have a place to sleep tonight."

His thoughts veered in directions that they shouldn't, thoughts that included her and a bed. Fewer clothes. Less talk.

"Before buying the house, I lived with roommates. Four of us in a small apartment. And before that I lived with a relative."

Relative—not parents? He wondered about that, but then she continued explaining.

"I'm happy to be on my own. You don't have to worry that

LORI FOSTER

I'll impose on you, not for any reason." She rocked to her heels a little, her fingers laced tightly, looking uncertain, self-conscious. "I'm grateful for the offer of a helping hand, and as reassuring as it is to know there's backup so close by, I want to do this, the rest of it, on my own. It's important to me."

Yeah, it had been important to him, too, so he understood. But understanding and believing she could do it were two different things. She lacked muscles, yet much of what needed to be done would be labor intensive, work that included heavy lifting, pulling and endurance. Given her clumsiness with the dolly, he doubted she knew her way around the toolshed. What her house needed would require more than a hammer or a screwdriver.

To be sure, he asked, "You have experience with remodeling?"

"No. But I'm not dumb. I can read instructions."

Instructions wouldn't really cut it, but rather than belabor the point, he merely nodded. "Let's go eat." He'd be glad to get that part of it over with. Whether his brother or nephew realized it, Honor Brown was going to be trouble. With her next door, their peaceful bachelor existence would soon be shot to hell.

Honor bit her lip. Her gaze dipped down to his chest, then shot back to his face. Her eyes were big and innocent when she said, "Only if you put on a shirt. Because otherwise, I just can't do it."

Jason sighed. And so it began.

2

HONOR WASN'T USED to eating with three men. It astounded her how fast the pizza got devoured. But then, she'd pretty much inhaled her own slice, too. Working up a hunger, it seemed, overshadowed other concerns—like feeling self-conscious and knowing she was an intruder despite their efforts to put her at ease.

They all chatted easily, except for Jason, who seemed introspective. He'd gone from staring to teasing, to warning, and now quiet.

At first she'd worried that she might have offended him. But how? Not by asking that he wear a shirt, because that was a request he'd ignored.

The man was still half-naked.

And it couldn't have been from accepting his help, because he was the one who'd bullied his way in and insisted on…being wonderful.

She rubbed at her temples. When she'd thought about neighbors, she never imagined any like these.

"You okay?" Colt asked.

A fast smile, meant to reassure him, only amplified the headache. "Yes. Just a little tired."

"She works too much." Lexie shoulder-bumped her. "I've

tried to get her to play a little, too, but she's the original party pooper."

Lexie, at least, seemed right at home. But then she always did. Confident, beautiful and fun—that described Honor's best friend.

They were polar opposites.

As if she'd known the guys forever, Lexie had heckled Hogan, teased Colt and praised Jason. She also repeatedly put her head back and drew in deep breaths, closing her eyes as she did so. With the scents of freshly mowed lawn, earth, flowers and trees all around them, Honor understood her reaction. Jason's backyard was a half acre, same as hers. But while hers was nearly impassable with weeds, his was park perfect.

A gigantic elm kept them shaded, and with the help of an occasional gentle breeze, the summer day became more comfortable. Honor glanced around at the neatly mulched flower beds, the velvet green grass and the well-maintained outdoor furniture. His garage was spectacular, matching his house. Every so often she caught the faint scent of oil, gasoline and sawdust.

She also smelled sun-warmed, hardworking male. Not at all unpleasant.

"Where do you work?" Colt asked.

"She's a stylist," Lexie offered. With a nod at Jason, she said, "Honor could do all sorts of amazing things with your hair."

Honor choked on her last drink of Coke.

Unaffected, Jason ran a hand through the dark waves. "I have a barber but don't make it there as often as I should."

"He's always working," Colt said. "He's usually out there in the garage before Dad and I even get out of bed."

"Good thing messy looks so sexy on him, then, huh?"

Colt laughed. "If you say so."

"I do." Lexie half turned to face the garage. "You guys have a lot of vehicles."

"The blue truck is mine," Colt told her. "Dad drives the motorcycle. Or when it rains, he takes the Escort. Uncle Jason has his own truck, the red newer one, and the gray SUV. The flat-bed truck he uses for deliveries."

Wow. Honor glanced over and saw that the two-story garage also housed a fishing boat on a trailer and another, older truck parked front and center.

"Who drives that one?" Lexie asked.

With something close to hero worship, Colt said, "Uncle Jason was hired to work on it."

"Hired?"

"Yeah, that's what he does. He fixes things. He's really good, too. All these old houses? They're always needing something repaired and usually Uncle Jason can do it. Everyone around here hires him for stuff."

"Sounds like it keeps him busy."

Colt snorted. "Yeah, sometimes too busy."

"I don't mind." Jason's gaze cut to Honor, and his voice deepened. "I enjoy working with my hands."

Honor felt like he'd just stroked her. She caught her breath, shifted in her seat and tried to think of something to say.

Clearly tickled, Lexie looked back and forth between them. "So you're a handyman?"

Again, Colt bragged. "More like a contractor. He can build things from the ground up, including the plumbing and electrical. Or make stuff like custom gates or stylized shutters, or repair just about anything."

"Nice," Lexie praised.

"He's a jack-of-all-trades." Hogan toasted Jason with his Coke. "Whatever's broke, Jason can fix it."

Jason gave him a long look. "Maybe not everything."

"Right. Can't fix big brothers, can you?"

Tipping his head slightly back, as if he'd taken that on the chin, Jason replied, "I only have one older brother, and far as I'm concerned, he's not broken."

Colt went silent, and God, Honor felt for him. Too many times she, too, had been caught up in the middle of family squabbles.

"So, with the truck," Lexie said, interrupting the heavy tension, "are you doing engine or body work?"

Before Jason could answer, Hogan said, "Why are you so curious, anyway?"

Lexie leveled him with a direct stare. "I was making conversation."

With a sound halfway between a laugh and a groan, Hogan sat forward. "We already covered that he can do anything."

"*Anything* is a big word. I mean, can he get the stick out of your butt? Because seriously, you're being a pill."

Honor frantically tried to think of a way to hedge the impending storm. Lexie wasn't reserved. If Hogan chose to be snarky, she wouldn't hesitate to give back tenfold. Worse, she might well drag Honor into it.

"It's a fascinating business," Lexie said, "though apparently you don't think so?"

"I'm proud of my brother."

"Yes," Lexie quipped, her tone dry. "That was so obvious."

Taken off guard, Hogan eyed her.

"But then, who wouldn't be proud of a handsome, accomplished, well-mannered man?" Lexie smiled with menace. "Speaking of that, I'm a fashion buyer for a boutique. If you ever want to step up your game, I could make some suggestions. And maybe Honor could update your hairstyle. You have the potential to be *almost* as hot as your brother."

Hogan's eyes flared, then narrowed.

"Lighten up." Jason clapped him on the shoulder. "And, Lexie, thanks, but honestly Hogan already has more dates than he can handle."

"Now, that is fascinating," Lexie said.

"He does both," Colt cut in, clearly not anxious to talk about his father being out on the market. "Uncle Jason, I mean. You asked about the truck?"

Lexie gave Colt a genuine smile. "So I did."

"He does body and engine work. But this time Uncle Jason's just tricking it out some."

Honor watched the back-and-forth conversation, noting the indulgent way Jason looked at his nephew, while also feeling the growing tension from Hogan. But why?

The quiet smothered her, especially with the palpable acrimony now flowing between Hogan and Lexie. After clearing her throat, Honor asked, "Is that what we interrupted? You were working on the truck?"

Jason shook his head. "Tractor." He nodded toward the side of the garage. "The owner of the truck is making up his mind between two options I gave him. Today I was repairing the tractor, but it needs a part I won't have until tomorrow. I'm at a standstill on both projects, so you didn't really interrupt. I was already done for the day."

Hogan ran a hand over his face, popped his neck and finally worked up a smile. "He built the garage a few years back."

"You helped," Jason reminded him.

"By help, he means I followed directions. No idea where Jason got the knack, because our dad wasn't the handy sort. But if there's an upside to us staying with him right now, it's that he's teaching Colt."

"And Colt does appear to have the knack," Jason added.

Both she and Lexie looked at the garage with new eyes. Wow. Just...wow.

Honor said, "It's unlike any garage I've ever seen."

"You should see the shed he did for Sullivan," Colt bragged. "And the gazebo for Nathan."

"Sullivan and Nathan?" Lexie perked up with interest.

"Other neighbors," Honor said before Lexie could get started.

She pushed to her feet while saying, "This was really wonderful. Thank you again, all of you."

When she started to pick up their paper plates, Colt took over. "I got it."

Unbelievable. She'd never known such a polite young man. "Are you sure?"

He grinned, looking like a younger version of his uncle. "Positive. It all just goes to the can." He gathered up everything and walked off.

Honor turned to Hogan. "You did an amazing job with him."

"Thanks. He's always been an easy kid. Smart, friendly and self-motivated."

Again, Honor wondered about Colt's mother. Had she taken a hand in molding such an impressive young man?

Hogan said, "I need to take off now, too."

"Big date?" The way Lexie asked that, it was clear to one and all she didn't expect it to be.

"Actually," Hogan said, "yes."

In an effort to stem new hostilities, Honor stepped in front of her friend. "I hope we didn't hold you up."

"Nope. I have a few minutes yet." His frown moved past Honor to Lexie. "Guess I need to go change, though."

Laughing, Lexie asked, "Need help?"

His dark expression morphed into a reluctant grin. "I think I've got it covered."

She nodded while yawning. "I need to get going, too."

"Gotta catch up on your beauty sleep?"

Honor almost groaned...until Lexie laughed again.

"Good one," she said, and then she held up her palm, leaving Hogan no choice but to high-five her. To Jason, she teased, "The differences aren't just in looks, I take it."

Jason lifted a brow. "No, they aren't."

Without comment, Hogan headed off for the house.

"Well." Honor watched everyone depart. Hogan went into

the house from the back door. Lexie headed off to the rental truck. And Cody hadn't returned from taking away their trash.

She and Jason were alone and with every fiber of her being, she felt it. Hoping not to be too obvious, she took a step back, then another. "I should get going, too. I need to drop off the truck tonight so I can get my car back. After I run Lexie home, I need to stop at the grocery. It's going to take me a few hours to get back here, and I still have to get things set up for the morning."

"What kind of things?"

"Alarm clock, coffee and I have to unpack enough clothes to get ready for work in the morning."

He had been looking down at the ground as they walked to the curb, but now his head lifted and he stared at her. "You have to work tomorrow?"

"Yes." But it wasn't a matter of having to. "I'll be taking all the hours I can get for a while. There are so many things I want to do to the house, but it all takes funds." Funds she didn't have. What money she'd saved would go to dire necessities, so overtime helped to pay for the extras she wanted.

"You have to be tired."

"A little." She rolled her aching shoulders, but resisted the long stretch. "I'm both excited and exhausted and I don't know if I'd be able to sleep in anyway."

"Excited?"

There were a hundred different reasons for her excitement, and one of those reasons was standing before her. Jason Guthrie was about the sexiest man she'd ever met. His careless hair, strong features, dark eyes and that body… Yup. The body definitely factored in.

But she also liked his intense focus, the way he smiled with pleasure at his nephew and his up-front honesty. That honesty had stung a little, since he clearly felt she was out of her league.

LORI FOSTER

Then again, he'd pitched in and done what he could to make her move-in easier.

How could she not admire him?

Naturally she wouldn't say any of that to him, so instead she shared other thoughts that would hopefully reaffirm for him that she was here to stay. "The move, the house—now that it's officially mine and I'm here, there are a million things running through my mind. What to do first, how much money I'll need, how to do it and when to do it." Forgetting her reserve, she whispered, "Tonight, I might just dance around and enjoy it all."

"Yeah? Since you don't have curtains yet, that could be interesting."

Heat rushed into her face. "*After* I get the windows covered, then I'll dance."

Amusement curled his mouth. "Spoilsport."

Their shoulders touched, electrifying Honor. She took a step to the side, ensuring that it wouldn't happen again. *Remember that he wants you gone. Remember that he wants you gone. Remember...*

"I get it," Jason said. "First big night in your own place." Lifting a brow, he added, "And yeah, curtains might not be a bad idea. Or at least tack up a sheet or something."

Maybe, Honor thought, he didn't dislike her as a neighbor as much as she'd assumed.

Stopping in the side yard, well out of range of everyone else, Honor looked up at him. Way up because he was so much taller than her.

He stopped, too, his expression attentive.

She shouldn't ask, but she had to. "When we first met...when I hit your trash can?"

"I told you, no big deal."

"I know, but...is that why you kept staring at me?"

Those gorgeous dark eyes caressed her face. He glanced toward Colt, then over to watch Lexie climb into the passenger seat of the truck.

don't tempt me

Finally his gaze came back to hers, and the impact took her breath.

"For one thing," he said, low, "you're attractive."

Without thinking about it, Honor smoothed her ponytail and tucked a few loose tendrils behind her ears. "Um, thank you. But I'm such a mess today."

His gaze warmed even more. "Messy and a mess are two very different things."

That deep voice made her pulse race. She was so unused to compliments from men she wasn't sure how to respond, so she just nodded and said, "Okay."

A fleeting smile teased his mouth before he grew somber. "I also recognize trouble when I see it."

She tucked in her chin. "Trouble?"

"You."

"*Me?*" The question emerged as a squeak.

"You don't fit the mold, Honor Brown. Not even close."

A rush of umbrage helped to steady her voice. "What's that supposed to mean?"

"A certain type of person moves here. Not just to the area, but to this particular block. Mostly single men who can handle themselves. Men with some contractor skills, with time and ability to do the repairs needed. What we don't generally see are young women—"

"I'm twenty-nine!"

"—who are completely alone, setting up house here."

It hurt to know he was right, that for all intents and purposes, she was alone now. She had Lexie, but that wasn't the same as a significant other, or family who cared.

"You're in over your head," he continued. "The work that needs to be done would be daunting for a man, but for a woman? Especially a woman like you?"

Sexy—and sexist. She firmed her spine. "Like me?"

"Small," he explained. "Soft."

"I'm not."

"You most definitely are. Playing house is all well and good—"

"I'm not *playing*." She was dead serious about it, all of it. She had to be.

"—but it'll take more than that to make it work. A hell of a lot more."

Honor huffed, then deflated with the truth of her situation. "Well, this sucks."

He hesitated, but finally asked, "What does?"

Putting her nose in the air, she stared into his beautiful brown eyes. "I haven't even finished moving in, and already I dislike my neighbor."

On that parting remark, she turned and strode away. But her heart was thumping and her hands felt clammy and her stomach hurt.

She was never that rude, especially when she knew someone acted out of concern. *What in the world got into me?*

Right before she reached the truck, she glanced over her shoulder and saw Jason still standing there, hands on his hips, that laserlike gaze boring into her.

Damn it. She turned to fully face him. "Jason?"

His chin notched up in query.

"I apologize. I didn't mean it." Immediately she felt better—even with Lexie now laughing at her.

Jason's hands fell to his sides and he dropped his head forward. She saw his shoulders moving.

Laughing? She wasn't sure.

But she smiled and started to turn away again.

"Honor."

She peeked at him and found his hands were back on his hips.

"You're still trouble, no doubt about it. But if you need anything, let me know."

Sure. When hell froze over. She smiled sweetly, waved and finally got in the truck.

More than ever, she was determined to do it all on her own. In the process she'd be nice to her caring, helpful, *gorgeous* neighbor—and she'd absolutely prove him wrong.

A week later, in the middle of painting her small bathroom a cheery yellow, Honor's cell phone rang. Since she didn't have the luxury of ever ignoring a call, she always kept the phone on her.

Juggling things, she dug it from the pocket of her sloppy pajama pants, saw it was Lexie and put it on speaker so she could leave it on the sink. "Hey, Lex."

"Dare I hope you're breathless for a good reason?"

"Painting."

Lexie blew a loud raspberry into the phone. "Not a good reason at all, damn it."

Honor shook her head. Lexie, more than anyone else, knew just how seldom she got breathless for the "good" reason. "With all this rain I haven't been able to get much done outside, so I've been painting everything inside. I have most of the rooms done now and tomorrow I'll start on the baseboards and doorframes. I want them to be a nice, bright white."

"Uh-huh," Lexie said, not real excited over paint ideas. "How's that hunky neighbor of yours?"

"Which one?"

"Love it when you play dumb." She laughed at her own joke. "One was too young for me to reference without feeling pervy, and the other was gorgeous but a complete pill. That leaves Jason."

"You didn't think Jason was a pill?"

"I thought Jason was awesomely *concentrated*."

True, and it had intimidated her just a little. "Well, doesn't really matter which one you meant, because I haven't seen any of them."

"Then you need to break something," Lexie suggested. "Or buy something, stand in the driveway and look helpless."

"In the rain?"

"What's a little rainwater if he offers his help?"

Not in this lifetime. "I don't think so." Honor was all about looking self-reliant, not needy. That had been her core desire all along, but now, on top of that motivation, she desperately wanted to prove Jason wrong.

Unaware of Honor's inner turmoil, Lexie said, "Well, you could just ask for his help. I'm sure there's something around the house that he could assist with. Maybe something in the—" fake cough "—bedroom?"

"You're impossible. Stop trying to be my pimp."

"Pimps get paid. I just want to see you glow."

A crack of lightning made Honor jump. She had to admit that Jason's warnings had her spooked. For most of her life she'd been an insomniac, but after him predicting doom and gloom and making it sound like she was a sitting duck to all sorts of despicable crimes, she could barely doze. There were a lot of unfamiliar sounds in her house and even though she'd reinforced every entry, she still went on high alert every time she heard a squeak.

"You didn't hang up on me, did you?"

"Nope." Honor climbed down off her stepladder and set the brush across the top of the can. "But you already know I don't want to ask for his help." Jason thought she was trouble, assumed she'd fail and expected her to somehow cause problems.

"C'mon, honey. Think about how much quicker you'd get things done."

She'd also prove Jason right, that she couldn't handle it on her own. No, thank you. "I'm happy doing it all myself."

Lexie blew out a breath. "That's a shame, because I was planning to visit tomorrow and lend a hand, as I'd promised. I'd have been there sooner, but we were restocking this week."

"I don't want to work you, but you know you're more than welcome to visit." Luckily Lexie lived and worked only half an hour away, in the downtown area. The salon where Honor worked was in the opposite direction, but not very far at all. "I wouldn't mind chatting with you while I get things done." Lexie was the ray of sunshine in her otherwise dull world.

"I promise to actually assist. What time will you get home?"

For too many years now, Lexie had been fighting her way around Honor's barriers. She knew from experience that it did her no good to resist.

Smiling, Honor said, "Around six—" and then her phone beeped. When she glanced at the screen, dread went through her bloodstream. "Shoot, I have to go. That's the facility."

"Of course it is," Lexie groused. "Don't let them wear you out. I'll see you tomorrow at six-fifteen."

Honor switched over the call, and while she listened she headed to her bedroom to change. She already knew what the call meant, what she'd have to do.

Looked like she'd be making a trip out in the downpour. The painting would have to wait. *It's only paint*, she reminded herself.

But it felt like so much more.

It felt like…her future.

Her curtains did nothing more than tease. Jason stood at the window, watching the storm. Or at least he had been. But as soon as Honor's bedroom light came on, his gaze shifted from the dark sky to her shadowy form…undressing.

The woman kept the strangest damn hours, heading out for work in the early morning, coming home after six, then regularly leaving again, sometimes in the middle of the night. On the quiet street he often heard her car door open and close. Other than those times, with the storms keeping everyone inside, he hadn't seen her.

Would her roof leak? Were the windows sealed? His gaze

shifted to one of the big trees in her backyard. The wind pulled at dead branches that could do a lot of damage if they landed wrong.

So much for her to do, and yet it seemed she was never home long enough to get to any of it.

"Spying again?"

Jason didn't bother to turn to Hogan. "It's really coming down."

"Right. Never knew the rain fascinated you so much."

"The creek might flood." He glanced at his brother, took in his clothes and knew the answer even before he asked. "Going out?"

Hogan rolled one shoulder. "Yeah."

Running. Always running. From one meaningless date to the next. Jason understood, at least to a degree. The past year had been hard on his brother.

But damn it, it had been hard on Colt, too.

He didn't want to judge, but right now it seemed Hogan had his head up his ass and was blind to everything except his own damaged ego. A million dates with easy conquests wouldn't fix anything. But how did he tell Hogan that?

He couldn't. Not yet anyway. So instead he concentrated on other, more tangible and less emotional issues. "How'd the interview go?"

"Same as the others. I'm fucked."

It was an awkward thing, being in the position of advising his older brother. For so many years Hogan had been the settled one. Gorgeous wife, check. Awesome son, check. Nice house, nice bank account and respectable job with benefits, check.

But over the last year, everything had changed and there were times Jason wondered if they'd ever get back to normal. He'd never been in love, never had a son and never lost his livelihood, so he couldn't pretend to know how Hogan felt.

But he loved his nephew and he knew, eventually, Hogan

would have to get his priorities straight. He was a good dad, always. But lately he'd been far too absent, physically and emotionally.

Running a hand over the back of his head, Jason said, "The bankruptcy?"

Disgusted, Hogan curled his lip. "Who wants to hire an accountant who was unable to manage his own finances?"

A definite problem. "Did you explain?"

That made him laugh. "Right. What would I say? That I didn't know my wife was boning two different guys while going through our money like water through a sieve? That elevates me from a bad accountant to a total moron."

Jason blew out a breath. Tough to go from six figures with elite and exclusive clients to unemployed without prospects. "Something will turn up."

"Maybe." Pulling on a wind breaker and turning up the collar, Hogan said, "If the night goes well, I'll be home in the morning."

"That's what you want me to tell Colt when he asks?"

Without meeting his gaze, Hogan said, "He won't ask."

No, Jason thought, watching Hogan dart out into the rain. Colt already knew his dad cared more about chasing tail than manning up and facing the reality of their situation.

But Jason wished like hell it was different.

Needing a new focus, he returned to the window. Earlier, Honor had been painting. Two at a time she'd carried in cans of paint from her car, getting soaked in the process. At this rate, the whole house probably had a fresh coat. He wondered at her color choices. Was she a bold primary kind of girl, or soft pastels? A continuous color like this house, or a rainbow of hues, each room different?

He'd bet on the rainbow.

A few minutes later when Honor's front door opened, Hogan was already gone. Propping a shoulder on the window frame,

Jason watched her as she stepped out, locked the door and double-checked it.

Smart.

She wore skinny jeans, sandals and an oversize top that mostly concealed her figure. Before stepping off her rickety porch she opened an umbrella—one that sported wide, bold stripes in every color imaginable.

Yup, rainbow colors.

He'd like to see the progress she'd made inside the house, but just as the rains had kept her inside, they'd kept him away from the yard. He'd worked either inside his garage or not at all. Probably for the best. If he got inside her house and saw her workload, he'd want to help.

He and his nephew were alike that way. But she'd already made it clear that his help was unwanted.

As Honor darted into the rain and to her car, he tracked her every move, and nodded.

Trouble—with a capital *T*.

Hours later, as Jason lay in the dark trying to sleep, he heard her pull in to the driveway. Her headlights cut across his window, briefly illuminating his room before she turned them off. She didn't slam her car door, but the sound of it closing echoed over the quiet streets. He glanced at the clock and saw it was 2:00 a.m.

Without giving it much thought, he threw back the sheet and strode to the window to look out. He had a better view from his dining room, with that view directly facing her front porch, but he was naked, so he stayed in his bedroom and lifted aside the curtain.

Sometime during the night the rain had stopped. Black clouds parted and moon shadows danced over the yard. The faint glow of her porch light showed the exhaustion visible in every line of her body. At the bottom step of the porch she paused and looked up, staring at the skinny crescent moon for a very long time.

While Jason stared at her.

His heart beat heavily and he felt unfamiliar things, things that only partially involved lust. Every day for a week he'd thought about her, watched for her, worried over her situation.

He wanted to lend a hand. It went against his nature not to. But she'd been pretty clear on her preferences.

Finally she lowered her head, rubbed at her eyes, then trudged up the steps and, after fumbling at her door for longer than should have been necessary, she went in.

Telling himself he'd only watch to ensure that she got inside safely, Jason waited.

Lights came on as she walked through the house to the kitchen, then out again when she went to her bedroom.

She must have undressed in the dark.

When all stayed quiet, Jason decided she'd gone to bed.

After a deep breath he dropped the curtain and did the same.

There were two types of problems.

The type where, if you just told someone, things could work out. People would have answers or suggestions, or they'd offer desperately needed help. You shared and others got involved and things got better. Honor had always considered it dumb when people kept their problems to themselves if sharing could make things easier.

Unfortunately she never seemed to have those types of problems. She had the other kind. The kind where no solutions existed and talking to others equated to whining because you knew they couldn't help. Sharing only drew them in and made them feel responsible, and then resentful.

Or worse, they felt sorry for you.

She never wanted anyone to pity her.

Once, in a moment of weakness, she'd explained everything

to Lexie—and learned a valuable lesson. Lexie had an overpro-
tective streak, which meant she griped nonstop on Honor's behalf. Even worse, Lexie's mean-spirited barbs put Honor in the
unpalatable position of having to defend her family.

She disliked that almost as much as the pity.

But she loved Lexie. She especially loved that Lexie was coming over that night. She could use a dose or two of laughter to
help her stay focused.

She'd awakened late after sleeping through her alarm. Luckily
sunshine cut straight though her makeshift curtains, which, as
Jason had suggested, were really tacked-up sheets. At the moment, she couldn't afford real window treatments.

Grateful for the beautiful day, she'd swilled coffee, hopped
in and out of the shower, brushed her teeth and hair, forfeited
even the most basic makeup and was now rushing out.

After securing all the locks on the door, she turned for the
porch steps—and drew up short at the sight of her trash…ev-
erywhere.

Oh no.

As she stared in horror, Jason righted the overturned trash can,
and then he and Colt began picking it all up. Hand to the top
of her head as if to keep her numb brain contained, gaze going
everywhere to take in the catastrophe, Honor strode out to the
yard. Feeling sick, she asked, "What happened?"

As if it didn't matter, Jason glanced at her, over her, then answered while getting back to work, "You didn't have a lid on
your garbage can, and winds knocked it over during the storm."

She was already late. *What to do?*

Standing, Colt noticed her shock. "Hey, no worries. You can
go on and I'll take care of it."

Bless him.

But then Jason slanted her a look. It wasn't exactly condem-
nation. Truthfully she didn't know what to call it; she just absolutely knew she couldn't walk away yet.

Mouth pinched to keep the groan contained, she dumped her purse, packed lunch and keys into the driver's seat of her small car and started grabbing up garbage. Luckily none of it was the nasty kind. Nothing too personal.

She chased down a piece of paper skipping over the lawn, and almost collided with Jason.

Of course the man was shirtless again.

Did he only own pants?

Rain or shine, he usually worked in the garage and his requisite outfit included some variation on jeans or shorts, athletic shoes or work boots—and no shirt.

Occasionally he wore a trucker's cap...backward.

When he wasn't too close, when she only spied on him through a window, she could take it. Barely.

But now, with only a foot between them? Awareness thrummed through her bloodstream, her skin went warm and keeping her gaze on his face proved nearly impossible. "I've got it," she mumbled, and started to reach for the paper.

Jason got to it before she could.

She quickly stepped back—and he followed.

"Honor?"

"Hmm?"

Taking her by surprise, he tipped up her chin and studied her face. "You look tired."

God, his fingers were hot, a little rough, and they sent her heartbeat into a frantic race. "No." Her false smile felt absurd. "I'm good."

His gaze dropped to her mouth, wandered lower—then came back to her eyes. "Yes, you are. Maybe too good—because you can't lie for shit." His hand left her chin but only so he could trace a fingertip along her cheekbone. "You've got dark circles under your eyes."

Deadpan, trying to hide her sizzling awareness of him as an ultrahot man, she said, "Yay. Just what I wanted to know."

LORI FOSTER

His mouth quirked, and he thankfully dropped his hand, allowing her to breathe again. "What time do you need to be at work?"

An innocuous enough question, especially after those light, bone-melting touches. "Twenty minutes ago." Then, because she never could be short, she explained, "I have clients coming in first thing, but the salon is only ten minutes away and I had time built in to store my lunch, go over my schedule, get my supplies ready, spruce up my area and..." She trailed off at his slight frown. "Sorry."

"Sounds like you have a lot to do."

"The salon where I work is small. Every stylist is responsible for her own area."

"Small, as in lacking business?"

She wrinkled her nose. "Small, as in superexclusive."

"So you have a lot of clients?"

Was he skeptical? Or just interested? She couldn't tell. "Don't judge my own sloppy appearance." Forgoing modesty, she admitted, "I'm in high demand."

He murmured, "I bet you are," while looking at her mouth again.

A rush of heat hit her and it had nothing to do with the humidity rising off the wet ground in waves. At this rate, she'd be mush by the time she got to work.

After clearing her throat, she said, "So..."

"You were out late last night."

Totally not what she'd expected from him. "How do you...?"

"My bedroom is closest to your house. I hear you coming and going."

"Oh." Well, that was embarrassing. Now she'd never be able to sleep for thinking about him that close...maybe listening to her. She didn't have time to explain, not that she'd know what to say anyway. Lexie's general explanation, that she was keeper of the zoo, didn't feel appropriate. "I'm really sorry. About waking you and—" she gestured at the yard "—about the mess."

"I'll keep an eye on things until the garbage truck comes by and picks it up in another hour. But you should get a lid for your can. That'll take care of it."

"I will." She searched the yard and spotted Colt. "Thank you," she called out to him.

Dropping a few things back into her can, he waved her off with a friendly smile.

Honor sighed. "He is such a great kid."

"Yeah, he is." Smiling, Jason added, "But he doesn't much like being called a kid."

He had the most gorgeous smile that put sexy little dents in his whisker-rough cheeks and crinkled the corners of his dark-as-sin eyes. That smile had the effect of making Honor smile, too. "I'll try to remember that." She back-stepped toward her car. "And the lid to the can."

Jason nodded.

And she'd especially remember to close her car door quietly from now on. Very, very quietly.

3

PROUD OF HERSELF for coming up with such a great scheme, Lexie arrived a few minutes before Honor should be there. As soon as she pulled up, she spotted Jason in the garage, hammering away on something that looked like a small house.

Perfect.

Honor deserved a nice but hunky guy, someone to pay attention to her, lighten her load a little and make her feel as special as Lexie knew her to be. Jason, with his simmering gaze and hot bod, seemed like a great candidate. From what Lexie had seen so far, the chemistry was strong. Enough sparks had bounced between them to start a forest fire.

With the top up on her convertible, she circled to the back passenger door. When she opened it, the stems of the large bird-of-paradise plant flopped out. Getting the thing in there had taken two men from the garden center and some creative stuffing.

Pushing her sunglasses to the top of her head, Lexie put on her best helpless face, glanced around, then zeroed in on Jason— willing him to look up.

"Excuse me."

Startled, she followed the sound of that smooth, deep voice and found herself staring into incredible cobalt-blue eyes...

...in a stop-your-heart handsome face.

…with an oh-my-God physique.

Done with her up, down and sideways analysis of his fine self, she smiled. "Hi there."

Dressed in loose athletic pants, running shoes and a snug-fitting T-shirt, he asked, "Did you need some help?"

She needed all kinds of things…

He nodded to the plant.

Forgetting all about Jason and her plan, Lexie quickly agreed. "Yes. Please. Thank you."

His polite expression never faltered—unlike her pulse.

Inhaling, Lexie looked him over again. Straight black hair, neatly trimmed but not overly styled. A firm mouth, strong jaw and those incendiary eyes. A lean, tall, finely honed body. "Where did you come from?"

"I live across the street."

He could've said heaven and she would have believed him.

Wearing a quizzical frown, he glanced at Honor's house. "I take it you're my new neighbor?"

Oh, she wished. It'd be worth giving up her very nice downtown apartment overlooking the river. The views around Honor's house were definitely better.

"My best friend is, actually." Belatedly she held out a hand. "I'm Lexie Perkins."

"Sullivan Dean." He carefully took her hand, his touch gentle and somehow more familiar because of it. "It's nice to meet you, Lexie."

Liking the sound of her name on his lips, she tried to hold on to him, but other than a long look, he didn't play along. Bummer.

From behind her, Jason said, "Hey, Lexie."

She turned—and couldn't help looking Jason over, too. Honor had struck gold with her location.

And to think she'd once considered the neighborhood old and stuffy.

LORI FOSTER

"Jason, just the guy I was hoping to see."

Wearing his intense, enigmatic expression and *not* wearing a shirt, Jason shifted his gaze to Sullivan.

Oh, crap. Lexie definitely didn't want Sullivan—*please let him be available*—to get the wrong idea. She had zero carnal interest in Jason…especially since Honor had already staked a claim, even if Honor didn't realize it and would never admit it.

To clear up any misconceptions, she explained, "I was going to ask you to carry in the plant I got for Honor. It's a housewarming gift. But it's a monster. No way can I get it up to her porch and in the house on my own."

Once she got Jason inside, maybe she could convince him to stay. If he got to know Honor, if he understood why she forced the issue of independence, Lexie felt sure he'd adore her as much as she did.

Things didn't go quite right when Sullivan stepped forward. "I've got it." In a beautiful display of muscles and fluid strength, he lifted the plant as if it were a bag of sugar. "Where to?"

Oh, those glorious biceps…

While Lexie quickly considered the twist to her plans, Honor pulled up. Exhaustion gave way to confusion as she hurriedly left her car and trotted toward them. "Lexie? What did you do? What's going on?"

Sullivan stared at Honor, smiled slightly and said, "I see. Now it makes more sense."

Jason shot him a look but quickly returned his attention to Honor.

Lexie had no idea what that odd exchange meant, and with so much accusation in Honor's tone, she couldn't figure it out right now. Given half a chance, Honor would send them all packing.

Her friend didn't like gifts any more than she liked help.

"Surprise!" Unwilling to let Honor put a damper on things, Lexie grabbed her hand and started hauling her toward the house. "Come on. Sullivan's carrying your housewarming plant for me and I don't want to test his goodwill. It weighs a ton."

"Sullivan?" Honor asked.

"Your smoking-hot neighbor from across the street."

Honor glanced back at him. So did Lexie.

Amused by the praise, Sullivan smiled at them both. "Hello."

Honor swallowed. "Hi."

Jason said nothing. He just watched Honor with near–predatory intent.

Lexie understood his expression, though it clearly went straight over Honor's head.

Pleased with things so far, Lexie continued to rush Honor until she got the door unlocked. Lexie stood back to hold the door open and Sullivan carried in the plant, bending his knees as he went over the threshold to keep from damaging the top leaves.

Jason still stood in the driveway.

Cocking out a hip, Lexie shook her head and said, "Come on, slowpoke. We might need your help. And even if we don't, you're the reason I'm here, so—"

"Lexie."

As Honor's fretful voice emerged from the house, Jason grinned and ambled up the drive to join them. Sweat gleamed on his naked shoulders, and muscles flexed in his thighs.

She understood exactly how he so easily flustered Honor. Most women would react the same.

Until he came in, Lexie hadn't yet looked around, but as soon as he cleared the doorway she did, and it blew her away. Honor had arranged everything so that the small room felt more spacious. Fresh paint on the walls brightened things and even her makeshift sheet curtains looked smooth and crisp and coordinated.

Lexie turned a complete circle before saying, "Wow. You've been a busy girl, Honor. It looks great."

Jason nodded his agreement. "The colors are really nice."

"Thank you." The praise took some of the tension from Honor's shoulders. "I like a lot of color, so I researched what would be right for this type of home. I wanted to stay true to the Cape Cod style."

"Perfect choices. It looks terrific."

She smiled with relief, then touched one leaf of the plant. "You shouldn't have, Lex."

Knowing it wasn't the problem, Lexie said, "If you don't like it, I can take it back and pick you out another."

"It's beautiful."

"It fits okay? Not too big?"

"It's *perfect*." She turned to Sullivan. "Thank you for carrying it in."

"Carrying in a plant was as good an excuse as any to meet you." He held out his hand. "Sullivan Dean. I live across the street from you."

Smiling, Honor indulged the requisite handshake. "Honor Brown. It's very nice to meet you."

He enclosed her hand in both of his. "I'll admit I was curious. We were all at Screwy Louie's the other night when Jason mentioned we had a new neighbor. With all the rain, I hadn't yet seen you."

She tipped her head. "Screwy Louie's? Is that a local place?"

"It's a bar and grill a few blocks down in the commercial area. You haven't been?"

"No."

"We'll definitely have to remedy that. Anytime you need a bump up from fast food, go to Screwy Louie's. Best food around."

"They have takeout?"

"Sure."

Still holding hands? "Sounds fun," Lexie said, making sure she wouldn't get left out. "Maybe we could all meet up there sometime."

"Since we go every week," Jason rumbled in a low voice, "I'm sure we could make it happen."

"Definitely." Sullivan finally let her go.

"So…" Honor shot a glance at Jason, then turned back to Sullivan. "You said Jason mentioned me?"

"With the trouble still in the area, he wanted to make sure we were aware of you."

"We?" Lexie asked.

"Nathan and me."

Honor wrinkled her nose. "Because I'm a woman alone?"

"A block or so down, there are a few older widowed women who've been in the area for twenty years or more. But yeah, a woman like you…"

"Like me?"

"Younger, single and attractive." He hitched a brow. "I think you're the first. If you ever need anything, feel free to give me a yell."

Lexie didn't miss a thing, including the territorial way Jason moved closer to the pair. She shivered. Alpha guys were so hot. It also struck her that Honor was again her usual bubbly, friendly self.

But when around Jason, she was very different.

"Why, thank you. I appreciate that," Honor said to Sullivan. "So far, so good, though. I think I've got it covered. And honestly I'm enjoying figuring out everything on my own."

Keeping her plan in mind, Lexie said, "I brought some snacks and drinks. Why don't you both stay and visit for a bit?"

Sullivan checked a thick black watch on his wrist. "I have thirty minutes before I need to take off."

Before she thought better of it, Lexie asked, "Hot date?"

His slow smile sent a spike of heat through her core. "Actually, no."

Lexie noted that her boldness didn't throw him, but it did turn his gaze speculative.

"I have an evening class and won't be back until late."

"So we'll make do with thirty." She'd find out about the class stuff later. "What about you, Jason? Got a little free time?"

Honor made a point of studiously examining the leaves on the plant, so she missed the way Jason checked her out—specifically her behind in her snug jeans.

When he realized Lexie was watching him, he drew his attention away to ask, "What?"

Around a laugh, Lexie said, "I'm going to take that as a yes."

His gaze went right back to Honor. "Yeah, do that."

"Perfect. I'll run out and grab the stuff from my trunk."

"Need a hand?" Sullivan asked.

"I'll take both, please." Lexie hooked her arm through his, taking him with her while saying over her shoulder, "You two behave, now. We'll be right back."

Jason's chuckles followed her out the door, but Honor just groaned.

Snickering, Lexie said, "She is so funny."

Without making a big deal of it, Sullivan freed his arm but put his palm at the small of her back. "Your friend Honor?"

"Yes." He had big hands. Even through her shirt she felt the heat of his palm. She wasn't Honor; a single touch didn't usually make her giddy.

But damn it, this time it did.

She looked up at his profile. "When Honor first showed up, you said 'I see,' as if you just understood something."

He shrugged strong shoulders. "At first I thought you were her and it didn't make sense."

"What didn't?"

"Jason's interest."

At her car, Lexie stopped and turned to face him. Hand on

her hip, she pretended a show of attitude. "You can't see him being interested in me?"

With his smile going cocky, Sullivan shook his head. "Not really, no."

Why that disgruntled her, Lexie wasn't sure. "Why ever not?"

He pinched her chin. "Let's just say she's better suited to Jason."

"No, let's don't." Lexie made a "bring it" gesture in the air. "Let's hear it. Why am I so unsuitable?"

"Unsuitable for Jason," he clarified, still all cocky and amused. "See, he's the home-and-hearth type and I figure you for a one-and-done kind of girl. You party, you have fun, you get what you need and then you move on."

Her jaw loosened. Wow. "You nailed me."

"Not yet." That hot blue gaze turned seductive. "But I'm not opposed to the idea."

Lexie started to speak, realized she had no idea what to say and sighed instead. "We need to table this discussion for now, at least until I get my bearings."

"All right. How about we get into it more next week? I can get out early one day."

"Early from what?"

She could tell he thought twice about sharing, then gave a mental shrug.

"I have a studio where I teach martial arts."

"That's pretty cool." And explained his shredded physique. Her thoughts jumped ahead and she asked, "Who can sign up? I mean, do you need previous training?"

"I do the training, so no. I have beginner classes up to pros."

Yeah, she was starting to like this idea. "You could teach me to kick butt?"

More serious than her, he gave one nod. "Sure. But I also teach how to avoid being in situations where you need to physi-

LORI FOSTER

cally engage. My school is as much about motivation and quiet confidence as it is life skills."

Lexie daringly looked him over. "Bet you have a lot of ladies in your classes."

He deliberately misunderstood that. "I train plenty of adults, but what I really enjoy is working with kids." Changing the subject, Sullivan glanced back at the house. "I know Jason's glad the place was bought, but your friend has a hell of a job ahead of her."

"Honor is strong." Too strong, in Lexie's opinion, because she'd always had to be. "She'll figure it out."

"She looked a little overwhelmed to me."

Lexie popped the trunk. "I think that was because of Jason. Honor's not really shy, but around him…well, it's like seeing her in high school again."

"You've known each other that long?"

She lifted out the big bag of mixed munchies and left the cooler for Sullivan. "Since middle school. She was always super-conscientious about things, but these days she spends *all* her time working and sorting out problems for her family. She never has time to date." Thinking he'd appreciate her cleverness, Lexie leaned closer to him. "I'm trying to lend a hand."

He lifted out the heavy cooler one-handed, then closed her trunk. "How's that?"

"The plant I brought over? I deliberately got one big enough that we'd need to ask for Jason's help."

Wearing a slight frown, his midnight eyes unreadable, Sullivan looked down at her. "So you manipulated things, but then I stepped in and ruined your plans?"

She didn't like the way he worded that. "It's okay. I think this will work out even better."

"How so?" He made no move to leave the curb.

The evening sun cast long shadows in the yard. Birds sang overhead. A fly buzzed near her ear.

And Sullivan stood there—more or less calling her manipulative.

Which, okay, was mostly true.

A little bemused, Lexie readjusted the bag in her arms. "A small group is less intimate, and that takes the pressure off her."

Still watching her, he said, "So we're avoiding intimacy?"

Lexie opened her mouth, closed it, then laughed. "You keep beating me at my own game."

"Flirting?"

"I was," she admitted. "Are you?" Something about Sullivan made it difficult to tell.

"I haven't quite decided yet." With his hand returned to the small of her back, he got her walking again.

Now, wait a minute! She stopped, but he didn't, so she had to hustle to catch up. She wanted to finish this discussion before they got inside with the other two.

"What is that supposed to mean?" If he thought she'd hang around, waiting and hopeful, he could think again.

"You like games," he stated, as if he knew her. "Me, not so much."

Lexie caught his arm to slow him down. "You were playing along with me," she reminded him, and then wondered if he'd admit it.

"I was." They reached the door.

"Well, then?"

He shocked her by cupping one hand to her face. "I think you're dangerous."

Dangerous? Her heart tripped as she stared up at him. "To a big, strong guy like you?"

"To a serious guy like me." His thumb brushed the corner of her mouth. "But hey. I did ask you about getting together next week. You never answered."

"Yes."

"Yes?"

"Yes, we should get together."

The small smile turned into a grin of satisfaction. "Let's exchange numbers, then, and we'll work it out."

Lexie's matchmaking efforts were like getting run over by a bus. If Honor could get her alone, she'd give her a cease-and-desist order. But so far, Lexie had stuck close to Sullivan.

At first, when she found herself alone with Jason, Honor had made the quick excuse of needing to change clothes. She had dye on her fingertips, and she knew she smelled like perm solution thanks to one of her older clients.

But while out of the room, she'd also brushed her hair and cleaned her teeth and freshened up the best she could without a shower. Then she'd lingered, but so had Lexie and Sullivan.

Finally she'd had no option but to reemerge.

In her absence, Jason had looked around her kitchen, pantry and living room. She'd found him examining the leaky sink, and when he came out from under the cabinet, the leak was gone.

Honor had stammered her gratitude.

Taking pity on her, Jason had mostly talked about the house. In fact, other than a few too many, too-long glances, she'd enjoyed chatting with him.

She was lucky that the furnace and air, the electrical and the plumbing were all in decent working order. He'd checked the warped back door and told her what needed to be done so that it would open and close properly. He'd even offered to do the work.

She'd politely declined.

And finally Lexie and Sullivan had rejoined them. Together they chatted about the renovation of the neighborhood, local venues of interest and the endless rain.

There was a slight lull when Jason told her, "You look tired."

Conversation died around them and Honor quickly swallowed her drink of cola, then choked.

Patiently Jason patted her on the back—and seriously that did *not* help. Honor didn't know what it was about the man, but he touched her and all the oxygen sucked out of the room, leaving her breathless.

"I'm okay," she wheezed, setting aside her drink. "Went down the wrong pipe."

"You do look tuckered out, Honor." Lexie gave her the critical once-over. "Have you been getting any sleep at all?"

Not much. "Of course."

"I don't see how," Jason said. "Not with the strange hours you keep."

That caught Sullivan's interest. "Strange hours?"

Before this got out of hand, Honor pointed at Lexie and said a firm, undeniable "No."

Full of mock innocence, Lexie blinked at her and played dumb. "What?"

"Not a word, Lex. I mean it."

Silently agreeing, Lexie pretended to lock her lips and throw away the key.

"A mystery." Sullivan smiled. "I don't know about you, Jason, but now I'm twice as curious about what she's been up to." He pushed back his chair at the little dinette table and stood. "Too bad I need to head out or I'd try my skills at interrogation."

Lexie unzipped her lips real quick, blast her. "You could interrogate me." Coy, she murmured, "I'm known to cave easily."

"Something else for me to think about." He nodded to Honor. "Remember what I told you. If you need anything—"

"I'm right next door," Jason finished for him.

At that, Sullivan almost laughed but instead turned it into a cough. "Right."

"I'll walk you out." As Lexie followed Sullivan, she used both hands to make a squeezing gesture in the air near his rear, then looked over her shoulder at Honor and Jason to mouth, *Oh my God!*

Jason laughed. "How does she know I won't tell him?"

"She's nuts and probably wouldn't care." Honor stared after them, even when the front door opened and closed.

"Honor."

That deep, dark voice drew her gaze back to Jason's. He looked both concerned and determined.

Idly turning his Coke can, he asked, "Will you tell me what's going on?"

"What do you mean?" She knew exactly what he meant. In a too-high, evasive voice, she claimed, "Nothing's going on." Her follow-up, negligent laugh sounded more like a nervous admission.

Jason's gaze sharpened as if he could read her thoughts. "You are such a mystery."

"No, I'm not." Mysteries sounded intriguing and exciting. Sadly Honor knew she was neither.

Even though his mouth stayed firm, his dark eyes teased her. "You know, sometimes I think you just like being contrary."

"No, I don't."

This time, he gave in to the laughter.

Great. Now she had him laughing at her.

Except that when he looked at her, there was nothing mocking in his gaze, and he was so devastatingly focused on her that she forgot to be annoyed.

As they stared at each other, the humor faded away to a slight, sexy smile. "Come on, Honor. Where do you go in the middle of the night, and what difference does it make if Lexie tells anyone?"

No way would she go into detail with him, but this time she couldn't think of an excuse to dodge out.

Trying not to sound rude, she said, "It's just…it's complicated."

Jason sat back in his seat and looked at her, his expression hooded, his inky lashes at half-mast.

When she finally escaped his gaze, her attention went all over his body instead. His flat, firm abdomen was pretty darn sexy, especially with that downy line of dark hair trailing from his navel down into his loose-waisted shorts.

He was the most casual, comfortable man she'd ever met.

She tried to get her gaze northward, but only got as far as his pecs. How nice would it feel to rest her cheek against that lightly furred chest?

"Honor?"

"Hmm?"

"Keep looking at me like that and I'm going to get ideas."

Her gaze shot to his.

Lifting a brow, he corrected, "More ideas, I should have said."

Wondering if he meant that to be teasing, Honor stared at him. Could he be as fascinated with her as she was with him? She licked her lips. "More ideas?"

"I've had a few already."

So had she. Too many ideas. *Impossible* ideas. "Oh." *Smooth, Honor. Real smooth.*

Keeping her gaze captive in his, he sat forward again, one strong forearm resting on the table, his other hand reaching out...

She held perfectly still.

He tucked her hair back. "You honestly do look exhausted. What's going on?"

He sat so close she could smell the scent of his big, semibare body.

His brows twitched. "Are you holding your breath?"

Oh, shoot. She released it in a long sigh. "I'm sorry." Regret put a stranglehold on her. It would be so nice to flirt as Lexie did, to be cavalier about an involvement. But she didn't know how. "You shouldn't do things like that to me."

He turned his head, and his voice went all sexy deep. "Things like what?"

Like touching her, but she wouldn't state the obvious. He knew what she meant. "It rattles me."

"Can't have that."

She started to relax.

"Can't swear it won't happen again, either."

So her awkwardness hadn't scared him off? It did most guys—not that she'd known any guys like him. If only she weren't so damn backward.

If only she didn't have so many obligations.

Getting serious, his tone gentle, he said, "Relax, Honor. If you're not interested, I'll back off."

Oh, she was interested all right. "It's not that," she dared to admit.

Satisfaction glittered in his dark eyes. "Then what's the problem?"

"The thing is—" A loud roar started in her backyard, cutting off the explanation she didn't know how to make. "What in the world?"

Leaving her chair so fast it nearly toppled, Honor dashed to the side door. Of course it didn't open, so she put her hands together on the thankfully clean pane and looked through the window. She couldn't quite see anything—but the noise was deafening.

From behind her, now crowded very close, Jason peered out over her head.

Good Lord, the man was hot. Literally. Heat radiated off his body and seemed to seep into her, making her knees weak and her nerve endings tingle. And his scent...heavenly. She'd never realized men smelled so good. Or maybe they all didn't. Maybe it was just him.

Or maybe everything about him appealed to her.

She bit her lip and concentrated on not leaning back into him.

What would it be like to have him actually hold her? Touch her, kiss her? Lexie would tell her to go for it, but she wasn't

Lexie, so instead she stood there, stiff and still, in awful inde-cision.

"That's the Bush Hog," he murmured, and his breath brushed her ear, making her shiver.

Get it together, she ordered herself. Giving a blatant show of her inexperience would only make her feel more like a doofus. She cleared her throat and asked, "Bush Hog?"

"Yeah." One of his large hands came up to rest on her shoul-der. "Colt must be home. Remember he told you he'd finish up when he could? The rain put him behind, but it's finally dry enough."

Colt was cutting her jungle of a backyard?

Incredulous, Honor forgot her hormones, turned—and found herself staring up close and personal at Jason's gloriously naked chest. Tanned, sleek skin, stretched taut over naturally attained muscles.

It took all her concentration not to lean in and nuzzle her nose against his chest hair.

Jason didn't back up, but he did lift her chin. And just that, a light touch with his rough fingertips caused a sweet ache to pool low in her belly.

"My brother is going through a really hard time, which means Colt is going through an even worse time. He's at loose ends, missing his friends from back home, especially the girl he'd been seeing. He has a part-time job, but he needs something more to focus on. I'd appreciate it if you let him help you with things."

What he said was so far from what she'd been thinking that it took a moment to register.

They stood close together, his hand still holding her chin, his warm breath on her face, his heated scent filling her head. The urge to kiss him made it difficult to think—especially when his attention dropped to her mouth.

His thumb moved over her bottom lip. "You're making me nuts, Honor."

The rough words were so low she barely heard them. "I don't see—"

Abruptly he released her and stepped back. "It'll help Colt if you let him stay busy. I try, but I just don't have that much for him to do."

The new space between them left her oddly bereft. Ridiculous. She barely knew the man, and what she did know confounded her. Clearly he found her incapable of managing her own home chores; he'd already said as much.

Did he resent her as a neighbor?

Want her as a woman?

She frowned at him. "And they say women are difficult to understand."

That earned her a brief self-deprecating smile. "I'll attempt to be clearer."

Oh. Anticipation set her heart racing.

"Colt is still finding his place here."

Well, darn. She'd wanted him to be clearer about those tantalizing touches and long looks. Then again, the fact that he cared for his nephew only added to his appeal, so she merely nodded.

"The busier he stays," Jason said, "the less time he has to dwell on changes out of his control."

She wanted to help, she really did.

Pretty much, she always wanted to help—which Lexie claimed to be one of her biggest weaknesses.

Drawn to Jason, she inched closer and only realized it when his attention went back to her mouth. "The thing is," she said, "I can't afford to pay him."

"No one asked you to." He shoved his hands into his pockets. "You really need to learn what it means to be neighbors."

Whoa. His jeans just slid an inch lower. She gathered her wits with an effort. "If it means clearing my yard and other hard work like that, then I have to do something in return for you."

His eyes flared, then narrowed. "If anything comes up, I'll

let you know. But for now, you're the one with the surplus of stuff that needs to get done."

"Stuff you keep claiming I can't do on my own, but I *can*." She just needed more time. Maybe more energy. And the right tools…

Did it annoy him that she hadn't yet gotten to the yard? Oh God, probably. He kept his own grounds pristine, and hers looked like a dump.

Shame put her shoulders back and stiffened her spine. "I promise that I'm getting to it as quick as I can."

"You'll get to it quicker if you stop being stubborn and let Colt help you."

It wasn't about stubbornness. It was about carrying her own weight so others, he especially, didn't resent her. "This is ridiculous—"

"I agree. So let him help."

"Fine."

"Great."

Thinking it might be a good time to redirect the conversation, she tossed out what she thought was a bland enough question. "So, is your brother divorced or widowed?"

Frowning, Jason turned away from her and muttered something low.

So low that she couldn't catch it but thought it might've been a curse. "What?" she asked with suspicion.

"It's complicated."

Was he throwing her own words back at her? "What exactly does that mean?"

When he said nothing, she got the message loud and clear. He could grill her, but she was supposed to mind her own business. Sidling around him, she said, "Never mind."

"Damn it," he whispered roughly as he caught her arm and turned her back to him. The seconds ticked by; tension expanded in the air.

"Honestly," she said, matching his tone. "It's fine."

Jason dropped his hand and blew out a breath. "After sixteen years of marriage, Meg cheated on Hogan, bankrupted him and while he was divorcing her, she crashed her car into a tree and died on him."

The bottom fell out of her stomach. "Oh my God."

He looked past her shoulder, his expression pained. "Through it all, he never stopped loving her."

Honor gave in to temptation and touched his chest. "You're right." Empathy made her voice softer. "It sounds very complicated."

4

LEXIE CAME IN loudly whistling, as if she thought she might interrupt something risqué.

Jason had to laugh when Honor gave a guilty leap away from him.

At least it broke that choking tension—a good thing, since he'd been a nanosecond away from kissing her.

Leaning in close, he teased, "We weren't doing anything."

She blinked fast and answered just as quietly, "Of course not."

"I wanted to." Even as he said it, Jason knew he shouldn't tease her. But the ladies were cute together, their personalities, like their physical appearances, opposite yet complimentary. "And so did you."

Hectic color rushed into her face. She took a halting breath— and nodded. "I did."

Well, damn. Forget nobility; he was about to reach for her.

"I'm coming in," Lexie called out.

Redirecting her attention, Honor growled, "I'm going to muzzle her."

Jason tamped down on his urges.

Since his brother and nephew had moved in, it seemed a perpetual gloom overshadowed everything. All their focus had been on Hogan losing…everything.

Well, *not* everything. He still had Colt and as far as Jason was concerned, that was where the focus should be: on his son. Everything else would fall into place.

But the struggle was real for all of them. So many things had changed almost overnight. They were family, so they'd get through it, difficult as it might be. Jason had to believe that Hogan would get it together soon.

Until that happened, their new neighbor proved a nice diversion.

Honor wasn't as problematic as Jason had imagined. She had a gentle way about her, both strong and fragile, that softened everything—even the obvious issues.

She was still weighed down with responsibility, and her schedule was a real mystery, but she was also a fighter. He admired that. A lot.

As Lexie stuck her head into the kitchen, she said, "You have some swoon-worthy neighbors, Honor. Present company included."

Because Honor stayed silent, Jason picked up the slack with some verbal sparring. "I could say the same about Honor's friends."

"Friend," Lexie corrected. "I'm numero uno with her."

"Noted." He'd already realized that no one else had ever visited her.

"So, Jason, tell me about this other guy, Nathan. Is he as studly as the rest of you?"

Studly, huh? "Not sure that's how I'd describe him."

She pointed at him. "You need to introduce me soon."

"I thought you were into Sullivan."

"Mmm… Sullivan. Yes. But a girl needs options." She transferred her attention to Honor. "I'm going to check out the rest of the house. Be right back."

After she'd gone, Jason shook his head. "She's so relaxed and funny."

"In ways I can't be."

Those words seemed to have significant meaning for her. "I never said that."

"You don't have to." Fighting off the awkwardness, she opened her arms and said, "Fine. Colt can do a few things. But don't pressure him. I'll talk to him myself, okay?"

"I appreciate it."

Honor twisted her mouth at the irony, then laughed.

The sound was light and easy and real. Not giggling, not too robust. He'd like to hear her laugh more often.

"On my next day off, if the weather cooperates and…and nothing else comes up, I hope to move outside and get started on the yard. You have to hate having all these brambles and weeds bordering your property."

"All the rain hasn't helped." Wanting to touch her again, he put a hand to her narrow shoulder. Though she went still, she didn't object or move away. "Mind showing me around, too? I'd like to see the rest of the house."

Proving she could hear every word, Lexie yelled, "Do, Honor! It all looks terrific."

They both laughed—and at last, Jason felt like some of the walls were coming down.

Now he just had to decide how far he wanted to take things. Because with every day, it seemed more likely that being mere friendly neighbors just wasn't going to cut it.

He wanted more. But how much more?

And where the hell did she go in the middle of the night?

Over the next week, the temps climbed into the nineties and Jason worried for Honor's AC unit. When they got old, anything could happen.

So far, so good, though.

Toward the end of the week on her day off, she cleared away a lot of brambles, working throughout the day with only a few breaks. She wore cutoffs so short he could see the bottoms of the pockets sticking out from the frayed hem. Her loose, oversize Kid Rock T-shirt looked at least a decade old. A big brimmed hat shaded her face, while rubber boots and gardening gloves kept her hands and feet clean.

Somehow, on her, the mismatched outfit looked pretty damn hot.

In fact, no matter what she wore, the sight of her never failed to fire his blood.

She stretched to knock cobwebs off her front porch with a ragged broom, and his breath labored.

She bent to pull weeds from the yard, and his abs clenched at the sight of her small rounded ass.

She smiled and waved at him, the epitome of the friendly neighbor, and all he could think about was getting her alone, preferably with no clothes at all.

Nearly every day for the past week he'd visited with her, but only for short spells because she was forever busy in one way or another.

He always offered to lend a hand.

She always refused.

And she never complained about the work.

She knew he wanted her, had admitted her own interest, but she didn't remark on it. Even though she kept things strictly casual, there was a new understanding in how she treated him. She watched him with big eyes and breathless awareness, making him feel possessive when no other woman had affected him that way.

Jason tried to give her room; she had a lot of remodeling ahead of her, an obviously busy job and those mysterious late-night visits.

When she wanted to move things forward, she'd let him know.

But damn, waiting wasn't easy.

Though she wouldn't let him fix a single thing for her, she held to their agreement a week ago and always greeted Colt's offers with a lot of gratitude. Many times while working in the garage, Jason could hear them chatting while they did a chore.

Earlier today Colt had helped her pull out two old, dead shrubs. Backbreaking work, especially in this heat, but she'd laughed when the shrub finally came free and she fell on her ass.

Colt had looked as bemused by that as Jason.

He'd wanted to join in, but he'd been finishing up an ornate doghouse for a customer. After he'd delivered it, he got home to see Honor raking up the last of the mess.

Shaking his head, he'd gone in for dinner.

Now, with the dishes put away, he stood at the dining room window watching her stuff refuse into a big, sturdy lawn bag.

"She's been at it all day," Colt told him, worrying.

"Yeah." Apparently she wanted to finish up before calling it a night.

"It looks better already with the dead shrubbery gone. She's anxious to paint. But the house will have to be scraped first. And the shutters are a loss. Not sure even you could fix them."

Maybe, Jason thought, he could use that as an excuse to visit. Going one further, he wouldn't mind making her some custom shutters like he had for his own house. He could follow Lexie's lead and present them as a housewarming gift.

Hogan crowded in next to them, drying his hands on a dish towel, since it had been his turn in the kitchen. "Has she lost weight?"

"Yeah." She was a little thinner, but still shapely.

"The place looks better every day."

"Yeah."

His brother gave him a funny look. "You've been staring at her so long that you can only manage one-word replies?"

He shrugged.

Over his head, Hogan and Colt shared a grin that Jason ignored.

"His brain is starting to rot," Hogan said. "There are easier women around, you know."

Colt shifted, uncomfortable with that particular topic.

It infuriated Jason that his brother could be that callous. While going through his own ordeal, it seemed he'd forgotten how it all affected his son.

The seconds ticked by in silence, and then Colt said, "I didn't tell her about the garbage yesterday. Did you?"

"Nope." Honor still hadn't gotten a lid for her can, and once more, her garbage had gone everywhere. Jason had woken early that day to see raccoons rummaging through it.

There'd been no sign of Honor or her car, so he and Colt had picked it up again. She hadn't gotten back home until that evening, and as usual, she'd looked limp with exhaustion.

For the past few nights, though, he didn't think she'd gone out. He was so attuned to her he'd have somehow known, no matter how she skulked about.

Sometimes he'd be working in the garage and sense her the moment she got near her house. A dozen times, occasionally during meals, once in the middle of a shower, he'd been drawn to the window and found her out there, either leaving, arriving or working.

She kept odd hours, she kept secrets—and still his hunger for her grew.

Suddenly she glanced up, saw them all clustered in the window, and she waved.

Colt waved back.

Hogan glanced at Jason. "She still rendezvousing in the middle of the night?"

Colt answered before Jason could. "Yeah, she is. But she's getting sneakier about it. Sometimes I hear her, and sometimes I don't."

Well, hell. He hadn't realized that Colt was aware of it, too. His bedroom was on the same side of the house as Jason's, so he should have expected it. Hogan, luckily, was on the opposite end, making do in Jason's den, sleeping on a couch and keeping his clothes on hanging racks.

"I never should have told her that we could hear her departures or arrivals." There were a lot of things he regretted telling her. Did she work herself so hard trying to prove something… to him? He hated that idea.

"Where the hell does she go?" Hogan wondered aloud.

Colt shrugged. "She hasn't said."

Suddenly Honor lurched back from the scraggly shrubs remaining in front of her house. Screeching all the way, her expression comical, she high-stepped it toward their house, jiggling and slapping her hands all the way.

All three men headed to the front door to greet her, with Jason in the lead.

He got the door open and she barreled into him, hopped and jumped around him in a ridiculous and awkward dance, and finally managed to gasp, *"Snake!"*

Jason caught her shoulders and held her still. "Snake?"

"In the bushes! Over *there*." She stiff-arm pointed toward her property.

Jason took in her abject horror, then his brother and nephew's wide-eyed astonishment. His smile cracked and once it did, Colt and Hogan roared.

They laughed so hard they couldn't stay upright. Doubling over, they fell into each other, and occasionally one of them would say in a ridiculously high pitched voice, *"Snake,"* while prancing in place.

Jason had to admit, it was pretty funny. And damn, he liked seeing Hogan like this. For too long it had seemed as if Hogan lost the ability to laugh when he lost his wife.

But he was laughing now.

Honor tried to shove away from him, and without thinking

about it Jason folded her in close, locking his arms around her. She quickly subsided. In fact, she went stock-still.

Worked for him. The heat of the day had intensified the musk of her skin and hair. He breathed her in. Her skin was silky soft, dewy warm and damp. Against his ribs he felt the plump cushion of her breasts.

Colt got it together first, but then he was more attached to Honor since he'd been working with her all week, so he'd naturally be quicker to want to guard her feelings.

Around spontaneous chuckles, he asked, "What kind of snake was it?"

Jason felt her lips move against his chest when she said, "The kind I don't want to see."

"Meaning any kind?" Hogan guessed.

"Pretty much." She snuggled in closer, turning so her cheek rested on him. "I'm sorry for bothering you with this. You told me to get a dog or a gun, and since I haven't done either, I just…came here."

"I'm glad." Jason smoothed her untidy ponytail, more than a little turned on. "If you'd had a gun, would you have shot the snake?"

"No, of course not." She tipped her face back to see him. "I don't want it hurt."

That got Hogan guffawing again, and Colt struggling to contain his hilarity.

All Jason could think about was kissing her. When she looked up at him like that, he was a goner.

With a sigh, Honor resettled against him. "Why are you always shirtless?"

"It's ninety?"

"So in the winter…?"

He shrugged. He wasn't big on bundling up unless he knew he'd be outside for a while. "Depends."

After a few seconds more, she inhaled and levered away. "Guess I made a fool of myself."

"Nah." Hogan further mussed her already disheveled hair. "You just showed us your dance moves."

She surprised everyone by reaching out to playfully punch Hogan in the shoulder while grinning. Her amusement faded and she shuddered. "Sorry, but I was using all my bravery for the bugs. Once that python showed up—"

"Python?" Colt asked.

"To me, every snake is a python." She hugged herself. "The one I saw was just gray. And not that big. But..." She mean mugged each of them. "It looked at me."

On another short laugh, Hogan shook his head. "Well," he said to Colt. "Should we go slay a dragon?"

"Sure." Colt gave Honor a crooked grin. "How about if we just relocate it?"

"Far away?" she asked hopefully.

"The woods on the other side of the creek should work."

That intrigued her enough that she lost her jitters. "You can get to it?"

"Yeah, sure. Be right back." He and Hogan walked off.

Leaving Jason and Honor alone.

As a reminder not to keep touching her, Jason again shoved his hands into his pockets. "Once your yard is in shape, you'll see that just beyond that line of trees is the creek. I put in a stone path to it from my backyard and built a little bridge to get over it to the other side. With all this rain, it's almost like a river."

"I didn't realize it was that accessible." Enthusiastic, she added, "I want to see it."

"Now?" He eyed her dirty knees and the scratches on her arms. She was certainly dressed for it.

"No, not while they're putting a snake there." She went back to hugging herself.

Did she think it would be snake free at some point? Jason stepped closer to her. "Could I ask a favor?"

Jumping on that, she replied fast, "Yes, of course. I'd love a way to repay you."

"I didn't mean... There's nothing to repay." He gave one shake of his head. "If you go to the creek, will you be sure to take one of us with you?" He held up a hand. "I know you're more than competent, but it's unfamiliar—"

Wearing a cheeky grin, she added, "And there'll be at least one snake there."

"—and it'd be better if you weren't alone."

They stared at each other.

She turned shy again. "You'd go with me?"

"Yes." Even as he reminded himself not to pressure her, he eased a step closer.

"Okay. Thank you."

Why did it feel like he'd just made a date for the prom? Unable to resist, he lifted a hand to her face and brushed his thumb over a smudge of dirt on her cheek. Silky, warm...would she be that soft all over? "I like your boots."

Dimples appeared in her cheeks. "Thank you. I didn't want my feet to get dirty." Her eyes widened. "Oh my god, my filthy boots! I tromped into your house." She turned a circle, looking everywhere for tracks, but then she slowed and breathed in awe, "Wow, your house."

Proud of all the work he'd done, Jason enjoyed watching her face, seeing her admiration as she visually explored.

She did another turn, taking in the cozy family room and peeking into the formal dining room. "It's *amazing*. I love your doors, and baseboards, and all the trim."

"The millwork is original to the house. When I remodeled and expanded things, I matched the existing trim with original moldings salvaged from area teardowns."

Eyes wide, she took in the higher ceilings and then the wide-plank wooden floors. "I'm blown away."

Her house was similar to his but smaller and without the major renovations. "Want me to show you the rest of it?" A tour seemed like a good opportunity to advance their relationship. He'd open up to her—and maybe she'd open up to him.

"Yes, please." Quickly she removed her boots and put them by the door. "Your place is twice the size of mine."

Jason stared at her small bare feet with the toenails painted pink. She'd only removed her boots, but it hit him like a striptease.

He forced his gaze back to her face. "I added to the length of the kitchen, one bathroom and my bedroom." Gesturing for her to go ahead of him, they went down the hall and started with Hogan's room. His brother wasn't particularly messy, but the setup—a somewhat converted den—made organizing tough.

"Hogan is camping out in here until he can make other arrangements. You can probably tell I'd turned the room into more of an office space. Things are shoved around now, mostly out of place."

Leaning in through the doorway, Honor admired the many windows, the floor and area rugs and the heavy masculine furniture. "It's gorgeous—and I think it's terrific that you and your brother are close enough to rely on each other."

"Family first," he said. "Always."

She beamed at him in approval, making him wonder again about her family.

Next he showed her the hall bath done in white subway tiles, dark wood and a grayish blue paint. Because Colt and Hogan tended to use the spare shower in the basement, the room remained nice and tidy.

At the other end of the house—closest to where she lived—he showed her Colt's room, which was predictably cluttered.

She took it all in and smiled. "Typical high school kid?"

"Been a long time since I was a high schooler, so I can't say for sure, but it seems to me he's a hell of a lot more mature than most. Messy, yes, but mature."

She grinned as she pulled the door shut. "He is pretty terrific."

"Agreed." Jason led her to the last bedroom.

His own.

"Until Hogan and Colt moved in, I'd never lived with a kid. Even at Colt's age, I was neat, and Hogan was never exactly a slob. But Colt..." He grinned. "I swear the kid could clutter up an empty lot."

"He's generous with his time." Guilt made her wince. "It seems I'm always working him now."

"With everything that's happened, I think he likes staying busy and being appreciated." He cupped his hand to her neck and moved his thumb over the side of her throat. "You're generous with your gratitude."

She moved nearer so that with each step, their bodies brushed together. "We haven't talked about anything too personal, but I know he misses his friends."

"The loss of his mom, the move—it's all disrupted his life in a big way."

"I can imagine."

Jason looked at her, but she kept her expression blank. "Since they moved in, a lot of the time has been transitioning here. Hogan still has business to wrap up in Columbus, and occasionally Colt can accompany him there, so he sees his old friends just enough to keep him from completely settling in here."

"Rough."

He nodded. "All in all, he's handled it well. At least from what I can see." Colt was a private kid. If he still suffered over the loss of his mom, he kept it to himself.

Honor shoulder-bumped him. "I'm glad he's here with you."

"Yeah, me, too." Pushing aside his never-ending worry for

his nephew, Jason opened his bedroom door and stepped in. "This is my room."

She balked at the doorway.

"Come on in."

She did, but instead of looking at the room, she looked at him.

"That's not playing fair," Jason murmured, doing his own share of looking. When he took a step toward her, she quickly got it together and jumped her gaze around the room.

"You have amazing taste."

"Thanks, but I can't take much credit. The furniture is antique. Mom was a collector. She bought this set ages ago, and Dad left it behind when he moved."

She stroked her fingers along the edge of an ornate mirror over the dresser. "I love it."

"Me, too." He'd repaired the pieces his father had broken in a depressive rant after his wife died.

Jason still missed her.

So how must Colt feel?

"The quilt is beautiful. Is it handmade?"

"Locally, yeah." Watching her walk around the room, touching some things, studying others, made it difficult for him to talk.

She looked out the windows to the backyard, then to the adjacent wall—where the window faced her house.

She glanced at him but said nothing.

The thought of leading her to the bed pulsed in his brain. Instead he said, "There's a bathroom through there."

Hesitantly she turned, opened the door he'd indicated, then sighed. "I'm so jealous." She disappeared inside.

Jason kept his distance. He was already at the ragged edge, and getting closer wouldn't help.

From inside the room she said, "Love your shower! It's huge. And the tiles are beautiful."

"It's one of the rooms that gained space when I added on."

When she emerged, she said, "You are so neat and clean. That shower looks like it's never been used."

"Use it every day," he promised.

She laughed at him. "Then you must dry it off each time."

"Guilty."

Walking around him, she headed to the door. "Show me the kitchen. They say it's the heart of the home."

For sure it'd be safer.

Taking her back down the hall and through the family room, they turned into the kitchen. The dining room had arched doorways that opened into the kitchen and into the family room, so that the three rooms flowed together.

Walking the perimeter of the room, Honor admired the cabinetry, the appliances and the natural stone counters. "It's beautiful."

She was beautiful, maybe more so while a little damp from yard work. He kept looking at the nape of her neck, where small curls had escaped the band of her ponytail.

He'd touched her there. Now he wanted to kiss her there.

He wanted to kiss her *everywhere.*

"You did all the work yourself?"

"Yeah." Realizing she'd caught him staring, Jason popped his neck and tried to focus. At this rate she'd think he was desperate. Or worse, that he'd never been laid. "I kept the basic design from my childhood, just bigger. This sink? It's the original. I updated the faucets but used the same style. My mom used to stand here doing dishes, and she'd watch Hogan and me in the backyard through the window." He gestured to the new island. "But back then, when the room was so much smaller, the sink was there."

Honor drifted to the sink and looked out. "I can almost envision that."

Almost? Jason looked at the length of her body, from the

gracefully bent neck as she bowed her head, down her spine to the dip of her waist, then the flare of her behind and hips.

Her softly rounded curves were perfect.

Feeling literally drawn to her, he stepped up close and put his hands on her waist. Through the big T-shirt he could feel the contours of her body. He let his nose tease her tantalizing nape. "Damn, you look hot grubby."

She made a rough sound of surprise—but she didn't move away.

"I like you, Honor."

She tipped her head to give him better access and said breathlessly, "You do?"

"Mmm." His lips just brushed the edge of her ear. "You like me, too."

"How do you know?"

Jason turned her to face him. Her eyes looked heavy, her soft lips parted. God, he needed her mouth. "You stare at me a lot."

"You're always half-naked."

So cute. "That's all it is, huh?" He smoothed back those wayward tendrils of hair. He *loved* her hair, so soft and baby fine, the color kissed by the sun. "Because you know, Mr. Westbrook a few doors down always cuts his grass in his Speedos, but I haven't seen you eyeballing him."

With the daze clearing from her whiskey-colored eyes, she snorted a laugh. "He's sixty-eight and…rotund."

"Rotund, huh? That's your nice way of saying he has a massive beer gut?"

Wearing a silly smile, she nodded. "I always try to be nice."

"Other than the time I pissed you off, you have been. And believe me, I deserved it then."

Scowling playfully, she poked him in the chest and said, "You didn't want me to move in."

He caught her hand. "I didn't think you could handle things."

How stupid he'd been. So far, Honor was the hardest worker he'd ever known. "Plenty of people have thought they could breeze in, do some cosmetic work and resell for a profit. Soon as they realize the scope of the job, they sell the property. And if they can't sell, they abandon it."

She tipped her head, studying him. "Is that what happened to my house?"

"Lucky for you, they'd already done repairs to the heat pump and plumbing." Winter might be a problem, because she'd probably need a new roof. But she'd likely figure that out, and how to deal with it, on her own, too.

She flattened a hand to his chest. "You know, you were right about a lot of things."

"Such as?"

"The noises at night, for one." She peered up at him and admitted, "I hear so many things."

"Things that scare you?"

There was a heartbeat of hesitation. "Let's just say they can be unsettling."

"Hey." Again he cupped her nape, this time with both hands. "You have my number." He wouldn't mind keeping her safe at night.

"Right." Her smile twitched. "So at two in the morning you wouldn't mind reassuring the insecure lady next door that the bogeyman doesn't exist?"

It wasn't the bogeyman she had to worry about, but real crime. "You can call me anytime." When her eyes searched his, he added, "For anything."

"So you're a good uncle—and a really terrific neighbor." Her gaze darted away. "But you already think I'm weak."

"Hell no." Bending his knees to draw her gaze back to his, he gave her the full force of his frown. "You've blown me away, Honor Brown. No one should work as hard as you do. You're…"

He straightened again and sighed. "You're not what I expected, because you're not like any other women I've known."

"Known a lot, have you?"

"I'm thirty-two and I haven't been a saint." He smiled. "But I'm also not a guy who feels challenged to get laid every weekend." Mostly because he was particular, and at heart he wanted what Hogan had once had…before it all went up in flames.

Her eyes flared at his blunt speaking. "Um…okay."

What exactly was it about her? "Every woman I've known would have been asking for help, not refusing it."

"I'd like to say I'm different from them." She gestured between them. "But I'm here because I ran to you terrorized by a snake."

"Well, hallelujah, you have a weakness."

Now she laughed. "I have many, if you must know."

"I'd like to know." He wouldn't mind learning everything about her, especially the reason for her midnight runs. "Speaking of that. Where do you go—"

Laughter and a closing door proclaimed their private time over.

Walking into the kitchen, Colt said, "You scared that poor snake so badly it had gray hairs—"

His voice dropped to sudden silence. Hogan almost ran into his back. Both of them stared, then ran into each other again trying to backtrack out.

"Sorry."

"Should've knocked."

Ducking away from Jason, Honor didn't let them get far. "You guys got the snake safely settled?"

After giving Jason a look of apology, Colt grinned at her. "We didn't tuck him in or anything, but yeah, we put him underneath a shrub on the other side of the creek."

"I hope he'll be okay."

They all stared at her, each trying to suppress a smile.

"The creek's high," Hogan said, just to fill in the silence. "I could almost hear the fish calling out to us."

The effort to joke didn't quite dissipate the sexual tension still stirring the air.

"So…" Feeling that tension, Hogan put a hand on his son's back and steered him to the doorway. "Colt and I are going to watch some TV. Carry on."

The second they stepped out, Honor turned to Jason, her eyes filled with questions.

"We got interrupted," he said gruffly.

"Yes, we did." She waffled, then came close and, in the barest whisper, asked, "Were you…you know. Going to kiss me?"

Damn right. "The possibility crossed my mind." Maybe after he got her to answer some burning questions about her frequent trips. He needed to know where she went during the night. The only possibility he could think of was her seeing another guy, and he hated it. Honor didn't strike him as the type to play that game, but he needed her to confirm it.

Before he could ask her, she bit her lip, nodded—then suddenly went on her tiptoes to lightly press that irresistible mouth to his.

Used to her usual reserve, the kiss totally took him by surprise. He registered the softness of her lips along with the gentle touch of her hands on his bare shoulders as she braced herself.

Needing more, he reached for her just as she dropped back flat to her feet. Looking shy once again, she whispered, "Thank you for saving me from the snake."

"Welcome," he managed to say around the surge of lust.

Flushed, she put a hand to her chest. "That made my heart beat harder than the snake did." She smiled—and turned to walk away.

Like hell. "Honor."

She paused, her back still to him.

"When's your next evening free?"

Looking over her shoulder at him, she asked suspiciously, "Why?"

"I want to take you out. Nowhere fancy. Maybe Screwy Louie's."

"Really? I've been wanting to go there." She turned to him again, and her face fell. "I don't really get nights off, though. I mean, not while there's still so much to do on the house."

"Take a few hours off for me and I'll help you get some things done." When she started to object, Jason closed the space between them, drew her in close and kissed her the way he really wanted to.

Keeping her still, he touched his mouth to hers. Her lips were full and warm, and Jesus, she smelled good. He touched with his tongue, teasing with shallow licks and small strokes until she parted and let him in, allowing the kiss to go deeper. Damp, hot.

Breath quickening, she pressed closer.

His cock twitched—from a *kiss*.

Against his chest, he felt her stiffened nipples and the rocking of her heartbeat. Or maybe that was his heart pumping too fast. Hard to tell.

He knew he should let up, but he couldn't quite convince himself of that. He wanted more. *Needed* more.

Given the way her fingertips dug into his shoulders, she did, too.

So damn sweet. God, her mouth was nice.

If kissing her was this hot, what would the sex be like?

When she gave a small groan, he pressed a hand down to the small of her back, gathered her in closer and this time he was the one groaning.

He'd been far too long without a woman, and his control wasn't what it should be. His brother and his seventeen-year-old nephew were in the other room. Most important, Honor had been too reluctant for him to take advantage of her now. *She'd initiated the first kiss.* He should relish that without pushing her too much; the last thing he wanted was for her to have regrets.

It wasn't easy, but he got it together and gently eased her away. Her eyes stayed closed and she breathed heavily.

Such a temptation.

"Make time for me." With lust roughening his voice, the request sounded more like a demand.

As if coming out of a fog, Honor blinked lazily, then blew out a slow breath. "That might not be a good idea."

"It's a terrific idea. You could use some fun."

She blinked fast. "Fun?"

"Screwy Louie's. Remember?"

"Oh, right." She hugged him tight and, sounding apologetic, said, "I don't know when I'd have time. I've still got so much to do to the house and then there's work and...other things."

Determined to find out about those "other things," Jason smoothed down her ponytail, kissed the top of her head and just enjoyed holding her because that, too, was damn nice. "You said you wanted to repay me." It was dirty pool, playing that card against her. But the way he felt right now, he'd do whatever needed to be done to win her over.

"I do, but—"

"No buts. I promise it'll be painless, and I promise you'll have fun. That's all I'm asking for." He tilted back to see her. "Just neighbors visiting, okay? No reason to worry."

"I..." She thought about it, but clearly couldn't come up with a reason to refuse. "Okay, fine." She went to step away, and he reluctantly let her.

"One thing, Honor."

"Hmm?"

Her eyes were still hazy with need and it nearly took out his knees. No woman should be so sexy and so incredibly sweet. "Don't make me wait too long."

Warm color mottled her cheeks, and as she started backing

up toward the door, worry showed in her beautiful eyes. "No problem there." She looked at his chest, his abdomen…lower, then quickly met his eyes again. "Apparently my willpower isn't that strong anyway."

For once in her life, Lexie hadn't shared with Honor, and she wasn't sure why. Honor was always supportive, never judged her and understood her quirkiness.

But for some reason, this felt…private.

Dumb. Especially since Honor had told her about "the kiss," as Honor called it. Lexie grinned thinking about it. For Honor, that had been a huge move—a move she rarely made. It usually took Lexie a lot of arm twisting just to get Honor to agree to a date. But close to a week ago she'd kissed her hunky neighbor in his kitchen with his relatives close by, all predate.

Silently she'd cheered. Not so silently, she'd told Honor to go for gold. So far, though, that hadn't happened. Hopefully soon.

She pulled up in front of the restaurant with a lot of anticipation. After too many conflicts with their schedules, she and Sullivan had finally arranged to meet for an early dinner, away from his neighborhood, closer to hers. Given the time, he'd told her he could shower at his gym and come straight from there. She'd been tempted to run by there, take a peek, see the setup. But that might have looked stalkerish, so instead she'd resisted temptation and put all her thoughts on what might happen later tonight.

After checking her lip gloss in the visor mirror, she turned off her car—and jumped when a tap sounded on her window.

Sullivan stood there, looking immeasurably hot in a black T-shirt and khakis. Smiling, he opened her door and Lexie stepped out.

The man had it.

All the good stuff. Machismo. Killer body. Charming smile.

It wasn't often a man could bowl her over, but Sullivan really did it for her.

Trying for her usual careless air, she said, "Hey, Sullivan. Perfect timing."

"Hey, yourself." His appreciative gaze boldly coasted over her. "Nice."

Since she'd specifically dressed for him, she liked his reaction to her simple black tank dress made snug enough to show off her every curve. She'd dressed it up a little with medium-heeled, beaded sandals and dangly silver earrings.

"I'm glad you approve."

"I didn't say that." Lifting one brow, he let his attention linger on her breasts, her belly, her upper thighs. "Looking like you do, you're liable to cause a riot."

Oh, such a flatterer. "I'll trust you to keep me safe." Copying Honor's example, she leaned into him and stole a kiss.

She was about to move away, but he caught his arm around her waist and locked her close. "Try that again," he said against her lips, "but this time do it like you mean it."

"A challenge?"

"If that's how you want to take it."

Loving this game, Lexie held his face, gently kissed his bottom lip, nipped it with her teeth, then teased with her tongue.

"Better," he growled while stepping his body against hers, pressing her to the car.

"Hush." She put her mouth to his and kissed him the way she'd wanted to since she first laid eyes on him.

His inky dark hair was still damp from a recent shower and she inhaled the scents of soap, aftershave and oh–so-potent male. Intoxicated, she forgot it was a game and got lost in the kiss—especially when Sullivan took over.

Add "excellent kisser" to the list with his other fine qualities. It had been a long time since something as innocent as a mere kiss got her this fired up.

When a horn beeped and someone laughingly yelled, "Get a room," they both recalled they were standing beside her car at the curb in full view of passersby.

His smile wicked, Sullivan whispered, "Now, that was a kiss."

Flustered, turned on and totally off her game, Lexie managed to say, "Oh, I have other tricks up my sleeve. But maybe not here."

His laugh showed beautiful white teeth and made his blue eyes light up brighter. He gave her another quick kiss, and even that, more of a teasing smooch than anything sexual, had her toes curling.

With his arm around her he led her to the sidewalk in front of the restaurant.

Far as Lexie was concerned, dinner couldn't end quickly enough—but hopefully the night would be long.

5

MIDWAY THROUGH HIS meal with Lexie, Sullivan knew he wanted her. Actually he'd known that from the moment she introduced herself. Her body language, her smiles, even her eyes made it clear that she was available, willing, even anxious to hook up.

He loved confident women.

On temporary occasions.

His still somewhat new business and his dedication to the kids didn't allow for any serious entanglements. And even if he had the time or inclination, which he didn't, Lexie was the opposite type of woman he'd be after. She was about the here and now, not the long haul.

Tonight that suited him just fine.

She suited him—except that she was his neighbor's best friend, and she'd already proven to be scheming. Not a great combo when what he wanted, what he needed, was that "one and done" attitude they'd already discussed.

Prior to setting the date, he'd weighed the pros and cons at length, but finally decided the cons didn't matter. Not enough anyway.

She wasn't his neighbor, so proximity didn't have to factor in. How often could she visit Honor anyway? And with the hours he worked, even if she was there every day, odds were he wouldn't see her. Today was an aberration, given he'd taken off early and left the last class with an employee. He never did that—the work he did with at–risk kids was too important to him.

But for Lexie he'd made an exception.

He needed a woman.

Lexie was a party girl, not at all clingy. He wouldn't have to worry about her making an issue of things. A good thing, since he wouldn't let any woman, especially a cunning, carefree flirt, mess with his long-term plans. The school was his priority. Helping kids to avoid his mistakes was a priority.

Chasing tail was not.

Luckily, with this particular woman, he hadn't had to do any chasing at all.

Watching Lexie now, he damn near throbbed with lust. From the second she'd stepped out of her car in that second-skin dress, he'd been on edge. Lust, pure and simple.

Easy to sate.

Her short pale blond hair, curling around her face, only emphasized her golden-hazel eyes—eyes that repeatedly ate him up.

Slender arms, a narrow waist and gorgeous, shapely legs, paired with that beautiful face and her innate confidence, had every guy in the restaurant checking her out. Luckily the hour was early enough that the place wasn't as packed as usual. He hadn't been joking about the riot.

Propping an elbow on the table, Lexie leaned forward and gave him a mouthwatering view of her cleavage.

No way could she be wearing a bra. He wasn't even certain about panties, given the smooth line of the dress.

Smiling lazily, she said, "Penny for your thoughts."

"Probably the same as yours."

The smile turned into a sly grin. "You think?"

She'd been as up front as possible, but to be sure, Sullivan teased one fingertip on the back of her hand. "I'm thinking this meal is taking too long and I need to see you naked."

After a sharp inhale, she sat back, tipped up her wineglass to finish it off and then met his gaze again. "You're actually better at this than I am, and that's a compliment because I consider myself more than adequate at the whole back-and-forth sexual banter."

"More than adequate," he agreed. Hell, she had him on the ragged edge.

"How about," she murmured, "we wrap this up, and then you can follow me to my place? It's closer."

That suited him. He'd prefer her apartment over his house. He didn't need anyone knowing his personal business, especially since Jason had a thing for Honor.

As an answer, Sullivan raised his hand and summoned the waiter.

Less than five minutes later they were on the road, and ten minutes after that he walked into her apartment. After looking around, he said, "Classy place."

She kicked off her shoes by the front door, dropped her purse on a foyer table and turned to him with hot expectation. Taking both his hands, she began back-stepping. "I'll give you the tour later."

"And now?"

"Now we go to my room."

Such a rush. He was used to women going a little slower, needing a little more attention. Not Lexie.

Knowing she had high windows that overlooked the city and the river, he wanted to take in the view, but he couldn't get his gaze off her. In his peripheral vision he noted sleek, modern furniture and minimal clutter.

Sullivan let her pull him down a short hall, past a small bathroom done in silver and cream, then into a lavishly decorated bedroom, mostly white but with accents of silver, black and sapphire.

Before she could head to the bed, Sullivan pinned her to the wall and slowly lifted her hands above her head.

She shivered, her golden eyes molten, her lips parted.

Ready.

He got that. He was so hard he hurt, burning up with need. He could take her right here, standing, but as bad as he wanted to be inside her, he wanted to taste her, too.

And he definitely wanted to watch her come.

Slowly he leaned in, detouring from her mouth to her throat. Lexie tipped her head back wantonly, making it easier on him. With open-mouth, damp kisses, he left a trail from her fragrant, silky neck to the bend of her shoulder, down her chest to one firm breast, where he nuzzled, then lightly bit the taut nipple straining through the thin material of her dress.

On a vibrating groan, she arched into him.

He transferred both her hands into one of his and stroked her body. His turn to groan. "No underwear at all?"

She looked at him through heavy, heated eyes. "See for yourself."

Damn, he loved her brazenness. "I think I will." He inched the dress up, caressing her skin along the way. Her thigh was smooth and warm and soft, and at the top of her hip he encountered one thin string.

Leaning away, he looked down and saw the skimpiest of thongs, barely covering her. Nostrils flaring, he stroked over her hip to her naked ass. Firm, satiny.

While palming one bare cheek, he took her mouth in a ravenous kiss. She stayed with him, her hips snuggling into his, stroking him through his khakis. Dangerously close to losing his control, Sullivan made himself slow, made himself think of Lexie, her need, and what he ultimately wanted—*her* out of control.

He released her wrists, stepped back and whisked that cock-teasing dress up and over her head. Breathing heavily, he took

LORI FOSTER

in the sight of her, flushed with desire, naked except for the tiny scrap of material hiding her sex.

"Damn." She had beautiful breasts. Not big, but round and firm, pale, her nipples a dusky pink. With both hands he cupped her, teased her with his thumbs, tugged gently.

The second he drew her into his mouth, her compliance shattered, gone in a rush of lust.

Pushing him back, she attacked his belt buckle, then yanked down his zipper and freed his cock. Sullivan breathed deeply, his arms at his sides, letting her touch him, stroke him as she pleased.

"You're ready," she murmured with satisfaction.

"Did you doubt it?"

"Protection?"

He quickly fished out his wallet and retrieved a lone condom. "One."

She smiled up at him. "If you do it right, one will be enough."

Laughing, he said, "I'll try my best."

Seconds later they were on the bed, both of them naked, entwined, and Sullivan got lost in the feel and taste of her. He found her boldness and confidence even more exciting when it applied to sex.

If he had more room in his life, if he wanted different things, she'd be the perfect woman.

Given the way she stirred him, she was perfect—for now.

After some frenzied foreplay, she sat astride him and carefully eased him inside her.

They both went still, breath held, bodies tight.

Sullivan moved first, gripping her hips and easing her up, then bringing her down slowly again.

"Sorry," she whispered, the words broken, "but I can't wait."

He stared into her eyes. "Then don't."

Needing no more encouragement than that, she proceeded to ride him hard while he enjoyed her breasts until suddenly, far too soon, she broke, her head back, a long, ragged groan tearing from her throat.

So fucking perfect.

Seeing her, hearing her, feeling her clamped around him, wet and hot, sent Sullivan over the edge, too. And it was so powerful it left him reeling.

Sometime later, his heart still hammering, with Lexie as a warm blanket over him, he heard her murmur, "You did it right, and then some."

Smiling, far too content, he thought, *What now?*

He should start making moves to go—but he didn't want to.

He should ensure that she knew this was a onetime shot—but he suddenly hated that thought. No way had he gotten his fill. Not even close.

Hell, if anything, he wanted her even more now. Crazy. Impossible.

He had to stop thinking about taking her again, right now, even though neither of them was yet breathing right. But he had no idea how to block those thoughts when the sex had been so spectacular.

When *she'd* been spectacular.

He turned her under him, took in her slumberous eyes and sated smile—and the cell phone in his pants pocket rang.

They stared at each other.

"No," she insisted softly.

He wanted to ignore it, he really did, but as a businessman he couldn't. It probably wasn't even seven yet, and it could be his employee with an issue. Something could have happened with a pupil. "One second. I promise." He stretched out an arm, snagged his pants, found the phone and saw it was Nathan calling.

He got a very bad feeling.

Swiping his thumb over the screen to answer, he sat up and away from Lexie, saying, "Hey, Nathan. I'm a little busy right—"

"Someone put a pipe bomb in your new neighbor's mailbox. Jason's not around, and she's apparently not home. Don't suppose you have a number for her?"

Shit. Just...shit. He looked at Lexie, so ripe, so anxious for him. They were out of condoms, but there were so many other things he could do to and with her.

Unfortunately, if he kept this from her, if Honor got home to a crime scene...

The decision made, he gave Lexie one last apologetic look, then said, "I don't, but her best friend is right here, and I'm sure she does."

Despite the way the day had gotten away from her, Honor pulled onto her street in a fairly good mood. It was barely seven-thirty, later than she would have liked, but she'd orchestrated the craziness to the best of her ability so that she'd have the rest of the night free. She'd already done her hair and makeup at the salon, taken care of an early visit and as soon as she changed into prettier clothes, she'd check with Jason to see if he had a few hours to visit.

Finally they'd have that date.

Just a date, she told herself. No reason to panic, no reason to worry. It wouldn't interfere with her impossible schedule, and there was no reason it had to be more than one date...right? Never mind what she wanted, what she wished could be.

She was a realist. Etching out time this evening hadn't been easy. Fitting in anything more than this one night would be damn near impossible.

So she'd take it, make the most of it and then she'd get back to her daily routine.

It had been so long since she'd been on a real date she wasn't sure she remembered how to behave. She hoped Jason was free, because she honestly didn't know when she'd get another opportunity.

She was lost in daydreams of kissing him again, maybe more, when the sight before her registered. Alarm shot through her bloodstream. Jason was there, wearing a button-up shirt with his jeans, talking to another man she didn't recognize. Sullivan and Lexie stood next to them. Gray smoke hung in the air and...

Ohmigod. Her mailbox was a smoldering pile of unrecognizable wood and plastic. Because the small crowd blocked her driveway, she pulled over to the curb in front of Jason's house. He glanced at her as she left the car, looked away dismissively, but a second later his gaze shot back for a longer look.

Eyes narrowed with puzzlement, he took a step toward her. "Honor?"

"What happened?" Heart in her throat and a sick feeling churning in her stomach, Honor stared at the ruins before her.

Jason stared at her.

She remembered that this was the first time he'd seen her not a mess. She wrinkled her nose and pushed past him.

"Hey." Lexie embraced her. "I hate to take you by surprise, but I tried calling twice with no answer."

Brows up, Sullivan stared at her, too.

Good grief. Had the men assumed she never wore makeup? That the only hairstyle she had was a sloppy ponytail? She was a salon stylist, after all.

In a rush, she dug her cell phone from her purse and saw she had two missed calls. "Must have been when I was..." Doing a preemptive run on her responsibilities. She swallowed back that explanation. Not that an explanation was needed.

Lexie hugged her. "I'm sorry."

"What happened?"

Another man stepped up to her. Tall, sandy brown hair, eyes hidden by dark sunglasses and shoulders broad enough to block her view of the chaos. He took off the glasses and hooked them to the front of his blue, button-up shirt. "You're Honor Brown?"

With his whole face revealed, she saw the thin scar cutting

across his right cheek from his temple to the corner of his mouth. Rather than detract from his good looks, it gave him a rugged, dangerous appearance that was also very sexy.

She blinked twice and nodded dumbly.

Expression dark, Jason moved over beside her, so close that they touched. "Honor, this is Nathan Hawley, our sheriff and neighbor."

Holy smokes. She was starting to agree with Lexie; there must be something in the water to grow the men so fine in Clearbrook.

Looking past the guys to her friend, Honor watched Lexie theatrically fan her face in agreement.

Silently Honor agreed—times ten.

Studiously ignoring Lexie, Sullivan pointed at her mailbox. "Someone blew it up."

"Pipe bomb," Nathan explained.

But…she'd only recently changed out the old rusted mailbox for a nice new shiny one! "Why would anyone do that?"

"Vandalism," Nathan said. "We get that around here. I'm guessing it was no more than that—"

Finally regaining her senses, Honor said, "That's more than enough!"

"I agree." Calm personified, Nathan looked at her house. "To be on the safe side, though, I'd like to check your house, too."

Her throat tightened and she squeaked, "Check it for what?"

"I just want to make sure everything is still secure."

Secure? Horrified by the thought of an intruder, Honor stared toward the dark windows at the front.

Jason put his arm around her. "The mailbox was intact when you left? Still closed? You didn't notice anything around your property?"

She hadn't really been paying attention, but surely she would have noticed otherwise. "Yes… I think so."

"When exactly did you leave this morning?" Nathan asked her.

Honor stepped around the men to look at the destruction. She didn't want to meet Lexie's gaze, and she was too rattled to look at the hunks surrounding her. "Before five."

"A.m.?" Jason asked.

Ignoring his disbelief, she nodded. "I had to run a few…errands before work." *To hopefully clear a path for our date.*

Nathan propped his hand on a holster.

A holster with a gun that she hadn't even noticed until now.

"We've had other mailboxes destroyed in the area."

"Today?"

"Recently."

"So." Honor tried a deep, cleansing breath to help her calm down, then asked with hope, "Random vandalism?"

"It's possible." Nathan's gaze cut to Sullivan's and then Jason's. "But we've also had some burglaries."

As if she'd been struck, Honor sucked in more air—then turned and ran for her house.

"Honor." Jason's hand caught her arm before she'd reached the porch. He pulled her up short, holding her securely. "Let Nathan do his thing."

"His *thing?*" All she cared about at the moment was her home. Had she been robbed? Her possessions destroyed?

Nathan stepped around her. "Let me see if the door and windows are locked, and we'll go from there."

Oh God. Fear robbed her voice of strength. "What if someone is still inside?" The words emerged so quietly it surprised her that Jason heard.

He drew her closer. "Odds are, if anyone even attempted to get inside, they'd be long gone now."

"You have those security lights, especially around the garage," Sullivan pointed out to Jason. "They light up half of Honor's yard, too, at least on this side. I can't see anyone risking it."

Stepping back off the porch, Nathan said, "The front's still locked up."

LORI FOSTER

When he started toward the back, Honor pushed away from Jason to follow. Everyone else fell into step behind them. The side of her house closest to Jason's was undisturbed. The back windows, too, remained locked.

Unfortunately, on the farthest side near the woods, where no neighbors existed, they found an open window.

Honor's knees wobbled.

It took Jason no time at all to say, "It was pried open."

"Yup," Nathan agreed. "The lock is broken."

She'd been so lighthearted and happy, looking forward to the evening, to a possible date with Jason.

She'd styled her hair!

Even painted her fingernails.

Now her throat felt thick and her eyes burned. She'd been invaded.

Nathan went into bossy sheriff mode. Holding out his hand, his green eyes direct, he said, "Your keys?"

He spoke with such quiet command that Honor automatically gave them to him. Lexie scooted up to her side, physically offering her moral support.

"I doubt anyone's hanging around, but I don't like taking chances."

Nodding, Honor agreed with him. "I'm not about to go back in there until I know it's safe." And even then…she shivered.

Lexie hugged her. "You can come home with me."

That'd be the coward's way, and even though at the moment it sounded pretty good, she knew she couldn't.

Honor didn't have to announce a decision right then. Looking somehow bigger and badder than he had just moments ago, Nathan stated, "I want you and Lexie to go next door. Stay there until Jason comes for you."

She nodded fast. "Okay." She was capable, but she wasn't stupid.

Lexie agreed. "Sure."

Neither of them actually moved.

"Jason, you and Sullivan stay here in case anyone tries to slip back out the window. But if you see anyone, no matter what, get the hell out of the way."

Sullivan made a rude sound.

Turning on him, Nathan said, "No fucking heroes," with iron command. "I mean it."

Sullivan, however, appeared unimpressed.

Lexie whispered, "When Alphas collide..."

"Shush," Honor told her.

"Go on, Nathan. We'll be fine." Jason turned to Honor. "Back door is unlocked."

The prompt got her moving. "Right." Dragging along Lexie, who kept looking back at Sullivan, Honor hurried to Jason's house. Nathan headed to the front.

Thinking of the significance of the black gun in his holster, she gulped as she moved behind some bushes bordering the back patio. If necessary, they could duck into the house quickly enough, but for now, anxiety gripped her.

Jason and Sullivan stood at the back corner of her house, able to see the open window but not in the direct line of anyone who might try to scuttle out. Honor could hear their quiet murmurs.

A dozen different what-ifs raced through her brain.

Lights came on inside, and with each one her heart lurched as she waited to hear a conflict or even possible gunfire.

Hunkered down next to her, Lexie whispered, "You didn't leave out anything personal, did you?"

Gaze continually sweeping from the windows to the front door, and then to the men at the back, she replied just as quietly, "What do you mean?"

"You know." Lexie nudged her. *"Personal."*

"Like my toothbrush?"

Aggrieved, Lexie sighed and started to speak.

But from behind them someone said, "She means a vibrator."

Screeching, Honor whirled to face the threat and ended up falling into the bushes.

Hogan, Jason's brother, frowned at her.

"Damn it," Lexie hissed at him. "Why are you creeping up on us?"

"I didn't creep," he said, lowering his voice theatrically to match hers. "You were too busy being nosy to hear me."

"Nosy?"

"Getting all up in Honor's business," he explained. "You should worry about your own vibrators and leave hers alone."

When Jason suddenly loomed over her, Honor groaned in mortification. How much had he heard? And how difficult was it going to be to explain?

Gaze carefully neutral, Jason took her hands and pulled her to her feet. "Are you okay?"

Honor jerked back around to the house and saw Nathan joining Sullivan, both of them on their way over, their steps unhurried, their posture casual.

Her heart thumped so hard she had to grope for a chair. "It's clear?"

"Apparently." He turned her to face him again. "I came to see why you screamed."

"Hogan snuck up on us," Lexie accused meanly. "That's why."

A wicked smirk spread over Hogan's face. "Actually they were whispering about sex toys, so they didn't hear me walk out."

"I didn't say a thing!" Honor protested in a shrill voice.

Jason glanced at his brother. "Quit heckling her." Then his speculative gaze landed on Honor and she just knew where his thoughts had gone.

Propping her elbows on her knees and putting her head in her hands, Honor ignored them all to catch her breath.

"Problem?" Sullivan asked as he rejoined them.

Hogan said, "They—*oof.*"

Honor looked up to see Hogan clutching his ribs while Lexie glowered. Then she shocked Jason's brother by explaining.

"Since Nathan had to go through her house, I asked Honor if she'd left out anything personal."

"And I," Honor assured them all, "was about to tell her that I don't have anything *that* personal."

"Seriously?" Lexie asked.

Hogan said, "See what you did? You embarrassed her."

Sullivan ran a hand over his face.

Nathan stepped forward to regain everyone's attention. "The house is empty, but someone was definitely inside."

"Oh God." Slowly Honor forced herself to stand again.

"I'm sorry," Nathan said, "but they did a little damage. I can't say if anything's missing, since I was never inside before, but—"

Not waiting around to hear anything else, Honor headed for her house. *They did some damage.* She felt violated, exposed, wounded; every step toward the property made her more anxious.

Jason stayed at her side, matching his pace to hers. They'd just reached her front yard when he took her hand. "I'm going in with you."

Like a lifeline, she held tight, grateful for the support. "Thank you. I have to see, but it sort of feels like I'm walking into danger. I know that doesn't make any sense."

"It makes perfect sense." He lifted her hand and kissed the back of her knuckles. "We'll figure this out, okay?"

The press of his mouth and his caring tone nearly unraveled her control. Throat thick, she nodded, because agreeing seemed easier than attempting to explain, yet again, that this was her responsibility and good or bad, she could and would handle it.

They went up the porch steps together. Dread clawed inside her.

"Take a breath." Jason put one hand to the middle of her back. "Do you want me to go in first?"

"No." She made herself say the lie. "I'm fine." Shoulders tight, she reached for the doorknob.

Nathan hadn't bothered locking back up, so the door opened easily, silently.

"Damn." Jason stepped ahead of her and righted the large plant Lexie had given as a gift. Leaves were broken and dirt had spilled on her floors, but otherwise the plant had survived.

Bastards. Unable to bend her mind around such useless destruction, Honor wondered aloud, "Why would anyone do that? How does knocking over my plant accomplish anything?"

"Who knows what motivates idiots?" He sounded enraged and held himself stiffly.

On her behalf? "Jason?"

He flexed his hands. "For once I'm glad you weren't home at a normal hour."

The mess momentarily forgotten, she stared at him in incredulous wonder. Only Lexie had ever reacted like that for her. Her family, what existed of it now, usually went the other way—outraged at her, not for her.

More than the vandalism could, his backup rocked her foundation. Breathing was harder, focusing on the damage almost impossible.

Was she really so starved for genuine emotion? No, she didn't want to believe that about herself, because that would make his initial assessment of her true—it would make her weak. She swallowed the lump in her throat, blinked the daze from her eyes and finally managed a nod. "Me, too." Her heart continued to beat too heavily, but Jason couldn't see that.

With a visible effort, he drummed up a reassuring smile. "It's just a little mess." He returned couch cushions, straightened a chair. "Nothing permanent."

"My TV is gone."

He rubbed the back of his neck. "It can be replaced."

Still staring at him, overwhelmed, she admitted, "It was small. Cheap. It wasn't worth this."

"I'm sorry, honey."

Honey?

"Come here." When her feet refused to move, he strode to her and pulled her in close to his chest, one big hand stroking down her spine, the other keeping her head against his shoulder.

He pressed a warm, firm kiss on her temple.

Honor felt that kiss everywhere—and though she knew it to be foolhardy, she wanted more. The conflicting emotions left her confused.

Mistaking her reaction, he hugged her once more. "Let's see the rest and get this over with."

Being pathetic, especially in front of Jason, infuriated her more than the damage. Straightening away and squaring her shoulders, she looked around again and saw it was all superficial. As to the television…well, she rarely had time to watch it anyway.

Taking Jason's hand, she went through the kitchen, the bedrooms and the bathroom. There was nothing too terrible except for her dumped jewelry box in the bedroom and her ransacked dresser drawers. A bra, panties and a few other pieces of clothing littered the room. Winter boots she'd stored at the top of the closet were now strewn across the floor.

Without a word, Jason pitched in, helping her to put things away. Honor went after her underwear first; they were mostly plain, utilitarian and very uninspired. She owned only a few sexier pieces—not that she ever had much opportunity to show them off.

When she reached for a boot sticking out from under the bed, her stomach clenched. Drawing back, she paused, swallowed, then made herself look.

Nothing under there except some dust.

She grabbed the boots.

"It's understandable to be nervous." Jason took the boots from her and easily stored them in the top of the closet before again looping his arm around her.

She was rattled enough already, but with Jason now upping the ante on familiarity, it was no wonder she still felt off-kilter. "Do you think Nathan checked everywhere?"

"Yes, but we can do it again right now if you want."

She did, but she hated for Jason to see her being such a weenie about things.

"For me," he said. "I'll feel better knowing for sure."

Her grateful smile made him smile, too.

Room by room, they checked every closet, nook or possible hiding place while also ensuring that every window locked securely.

When they'd finished, Honor finally felt some of the stress ease from her muscles. "For once, I'm glad I don't have a basement."

"In these old houses, believe me, there are other reasons to be grateful."

"Leaking?"

"That'd be number one." Again with his arm around her, they left the house. On her porch he stopped and turned her toward him. Hands loosely laced at the small of her back, he kept her very close—right where she wanted to be. "You look nice, Honor."

For some insane reason, she blushed.

That made his mouth inch up in a sly smile. "Don't misunderstand me, you always look hot." His gaze narrowed on her eyes, then her mouth. "With or without makeup."

"Bull," she teased. "You almost didn't recognize me."

He lifted a hand to toy with her hair. "I'm used to your cute ponytails." Taking her by surprise, he brushed his mouth gently over hers. "Now," he whispered against her lips, "I know what you look like with your hair loose, and it's even better than I imagined."

He'd imagined it? She wanted to ask about that, but she mostly wanted to kiss him. Unable to resist, she closed the scant inch between them so that their mouths touched again. It was gentle, tentative, searching—until suddenly Jason's hand cupped the back of her neck and he turned his head for a better fit.

His tongue...oh, wow. The man knew how to do wicked, wonderful things with that tongue.

True, she didn't have a wealth of experience, but she had been kissed. Just never like this. Never with a guy like Jason.

He teased, stroked, made her breath catch and turned the kiss scorching.

Holding on to him, Honor lost herself in the pleasure of his touch, his hot scent, the comfort of his strength. It was so much better than fretting over minimal damage caused by a stupid prank, or the fact that it was going to take her a very long time to again feel secure in her own home.

Beneath her hands on his chest she felt muscles shifting and his steady heartbeat. One broad hand traveled down her back, lingered at her hip, caressed, then scooped over her bottom, cuddling, squeezing.

Honor gave a low groan.

Slowly Jason ended the kiss but stayed near, his forehead to hers. "Damn," he whispered. He caressed her behind one last time, gripping her in close to his body, then loosened his hold and instead lifting his hand to the side of her face. "I'm a bastard for taking advantage of you."

"You didn't."

His half smile melted her heart. "Are you okay?"

It took a second for Honor to realize she had her hands fisted in his shirt, holding him with near desperation. "Right now?" Intoxicated with lust. "I'm fine."

"Very fine."

Her face warmed. "I guess we got carried away." Although she never had before.

With a rough laugh, he hugged her. "Kissing you is a revelation." He came back for another warm taste, saying gruffly, "You burn me up, Honor."

Oh. *Nice.* "Same here."

"Perfect ass, too."

She had no idea what to say to that. *I'm glad you like it* didn't seem appropriate.

His thumb teased over her jaw. "Is there a reason you fixed yourself up?"

So much attention to a little makeup and styled hair left her even more flustered. "I was hoping for a date."

His brows came down and he asked, low, "With who?"

"You."

Surprise pushed his brows back up. "Yeah?"

Now she felt forward and rushed into explanation. "You had mentioned Screwy Louie's, remember? I thought maybe—"

Another kiss, then one more, and he said, "Great idea. Let's do it."

"But..." She gestured at her door. "My house...? And it's probably getting late—"

"Come on." Holding her hand, he led her off the porch and around to his backyard.

Lexie and Hogan were still at it, ribbing each other mercilessly while Sullivan did his best to referee.

Nathan stood a few yards away on his cell phone. Agitated, he paced the yard, but when he noticed Honor, he ended the call and pocketed his phone.

When he reached them, he asked, "Anything important taken?"

Sadly she didn't have much of importance. "Not really, no."

"Good." He turned to Jason. "I take it you weren't around today?"

"Unfortunately no." In front of everyone, Jason put an apologetic kiss on her temple. "One damn day I'm off looking at an on-site project, and this happens."

Bemused at this new intimacy, Honor didn't know what to say or do, so she chose to do nothing. Lexie grinned hugely at her.

Seeing nothing amiss, Nathan asked Hogan, "What about you?"

"Colt was working, and I had a meeting. Got home just a few minutes ago. Sullivan filled me in on what happened."

"Someone must've realized you were all gone." Nathan gave his attention back to Honor. "At a minimum, you need security lights and better locks on your windows."

"Trust me. It's on the list of things to do first as soon as I get my next paycheck." Which wouldn't happen for another week, and until then, she'd figure out a way to make every ingress more secure.

Hogan tipped his head. "You look different."

Rolling her eyes, Honor brushed her hair back. "I had hoped to take the night off, maybe visit Screwy Louie's." Very aware of Jason beside her, knowing he thought her plans shouldn't change, she said, "But now it's getting late, and I'm thinking of nailing all my windows shut."

Hogan checked his watch. "You have hours yet before they close. And seriously, you don't want to go damaging the window frames."

"Definitely not," Nathan said. "The wooden trim is original to the house."

Jason added, "And there are better ways to secure them until we get new locks."

We? Absently Honor said, "I can get my own locks." Then she looked from one concerned male face to another. Without an ounce of humor, she laughed. "Someone was *in my house*, and you're all worried about the preservation of my window frames?"

Wearing identical worried expressions, the guys all deferred to Jason. She shook her head in disbelief. Did they expect him to reason with her? To calm the hysterical woman?

She supposed he could kiss her again. She tended to forget everything when he did that, even scary intrusions.

Jason reassured the others, saying, "She's not going to do anything drastic. Honor doesn't operate that way."

Well, damn it, how could she be extreme now, after he'd given her a vote of confidence?

"Why don't you go on?" Lexie sidled over next to Sullivan. "I can hang around to keep an eye on things."

Sullivan frowned over that.

"We have those extra floodlights in the garage," Hogan reminded Jason. "Colt will be home soon, then he and I can mount them on poles. Won't look great, but at least the yard will be lit up."

"If you don't mind," Nathan told her, "I can secure the windows temporarily."

"I'll lend a hand," Sullivan said.

Honor didn't know what to think. They were all so sweet, so caring. *Her neighbors.* She realized that meant something, but it wasn't anything she was used to and she seriously didn't know how to react so she reverted to old tactics of independence. "I can't impose that much."

Immediate arguments countered her statement. They were each insistent, and she felt very unsure on what to do.

After being mostly alone for so long, she suddenly felt like she was part of something bigger. It was a little scary, and a whole lot amazing.

Smiling, Lexie reminded her, "One step at a time, honey."

She didn't want the men questioning her about that, so she shook her head. "I... I don't know what to say."

Jason squeezed her. "Let them feel useful. Say you'll let them help."

"Do," Lexie encouraged.

Overwhelmed, Honor felt the wetness in her eyes and willed it away. She absolutely would not cry in front of them. They were all strong and intelligent and she wanted, *needed*, their respect.

Two blinks and one quiet sniff, and she felt marginally more composed. "You're all too wonderful. Thank you."

Lexie grabbed her arm and started for the house. "Give us five minutes," she told the men. "We'll be right back."

6

LEXIE WAS A devious woman, Jason would give her that.

Just as Honor had gotten emotional, ripping his heart out by the way she'd struggled to accept a little caring, a few helping hands, Lexie had led her away—then returned her in a killer outfit that made it nearly impossible for Jason to think about anything other than stripping the clothes back off her.

They'd taken his truck to the diner, and the drive had been a lesson in concentration. What he'd most wanted to do was stare at Honor.

Or better still, detour away from Screwy Louie's to someplace more private. He wanted to get his hands under that shirt, or back on that perfectly cushy rear.

With hands and mouth, he'd love to learn her each and every curve.

Unfortunately no place private came to mind. More than enough company congregated at his and Honor's houses to ensure they wouldn't get a moment alone.

Screwy Louie's certainly wasn't any better.

Neighborhood regulars crowded the outside dining area, so Jason led her inside.

Everywhere she went, Honor turned heads.

To him, she always looked incredible. But tonight, in denim capri leggings, heeled sandals and a sleeveless white crochet top that fit to her breasts but fell loosely around her waist—meaning getting his hands under there would be easy—she'd ramped up the overt sexiness a lot.

He wasn't a caveman, but Jason found himself sticking close as they maneuvered across the floor to an empty booth. He wanted anyone who saw Honor to know she wasn't alone.

Her hair brushed his arm as she looked up at him. "Is it always this busy?"

"This time of night, yeah."

She slid into a seat, folded her arms on the booth top and looked around in awe.

Jason looked at her. At the fall of her hair, the length of her lashes, the sparkle in her tawny eyes.

And her cleavage.

She busted him looking, started to hike up the neckline a little, but he caught her hand. "You have no reason to be modest."

Color slashed her cheekbones. "Lexie picked this out." She waffled, then said, "It's a little more daring than what I usually wear."

"You look good enough to eat."

Her blush intensified.

Enjoying her, Jason kissed her knuckles. "I'm guessing that was Lexie's intent, so let's not spoil it for her, okay?"

With her bottom lip caught in her teeth, she subsided. "If you're sure I'm not inappropriate…"

"You're a fantasy." *His* fantasy. "Go with it."

A little laugh snuck out, she ducked her head, then shyly met his gaze again. "I've been thinking about that kiss."

"Yeah? Me, too." Nonstop.

The jukebox blared, a few people pretended to dance and a continual drone of voices and laughter filtered around them. They paid no attention.

Jason kept thinking, what if she'd been home alone when the intruders broke into her house? It wasn't really enough, but he kissed her hand again, on her knuckles, then on her wrist, assuring himself she was unharmed.

Her lips parted.

Unfair, he knew, to bring her here and then keep teasing. Unfair and torturous. For them both.

"For now, let's relax." Jason settled back in his seat. "We'll return to this later."

She closed her eyes long enough to drink in a deep breath, then smiled at him. "Okay." But she reiterated, "Later," like a promise she intended him to keep.

People bumped into their booth, said a quick apology and kept going. Across the room, a tableful of people laughed loudly, drawing Honor's attention. She watched them with something close to envy.

So many things about her touched his heart. One moment she'd come across indomitable, and in the next she'd be so incredibly vulnerable that it hurt him.

It was easy to see that she cared about his nephew, but she kept secrets, too.

Her crazy hours would give him no end of worry. What if she came home in the middle of the night to more intruders? He usually heard her, but what if he didn't?

Given the superficial destruction inside her house, Nathan assumed knuckleheaded youths were responsible. But neither he nor Jason would take anything for granted. They'd both be keeping an eye out.

Jason knew that before he returned with Honor, Sullivan and Nathan would have her windows temporarily rigged to ensure they couldn't be opened, and Hogan and Colt would have floodlights erected, especially on the darker side of her house.

He'd aim one of his own security lights toward her side door, even though that door still hadn't been repaired and wouldn't open without a lot of effort. Eventually he'd plane it down for her and change the hinges.

That is, if he could ever talk her into letting him do it.

He'd just slid his feet to either side of Honor's, caging her in, when a cute server stepped up to their table. "Sorry for the wait. What can I getcha?"

Honor looked first at him, then to the server. "Oh, um…"

Grabbing the menu kept tucked between the napkin holder and the condiments, Jason slid it toward her.

"Oh, sorry. I didn't realize it was on the table." She opened and began perusing.

"Still no ribs?" he asked the server.

"Sadly, no. Violet's been looking for a new barbecue cook, but it's not going well."

"How about bringing us a couple of drinks while we figure out our orders?" He glanced at Honor, seeing her pursed mouth as she read the options. "Sweet tea sound okay to you?"

Nodding absently, she said, "Perfect, thank you."

After the server departed, he told Honor, "The wings are good. The burgers, too."

Laying the menu on the table, she tipped her head at him. "What are you going to get?"

"Loaded burger and fries."

"Hmm…" She lifted the menu again.

Jason had to laugh. "Having trouble deciding?"

"It all sounds so good and I'm starving."

The server returned with their drinks. "Need a little more time?"

Jason lifted a brow at Honor.

"Nope." She closed the menu. "Two loaded burgers and fries."

"Big appetite," the server said with a grin.

"Oh." She laughed. "No, that's one for me and one for him. Jason assured me the burgers are great."

Jason took her hand and said to the server, "It's her first time here and she had some difficulty deciding."

"Well, you chose right. The burgers are awesome." She

reached past them to tuck the menus away, then left with a quick "Be right back with your food."

"How old is she?" Honor asked.

The quick switch threw him. "Who? The waitress?"

"She's really cute, isn't she?"

Jason automatically looked to where the girl, with dark, shoulder-length hair and a slim build, hip-bumped a guy standing in her way. They laughed, and she patted his arm, then disappeared into the kitchen. He shrugged. "Yeah, I guess so."

"Has Colt met her?"

Ah, now he knew the train of her thought. "She's at least nineteen to work here, since they serve alcohol, too, but I'd say she's closer to twenty-one or so."

Honor's face fell. "Well, darn."

"Playing Cupid?"

"I don't like seeing him unhappy."

Damn, but she pleased him. "Don't let Colt's laid-back attitude and manners fool you. He has no problem getting female attention when he wants it."

"I can believe that." Her smile quirked. "He's a lot like his uncle."

Jason grinned. "Colt thinks he's carrying a torch for the girl he left behind."

"You don't agree?"

He shook his head. "She was part of what grounded him when everything else went to shit. One day he had the ideal situation with the perfect attentive, happy and dedicated parents. Next day he found out his mom was discontent enough with his dad that she'd cheated with more than one guy, his dad was in a constant fury, they were gearing up for divorce..."

Honor squeezed his hand, her voice low with sympathy. "And then his mom was gone."

"Hogan tried to work it out, I'll give him that. But Meg had not only cheated physically, she'd cheated with their funds. Bank accounts wiped out. Checking account overdrawn." Jason still had a difficult time bending his brain around it. In some ways it seemed Meg had suffered a mini breakdown. She'd had everything—and thrown it all away. Including her life. "She'd even emptied out Colt's college fund."

"Oh no." She covered her mouth. "I'm so sorry."

How the hell had they gotten onto this? He didn't want his first date with Honor tainted with sadness. "Kids are resilient. When Colt's ready, he'll find his place."

"When school starts?" Pensive, she looked away. "Maybe you never had to be the new kid at school, but it can be really awkward and uncomfortable."

Grabbing on to that, Jason asked, "You know from experience?"

She tucked her hair back behind one ear, and damn, even that turned him on.

He waited on her answer.

But far sooner than expected, their server returned with a small platter, letting Honor off the hook.

"Compliments of the house," she said as she set down the overloaded sampler. "Violet said with you and your brother being such good customers and all, and since your date's new, she should try a little of everything."

Honor stared at the potato skins, wings, onion rings, fries, grilled cheese balls and a variety of dipping sauces. "Wow."

"The burgers will be right out." Again, the waitress took herself off.

Wide-eyed, Honor leaned toward him to ask, "We're supposed to eat all this *and* burgers?"

Jason handed her a chicken wing. "Better get started."

"Okay." But rather than take a bite, she held the wing and asked, "Who's Violet?"

The really beautiful, redheaded hottie who runs this place. He cleared

LORI FOSTER

his throat and tried to look nonchalant. "Violet Shaw. She's the owner."

"Hmm." She dipped the wing in sauce, then nibbled. "You know her well?"

"Sure." Jason didn't exactly hear jealousy. More like sharp curiosity. The fact that he and Violet had gone out a few times didn't factor into anything. "She's a nice lady." True. "Twangy voice." Very true. "She's friendly with everyone."

Soon as he said it, he winced because it sounded bad. Violet *was* friendly—but she'd been a whole lot friendlier with him. Mostly, he figured, from loneliness. He knew for a fact she wasn't hung up on him—or him on her.

Honor took in his expression, then fought a smile. Pointing at him with the wing, she said, "You two had a thing?"

Because he wouldn't lie to her, Jason set aside the cheese ball he'd been about to devour. "Yeah. Nothing serious and nothing that lasted. But we did go out a few times."

As she ate, Honor considered him. "So...went out, as in got intimate?"

He answered her question with one of his own. "Is that a problem?"

Her slim brows climbed high. "I never thought you were a virgin. I'm not dumb. As long as you're not still involved—"

"We're not," Violet said as she stopped at their table. She eyed Jason. "Where's your reprobate brother?"

"Home with Colt." Knowing how she'd react, Jason teased, "Missing him?"

"Ha!"

"You know you like him." Soon after Hogan moved home and Violet met him, sparks had flown. Luckily that was well after Jason and Violet had ended their brief fling. The interest was shared by them both, Jason was sure of that, but since Violent was a proud, self-sufficient woman, she kept some distance with Hogan. If Jason's idiot brother would quit repairing his wounded ego with one-night stands, he just might have a chance with Violet.

She shrugged. "He has moments of humor, and physically he shares your excellent genes, but I like mature adult men, not testosterone-driven idiots."

"Give him time."

Smiling, she asked, "Now, why would I want to do that?" Done with that topic, she turned to Honor. "So you're my new customer?"

Quickly dabbing her mouth with a napkin, Honor nodded. "You're the owner?"

"Yes."

Wary, Jason waited to see how things would play out.

Honor grinned. "Thank you for the platter. The food is delicious."

Violet gave a sideways glance at Jason, then laughed. "Relax, big boy. She's not the jealous type."

"No, I'm not." Honor's gaze touched on each of them in turn. "As long as I'm not stepping on any toes…?"

"By mutual agreement, Jason is now just a good friend."

"Then from my perspective, it's all good."

With his concerns allayed, Jason did the introductions. "Violet Shaw, meet Honor Brown, my new neighbor."

"Lucky you," Violet teased.

With a small smile, Honor looked toward him. "You know, I was just thinking that very thing."

By the time they left the diner, a crescent moon shone bright against a velvet dark sky. The crowd had thinned, the air had cooled and despite the break-in at her house, Honor floated on a cloud of happiness. There'd be plenty of time to fret, plenty of time to give in to her fear, after they ended the night.

Though she'd left her cell out so she could hear it, she hadn't gotten a single call, not from her family, the facility or the friends ensuring her house's security. While they'd eaten, several people stopped by their table to chat with Jason. Some thanked him for the help he'd given in repairs or for things he'd built them, while still others asked about hiring him for various projects.

Obviously he was well liked and respected. And why not? Far as Honor could tell, he didn't have a single flaw.

When she thought of how guarded he'd acted during Violet's brief visit, she nearly smiled. She understood his concern. Violet Shaw, with her striking red hair, creamy skin and vivid blue eyes, was incredibly beautiful. She'd looked slimmer than Honor, more petite, but still shapely. She had a very inviting country accent, and was supernice to boot.

Jealousy would be a natural reaction. But Honor intrinsically trusted Jason, and he said there was no reason for it.

For the first time in a long while, she felt free and she wouldn't let any ridiculous envy spoil things.

Jason drew her around to face him, then backed her up a step to something solid—and she realized they'd reached his truck. Bracing his hands against the roof at either side of her shoulders, he surrounded her.

They stood at the outer edge of a bright streetlamp with heavy shadows concealing them. Music from the diner barely stirred the air. His unreadable gaze moved over her face. "Worrying about your house?"

Mostly about being alone there, but she didn't say so. "Just a little." This close, his heat and scent touched her everywhere. She loved breathing him in, and she especially loved the relaxed, almost possessive way he looked at her.

Giving in to temptation, she put her hands against his chest. The contrast of solid muscles under the soft cotton of his shirt stirred butterflies in her stomach. She peeked up at him. Rather than concentrate on problems, she said, "I like your friend."

His eyes glimmered. "Which one?" he asked, as if he didn't know exactly who she meant.

don't tempt me   121

"Violet."

His attention zeroed in on her mouth. "She's a very nice person."

"I assumed so, or you wouldn't have dated her." At least, probably not more than once. But anyone could see they'd shared more than a one-night stand. "Why didn't it work out?"

Leaning in, he teased his nose over her cheekbone, her ear. "Neither of us was looking for anything serious, so there was nothing to work out."

Was the same true for her?

Being realistic, she knew a relationship would be pretty tough for her right now. As it was, she could barely keep up. She couldn't see a man like Jason waiting around for her to find the occasional evening free. But did it really matter? She was tired of fighting her attraction for him. She needed to know how it would be with him, even if only for one night.

Burdened by the restrictions of her life, she sighed. "Is it evil of me to say I'm glad you're not still involved?"

"No." He kissed her gently. "Because I'm glad, too."

So he felt the same? Need pushed aside all other concerns. She'd much rather focus on Jason than petty vandals, vindictive family or constraining responsibilities.

She could almost hear Lexie saying, *Go for it*, and so she did, accepting him with a smile.

And that made Jason's mouth tilt, as well. "I like seeing you like this. More relaxed, less worried. A little happier."

She twined her arms around his neck, getting closer still. The warm skin of his nape and his unstyled hair teased her wrists. "It makes me happy for you to kiss me."

"Is that a hint?" Keeping her gaze caught in his, gauging her reaction, he slipped his big hands to her waist—under her shirt.

The way he watched her, as much as his touch, made it seem far more familiar, to the point of being intimate. "Yes."

As his mouth touched hers, his fingers spread, covering a lot of skin, exploring along her back, her ribs, down to her hips above her low-fitting capris. After that long, leisurely stroke over so much skin, she almost felt naked, and that made the kiss even more intimate.

Her thoughts scattered at the heat and roughness of his palms, and the fierceness of his kiss. With Jason, she felt positively tiny, but still protected.

Plenty of times in her life she'd felt small. Too small. Ineffectual. Even invisible.

But not since her grandpa's mind had faded had she felt so safe.

With obvious reluctance, he ended the kiss. That was appealing, too, how circumspect he could be.

Swallowing wasn't easy. Neither was breathing. "Jason?"

"You feel it, don't you?"

She nodded.

"I want to have you alone, Honor." He kissed her jaw, her temple. Under the loose-fitting shirt, his thumbs brushed just below her breasts.

Oh God. Anxious for more, afraid she might never feel this way again, she snuggled in. "I want that, too," she confessed. "So much." *Please don't let my phone ring. Please let me have tonight.* Knowing there'd be no guarantees, she almost wanted to rush Jason to someplace private, to somehow ensure the moment wouldn't be robbed away.

She'd worried about a thief being in her house, but what she felt right now with Jason was far more valuable than any possession she owned.

Others left the diner, their laughter and conversation intruding. Attempting to be proactive, Honor asked, "Do you want to come to my house? I know the whole situation might not be very romantic, not after intruders were in there, but—"

His nostrils flared, fascinating her. "I'm ready if you are."

She added quickly, "You think it's okay with Colt being right there? I wouldn't want to do anything that might—"

He kissed her quiet, obliterating her concerns, but given they were still so close to the diner, it wasn't the way either of them really wanted to kiss. With his forehead to hers, he growled, "Colt is old enough to understand." Straightening, he opened the door and helped her into the truck.

They drove home in near silence, anticipation humming between them. And with every minute that passed, Honor grew both more excited—and edgier with nerves.

"Jason?"

Mired in graphic sexual images of Honor naked in a bed, waiting for him, Jason couldn't manage anything more than "Hmm?"

Silence.

He glanced her way, and found her biting her lip, her eyes big and luminous, filled with anxiety. "Hey." Reaching out a hand, palm up, he waited.

It took her a few seconds before she laced her fingers with his.

He tried to smile, but he was so tightly strung it wasn't easy. "Tell me what's wrong, honey."

She nodded, but said, "It's dumb."

"I don't believe that." Hoping to soothe her, he moved his thumb over her knuckles. "You can tell me anything."

Another nod. "It's...well..." She glanced at him, then away. "It's been a while for me."

His muscles clenched. "You mean sex?"

She half smirked, half choked. "Sex, yeah. And pretty much everything else."

Incredulous, he worked those words through his brain, but they still didn't make sense. "Explain 'everything else.'"

Fidgeting, she crossed her legs, uncrossed them. Glanced at him and away, then blurted, "I haven't had a date in two years."

His brain went blank. Before he could assimilate such a thing, she spoke again.

"Haven't been kissed."

No fucking way.

She lifted their entwined hands. "Haven't even held hands."

His head swam with a tidal storm of emotions.

Honor wasn't outspoken, but he wouldn't call her timid, either. Understated, but not exactly shy. Her sensuality wasn't in-your-face, but it was there all the same. What man could look past a woman so energetic, earnest and unfailingly sweet?

On every level, she appealed to him, and he knew it must be the same for other guys.

That meant the decision to be alone was hers. But why?

"You want to tell me how that happened? How does a woman go two years with no involvement?"

"It wasn't exactly on purpose. I work in a salon, so I'm mostly around women. Plus, I've been so busy..."

Her voice trailed off, so Jason prompted her with "And?"

Her skittish gaze jumped to him. "And... I guess no one really interested me enough to bother. Until you."

Satisfaction slowed his racing heart and expanded the protectiveness he felt for her. "Until me."

"I just thought you should know. In case I...blunder or anything."

She warmed him clear down to his soul. Bringing her hand to his mouth for a kiss, he murmured, "Don't be nervous, okay? Not with me."

She laughed. "Easier said than done. I'm—" her nose wrinkled "—rusty."

"Not rusty at all. More like soft and so damn pretty, so incredibly sexy I've thought about getting you naked every day since I met you."

As she watched him, the tension blossomed between them. "Yeah, see, that's not really doing much to help. I mean...you sound ready, and I feel awkward."

Jason hesitated.

Quickly she added, "Not awkward like I want to wait."

Thank God.

"Awkward like I'm not sure what to say."

"You don't have to say anything. But, Honor?" He waited until those beautiful amber eyes met his. "There's no rush here. Today was a bitch, what with your mailbox being destroyed, and people in your house. If you need more time, I promise, honey, it's—"

Groaning, she dropped her head back against the seat and tossed up her hands. "See, that's what I mean. I'm already screwing this up."

"You're not screwing up anything."

She came forward in a rush, her hands attempting to wrap around his upper arm. "I want you, Jason Guthrie. A *lot.*"

He nodded, because damn, hearing her say it felt like a stroke in the right place.

"Tonight. Despite my mailbox and idiot vandals and…and everything else."

Everything else being *what*? he wanted to ask.

But then she said, "I want you *tonight.*"

Choking on lust, he nodded. "Thanks for the clarification."

Her eyes narrowed. "Are you laughing at me?"

Finally home, he pulled into the driveway, drove past where he saw his brother, nephew and Nathan sitting around a bonfire blazing in the pit, and then into the garage. Soon as he killed the lights and turned off the engine, darkness folded in.

Fortunately he didn't need light to see—he knew exactly what he wanted.

Hauling Honor close, he kissed her hotly, wetly, his tongue moving against hers, his teeth nipping her bottom lip. He held her face and said against her mouth, "Not laughing, no. I want you, but I want you comfortable. I want you ready. You've already been through the wringer tonight. All I'm saying is that if you need more time—"

LORI FOSTER

She closed the scant space between them, this time the aggressor in the kiss. And when she let up, she whispered, "I want you right now."

Jason started to relax.

Then she said, "How do we get past the audience outside?"

Damn. Figured they'd be congregated around the fire pit when he wished them all inside. "Let me handle it."

Honor realized that Jason's way of "handling it" meant making a beeline for her front door. Though the others smiled toward them, Jason said nothing. He didn't even acknowledge them.

When she heard Hogan chuckle, heat crawled up her neck and into her cheeks.

She put on the brakes and turned to face the men, trying her best to look innocent instead of turned on. "Hey, guys. Where's Lexie?"

Aggrieved, Jason muttered, "Damn," but he stood there with her.

Around a deep drink of beer from a longneck, Hogan eyed his brother critically. Lowering the bottle to the side of his lawn chair, he fought a knowing grin and said to Honor, "She left when Sullivan did."

Just that, nothing more.

Honor couldn't get a clue from any of their faces, so finally she asked, "They left together or separately?"

Hogan shrugged.

Folding her arms and cocking out a hip, Honor frowned at all of them. "Seriously? You have no idea if they—"

"Sullivan said he had an early appointment." Nathan spoke while poking the fire with a stick. He settled back in his seat and picked up his own beer. "Your friend watched him leave, then she got in her car and took off."

Bummed, Honor unfolded her arms and glanced at Colt. He was busy texting on his phone.

Nathan tipped his head toward Colt. "He's sexting."

Colt's head popped up, he scowled, then went back to thumbing in a reply.

"Secured your windows." Holding the neck of the bottle between two fingers, Nathan considered her. "You shouldn't worry, okay?"

Honor smiled. "Thank you so much. You don't know what this means to me. Really, I appreciate it more than I can say."

"I jog early most mornings. I'll make a point of coming this way instead of my usual route, just to check on things."

Gratitude made her smile wobble. "I should tell you not to go out of your way, but—"

"I'd do it anyway," he assured her.

"Then thank you again. Sincerely."

Smiling, he gave her a nod.

She indicated the floodlight aimed at the side of her house. "Hogan and Colt, thank you both for this, too."

Without looking up, Colt said, "Welcome."

Looking beyond her, Hogan asked, "Something wrong, Jason? You look…impatient."

Nathan turned a laugh into a cough. "Noticed that, too."

His tone almost combative, Jason spoke to them both. "I'm going over with Honor."

Feigning umbrage, Hogan quirked a brow. "Should I ask about her intentions?"

"Look at her," Nathan said with a sly smile. "I'd say her intentions are pretty clear."

At that, Colt glanced up, grinned and said, "Go for it."

Oh. My. God. They were all insane. And outrageous. And when did Colt start sounding like Lexie? Honor sputtered around her embarrassment but couldn't get a single coherent word out.

"You're the one who stopped," Jason reminded her as he put

a hand to her back and urged her toward the yellow porch light at the front of her house. Behind her, she heard the low chuckles…that grew into outright laughter.

Hands to her cheeks, she whispered, "That was so uncomfortable."

"Might as well get used to it." He paused long enough to kiss her. "There's no avoiding them, and I don't plan on this being a onetime thing."

That diverted her. "You don't?" But…what if she only had this one time?

"Hell no. If that's what you're thinking, forget it. One time won't be enough."

"I wasn't thinking that at all," she lied, afraid to think much beyond the stolen moment they had right now.

"Good." He brought her with him up the porch steps, and his voice went deeper. "Because a week's not going to cut it, either."

A week! He expected her to free up enough time for a week? Not possible.

Was it?

Jason took her keys from her and unlocked the door before facing her again.

Her nipples tightened as he looked at her breasts.

Then her stomach hollowed out as his gaze moved lower, down her body to linger near the top of her legs, before finally returning to her face. "Honest to God, Honor, I'm not even sure the rest of the summer will be time enough."

She knew she should play it cool instead of desperate, but her heart soared at the promise in his deep voice. *The whole summer.* If she could somehow make it work, well, then, it sounded like a fine plan to her. For right now, she'd just hope for the best and take it day by day. "Okay."

He didn't touch her. "You're tense. We'll work on that first."

"First?"

"Sex has a way of relaxing everyone."

Talking about it only made her more anxious, so she nodded.

His smile quirked, and with a warning in his tone, he said, "Then we're going to work on all these secrets you're keeping. No, don't say anything yet." He stroked his fingers over her cheek. "Let's just wait and see how agreeable you are in the morning."

God, Honor thought, as she followed him inside. He wanted answers, and she didn't even know if she'd be around in the morning.

7

JASON WENT IN FIRST, turned on a few lights, then closed the door behind her. When the lock clicked into place, she jumped.

Huddling close beside him, she darted her gaze everywhere around the house—maybe with worry, and then all over him—probably still with worry.

Two years. It didn't make sense to him. And yet, at the same time, it ramped up his need for her tenfold, a need that he knew wasn't just physical.

Sex hadn't been a priority for her.

Apparently she found him special.

Nice, because he certainly felt the same about her. And that's why the secrets would have to go. He liked her, a lot. But he wouldn't start a relationship without honesty.

Trying to be patient, he cupped her shoulder. "You okay?"

Idly she waved a hand to indicate the house. "It was easier not to think about it when we weren't here. But now that we are, it's hard not to focus on the fact that someone broke in here earlier today."

He wanted her at ease, but at the moment she looked jittery enough to jump out of her skin. "How about a drink?"

"Yes, of course." Given a purpose, she marched toward the kitchen, flipping on lights as she went.

At a more sedate pace, keeping several feet between them, Jason followed. With her head stuck in the fridge, she called, "I have tea, cola or juice."

No alcohol? That shouldn't have surprised him, since he'd never seen her drink. "Iced tea sounds good."

Hearing him so close behind her made her jump again, and she smacked her head on the door.

While she rubbed it, Jason said, "Let me," and he reached around her for the half-full pitcher. "Glasses?"

"Right." Still looking disgruntled and mumbling about clumsiness, she went on tiptoe and got down two mismatched glasses from a cabinet. "Ice?"

"Sure." Staying busy might help distract her.

He wasn't a kid. He didn't need to rush her to the bed, especially when he also enjoyed talking to her.

Yeah, he'd rather talk later, but he'd survive.

She filled the glasses with flower-shaped ice cubes and set them before him, waiting while he poured in the tea.

Beside her, Jason propped a hip on the counter and sipped.

Honor just watched him.

It almost made him smile. If he were more gallant, he'd insist they wait for another day regardless of what she said. But he wanted her too much, she'd been insistent and he had to believe that once they got together, it'd be okay.

As he'd told her, sex was the best way he knew to shrug off tension.

Honor surprised him when she blurted, "Will you look around the house with me?"

Her eyes were big, her cheeks flushed, her lips trembling. She still hadn't touched her tea. Concerned, Jason nodded. "Okay."

Her shoulders relaxed. "I'll feel better, you know?"

Something about how she said that didn't mesh, but he let her take his hand.

"Honestly I don't really think anyone could be here, not with the guys watching over things." She tugged him with her into the hall. "But I'm a little creeped out anyway."

Creeped out was not a good beginning to the strongest sexual attraction he'd ever had. Her hand in his felt so small and fragile, but she kept her spine straight, her shoulders squared. Soft and strong. Sweet but determined. He enjoyed the various aspects of her personality a lot.

Every few seconds, she stole a look at him.

And each time, the lust coiled tighter.

Wondering at the secretive smile she wore, he went with her through the small bathroom, the guest rooms and then into her bedroom.

Every heavy beat of his heart reminded him how close he was to her bed—and to having what he craved.

Here where she slept, he picked up her fresh fragrance, light and sweet. The arrangement of nicked, mismatched furniture somehow worked perfectly, especially paired with a fluffy, butter-yellow coverlet and an array of pastel-hued pillows on the bed. Throw rugs and more sheets for window coverings perfectly represented Honor's personality—tidy but not flawless, colorful while still subdued, pretty without being pricey.

Damn, she got to him in a dozen different ways.

When she moved around in front of him, he forgot his perusal of the room and focused solely on her.

Biting her bottom lip, she caught the hem of that awe-inspiring, sexy top and tugged it off over her head.

Holy hell. Anticipation spiked his pulse.

She stood before him in nothing more than a flesh-colored bra and very low fitting capris. Her creamy skin and killer curves caused a near-spontaneous reaction.

He couldn't tear his rapt attention from her body. "God, you're gorgeous."

"You kept waffling," she said in an uncertain rush. "Like maybe you wanted to…wait?"

That's what she thought? "No," he assured her with sincerity.

"Good, because I *can't* wait. Not anymore." She tugged down her capris as she spoke, stumbled a step as the tight material hindered her, awkwardly kicked free, then faced him—and he saw that the panties matched the bra.

Translucent lace over perfect nudity.

Without even thinking about it, he moved toward her, but she turned away and threw back the coverlet.

Seeing her scramble up onto the bed on her hands and knees nearly gave him a heart attack.

She hurriedly turned to him again, lifted her chin and like a challenge, flicked open the front catch of her bra. The cups parted around full breasts, framing them in lace.

Her nipples, a dark, dusky rose, were already tight.

She'd gone from what he thought was timidity to Mach-speed urgency, and it fired his own need to a razor sharpness.

Done playing the voyeur, Jason strode to the bed while kicking off his shoes and yanking off his shirt. He was more than ready to be an active participant.

Her nudity, her need, gave him a buzz like one drink too many. The periphery of his vision faded until all he could see was Honor, the soft fall of her hair, the wild pulse in her throat and that incredible, almost bare body.

Taking her shoulders, he lowered her down to the mattress as he covered her, his mouth already on hers, his body on fire. Her warm, tender lips opened at the touch of his tongue. He licked in, tasting her deeply, going on sensory overload with the feel of her small body under his, cushioning him in all the right ways.

Trailing a hand down her side, he touched all that silky skin, over her hip, to the thin material of her panties, until he reached her slender thigh. Cupping his hand behind her knee, he urged her leg up and out until he could settle fully against her.

She gave a muted sound of pleasure and lifted into him.

Jason stared down into her smoldering gaze and gently rocked against her. Her eyes were heavy, her lips swollen and wet from his kiss.

"One of us," she rasped, her fingertips digging into his shoulders, "is wearing too many clothes."

Jason ignored that. If he shucked off his jeans, he wouldn't be able to control himself. Better to leave them on for now.

Just looking at her was a turn-on and he wanted to enjoy it. He smoothed back her mussed hair, brushed his thumb over her bottom lip, and bent to kiss her neck, drawing in her soft skin before soothing with his tongue.

Her breath hitched, then released in a throaty moan of pleasure that he felt in his pants.

Sensitive neck, noted.

He couldn't wait to see where else she might be sensitive, to figure out everything she enjoyed.

Trailing wet, open-mouth love bites down to her shoulder, then on to her breasts, he immersed himself in the taste and feel of her fragrant skin. Her breasts were plump, her legs restless, her hands continually touching him…keeping him close.

With her thighs now open around him, he cupped both breasts. *So soft.*

She tipped her head back, going still in anticipation.

Knowing his whiskers rasped her sensitive skin, he carefully nuzzled, drawing nearer to a straining nipple. Her legs shifted, tightening.

He traced her with the tip of his tongue.

"Jason," she whispered, pressing up to him, trying to urge him to her.

He blew against her and saw her nipple tighten more. Her hips began a rhythmic rocking, making him a little crazed. He licked…then drew her in, sucking softly.

Ripe need vibrated in her quickening breath. She tangled her fingers in his hair, holding him to her while her hips continued moving, faster now.

And Jesus, he loved it.

He'd expected her to be shy, reserved.

But as usual, she was the opposite, her sensuality open and honest.

He kissed his way over to her other breast, realized she was holding her breath and instead of drawing her in he carefully caught her with his teeth—and tugged.

Groaning, she slid a calf up his side, then around his waist, locking herself to him as she continued that sensual grind against his erection.

He tugged again, insistently, flicking the very tip of her nipple with his tongue.

Her movements became more urgent, and he loved it. He loved teasing her, pushing her to the edge, the scent and feel and taste of her.

Holding back wasn't easy, not when she continually stroked her heat against his straining dick. But her breasts were so soft, her reactions so satisfying, that he tamped down his own need in favor of hers.

Minutes later, to his surprise, she went taut with release.

Stunned, Jason remained still, letting her ride it out against him, but lifted his head to watch. He'd never seen anything as hot as Honor Brown lost to a blinding climax. There was no artifice, just the very real twisting of pleasure, her face tight with it, her cries guttural, harsh and real.

As she gradually went looser, then limp under him, Jason sat up beside her. Lust had him in knots, but insanely, tenderness took precedence.

It was a first for him.

Looking her over, he appreciated the picture she made with her bra tangled around her slim, lax arms, the blush of her dewy skin, her tight, wet nipples and parted legs. The scent of her, now richer, filled his head.

Idly he trailed his fingertips over the subtle curve of her belly, hipbone to hipbone, and saw her twitch. He glanced up at her eyes and caught a look so sultry it left him singed.

"Get naked," she whispered, "and let's try that again. Maybe with you inside me?"

The words made him shake, but he said only, "Soon." Drifting his palm down her body, he slowly, deliberately, wedged it between her open thighs.

Her eyes closed. Her lips parted.

Against his fingers, he felt wet heat. "Nice," he whispered, the word hoarse with need. He idly stroked her, and her panties got wetter.

"Jason…" Once again, she lifted into his touch. "I need you."

"All right." Getting naked sounded like a plan, so he straightened away from the bed and, after taking another leisurely look at her body, pushed off his jeans and boxers.

Honor lazily came up to her elbows to watch. She licked her lips and whispered, "I've thought about seeing you like this so many times."

Far from shy, he went about fishing his wallet from a pocket, located the condoms he'd put there earlier and set them on the nightstand. "Whenever you want to see me, honey, just let me know." He caught his fingers in her panties and said, "Rise up."

Her hips lifted and he skimmed them off. For only a moment he touched her, slowly brushing the backs of his fingers over the neat triangle of her pubic hair, then lower, finding her sleek wetness. He teased over her with two fingertips.

"Jason," she pleaded, her voice trembling and soft.

Silently he took her arm and flipped her over to her stomach, taking a few seconds to fondle that amazing ass before freeing her arms from the tangled bra straps.

Finally—he had her completely, beautifully naked.

When she started to turn to her back again, he stilled her with one hand on the small of her back. His spread fingers spanned the width of her from hip to hip. So small, but still so damn shapely. Visually he traced the length of her graceful spine down to her full, rounded bottom.

On her elbows, she sent a curious look over her shoulder. "What's wrong?"

Rather than answer, he bent and kissed her lower spine, lightly bit one plump cheek, moved his whiskered jaw over her—and she lurched away with a yelp.

She'd been so bold, so openly sexual, it took him by surprise when she scampered to her back, clipping him in the nose with her knee.

As he rubbed away the sting, she frowned at him with accusation. "Nothing kinky, okay?"

The prim indignation made Jason grin. There was the quirky, adorable, modest neighbor he lov...

Those appalling thoughts hit a brick wall and stalled.

Jesus. He hadn't known her long enough to be thinking things like that.

Sure, he couldn't get her off his mind. And with her sitting there naked in front of him, his need for her had escalated through the roof. Her satiny curves hid a will of iron, and any man would be drawn to that.

Sex. That's what he needed.

Once he had her, he'd clear out the fog of lust and be able to think clearly again.

"What?" Concern blooming, Honor glanced down at herself, then folded her arms over her breasts. "You're making me feel naked."

Belatedly, his brain kicked back into gear. "You *are* naked." Looking at her smooth belly and thighs, and her now-damp sex—which she hadn't bothered to conceal—he opened the condom. "Did you forget?"

"What? No." She watched in fascination as he rolled on the rubber. "But you gave me a funny look."

"I'm on the ragged edge." He stretched out beside her, smiled

LORI FOSTER

and kissed the mulish set of her mouth. "I can barely think, so don't hold a single look against me."

Her frown smoothed out. "Okay, it's just…"

Jason took her hands, kissed each one, and pressed them to either side of her head. "I like looking at you, honey. Every part of you. You're perfect."

Modesty colored her cheeks. "No, I'm not. I have more flaws than I can count."

Because he didn't want to debate it, he kissed her forehead and said, "You're perfectly flawed, then, and every part of you is sexy."

"I'm glad you think so."

Done talking, Jason eased her into a carnal kiss. He took a moment to play with her breasts, to tease over her stiffened nipples, then stroked down her ribs and over her belly, wedging his hand between her thighs.

She made a sound of pleasure and curled toward him, taking the kiss ravenous.

Suited him. He loved her mouth, how she tasted and the heat of her.

And speaking of heat…carefully, forcing himself to go slowly, he explored her with his fingertips, each touch a little bolder, a little deeper.

Getting wetter.

She'd already come once, and knowing she'd be sensitive, he kept the touch light as he stroked his now slippery fingers over her clitoris.

She gasped, retreated a moment, then pressed to him again.

"Easy." He felt a new rush of moisture and knew he wouldn't last much longer. "I love how you feel, Honor."

Eyes closed, head back, she breathed, "I want to touch you, too."

"Sure." Later. If she got her hands on him now, he'd be a goner. "In a bit."

"But...*ah*." She arched her neck and whimpered brokenly.

"Damn." At the end of his control, Jason hooked an arm under one of her knees and opened her legs as he rose over her. Her tender inner thighs cradled his hard hips, and her breasts cushioned his chest. "Honor, look at me."

She lifted her lashes, her eyes dark and dazed.

"Yeah, just like that." When Honor stared into his eyes, he didn't even care that he was falling fast.

Secrets, he reminded himself.

They existed, but no way in hell would he worry about them now.

He reached down between their bodies, positioned himself and slowly, relentlessly, pressed into her, filling her up as she squeezed him tight.

Two years. God, she was snug and it made him shake.

"Don't move yet," she whispered, adding, "You feel good, but..." She shifted, trying to accommodate him. "You feel big."

Choking on a laugh, Jason locked his jaw and struggled to stay still against the overwhelming urge to thrust.

Hard.

It wasn't easy, but never would he hurt her. Then *she* moved, wiggling and adjusting—torturing him.

She touched his jaw, her fingertips brushing over his beard stubble, then down to his chin. "You're the one who's gorgeous."

"You're killing me, Honor." He *needed* to move.

Her serious gaze warmed even more, and she whispered, "I'm not a very sexual person, but I swear, I could almost come just from looking at you."

Groaning, Jason took her mouth and gave in to the cravings. He opened a hand on her lush hip, his hold secure as he gently guided her to match his slow, careful thrusts. At each retreat her body squeezed him, and at each glide in, the wet, hot friction tried to drive him over the edge.

As their rhythm meshed, he braced on his forearms over her.

Her breath labored, deeper, faster until each gasp became a short, desperate cry.

Her slim legs came around him.

Her arms held him as tightly as she could.

He rode her harder, heard her groaning, felt the frantic clench of her sex around his erection. Their skin grew damp and heat blanketed their bodies.

Suddenly she stiffened, and her sharp cries did him in.

Losing the battle, Jason gathered her closer to his heart, put his head back and gave in to his own thundering release.

Honor floated in a lethargic haze of pleasure. Nerve endings still pulsed and she couldn't get rid of her small, content smile. Jason rested over her, his big body bearing her down into the mattress, his breathing now slow and even.

Loving it, she hugged him a little.

If sex had ever before been that amazing, she probably wouldn't have given it up so easily.

Pleased, stress free and sated, she stroked her fingertips up and down his broad back.

She loved the feel of him, his rich masculine scent, and she especially loved having him on her, around her, inside her. He wasn't hard now, but the connection went beyond physical—at least for her.

He shifted as if to move away. Not yet ready, she squeezed him and he settled again without argument.

His shoulders were so impressive, his strength more so.

Especially his strength of character.

He was such a good man. Thinking of the amazing orgasms she'd just had, she mentally tacked on *Good in every way.*

Groggily he asked, "What are you thinking?"

She pressed a kiss to one solid shoulder. "How awesome you are."

He huffed a low laugh. "So speaks a satisfied woman."

"Mmm. Yes, very satisfied." Trailing a foot up the back of his hairy calf, she purred, "You're pretty good, aren't you?"

Laughing again, he came up to his elbows and gave her a wicked, teasing smile. "If you want to think so, I won't dissuade you."

"I came twice."

The smile turned into a grin. "Trust me, honey, I noticed." He nibbled at her lips, then whispered, "You're easy."

"Hey!" Grinning with him, she denied that. "I never was before."

He tipped his head, still smiling but more serious. "No?"

Now that he had that intense focus on her, she went shy. Why had she started this? She shook her head. "I always had a hard—" *like almost impossible* "—time with it. Guys get impatient."

"As I recall, you were the impatient one." Somber, *sexy*, he kissed the bridge of her nose, her cheekbone and jaw. "I wanted to enjoy you more." He kissed his way down her throat.

Surprised, Honor pressed him back. "What are you doing?"

"Seducing you. Now hush."

"Again?" He couldn't be serious. "Now?"

"You're tired?"

"No," she said too fast. She wasn't tired, she was anxious. Anxious to grab as many moments as she could before they got interrupted, anxious to feel what she could, to wallow in the freedom and sense of security he gave her.

He lifted a brow with cocky satisfaction. "Love the enthusiasm."

Honor sighed. "You are good, but also dangerous." *To my heart.* "You know that, right?"

"Just hush and go with it."

Holding her face in his big, strong hands, he kissed her so gently, with so much…well, it felt like emotion, need and all things wonderful. Already her body tingled in expectation.

"Don't move." With one more kiss, he sat up.

Honor sighed again. She was a complete and total goner and she knew it. Scary. But she wasn't a wimp, so after Jason removed the spent condom and reached for another, she took it from him, pushed him to his back and said with daring, "My turn."

Jason woke before dawn and automatically reached for Honor.

He'd already gotten comfortable with the way she'd curled against him, her legs tangled with his, her breath teasing him all through the night. He'd never before been a cuddler, preferring his own space when he slept. For that reason, he'd rarely asked women to stay over.

But that was before Honor.

And now...he realized the bed was empty.

Sitting up, he fumbled for the lamp on her nightstand, then winced at the brightness.

She wasn't in the room.

Naked and not caring, he left the bed and strode down the hall to the silent living room, the dark kitchen, back to the bathroom and the guest rooms...all empty.

Son of a bitch! He was a light sleeper, so how the hell had she gotten away without him knowing? Even from his own house, he heard her car—

A new thought struck him.

Rushing to the front door, he opened it—and saw her car was gone, too.

Quietly closing the door and relocking it, he forced himself to sort it out. Honor had snuck from the bed, presumably carried her clothes into the outer room to dress and literally left her house without making a sound.

She must have been extra cautious.

Meaning...extra sneaky.

But why?

He scrubbed a hand over the back of his neck and growled out his frustration.

Pacing, he tried to decide if he should wait. But that felt as wrong as waking alone.

In *her* bed.

They'd made love twice. She'd climaxed four times.

He inhaled sharply, remembering everything, how she'd looked and the heady scent of her release, the sounds she made in her pleasure, and damn if he didn't get semihard again. He frowned down at himself and said, "No."

Given her absurd hours, she could be back in minutes, or late tonight.

Decided, Jason stalked back to the bedroom and grabbed up his discarded clothes. Sure enough, her clothes no longer littered the floor.

He'd planned to uncover her secrets this morning, and instead she'd skipped out on him. He'd go about his day, but when she returned they would damn well talk.

There'd be no more skulking around. He needed total honesty, and one way or another he'd get it.

Lexie wasn't a timid person, but damn it, as she waited for Sullivan to answer, she couldn't make herself stop pacing.

Last night he'd treated her like…what?

Someone he hadn't slept with.

Usually that would have suited her just fine; she could be as commitment-phobic as any guy. But she liked Sullivan. Maybe more than liked him. So often she felt like the stronger personality with men—but not with Sullivan. He matched her, even exceeded her, in boldness, in flirting…and sexually. Thinking of it made her shiver.

She knew she was sometimes—okay, *most* times—outrageous. But it didn't scare off Sullivan. If anything, he just upped the ante, giving as good as he got.

She got the feeling that not much scared Sullivan Dean. She

wanted to know more about him, his background, what made him tick.

She wanted to see him again, damn it.

All morning she'd been waiting, hoping he'd call. She made it until her lunch break and then gave up and called him instead. Screw waiting. She was an accomplished woman with a mind of her own and—

"Hello?"

She froze, then squeaked, "Hi."

Tension-filled seconds ticked by before he said, "Lexie?"

"Yes." Rolling her shoulders, she tried again. "How are you?"

"The same as I was yesterday."

What the heck did that mean? "We got interrupted yesterday."

"How's Honor?"

Changing the subject? Lexie held out the phone, stared at it and then put it back to her ear. She loved Honor, but that wasn't why she called and he knew it. "I haven't talked to her yet today."

"Huh. With you two being friends, I just assumed…"

Condescending much? Her back went straight. "She was pretty psyched about going out with Jason, so I'm giving her space this morning. She'll call me when she's ready."

"I hope the break-in didn't shake her up too much."

"She's dealt with a lot worse, believe me."

"Really? How's that?"

Knowing she'd just said too much, Lexie clamped her lips together. Honor would kill her if she blabbed about her situation, so she did her own quick shift in topic. "Listen, I had a great time with you. Really great. But the evening definitely got cut short."

Silence.

"I thought maybe we could get together again." For once in her life she struggled to sound careless. "My place? I'm free tonight."

Another long hesitation made her chest tight.

Finally he said, "Thanks, but I'm going to be slammed for a while. Work. This is a busy time."

Too busy for sex? "Bummer," she said, knowing it sounded flippant. "Guess I'll just see you around Honor's house, then." Before he could even try to dispute that, she disconnected. "Jerk."

Refusing to mope, Lexie put all her attention into her work… and by the end of the day she'd come up with a plan.

Sullivan could run, but he couldn't hide—because she knew where he lived and where he worked. She was relishing the deviousness of her plan when her cell rang.

For one heart-stopping moment she hoped it was Sullivan calling back to apologize and explain.

She wasn't all that disappointed to see that it was Honor instead. Really. She loved Honor, so she answered with "Hey, girl, tell me all the juicy details."

"I need you, Lex."

Hearing that broken voice, Lexie grabbed up her purse and headed for the door. She wouldn't officially be off work for another twenty minutes, but that didn't slow her down. "I'm on my way. Home or facility?"

"My house."

Knowing that could only mean one thing, Lexie's heart broke. "Hang on, honey. I'll be there quick as I can."

The entire day had slid away and still no sign of Honor. Jason waffled between annoyance, worry, fury and insult.

She'd wrung him out with sex, slept tangled with him…then left him without a word.

He honestly didn't know what the fuck to feel or think.

In a bear of a mood, he'd plowed through a job in record time, building an entire doghouse from floor to finished roof in just a few hours. With that done, he started on shutters for Honor's house. He made two sets for the windows at the front of her house, but wouldn't make the rest until she approved the design. Still with too much pent-up, annoyed energy, he scrubbed out the garage, washed his trucks and then…just stewed.

It was damn near time for dinner when she finally got home.

This time he heard her car and immediately went to the window to look out.

Without once glancing toward his house, she got out of her car with her head down, her arms hugged around herself, her posture…defeated. She made a beeline for her front door, almost as if escaping.

Hogan, who'd been doing the laundry in the basement, paused beside him. "I thought you were past the stage of suffering in silence."

After Honor went into her house and closed the door, Jason turned to his brother. "I'm trying to give her some room, so shut up."

"Damn," Hogan breathed, his mockery changing to concern. "What the hell happened to you? You look like the Grim Reaper, if he got his ass kicked."

"Yeah, feel like it, too." Jason eyed his older brother, a man he respected despite the current circumstances, and he gave it up. He needed to talk and he couldn't think of anyone better to listen. "She walked out on me."

"Who?"

"Honor."

Confused, Hogan crossed his arms and frowned. "When was this? You didn't come home last night, so I assumed—"

"This morning." Feeling like a jackass, Jason admitted, "I woke up alone."

"In *her* bed?"

Jason glared. It sounded even worse coming from his brother's mouth.

"Whoa." Hogan dropped his arms. "Okay, so…you said something to piss her off?"

"No." He shifted his tensed shoulders and, forgoing details, summarized the evening in three short words. "Things were amazing." And if Hogan didn't understand that, he'd—

"Since she just got home, have you considered asking her about it?"

"I told you, I'm trying to give her some room."

Hogan raked him with a disbelieving look. "Who needs the room? Her…or you?"

Discomfort prickled the back of Jason's neck. "I like her."

"News flash—everyone already figured that out."

Right. "The thing is… I more than like her."

Hogan's brows went up. "Yeah? How much more?"

"Around her I feel… I don't know. Territorial. All the damn time. She's modest and still I want to keep other guys—even Sullivan—away from her." He didn't add that much of his tension came from not knowing where she went or why.

"You're a civilized guy, Jason. You know how to behave."

Of course he did. And he respected women too much to ever get pushy. But that wasn't the point. "I don't like feeling this way."

Grinning, Hogan clapped him on the shoulder. "I really don't see the problem. So you're falling for her? That's terrific. God knows she's close enough for convenience."

"Don't be an ass."

"She's also cute, has a great attitude and sweet personality."

All true. And if that wasn't enough, she was also scorching hot in bed.

At least with him.

He paced away two short steps, then stomped back. "I haven't known her long enough to feel like this."

"How long is long enough?"

"No idea." Jason stared out the window toward Honor's

house. He saw nothing. A day of tormented thoughts made his voice shallow. "What does it take to really know a woman?"

Hogan hesitated before asking, "What does that mean?"

Jason didn't want to say it aloud, and in the end, he didn't have to.

"You're talking about Meg."

Of course he was. Hogan's wife had always seemed one way—and turned out to be entirely different. Jason kept his focus on Honor's porch.

That's why he didn't see the shove coming.

He staggered, then glared at his brother. "What the hell!"

Hogan pointed at him. "Do *not* let my example scare you away."

"Why not? It's one hell of an example."

Usually Hogan went out of his way to deny his pain. This time, he let Jason see it.

"Shit." Feeling like a complete bastard, Jason said, "I didn't mean—"

"You did, and it's okay." Hogan dropped back to rest against the wall with a weary sigh. "Truth is, I never, not once, doubted her."

"We all thought we knew Meg."

Hogan just nodded. "Having her affairs thrown in my face demolished me. And before I could even begin to forgive her for that..." His mouth flattened.

Jason doubted his brother ever could have truly forgiven her—but that didn't mean he'd wanted her dead. Taking up space on the wall next to his brother, Jason let their shoulders touch.

"Short of something happening with Colt, I can't imagine a situation more devastating."

Jason had no idea what to say.

"You know, one reason it hit so hard is because I loved the whole home-and-hearth gig. Honestly? Being a bachelor sucks." Hogan slanted him a look. "Relying on you sucks even more."

Guilt burned through Jason. Had his brother felt his impatience with the whole situation? "Hogan…"

He smiled. "No, Jason, it's not you. It's me, one hundred percent. But eventually I'll work it out, I swear."

"I don't have a doubt." Willing Hogan to believe it, he said, "Until then, know that I'm glad to have you and Colt here."

"Thanks." For a moment they both stayed silent, and then Hogan turned, leaning on one shoulder now so he could face Jason. "This is odd, but nice."

"What's that?"

"The old familiar dynamic. Me getting to be the big brother again. I figured I'd lost that along with everything else."

"Not a chance."

After a fleeting smile, Hogan said, "The thing is, I knew Meg for a hell of a long time, and in the end it didn't matter. But remember Mom telling us how she fell in love with Dad overnight?"

"Yeah." Their mom had been a true romantic. "She always said it only took one date for her to know Dad was the one."

"They were together until the day she died, and I think one reason Dad moved is that he still loves her. Being here, where everything is so familiar, is just unbearable for him."

Maybe Hogan better understood all that, because he'd felt the same in his old hometown. Had it been a blessing for him, leaving behind the memories he and Meg had built together?

If so, Jason was doubly grateful he could help out.

Hogan clasped his shoulder. "As your big brother, I'm telling you not to blow it. If you think she could be the one, you need to work it out."

When Lexie pulled into Honor's driveway in a rush, they both turned to watch.

She jumped out of her car and jogged up the walk to the front door, which had already opened.

Jason gave up being circumspect.

He wanted Honor. He wanted to care for her.
She needed to know that.
"Go," Hogan told him.
But Jason was already on his way.

8

LEXIE HUGGED HER FIRST, then pressed her back to search her face. "What's happened?"

Choking on her hurt, Honor dragged Lexie in and to the sofa so they could both sit. She'd been up for too many hours now, hadn't eaten and honestly didn't know what to do. "Grandpa took a turn for the worse. He's fading right before my eyes and I know this is it."

"Oh, honey, I'm so sorry." Lexie rightfully looked confused as she tried to understand. "You could have called me while you were at the facility."

Honor shook her head, twisted the tissue in her hand and admitted in a rasp, "They threw me out."

Going stiff, Lexie growled, "Who did? Those creeps you call family? Did someone leave the zoo cages open?"

For once, Honor didn't have the energy to chastise her on the insult. "Yes. They...questioned my motives."

Fuming, Lexie shot to her feet. "Those *bitches*. You," she raged, her finger jabbing toward Honor, "are the only one who has cared for him. Sometimes day and night. You've been his caretaker since the dementia got bad. They've relegated *everything* to you, and now they want to accuse you of being a user? The nerve!"

Disregarding the defensive anger, Honor shoved her hair back and sighed. "I need to be with him, Lex." More tears blinded her, and her heart felt literally crushed. "I'm the only one he recognizes and they won't let me in!"

"What can I do?" In proactive mode, Lexie grabbed her hands. "Can we go and talk to the administrator?"

"I don't know." She fought from sniffling. "I tried to say that, I really did. But it surprised me when they showed up, they so rarely visit him. I guess the facility called them, too."

"Dumb move."

"Lex." She couldn't let that one pass. "They've been so good to him there."

"Sure, but they know how the relatives are."

"If they didn't, they do now." Remembering left Honor crushed. "Things got so ugly so fast I didn't know what to do except leave. I needed to think."

"You needed me," Lexie said. "Your *real* family. And believe me, hon, I will happily battle all of them for you."

God love her. Honor laughed around fresh tears. For so long now, Lexie had been there for her. And luckily the burden of it hadn't chased her away. "I want to go back. I guess..." It was a terrible admission, but she gave it anyway. "I just needed someone to reassure me."

A new voice intruded. "I wouldn't mind helping with that."

Appalled, Honor jerked back and found Jason standing in the open doorway. Panic tried to blossom from deep inside her. Things were bad enough, hurtful enough. She couldn't take having him see like her this. She wanted, needed, for Jason to know she was a self-sufficient person, that he'd never have to take care of her because she could take care of herself.

Allowing Lexie to know her weaknesses was not at all the same. Lexie had known the real her for a very long time.

Quickly swiping the tears off her blotchy cheeks and hoping to swallow the lump of heartache, Honor struggled to get herself together.

Didn't work. As Jason stood there, watching her with an inscrutable familiarity, more tears welled up and that damn heartache wasn't budging. Oh God. She curled in on herself, disgusted with her own pathetic weakness.

"You need to leave," Lexie ordered him.

Very simply, without animus, Jason said, "No." And stepped farther into the room.

Understanding Honor's embarrassment better than anyone else could, Lexie jumped into his path. "This isn't the time, Jason. Honor detests pity and—"

"I don't pity her." Jason pressed forward despite Lexie's attempts to block him. "I respect and admire her."

What? Honor blinked fast and bit her bottom lip to still the trembling.

"Good or bad," Jason said softly, "family is family. You deal with it, always."

"How long were you listening?" Honor asked.

"Long enough to understand."

"Hmm," Lexie said, looking back and forth between them as if to gauge each reaction. "Yeah, I think I'll just..." She sidled out of the way.

Honor gulped down her emotions and she, too, stood. "I was going to call you later."

Jason said nothing; he only watched her.

Humiliation tried to level her. "I'm such a mess."

An indulgent smile touched his mouth while his dark eyes held her captive. "I keep telling you, honey, our descriptions on that don't match." Cupping her face, he used his thumbs to remove the tracks of tears, then kissed her forehead. "You're always beautiful."

Lexie sighed. "This is a regular Hallmark moment. I'm positively melting."

Honor laughed again, albeit shakily. Her crazy friend.

"Better," Lexie said. "Now, how about you freshen up and we'll *all* go tackle the angry mob?"

No, no, no. She couldn't let this happen. The last thing she wanted was to impose on Jason. He and his brother and nephew had already done so much for her. *Too much.* Involving him in this would completely cross the line. "I'm fine now, I promise." Somehow she'd make it true. "Neither of you needs to go with me."

"It's not about need. It's about want. And we *want* to go." Cradling her close, Jason gave her a brief hug, then levered her back, his expression stern. "I only need five minutes. Do not leave without me."

Honor didn't know what to say or do. In her battered heart, a bubble of hope floated. But fear tamped it down because, damn it, she knew better than to lean on anyone. "We talked about this," she said. "My independence is important to me."

"Everything between us is different now."

Lexie whispered, "Whoa. Does that mean what I think it means?"

"It's a long story," Honor said.

"No," Jason corrected. "It's a short story. We're involved." Cutting off her chance for denial, he added, "I'm not trying to take over. I understand why you want to do things on your own."

She was pretty sure he didn't.

"But not this, Honor. Not now. You can't go from being with me last night to telling me to back off today."

No, she probably shouldn't.

"Last night mattered," he insisted.

"Yes." To her, it mattered a whole lot more than he realized. "But it doesn't mean you have to take over my life for me."

An unreadable emotion darkened his eyes. "Caring isn't the same as taking over. You want to continue struggling on your own, fine. I'll respect that. But this is different."

"This," she agreed, "is a very personal problem." It was the kind of problem people hated the most. Superficial stuff could be easily dealt with. But the personal baggage was more bothersome.

Jason said, "We now have a personal relationship."

That stymied her, but only for a moment. "I could be at the facility all night. Maybe longer." Needing him to understand, hopeful of salvaging what they'd started, she said, "This isn't something you want to be dragged into."

"Pretty sure you don't have a clue what I want."

Her mouth opened, but nothing came out. Desperate, she looked at Lexie and whispered, "I don't know how to do this."

Lexie stepped forward with encouragement. "I know, honey. But we've been working on that, right?"

She knew Jason didn't understand. He stood there, the epitome of patience while also ready to impose his will. Honor closed her eyes and tried to make sense of it all.

Leaning in close, her voice hushed, Lexie said, "Think about what you'd want to do if it was me. How would you react?"

When all else failed, Lexie always knew how to sway her. Nodding, Honor admitted, "If it was you, I'd want to help. I'm just not sure how—"

"I'm going along so I can do just that," Lexie cut in. "Helping in whatever way I can." She rubbed Honor's shoulder. "And I vote that Jason gets to go along, as well."

But Jason wasn't Lexie. Her…association with him was new and uncertain. It would be asking a lot to want him to stay involved after meeting her relatives.

With Honor's long, agonized hesitation, Lexie retrenched. "Unless you really don't want him there for some reason. Then I'll personally run him off. No matter what, I'm on your side, hon. Always."

Jason frowned at Lexie. "Stop helping."

Holding up her hands, she backed away again.

Belaboring the point just made Honor feel…mean. She'd never intended her independence to be off-putting to others. Just the opposite. She'd always hoped it'd make her more appealing.

"I need to be with you." Unrelenting more than cajoling, Jason insisted, "Say yes, Honor."

How could she possibly refuse him? Trying a small smile, she nodded. "Okay. Thank you."

"Holy guacamole," Lexie breathed. "This is potent stuff."

Jason surprised Lexie by hugging her off her feet. "I'm glad she has such a good friend."

Dazed, Lexie put a hand to her heart. "You are the most unpredictable man."

Honor was trying to assimilate all that had just happened when her cell phone rang. Frantic, she nearly dumped her purse to get to it and when she finally answered, an unfamiliar voice asked, "Honor Brown?"

Fear smothering her, she sank to sit on the couch and was immediately flanked by Jason and Lexie. With dread, she said, "Yes?"

"Hello. My name is Neil Mosely. I'm a very good friend to your grandfather, as well as his lawyer."

Her throat tightened until all she could get out was a strained, horrified whisper. "Is Granddad…?"

"Oh no, no! I'm sorry if I alarmed you. There's no current change."

Breath left her in a whoosh, and even though she sat, she reeled. "Thank God."

"I'm calling to inform you that, through Hugh's wishes, you're the only family member listed to visit him. He took care of that well before the dementia took over."

Her eyes rounded. "He did?"

"It's the others who are trespassing, not you. Never you. And because time is clearly limited, I'm hoping—"

She surged to her feet again. "I was just about to head back."

Satisfaction lightened the gravity of his tone. "Good, good. I'm pleased to hear it." He paused before pressing forward. "I realize it's a very emotional time, but could I meet you there in say, half an hour?"

Honor didn't understand that at all, but he claimed to be her grandfather's friend, and that made him special. After she met him, she'd find out why she hadn't known him sooner. Right now, with timing so urgent, she only wanted to concentrate on getting back to her grandfather. "Yes, of course."

"Excellent. You'll find me at his side."

When the call died, she looked at Lexie.

"I heard," Lexie said, as astounded as Honor. "You've never heard of him?"

She shook her head. "No, but I never got involved in Grandfather's business contacts, so... I don't know what to think."

Clearly Jason had heard as well, given the way he took her shoulders. "We can sort it out later."

We again. Each time he said it, it stunned her anew—but she was starting to get used to it, at least a little.

"While you get yourself ready I'm going to go grab a shirt and slacks. I'll drive and along the way you can tell me everything."

Everything. She wouldn't even know where to start, but she wouldn't waste more time battling, not when she needed to get back to the facility. "Okay." When things changed, she'd deal with them—

"Trust me, Honor." He smoothed her insanely messy hair. "I don't scare easily."

She watched him leave with a purposeful stride.

So did Lexie, until she finally got herself together. "Come on. I won't let you face them looking so upset, and Jason will be right back. Men are always faster at prep work than women."

Honor allowed herself to be dragged into the bedroom. Then she stalled.

Her bed was neatly made.

Meaning Jason had made it before he went home.

Awwww. Her heart had taken one blow after another today, first from the predawn call telling her that her grandfather could go at any minute. Then the chaos with her insane relatives. And now this.

This...*hope.* Long ago she'd learned how dangerous hope could be. It built you up, often just to let you down. It kept you from accepting the inevitable. But she felt it all the same.

Hand to her heart, she said, "He made my bed."

"Yeah." Lexie went straight to the closet. "I'm anxious to hear all about that." She riffled through Honor's clothes until she'd chosen a pretty but casual summer dress, a lightweight cardigan and comfortable sandals. "You can give me the deets while you change, but we have to hurry or I won't have a chance to fix your hair and makeup."

As Honor stripped off her clothes with haste, she said, "I can fix my own hair and makeup. I'm a stylist, remember?"

Lexie ignored that to say, "So you slept with the stud next door."

Popping her head clear of the dress she'd just pulled on, Honor said, "Yes, and it was amazing."

"Awesome-sauce!"

Honor stepped into the sandals, turned to the mirror over her dresser and cringed.

"Don't worry." Lexie snatched up a brush. "We have time to repair it all. But while I work, you talk. I want to know *everything.*"

Honor headed for the bathroom. "I've already given you all the details you're going to get. Just know that it was well beyond my expectations."

"Unfair! I always tell you about my sexcapades."

Mostly true, but Honor's involvement with Jason didn't feel like a sexcapade. It was a precious moment in time that she wanted to cherish and protect. While holding a cold wet washcloth to her eyes, Honor said, "You didn't give me details on Sullivan."

"Eh." Lexie dug through Honor's makeup bag. "I haven't yet found the right words, or I would have."

Honor lowered the cloth. "That good?"

With a dreamy smile, Lexie nodded, then almost immediately shook herself. "Stop trying to divert me. We're talking about you."

It took Honor all of thirty seconds to finish removing her ruined makeup. "I, um… I snuck out on him."

"No way."

"I know." She took the brush from Lexie. Her thoughts, her feelings, were all in a jumble. As she brushed, she explained. "He stayed with me, and all night long, whenever I'd move, he'd hug me closer, and oh God, Lexie, I loved it."

"Snuggling is good," Lexie agreed. "So, how'd you sneak out?"

"He was asleep when I heard my phone beep. I'd forgotten it and my purse in the living room, so luckily it didn't wake him." She lowered the brush. "When I first went to slide away, his arms tightened." And it had felt so good, so comforting, Honor had badly wanted to stay put. But she loved her grandfather and she knew what the phone call might mean. It was why she always answered.

Lexie fixed a headband into her hair. "Quit beating yourself up, Honor. So you were extra sneaky? It's okay."

Inch by inch, she'd freed herself from Jason's embrace. "I took my clothes and stuff with me when I crept out, and after I got the message, I…"

"You went to your grandfather." Lexie turned her, looked over her hair and nodded approval. "I'm sure Jason understands."

Feeling haunted, she closed her eyes. "I didn't even write him a note."

Lexie paused, but only for a moment. "Yeah, sorry, hon, but

that's pretty much a dick move. If the situation were reversed, I'd be furious on your behalf."

Slumping, Honor said, "I know."

"I'm not all that well acquainted with men like Jason, but it seemed to me he wasn't holding a grudge."

"I'm not."

They both jumped.

Forgetting to be contrite, Honor turned and said, "Stop sneaking up on me!"

Wearing khakis and a white button-up, Jason stepped in, tipped up her face, searched her eyes, and gave her a soft, gentle kiss. "Ready?"

His personal brand of affection made her knees wobbly.

"Yes." She grabbed her makeup bag from Lexie. "I'll do repair work during the drive."

"Speaking of that..." Lexie set aside the brush and smiled at them both. "I'll take my own car. It's only a ten-minute drive, so it'll give you both a chance to talk."

"That's actually a good idea, because it could run late." With that perfect opening, she faced Jason and tried again. "Maybe I should drive, too. That way if I decide to stay—"

Jason scooped an arm around her. "We already covered this, honey. Let's go."

Honor had all kinds of objections, but she couldn't seem to remember them. And then they were on their way and she had so much to think about it, she gave up the fight.

It amazed Jason how easily Honor applied a few touches of makeup while he drove. Her hair swung loose around her shoulders, soft and smooth, and though she used concealer to hide the shadows from her upset, the slightly wounded look remained in her expressive eyes, gnawing at his protective instincts.

He had a very bad feeling about things. He'd like nothing more than to bundle her back to his place where he could insulate her from any and all ugliness. But she'd been so resistant to him accompanying her he wasn't about to do anything to press his luck.

Dividing his attention between the road and watching her, he considered what to say. Every so often she visibly rallied, pulling herself together while pushing aside sadness.

"We'll be there soon."

She nodded. "I should probably prepare you. My relatives can be…difficult."

Given what he'd overheard from Lexie, "difficult" was a massive understatement. "Why don't you tell me about them? I'd like to understand." He needed the lay of the land before facing off with them.

Ill at ease, Honor pleated the hem of her skirt before smoothing it out again. "Granddad is everything to me. He took me in when I was twelve and raised me as his own."

"I didn't realize." He remembered when she first moved in, she'd claimed to be alone except for Lexie. At the time, he hadn't known her well enough to push. But now, as he'd told her, they were involved.

Even if she wanted to deny it.

He put a hand on her slender thigh. "Your parents passed away?"

"Not back then, no."

Needing the contact, he put his hand under the bottom of her skirt so he could feel the warmth of her bare skin. "How about you elaborate a little on that?"

She stared blindly out the window. "My mother left my dad and me."

That scared him and he asked, "She was abusive?"

With the slightest of smiles, rife with bleak sadness, she shook her head. "No. She was a wonderful mother. We did everything together. But then she met someone else and I guess he was more important to her. She told me she loved me, that she'd get in touch, but she never did."

Jason so badly wanted to pull over so he could hold her, so he could somehow make up for what her mother had stolen. But her grandfather was her current priority, and so it became his, as well. "Your father?"

She shrugged. "Dad took care of me for a while. He was solemn, but otherwise the same. A workaholic, kind but distracted. I think he tried, but it was just too inconvenient and one day, when I left school, Granddad was there to pick me up. He explained that I'd be living with him from now on." She chewed her trembling bottom lip, then swallowed and continued. "Granddad said that my father loved me, and that he knew I'd be well cared for. He told me we'd have an adventure, that he wanted to get me all new things, better things. I left my school, my town...everything."

Empathy got a death grip on him. "That must have been an awful adjustment for you."

She was quiet, introspective; then she said very softly, "Granddad did whatever he could to make it easier. I had a fancy new bedroom twice the size of my old room, filled with new clothes, computers, games...whatever he could think of that I might want or need. It meant so much to him that I tried to be happy."

For her grandfather, she'd buried her grief. Jason couldn't imagine a woman more innately caring.

When she looked at him, her eyes were damp. "One night he caught me crying." When she blinked, the tears trickled out and she quickly swiped them away, then smiled. "He was so upset that I ended up comforting him. You see, he felt the pain of what his daughter had done in walking away. He told me that it was his failing, not mine, and I realized that he was hurting as much as me, maybe more. I think that, in part, made us even closer. We relied on each other then—and we still do.

Just because he's forgotten most of it doesn't mean I'll ever turn my back on him."

Jason probably wouldn't be so drawn to her if she could. "I get the feeling that you've really condensed the whole story."

"I shared all the pertinent parts. There's no reason to go into a young girl's melodrama."

That was how she saw her hurt and disappointment?

Understanding her pride, and that she needed to be strong now, he let it go. "So the other relatives you mentioned, the ones who might be at the facility?"

"There's no might to it. They'll be there and unless someone has drugged them, they'll still be fired up."

At a time like this, he couldn't imagine anyone treating Honor with less than kid gloves. "How are you related?"

She rested her head back. "Two aunts, a cousin and a great-aunt. All on my mother's side, of course. I've never really known my father's family. He wasn't close with them and they didn't live nearby."

"So the relatives at the hospital, you don't get along with them?"

"My great-aunt, Granddad's sister, gets impatient, but for the most part she tolerates me. The aunts, though..." She made a face.

Jason patiently waited as she searched for the right words.

"In some weird way, they blame me for my mother taking off. And they really dislike that Granddad showed me so much attention."

Attention they thought should be theirs? "And the cousin?"

With a humorless laugh, Honor said, "She really, *really* dislikes me."

Impossible. In the time he'd known her, Honor hadn't shown a single objectionable trait. "What's her issue?"

Talking about her family had left her neck stiff, her hands balled tightly together in her lap. "Mostly she just follows her mother's lead. They think Granddad favored me, and it's partially true. We are…*were* really close. But that's because I spent so much time with him. The others missed every holiday, even his birthday. They'd only come around when they wanted something."

He'd be willing to bet Honor had never missed a chance to show her love and appreciation, especially on holidays. "What would they want?"

"Usually money." She shrugged. "He's fairly well off. I think they all expected him to be more generous."

One thought immediately struck Jason: if her grandfather was wealthy, Honor hadn't taken advantage of that fact when she purchased her house. "You didn't expect the same?"

She shook her head. "The family forever accused me of using him, even when I was a kid. They thought my folks had dumped me on him as a way to get to his bank account. Though how that would work when they've never come back around, I have no idea. And I've always tried to be as independent as I can."

That explained a few things about her, especially her determination to do things on her own. "You wanted to prove them wrong." Just as she'd wanted to prove him wrong.

"Maybe a little. But mostly I wanted Granddad to know that I loved him for *him*, not for any other reason."

Maybe she was also afraid that if she leaned on her grandfather, if she became a burden in any way, he'd also leave her.

What a terrible assumption for a kid.

"Was he proud of you for getting your own home?"

Her fretful hands opened and smoothed over her skirt. "He would have been, I'm sure. Though we probably would have argued about it." She flashed a brief smile. "He always wanted to make things easier for me, and I always wanted to prove I could do everything on my own."

"Even if your way was difficult?"

"Everything worth doing is. But since it's my responsibility, I don't mind. Until he got too sick, Granddad worked really hard every single day." Her voice softened. "And still he always had time for me. I didn't want to make it any harder on him than it already was."

Something occurred to Jason, and he asked, "The location of your house...?"

"It's a lot closer to the facility than I was before."

And he'd made that move harder on her. Feeling like a bastard, Jason imagined her as a young girl, so lost and alone, everything familiar to her gone, discarded by the people who should have made her a priority. He stroked her thigh with his thumb, offering what little comfort he could. "Your grandfather doesn't know about the house?"

"He's had health issues for a while now. His heart, his lungs, cholesterol, blood pressure...and with every issue his dementia got worse. It's been pretty bad for about two years now."

The same amount of time Honor had gone without a date. "I'm sorry." *For many things.*

"These days he rarely recognizes anyone, and he's often afraid, even paranoid." She put a fist to her chest. "But he feels safe *with me.*"

And so she stayed at his beck and call. Pieces of the puzzle were starting to fall into place. "That's where you go during the night? To see him?"

"He's so frail, Jason. When he tries to escape the facility and fights the nurses, or my aunts or cousin, they have to strap him down. He ends up all bruised and..." She swallowed hard. "I can't stand that. He was always such a gentle man that seeing him hurt destroys me."

"The other relatives don't help?"

"They sometimes show up. But he doesn't recognize them anymore, so he doesn't trust them." She paused. "Actually I guess he never entirely trusted them. But now he almost fears them, like he thinks they're trying to hurt him somehow. For the most part, it's easier on all of us if they just stay away."

"So it all falls on you?"

She shook her head. "Don't misunderstand. They're all in different circumstances than me. I'm single—"

"By choice." Venturing a guess, he said, "I assume so you could care for your grandfather?"

Her mouth flattened. "For the most part, the family thinks I'm there because, as they put it, I want to rip him off in his dying days. But honestly whatever money he had, I assume, was needed for medical care. Only they don't seem to understand that."

Idiots. All of them. "Who ensures payment to the facility?"

"I don't know exactly, but he had all that prearranged. Granddad was always a planner. He never wanted to leave things to chance, and he said he never wanted to burden me with it."

Like Honor, he hadn't wanted to impose on others. She'd probably learned to go it alone from her grandfather. "Your mother knows he's ill?"

"She passed away in a car accident when I was twenty. We only knew about it because Granddad had to pay for her funeral. I have no idea about my dad. Granddad said he could track him down for me if I ever wanted, but I didn't see the point. Dad knew where I was, but he'd never, not once, come back to see me."

Jesus, his heart broke for her.

"My great-aunt, Granddad's sister, used to say that at the very least he should track down Dad and make him pay my share of living expenses. She called my parents leeches, and me a leech by extension. They ended up in an awful argument over it. More than a month went by before he talked to her again. I don't think she's ever really forgiven me for that."

For *what?* Being a kid in need?

Knowing she didn't need his anger right now, he suppressed it. But it wasn't easy. "I'm glad you had your grandfather."

"Me, too." She curled her fingers over his. "And now he has

me. It doesn't matter how many times I have to get out of bed or rearrange my schedule, I'll be there for him through his last day."

As Jason pulled into the parking lot, he asked, "That could be soon?"

She lowered her head. "I'm afraid so. These last few months he's suffered and each day seems more difficult than the one before. He's so…blank now. In my mind, I know that it's his time. But in my heart—"

"I understand." When Hogan's wife died, Jason had been filled with both sympathy and anger. He'd grown to despise Meg for her cheating, but regardless she'd been Colt's mother and seeing his grief had hurt.

Seemed the heart and the head often did battle.

To help Honor keep her composure, Jason redirected her thoughts with a question. "How do you usually deal with the relatives?"

"I do my best to be kind, but still firm. If I'm not, they get bolder and everything escalates."

"Like it did today?" The news that her grandfather was almost gone had left her more vulnerable, and they'd pounced.

She looked away. "Yes."

Jason parked near the front and turned off the truck. "Should we wait for Lexie?"

Honor glanced in her side-view mirror. "She's here." Then she turned back to Jason. "Are you sure you want to—"

"Yes." He left the truck with Honor, taking long strides to keep up with her rushed pace. The circular sidewalk led to and from the main entrance with attractive plants and occasional seating along the way. Lexie caught up at the widest curve.

It was the first time Jason had ever seen her so serious, even grim.

She muttered, "There's a gargoyle keeping watch," and nodded toward the entrance.

Jason looked up. Right outside the double entry doors, a

woman in her midsixties watched their approach. Her high-lighted brown hair swung over her shoulders when she jerked around to face Honor, a glowing cigarette in one hand, a cell phone to her ear and a look of venom in her eyes.

Jason felt Honor's tension, but she didn't slow. Voice low, she told Lexie, "Behave."

When they were close enough, the woman flipped the cigarette to the ground and stepped in front of them. "Why are you back?"

"To see Granddad, of course." Honor started around the woman but got blocked again. Resolve squared her shoulders.

"You think just because you brought backup—"

"I'm going in, Aunt Gina. I'd prefer to keep things peaceful, you know that. But one way or another, with or without a scene, I will see my grandfather."

"You'd do that, wouldn't you? Show up here with your side-kicks, pushing your way in, causing problems."

Honor met her angry stare without blinking.

Giving up the intimidation tactic, Gina transferred her gaze to Jason. "Who are you?"

"He's with me." Honor moved forward, reaching past Gina for the door handle and forcing her to step aside.

Jason half smiled. Had he really thought Honor would need him to defend her? She was doing pretty damn good on her own.

Air-conditioning hit them the second they entered the building. They could all hear the woman on her cell, loudly proclaiming that the "little witch" had returned.

They stood in an interior entryway separated by a glass wall from the main foyer. Jason assumed the double entry was to help ensure that the patients inside couldn't wander off.

"Do you want to wait in the foyer?" Honor asked him.

"Not a chance." Jason helped her slip on her cardigan.

"It's only going to get worse."

He'd assumed as much. "I'm a big boy. I think I can take it."

Lexie shoulder-bumped him. "He's sturdy, Honor. He won't wilt under the maliciousness."

She shook her head and again started them on their way. "Fine. But I need you both to let me handle things."

"That's a tall order, but I'll do my best," Lexie said, and Jason silently agreed.

He wasn't surprised when, at the end of a long private hallway, two more women showed themselves. Another aunt, he assumed, given her resemblance to the woman out front, and probably the cousin who looked five or six years older than Honor.

Taking the offense, Honor said, "Aunt Janet, Terry. How is he?"

"Like you care." The younger woman sneered.

As if she hadn't spoken, Honor said, "I'll talk with the nurse after I've checked in on him."

"Hoping he'll go soon so you can collect?"

Good God, Jason thought, they were all vile. Lexie sure as hell hadn't exaggerated.

Honor said only, "Will we get along civilly or not?"

"Not," the woman snapped.

The older of the two glared. "I thought you'd stay home and cry into your pillow, but instead you came back with your little entourage."

"They're friends."

"It's bad enough that you have that one with you," she said, stabbing Lexie with her disdain. "Now you bring a boyfriend, too?"

There were no social niceties, no introductions or handshakes or even a measure of civility.

Honor said, "He's a neighbor."

"And you brought him *here?*" Ugly in her anger, the woman crowded Honor, her voice a hiss. "Isn't it enough that you've tried to cut out his family? Now you have to disrespect him by bringing a stranger to his deathbed?"

A door opened and a stately, much older woman stepped out, her narrowed gaze sweeping first over Jason, then everyone else. She pulled the door quietly closed behind her. "Janet, please shut up. And, Terry, you'd be wise to be silent now, too."

Both of the relatives clammed up.

Honor said, "I hope we didn't disturb you, Aunt Celeste."

"*You* didn't," Lexie grouched.

Jason could understand Lexie's inability to stay out of it. Already he clenched his teeth so tightly his jaw ached. But Honor didn't need added pressure, so he nudged Lexie, encouraging her to keep it together.

The other women all had varying shades of light brown or dark blond hair, similar to Honor's. But this woman—Aunt Celeste—had probably been steely gray for years. She shared a few features with the others, but was taller and notably thinner.

Because she wasn't glaring, Jason stepped forward and held out his hand. "Jason Guthrie." Following Honor's example, he explained, "I'm Honor's neighbor and friend."

"Celeste Mefford." She accepted his greeting, her hand fragile despite the strength of her manner. "I'm Honor's great-aunt, and I trust you're a tad more than a neighbor?"

"Yes."

She tipped her head at Honor. "I did wonder if you'd go home, compose yourself and then return. I see now that you returned with reinforcements."

"She doesn't need reinforcement," Lexie said. "But we insisted."

"Honor is strong-willed enough that you could insist until you lost your voice and if she didn't want you here, you wouldn't be."

Jason lifted a brow, and conceded, "Very true."

That made the old gal smile.

A bit more flustered, Honor said, "I'd like to see Granddad now."

"I assumed as much." Celeste stepped aside, deliberately positioning herself in front of the other two relatives. "If he wakes, and if he recognizes you at all, he'd enjoy meeting your friend."

"You two go on," Lexie said, taking a militant stance facing the others. "I'll wait here and ensure no one barges in with an Uzi."

When Jason looked back at her with concern, Celeste said, "Go on. She'll be fine."

Given the temperaments of the relatives, he wasn't so sure about that, but at least he'd get to stay with Honor.

9

HONOR FORGOT ABOUT the family as she stepped into her grandfather's suite at the facility. His bedroom blended with a seating area with only a bathroom providing privacy. With the curtains drawn and the lights low, she saw her grandfather's form as a faint shadow in the bed. He was so still that her breath froze in her chest.

"He's still with us."

Tears clouded her vision, and maybe that was why she hadn't at first seen the elderly man standing just inside the door. His hushed voice drew her attention real fast.

Black eyes in a dark, wrinkled face took her measure. He stood a few inches taller than her, mostly bald with only a little closely cropped gray hair remaining. Dressed in an expensive suit and carrying a cane, he smiled, showing incredibly white teeth and, at least to Honor, looking very kind.

Keeping her voice as low as his, Honor asked, "Mr. Mosely?"

"Call me Neil, please."

Honor stepped forward in a rush, her hand extended. "I'm Honor."

Hooking his cane on his wrist, he took her hand in both of his and held on. "Of course you are. Your grandfather has spoken of you often, and shown me many photographs. You're every bit as pretty as he said."

Meeting him was too confusing, and too significant, for her to smile. "Mr. Mosely—"

"Neil."

"Neil, this is my neighbor and very good friend, Jason Guthrie."

Neil turned his megawatt smile on Jason. As if telling a secret, he leaned in and whispered, "Celeste and I heard through the door."

Honor had forgotten how little privacy the room actually provided.

Waving a hand, Neil said, "She heard 'boyfriend' and high-tailed it out of here real fast, fearing she might miss the introduction, or that the others might scare you off." He released Honor to offer his hand to Jason. "I'm glad to see that wasn't the case."

"No, sir."

"You're a bruiser, aren't you? Physical job?"

"Mostly," Jason confirmed. "I build things."

"Just about everything," Honor added. "He's really talented."

Neil smiled at them as if greatly pleased. "Hugh would be so happy."

Why did they all assume that she and Jason were that involved? "Mr. Mosely—"

"Neil." He gestured toward the seating area. "Since Hugh is sleeping, could we talk a moment? I'll need to be leaving soon."

Honor wanted to keep vigil by her grandfather's side, but how could she refuse one of his close friends? After another long look at Granddad, she nodded. "Of course."

She wasn't sure, but she thought he might be around the same age as her grandfather, in his late eighties. Once he'd seated himself on the very edge of the soft padded recliner, his hands resting over his cane, she and Jason took up the loveseat.

Jason didn't put his arm around her, but he did sit near enough that their shoulders and thighs bumped, reminding her that at

LORI FOSTER

least for this visit, she wasn't alone. "You said you were friends with my grandfather?"

"For a long time now. Hugh and I met twenty years ago. I was around when he moved you in, and when he buried his daughter. He was there for me when my wife passed. I know you're probably wondering why you and I never met, and that's part of what I'd like to explain."

It did seem curious. Honor was well acquainted with many of her grandfather's friends and a few of his business associates. "If Granddad never mentioned you, I'm sure he had a reason."

Lines creased Neil's face as he smiled. "That's one of the things he's always loved most about you. Your unwavering belief in him. More than the others—" he glanced at the closed door "—you've always been there for him."

"I love him."

"And it's obvious." Neil turned to Jason. "Hugh used to complain that Honor turned his hair gray with her stubbornness, and in the next breath he'd brag on and on about her, saying she was the most like him."

"If that's true," Jason said, smiling at her, "then he must be wonderful, as well."

Neil's dark eyes gleamed with satisfaction. "Yes, wonderful." He slipped a hand to the inside pocket of his suit coat and withdrew a standard-sized white envelope. "I told you I was also Hugh's solicitor as well as his friend and I've had several duties to fulfill, including acting as his power of attorney to maintain the financial upkeep on his properties and holdings, as well as handling the payments on this facility. He entrusted me with very strict instructions—"

Honor closed her eyes. She didn't want to hear about her grandfather dying. Not yet.

"—which included this particular talk."

Jason kissed her temple. "Would you like me to wait outside?"

"*No.*" She grabbed his hand, realized what she'd done, and balked. "I mean, that is, if you want to go——"

His thumb smoothed over her knuckles. "I'd prefer to stay right here by you."

She didn't mean to, but her hand tightened on his. "Thank you."

Neil nodded. "Good. Hugh will enjoy meeting you. For so many years he feared Honor would spend her entire life alone. I'm glad he'll get to see that's not the case."

She didn't dare look at Jason. He probably had no real idea just how alone she'd been. And now her dying grandfather's solicitor was making it sound as if they were practically engaged.

At the moment, she wasn't up to explaining.

Neil didn't yet hand over the envelope. "Hugh knew years ago that his health was failing, and of course he knew about the onset of the dementia. That's when I became more important in his life. He knew his passing would be difficult in many ways, and he wanted to spare you the legalities of it. He never wanted to be a burden to you."

"He's not! He never could be."

As if she hadn't spoken, the lawyer continued in his best official voice. "Because of that he kept us separate, ensuring that you wouldn't know of his plans, of the ways he tried to protect you."

"I don't understand."

"Hugh took incontestable legal measures…and named you his beneficiary on all his cash accounts. They're set up as POD." He took a second, his mouth firming as he struggled for composure, before he murmured softly, "Payable on death."

Unable to take it in, Honor shot to her feet—then just stared, her thoughts scrambling, her stomach already knotting from the awful loss soon to come.

Jason slowly stood behind her, his strong arms coming around her, holding her close.

Neil struggled to his feet as well. "I've served as his medical power of attorney, but we were both certain if you knew, you'd try to help with that. Hugh trusted you, always, but he also understood exactly how much you love him—just as he loves you. That's why he details in his letter to you, at this point in his illness he doesn't wish to be resuscitated."

Pain turned her denial into a whisper of sound. *"No."*

Neil put a hand on her shoulder. "This saddens me, as well. I'm not ready to lose my dear friend. But this is a reality, and he knew you, above everyone else, would respect his wishes."

When she started to tremble, Jason turned her into his chest. She felt him kiss her temple, felt his big hands stroking down her back, and she concentrated on that instead of her grief as she tried to compose herself.

When she finally had herself together, she turned back to Neil, firm in her decision. "I don't want his money."

Tapping the envelope to his thigh, Neil scrutinized her. "Now, you listen to me, young lady. Hugh knew you would say that, just as he understood the difficulty this will cause you with the others. They inherit, but it's property and will have to go through probate. What he's given you, you can take immediately."

When he's gone. Honor squeezed her eyes shut and shook her head. "I can't."

"Read his letter and you'll see that it's not about what you want. It's about what *he* wants." Holding out the envelope, Neil emphasized again: "Hugh knew you would respect his wishes."

Reluctantly Honor took the envelope from him. She'd expected a packet of papers, but it seemed only one sheet might be inside. "It feels…thin."

"That's our Hugh, short and to the point." Neil offered his hand. "Should you ever need me, for any reason, my card is also included. Anything at all, please let me know."

Both she and Jason shook his hand.

Celeste stuck her head in the door, looked at each of them, then asked Neil, "Is it done?"

"I told her, but she hasn't yet read the letter."

Celeste said something to the others before stepping inside and pulling the door closed behind her, keeping a hand on the knob. "Well, now." She studied Honor critically. "You're still upright."

Urgently apologetic, Honor said, "I never—"

Celeste waved that away. "I love my brother, Honor. We've had our differences as all siblings do, though being an only child you might not have understood that. With all his faults, and all of my own, we were still brother and sister. Nothing would change that, not even disagreements over you or your reprobate parents."

Reassured, Honor nodded. "I'm glad."

"Of course you are." She held tight to the door when someone tried to open it. "You know, I always hoped you'd get some gumption to you. That you'd stand up and curse your terrible parents, because they *were* terrible and you deserved better. I wanted to see you cast some blame." She lifted a fist. "I wanted you to grasp what was yours. But you never had that fire."

"She has fire," Jason said, his voice tight.

Honor patted his hand on her shoulder. She didn't understand any of this, especially why Celeste was suddenly so different. She was usually all blame, without explanation or clarification. But now it seemed that she wanted Honor to understand. "Aunt Celeste—"

Opening her fist, palm out, Celeste indicated that Honor should shush. So she did.

"Perhaps your young man is right. Hugh always insisted that your fire was inside, subtle but there. I trust that's true because you're going to need it now."

"I don't want any conflicts."

"They'll be unavoidable, I'm afraid. Your mother's sisters,

LORI FOSTER

Gina and Janet, and your spineless cousin Terry will all be rabid over the idea of waiting for any inheritance while you get to collect the cash and move on."

"I don't want it."

Celeste looked at Neil, who shrugged.

"All the same, it's yours, as Hugh wanted it to be. Gina and Janet have bled him for years. Your mother, Honor, chose to walk away instead. Hugh felt he owed you everything he would have given to her—"

"He doesn't!"

"—and everything you refused to take while under his guardianship. And so you *will* take it and that's that." She gifted Honor with one of her very rare smiles that somehow still managed to be quite firm and insistent. "I believe I'll tell the others now— once I get them outside. You stay and visit with Hugh."

Confused, Honor stared at the closed door.

Neil patted her arm. "I've already said my goodbyes to Hugh."

Meaning he'd go soon, and she couldn't bear it.

"I'll go with Celeste now, just in case there are any questions of legality." Using his cane, he made his way out the door, closed it quietly behind him and still Honor stood there, the letter clutched in her hand.

Jason stroked over her hair. "Are you okay, honey?"

"He's already given me everything I ever wanted." Which was mostly to be loved, to be important enough to someone to matter.

"I know." Jason bent his knees to look into her eyes. "He loves you. He wanted to leave you something. You should honor him by agreeing, don't you think?"

A small noise drew their attention and they both looked toward the bed. Her grandfather's eyes were open, gazing at her without really seeing.

"Granddad?" Honor shoved the envelope at Jason and then hurried to the bed.

"Honor, dear." He smiled wearily as she gently held his hand. "You look so pretty. Did you get a date to the dance after all?"

Tears clogged her throat. "I did, Granddad. I went and I had such a nice time in the dress you bought me."

"Bah." His hand remained limp in hers. "If you finally accepted a date, I'm glad." He looked past her to Jason. "You never went to the dances."

Honor didn't know what to say. Whenever her grandfather drifted back to the past, she happily went along rather than confuse him further with corrections.

He squinted his watery eyes. "Who's that with you? Come closer so I can see you."

Jason stepped up next to the bed.

Honor was still debating what to say when her grandfather smiled.

"You're with my Honor?"

"Yes, sir."

"She's special," Granddad warned.

"Very special," Jason agreed.

Granddad considered him a moment, then sighed and closed his eyes. "Finally."

Sitting forward, Honor clutched his hand. "Granddad?"

In a faint voice, he murmured, "Go on out and play now, Honor. I need to rest."

She started to panic, but Jason curved his hand around her nape. "He's sleeping, honey. See his chest rising?"

Her spine turned into a noodle. She had a little more time... but she knew it wouldn't be enough.

"You don't need to stay," she whispered to Jason. "He might sleep for hours."

"You're here." He brushed his knuckles over her cheek. "There's nowhere else I'd rather be."

Lexie poked her head in the door. "Everyone else left." Seeing Honor and Jason so close, she asked, "Am I intruding?"

Honor waved her in and told her the same thing she'd told Jason. But just as Jason had done, Lexie, too, refused to leave her.

A very kind nurse brought in two more chairs and they waited together, sometimes talking quietly, sometimes sitting in comfortable silence.

With Jason's arm around her, Lexie's knees touching her own, she finally read her letter. As Neil had said, it was short and to the point. Granddad already had a burial plot and a headstone ready to complete; she didn't need to fuss about anything. He loved her, always had. He claimed she'd given him more than he ever could have returned, and thanked her for making an old man happier than he deserved.

A paper clip held Neil's business card to a short note that explained her grandfather's current cash balance amounted to a little over five hundred thousand dollars.

He'd left the staggering amount all to her.

Numb, Honor put the note away.

A little after midnight, her grandfather left her.

Jason woke to the sound of a lawn mower. He jolted, then realized that this time Honor was still burrowed close, her hold on him almost desperate.

For the longest time last night, she'd been strong. Too strong. While sitting with her grandfather's body, she'd shed a few quiet tears—and then she'd notified the others. Celeste had stood stoically by the bedside, but the aunts and cousin, lacking Honor's quiet way, had wailed and carried on with effusive emotion, alternately sobbing and blaming Honor.

It had infuriated Jason, but Honor had gone about dealing with the facility and contacting the funeral home. At one point her cousin tried to take over, but Celeste pointed out that Honor was the one in charge.

It was hours before they'd left, and Jason knew she held a wealth of sadness inside her.

She kept herself so contained, and so shut off from others, that it worried him—especially when she continued to urge him to go. Both he and Lexie had refused and by the time they'd gotten to her house, she'd given up insisting. With very little effort, he'd talked his way into her bed while Lexie took the couch.

He was starting to understand Honor. For much of her life she hadn't had anyone except her grandfather. Even Celeste, with her warped encouragement, had slighted her. She and Lexie had been friends a long time, but just as she'd hesitated to burden her grandfather, she hadn't wanted to take advantage of Lexie's friendship.

Her parents had taught her not to rely on anyone. Her other relatives had taught her not to hope.

Looking down at Honor now, with only the dim morning light filtering in through the sheets over the windows, he saw the paleness of her skin and the smudges under her eyes. He wanted to insulate her from hurt, protect her from hardship and at the same time show his respect for her strength.

He tucked the blankets up around her and pressed a very soft kiss to her forehead.

Limp with exhaustion, she barely stirred as he eased away.

He stood there at the side of the bed, watching her sleep, and he knew he was falling in love.

The timing sucked. He couldn't tell her how he felt, not when she spent every other breath trying to force distance between them. She had so much to deal with, and she'd taken great pains to prove her independence.

Instead he'd just be there for her and help her every way he could—meaning as much as she'd allow.

Lexie was still passed out facedown on the couch, a pillow over her head, when he slipped into the kitchen to make coffee. All he could see of her was her feet, poking out from beneath the rumpled blanket.

The scent of coffee must have roused her, though, because

just as the carafe filled, he heard sounds of grumbling. When he peeked into the living room, she sluggishly sat up, her hair a little wild, her mouth open in a jaw-breaking yawn.

"Morning."

She finished her yawn, got one eye open, groaned and flopped back down. "Unfair that you could look so good right now."

Jason gazed down at his wrinkled slacks and bare feet, but decided not to ask. "Coffee?"

"God yes." She didn't move.

"Will I need to pour it down your throat?"

"If you put it at the table, I'll crawl in and be forever in your debt." After two tries she finally got off the couch and schlepped down the hall to the bathroom.

Jason fixed his own cup, poured one for her and set cream and sugar on the table. When Lexie returned she looked a little more human—and cute in a bedraggled, underdressed way.

"I'm not a morning person," she explained as she slouched into a chair.

The nightshirt she wore—one Honor had lent her—barely kept her modesty intact. Under better circumstances, Jason would have imagined it on Honor. But right now caring trumped lust. "Especially when morning comes on the heels of last night?"

"Something like that." She sipped the coffee and groaned in near bliss. "You're so freaking perfect you suck."

"All things considered, I'm feeling pretty imperfect this morning."

"I know what you mean." She rubbed her face. "Did Honor get any rest at all?"

"It took her a few hours to fall asleep, but she's out now." And while she remained so, he had some questions for Lexie. "You've known her how long?"

"Since middle school, after she moved in with her grandfather." She drank more coffee and propped her head on a fist. "I consider it my greatest feat because Honor doesn't accept friendship lightly. I had to practically force myself into her life. But it was worth it." She eyed Jason. "*She* is worth it."

"I agree. There's something about her, this gentle, caring—"

"And ferocious loyalty."

"All mixed with pride and grit and humor."

Lexie smiled. "She's the real deal, when so few people are."

Yeah, he understood that all too well. "Her grandfather asked her about a dance. I got the impression she didn't go out much in high school."

"High school, trade school…basically since I've known her. Honor doesn't trust lightly. She's friendly to everyone, but only to a point. So even though a lot of guys have asked her out, I could count on one hand the number of times she's said yes."

Meaning he was special, regardless of the many ways Honor tried to keep him at an emotional distance. "Anything else you want to tell me about her?"

"Sure. She's dependable to a fault," Lexie said around another yawn. "But she never expects anything in return."

"I got that yesterday, listening to her relatives and her grandfather's lawyer." He hesitated, but knowing they were such close friends… "You knew about her parents?"

"Douches," she said with feeling. "Honor would never admit it, and if you tell her I said so I'll have to maim you, but they devastated her and she's never gotten over it. I mean, how does any kid ever get over a thing like that? Her parents literally dumped her and walked away without a backward glance."

Every time he thought of it, Jason's heart ached. Through it all, Honor had remained an incredibly genuine, honest person.

"She's learned to deal with it," Lexie said. "But it was a crushing blow and sometimes I think it's left her forever wounded."

No, Jason wouldn't accept that. "She's got more inner fortitude than anyone I know."

"She's never been given much choice. Except by her grandfather."

"And you," he said.

She half smiled, then asked, "And now you?"

"Yeah."

When they heard the bedroom door open, they both fell silent in expectation. Half a minute passed. They heard the toilet flush, water running in the bathroom sink and then Honor came into the kitchen, her hair lank, her eyes puffy—and she froze when she saw them.

Jason stood. "Good morning."

"What are you guys doing here?"

Lexie flattened both hands over her heart and flopped back in her seat. "I'm wounded."

It struck him that Honor had honestly expected to face the day alone. "You figured I'd leave without telling you?" *As you did to me.*

Defensive, she lifted her chin. "I thought you'd get on with your day."

His day would be about seeing to her, but he didn't bother telling her that yet. "Coffee?"

Her apprehensive gaze searched his. "Thank you." She sat next to Lexie.

While pouring her coffee, Jason watched out of the corner of his eye and saw Lexie stroke her hair, then take her hand.

"You okay, hon?"

Honor nodded. "Yes, of course. Thank you."

Extreme politeness seemed to be her defense—and it made him grind his teeth.

Lexie, however, wasn't deterred. But then, she'd known Honor a lot longer and was probably used to her means of coping. "I can take the day off—"

"No." Honor accepted the cup he handed to her, then absently stirred in sugar. "I appreciate the thought, Lexie. But there's no need for you to miss work. I promise, I'm fine."

Still looking worried, Lexie said, "You'll have to make arrangements."

"I know. It'll be a busy day." She glanced at the clock and made a face. "I'm sorry, but I do need to call off work." Taking her cup with her, she stood and said, "If you'll both excuse me, I…" She trailed off, then disappeared down the hall.

Jason turned to Lexie. "You going to be here a few minutes more?"

"Unless she shoves my lifeless body out the door. Why?"

"I have a few quick things to do. Don't let her leave without me. Okay?"

"Sure. But don't worry about it. I know Honor. She doesn't mean to be rude, but she's on autopilot today. It's a defense mechanism for her. She'll try to stay busy doing, so she doesn't have to feel." Lexie tipped her head. "You're going to stay with her?"

"One way or another."

She toasted him with her coffee. "Sounds like you have it covered. But if at any point she needs me—"

"I'll be sure to let you know."

While Honor remained on the phone in the bedroom, making one call after another, Lexie swilled a second cup of coffee. She was starting to come awake, but it'd take a whole lot more—beginning with a hot shower—before she'd be ready to face the world.

She headed back to the couch, dug out her phone and called her job to say she'd be late. Like…not-until-the-afternoon late. Because she had such a great track record for punctuality, it wasn't a problem.

The pillow and blanket called her name and she was just about to collapse again when a knock sounded on the door. She could still hear Honor on the phone, so she answered it herself.

Sullivan stood there.

Dark sunglasses shielded his eyes from the rising sun, but when his head dipped, she knew he looked her over.

And she wanted to cringe.

He stood there in a snug, snowy white T-shirt that hugged all those lean sexy muscles and black athletic pants, freshly shaved with his black hair combed back.

In one of Honor's very uninspiring nightshirts, her hair destroyed and her makeup nonexistent, she looked like a rat.

Copping an attitude, she put her hand on her hip and glared. "Your timing stinks."

He pushed the glasses to the top of his head, and those heated blue eyes went over her again before looking behind her at the bedding on the couch. "You stayed over."

Lexie pointed to her car at the curb. "You didn't notice?"

"No." He glanced back, frowned at her little convertible, then leaned a shoulder on the doorframe. "I thought Jason stayed over."

"He did." She smirked. "But I slept separately from them."

"Knowing Jason as I do, I didn't have a doubt."

Meaning he wouldn't put a threesome past her? "You're a funny guy this morning."

With his gaze somehow both intimate and grave, Sullivan frowned. "Sorry. How's Honor doing?"

"She's on the phone in her bedroom, making necessary arrangements." *And pretending both Jason and I are useless.*

"Damn."

Rather than invite him in, Lexie stepped out, forcing him to back up. She pulled the door partially closed behind her. "You heard?"

"Yeah. Hogan told me Jason went to the hospital with her last night." Brows up, he looked around as if concerned others might be nearby. "Is she okay?"

"Word sure does travel fast in this little Mayberry town, doesn't it?"

Inky lashes went to half-mast over his incendiary blue eyes. "Did you wake up on the wrong side of the couch?"

Men. Tunneling both hands through her insane hair, Lexie squinted up at him. Amazing how the sun put a damn halo around his dark head. She huffed. "I was up most of the night, my best friend is hurting, her couch is too short and I feel utterly useless. Then you show up and see me like this."

His jaw worked but he said nothing.

Lexie crossed her arms. "Well?"

His attention dipped to her breasts before he visibly forced it to her face. "What?"

"You could apologize."

"For...seeing you?"

"Like this." She swept her hands down to indicate the wrecked picture she presented. "Yeah."

Instead his nostrils flared—and suddenly he leaned in and kissed her.

Shocked, Lexie tipped her head back. "What—"

He stole that small distance from her, kissing her again, slowly gathering her close. Just as she started to melt against him, footsteps sounded on the porch.

"Break it up, you two." Jason moved past them. "Or take it somewhere private." He went on in and Lexie heard him call out for Honor.

Flummoxed, Sullivan stared at her.

She snickered, but quickly sobered. "Oh God, I'm an awful person."

Bemused, Sullivan asked, "How do you figure that?"

"Honor needs me, but I'm out here playing kissy face with you, then enjoying your reaction when you realized *you* started it. Kissing me wasn't your intention, was it?"

He inhaled deeply—probably reaching for patience. "No, it wasn't. I needed to talk to Jason."

"Bad timing," she said. "Again." And in case he didn't understand, she explained, "With the kiss—"

"Yeah, smart-ass. I got it." He stroked her with his gaze. "I'm not taking all the blame when you come out here half-naked, looking like you were just tumbled."

"Tumbled?" She blinked at him. "Please tell me you didn't just say that." It was sooo cheesy…and yet somehow charming, too.

"I said it." He locked his jaw. "You look like you were just properly laid." While she remained speechless over that, he reached past her to knock on the door.

"Sure," she finally said. "Intrude."

Jason answered, looked at them both, then asked, "All done?"

"I need a second. It's important."

He nodded and stepped out, saying to Lexie, "She's on the phone with Neil. I'll just be a minute."

"Right. This is a meeting of the boys' club. Got it." She went in and shut the door, then decided she should use the time to make herself more presentable…just in case Sullivan hung around.

They stepped out to the yard, far enough away from the porch for a little privacy, but still close enough that Jason could keep his eye on the door.

Anyone could see that he had a million things on his mind, so Sullivan got right to the point. "Last night, a couple of hours before you guys got back, someone was snooping around Honor's house."

Jason's attention sharpened. "The hell you say. Who?"

"Sorry, but I don't know. I was sitting out front and when the floodlight on the side of her house went out, it drew my attention. I spotted a couple of people moving near the woods, using a penlight. They were dressed in dark clothes, and they were definitely checking out her house."

"Son of a bitch."

"By the time I'd crossed the street to check it out, whoever it was had run off. I got hold of Nathan, and he came down to look around." Sullivan put a hand to his shoulder. There were few things worse for a man than to feel helpless. "The cord to the floodlight was cut."

"They were near the same broken window?"

"Seemed so. Nathan and I are thinking it was maybe the same people, trying to get back in."

"If it is, they probably know she's a woman living alone." Livid, Jason ran a hand through his hair while pacing. "She already has too much to deal with. She doesn't need this crap, too."

"I know, and I'm sorry. I made a point of keeping an eye on things until I saw you bring her back. I knew you were with her so I let it go. Besides, by then it was damn near morning."

"Thanks. She'd planned to get something more permanent in place, but now—"

Understanding, Sullivan asked, "It was her grandfather who passed?"

Jason nodded. "He was her closest family, the one who mostly raised her."

Rough. Sullivan started to speak, then he noticed Lexie moving around inside. He was so preoccupied with her that it made him nuts.

They were total opposites; after many past mistakes he'd learned to take life more seriously, whereas Lexie seemed to embrace a life free of responsibility. At first that had drawn him because he'd stupidly thought he could indulge in a fling with her and then move on. But after only one taste, he knew she affected him too much. Already he wanted more. A lot more. But when—if—he ever got seriously involved, it'd have to be with a woman who shared his commitments.

In the long run, Lexie would be totally wrong for his life— a life she knew nothing about, with priorities she'd never understand.

He'd already made up his mind to steer clear of her. Of course, he hadn't been thinking of steering clear when she stepped out looking so sleepy but still sassy, her naked mouth soft, her eyes heavy.

She paused in the window, looked out and blew him a kiss.

Getting himself back on track, Sullivan frowned and focused on the topic at hand. "Honor needs security lights that'll come on with movement. I know that means it'll catch every animal in the area, too, but it should at least scare off intruders."

"I'll take care of it."

Interesting. He knew Jason was seeing her, but he was starting to think it might be pretty serious. "Let me know what I can do to help."

"You already did it." Jason started to leave, then paused. "Don't say anything to Honor. I'll let her know about it once she's gotten her bearings again."

"And in the meantime?"

Jason started back to the front door. "I'll be with her."

Yup. Very serious.

Before he broke down and sought out Lexie again, Sullivan headed back to his own house. A group of "priorities" were counting on him, and he refused to ever let them down.

10

WITH HER HAIR and makeup done, Honor grabbed her purse and headed to the front door—but drew up short when she found Jason standing there, arms crossed, posture arrogant.

"Jason. I thought you'd gone home."

He nodded. "I came back."

Dressed in gray slacks and a black pullover, he looked amazing. She felt a terrible pang at knowing her newfound closeness with him had been so badly interrupted. She'd slept with him last night, and hadn't even thought of sex. Her buzzing brain and the strangling emotion had kept her thoughts centered only on her loss, on what she'd have to do to move forward, and what was needed to keep from letting down her grandfather.

Through the night, Jason's arms around her, the steady thumping of his heartbeat, had helped to quiet those turbulent thoughts, but they hadn't penetrated beyond that.

How amazing that *he* hadn't tried to initiate things.

And now he stood there, looking as if he expected certain things from her—none of them sexual.

So then…what?

She hitched her purse strap over her shoulder. "I'm meeting with the funeral director this morning."

He looked away, his brows twitching down as he worked

through some internal struggle. Finally, brows together in concern, he asked, "Would you like company?"

Everything in her went mushy with gratitude. When she'd bought her house, she was looking forward to standing on her own two feet, financial stability and the pride of ownership. Not once had she considered gaining a neighbor who could not only melt her in bed, but also devastate her with kindness. "You are so nice to offer, but—"

"I'm not *nice*." Pushing away from the door, he stepped up to her and cupped her face. "You shouldn't be alone right now."

Feeling the brush of his rough thumbs over her cheeks pierced the grief and made her skin tingle. "Neil will meet me there. He insists we..." God, it hurt to think it, much less say it.

"He wants you to take care of the financial transfers?"

She nodded, clenching her muscles to push away the weakness. "Yes. He said that's what Granddad wanted." She tried a smile that fell flat. "Many, many things to take care of today."

"I could help."

"You already have, so much." Briefly she rested against him while giving him a tight hug. "But this is something I need to do."

"Not alone."

"Yes." She sighed, then levered back again. It wouldn't do to start leaning on him. Despite his giving nature, their relationship was too new for her to dump all this on him. Grief, sadness, paperwork, funeral arrangements...it was almost too much for *her*, so it'd definitely be too much for an outsider.

"Honor..."

Her control felt fragile at best and if he showed too much concern, if he was too kind, she'd crumple and start bawling and that would be more humiliation than she could bear.

Taking his hands in hers, she stared up at him and whispered, "Please understand."

It took a few tense seconds before he nodded agreement. "I'll back off, if you promise me you'll let me know when and how I *can* help. With anything." He stroked his fingers through her hair, and tenderly kissed her forehead. "Anything at all. Okay?"

"Yes, thank you." God, if she didn't go now, she'd lose it. Biting her lip, she said, "I'm glad you slept with me last night."

He gave a brief, subdued smile. "That was my pleasure."

And hers. She nodded and fled, because if she didn't go now, she'd start accepting his offers and that wouldn't be fair at all. Worse, her neediness just might drive him away.

And she was far from ready to let him go.

After hours spent at the funeral home Honor got everything arranged. Her grandfather had enough caring friends and close associates that an extended viewing and visitation would be considerate. Closely following that would be the funeral. With some guidance from Neil and a little assistance from Celeste, she sent out notifications to the various papers.

The financial end of things took even longer. The sums were staggering and she honestly didn't know what to do with the money. Neil suggested depositing it for now and worrying about financial and retirement planning later.

It boggled her mind. She'd spent so much time living paycheck to paycheck, saving for every little thing, buying second-hand whenever possible, making it entirely on her own, and now…she didn't know what to think, so she decided not to. Pretending the money didn't exist was easier, especially since it was a reminder of what she'd lost.

By the time she got home, the sun hung low in the sky, a giant red ball surrounded by hues of purple and pink. A beautiful sunset. She was just pulling into her driveway when Lexie called. Again.

Throughout the day her friend had repeatedly checked on her.

Shaking her head, but also smiling, Honor answered with "Yes, I'm still okay."

"Of course you are. You're one of the strongest people I know. So, what do you think about ice cream? I could pick up a pint, maybe bring a cheesy movie for us to watch."

"I love you, Lex. You know that. But honestly tonight I just want to collapse." And knowing what Lexie's reply to that would be, she added, "Alone."

"Uh-huh. You know, honey, I don't mind playing second fiddle to a hunk of burning-hot man candy. If you'd rather spend the night with Jason, you have my approval."

"It's not that," she said honestly...but the thought tempted her.

"Okay, one quick lecture from me and then I'll leave you alone until lunch tomorrow. Men have an amazing way of making some things better. Trust me on this. Jason wants to help, so if everything starts to get to you, please—*I'm beggin' ya*—please let the man know. I guaran-damn-tee you he'll be happy to oblige. And few things can chase away the darkness like another warm body to touch."

"You're nuts," Honor said, but her thoughts rioted around the images she'd provoked.

"Sure I am. But I'm also right." Lexie sighed. "Love you, Honor."

"I know. And I love you, too."

After she'd disconnected the call and returned the phone to her purse, she glanced at Jason's house.

She didn't see him, but Colt was headed toward her. With his tall, lean, muscular build, he looked easily twenty-five, and he wore only shorts and held a leash attached to a big dog that she'd never seen before.

Thoughts diverted, she left her car and greeted him. "Hey, Colt."

With a confidence she rarely associated with teenagers, he came right up to her and drew her in for a one-armed hug.

Feeling indulgent, she smiled as she patted his bare shoulder. "You get more like your uncle every day."

Taking that as a compliment, he said, "Thanks." His concerned gaze moved over her face. "I heard about your grandpa. I'm really sorry. If there's anything I can do—"

"I'm fine." Kneeling, she greeted the dog because that was easier than seeing the sympathy on Colt's face. "And who's this handsome fellow?" She let the dog sniff her hand, then stroked down his neck and back. She didn't know much about dogs, but she thought he had the look of a German shepherd mix.

"Well, that's the thing," Colt hedged, before launching into explanations. "After people were tampering with your house again last night, I figured you needed more protection."

Honor jerked so hard she landed on her butt. The dog loved it, taking it as an invite and wiggling onto her, bestowing wet doggy kisses to her face.

She caught the collar, held the dog back and lumbered to her feet in a rush. "What are you talking about?"

The dog sat, then leaned on her, almost throwing her off balance.

"You don't have to take him right away," Colt said, still talking fast. "I know you have a lot going on right now. I'm going to take care of him until you're ready, and Dad said he'd help me get what he needs. But he's a really good dog. Some jerks dropped him off at the shelter because they had to move and said they couldn't take him with them. Bastards."

Surprised by the profanity, Honor temporarily forgot her own surprise. "That's a terrible reason to give up a pet."

"I know. Guess he was never a real part of their family."

Honor read far too much in Colt's expressive eyes. "Guess not."

"But he could be part of yours. I know it's asking a lot, but Nathan knew about the dog and—"

"Whoa." Because the dog kept wiggling closer to her, Honor took the leash from Colt. "We'll figure that out in a minute." How, she had no idea. Taking care of herself was, at present, overwhelming. Adding in a big dog would only complicate things more. "Right now let's talk about my house. You said someone was messing with it again?"

"You didn't know?" Scratching his ear with concern, he glanced around but they remained alone in her driveway. "Yeah, well, see, Uncle Jason said Sullivan told him about it this morning. I just assumed..."

"That your uncle would tell me? Yes, that would be an obvious assumption."

Colt cleared his throat. "Um..."

Jason came around the farther corner of her house, the side closest to the woods, and obviously he'd overheard because he said, "I've got it, Colt. How about you go around back and help your dad finish up?"

When the dog tried to follow Colt, it almost pulled Honor off her feet. Jason relieved her of the leash, then took a moment to stoop down and reassure the dog. "You're okay, now, Diesel."

"Diesel?"

"His name." Jason held the dog's face. "One way or another, you're sticking with us."

So if she didn't keep Diesel, he would?

The dog thumped his tail on the ground, looked at Honor, then came to lean on her again.

Had they somehow coerced the animal into helping with their plan?

Unable to resist, she put a hand on his scruff and glared at Jason. "Care to explain?"

"Which first? Diesel or house?"

"House." Thinking about the dog made her want to weep for some reason.

Maybe because he'd lost his family, too.

She filled her lungs with deep, even breaths to fight off the depressive emotion. No one, least of all Jason, wanted to suffer her excesses.

Cupping a hand around her nape in a now familiar gesture, he scrutinized her. "You know, Honor, you don't have to do this, not with me."

It felt like he looked clear through to her soul, and that made her a bit panicky. "This?" She needed to get away from him before she lost it. "What is that supposed to mean?"

His hand began kneading her tensed muscles. "You're not impervious to hurt, honey. Everyone suffers it."

Deliberately Honor stepped out of his reach. It wasn't easy, but she kept the defensive glare off her expression. "You were going to tell me something about my house."

Slowly, as if measuring her response, he nodded. "Okay, sure." He kept her gaze held in his. "Last night, Sullivan saw someone lurking around by the woods. They took off when he spotted them, but it's still a concern."

She did her utmost not to react, but damn, it made her knees shaky. Ever since her parents dumped her, she'd prided herself on being a strong person. In no way, not financially and not emotionally, did she infringe on others.

But things were piling up, weighing her down, and she needed privacy. Like…now. She choked down the fear and nodded. "I see."

"The cord for the floodlight was cut, and I knew you'd be busy with…other things today. So I got some actual security lights and Hogan and I got them wired. They're motion-activated, so if anyone gets near, they'll come on. Animals might also trigger them, though, so if the lights do come on, I don't want you to worry."

Making her mouth smile wasn't easy. "You shouldn't have, but thank you." She took a step back. "How much do I owe you?"

Frustration tightened his expression. "Don't insult me, honey."

As if a thin thread of rationale suddenly snapped, anger surged. "Insult you? You insult *me* by constantly assuming I can't take care of myself! You overstep, *often*, and I'm just supposed to be *grateful?*"

On each stressed word, her voice rose until she became aware of both Hogan and Colt stepping around the house to watch.

She felt like a spectacle. And oh God, she felt weak.

Worse, she felt ungrateful.

"I want receipts," she said in an unsteady voice. "For all of it."

Jason gave one small nod. "I understand."

The gentleness in his tone crushed her because it told her he understood more than the obvious. Even now he continued to treat her with kid gloves—while she acted like a bitch. Trying to moderate her reaction and her unruly emotions, she said, "I know you want to help—"

"That's what friends and neighbors do."

"—but I promise, I can handle things on my own." I don't *need* you. *I refuse to need anyone.*

She stepped away from her own thoughts, fighting the urge to run. "Thank you for what you've done. But going forward, please know that I—"

"I do," he said softly.

He'd given her an out from the impossible situation she'd just created. For only a second, Honor closed her eyes. When she opened them again, she saw Jason stroking the worried dog.

Her heart squeezed for the animal. He, too, had been through enough. "We can talk about him tomorrow."

"All right." Jason didn't move. "We'll be done with the lights in another ten minutes, and then I'll back off."

It sounded incredibly lame when she said, "Thank you."

"But..." Taking her by surprise, he moved in for a quick kiss, his hand on her face, his body heat enveloping her like a gentle hug. "If you decide there's anything I can do to help, anything at all, I'd appreciate it if you let me know."

Without giving her a chance to reply to that, he stepped

around her and, taking the dog with him, went back to the side of her house.

To put up security lights for her.

Lights that she hadn't paid for.

The panic bloomed inside her until she couldn't stay still. Too quickly, she strode into her house, closed and secured the door behind her...then slowly sank to sit on the floor, her head on her knees, shaking from the inside out.

The fact that she could now afford security lights and more only added to her tension. She couldn't think too much about the money without getting irrationally angry. It was like a giant exclamation point to her lopsided relationship with her grandfather.

He'd given her everything, and she'd had nothing at all to give.

Except...in his letter he'd told her what her time with him had meant.

Over and over her thoughts played with that idea, and with every fiber of her being she hoped her grandfather had truly known how much he'd meant to her, that she'd been able to show him how much she cared.

Neil promised her that she had. And he'd invited her to visit him as well. She thought she just might do that. Lunch with him would be the closest thing to seeing Granddad again.

When the outside hammering ended and she heard voices as Jason, Hogan and Colt crossed her yard to return to their own home, she stopped wallowing in indecision and went to investigate.

The second she stepped to the side of the house, the lights came on, spreading their glow in a wide arc. She peeked around back and saw more lights installed there, as well. Jason hadn't just stuck in ugly floodlights. No, these were beautiful lights that matched the character of the house.

They were lights she would have chosen herself if, as Jason

said, she hadn't been so busy dealing with the details of her grandfather's passing.

While looking at the lights, she also noticed the broken window had been repaired.

Conflicted, she went back inside and locked the door again. Why would Jason continue being so considerate? She should have somehow figured out how to do the repairs before he'd felt obligated to do them for her.

When it suddenly struck her that she still hadn't gotten a garbage can lid, either, she closed her eyes in regret. She was failing, so he felt he had to pick up the slack for her.

Vowing to do better, she began on a mental agenda. Tomorrow she'd get started on it.

Because tonight she needed a shower, wanted to change into her big loose nightgown, and she should probably eat whether she felt hungry or not.

By rote, she accomplished everything, and finally at ten o'clock, she tried to turn in.

It hit her then, truly hit her; *she was alone.*

Hollowness left her aching and again near tears.

She tried to block it, but the silence closed around her like a strangling fist until she began gasping for each and every panicked breath. Unable to stand it, she threw back the covers and launched from the bed.

Dragging in air, she frantically looked around her dark room. It had once felt like independence but now just seemed cold and incredibly lonely.

Last night, with Jason, she'd found some quiet within her own brain, so it made sense that her anxious thoughts veered to him.

She remembered what Lexie had said and, disappointed in herself, she strode to the nightstand, snatched up her phone and called him. Her trembling hand gripped the phone too tightly and she held her breath…

He answered before the first ring had completed.

"Honor."

That deep voice, gruff with concern, stole the remainder of her strength and she sank to sit on the side of the bed. For two seconds, her throat closed up and she couldn't speak. When she finally managed to ask, "Were you asleep?" she sounded incredibly pathetic.

"No," he promised. "Just sitting here hoping you'd call."

Was that true, or did he only want to make this easier for her? Didn't matter. "Would you…want to come over?"

"Already on my way."

Surprised, she ducked to the window to peek out. Sure enough, her porch light and his combined to show him halfway across the yards. When she couldn't see him anymore, she rushed to the living room, turned on one low light and opened the front door.

They each still held their phones to their ears.

His eyes were dark and filled with scrutiny. Pressing a button, he returned the cell to his pocket, then stepped in. Slowly she lowered her own phone.

With his gaze caressing her face, he smoothed her hair. "You were in bed?"

She nodded.

"Could I sleep with you?"

In every single way, he eased the hardship. "I was going to ask." But now she didn't have to, so instead she went in a different direction. After putting her phone aside, she stepped up against him, her nose to his naked chest. The soft hair there teased her, and she breathed in his comforting scent. "You enjoyed sex with me?"

Carefully, biceps flexing, he closed his strong arms around her. "Very much."

"Good." Needing no more encouragement than that, she pressed her lips to his skin. He was always so warm, she thought, losing herself in the nearness to him, lightly kissing her way up to his collarbone, then his throat. "You smell good."

His broad hands were still on her back, his entire big body held in uncertainty.

Yes, this was what she needed. A sultry diversion, sensation powerful enough to muffle the grief.

She nibbled her way along his hard jaw, his whisker-rough chin and finally to the delicious firmness of his mouth.

He passively allowed her to kiss him, but as she trailed one hand down his abdomen to the waistband of his shorts, he resisted. "Honor," he chided.

"Please." She couldn't talk about it. She absolutely could not suffer his pity. One breath, another and she begged, "Please, Jason."

For two agonizing seconds he considered her. She saw the heat ignite in his dark eyes right before he crushed her in so they touched chest to pelvis, his mouth hungry on hers, his hands stroking everywhere. Finally, *finally*, the bad thoughts receded.

Through her nightgown, he fondled her behind, lifting her to her tiptoes and repeatedly moving her against the solid ridge of his erection.

It thrilled her that he was already hard.

"Tell me what you want," he whispered, then kissed her again, deeper, hotter.

"You. I want you, Jason."

He switched to her neck, drawing in her skin, giving soft bites to every sensitive spot he found.

Turning, he pinned her to the door, his hands getting bolder as he squeezed her breasts, thumbed her nipples through her nightgown. Somehow he got one leg between hers, and she gladly moved against him in a frenzy of need.

"So hot..." Scooping an arm under her backside, he easily lifted her, and his mouth closed over one nipple through her nightgown.

Sharp need made her cry out.

She realized they were moving and then Jason laid her on her short couch. Before she could suggest the bed instead, he tugged her nightgown up above her breasts, stripped away her panties and sat between her legs, just looking at her in the low light.

And oh, how he looked at her.

Nothing bad could intrude, not now. Not with Jason.

Smiling slightly, Honor put her hands above her head and got comfortable.

"Jesus, you're beautiful." He caressed both breasts, repeatedly tugging at her nipples, bending several times to suck at her.

Escalating need made it impossible to stay still. She loved the way he teased her breasts, but she wanted him to touch her in other ways, too.

Hoping to let him know without words, she squirreled against him.

"Not yet," he whispered, proving he understood. Again he returned to draw on one nipple until she was so sensitive, each soft suction was felt in her womb.

She threaded her fingers through his hair, and she wasn't sure if it was to pull him away or hold him closer.

Abruptly he shifted, his hands on her hips to keep her still as he put a hot, damp love bite against her ribs, then down to her waist, over to her belly, where he prodded her navel with his tongue.

She was too surprised, too turned on, to be ticklish. "Jason?"

"Shh. Let me take care of you."

She wasn't sure what that meant, but she felt the damp heat of his mouth on her inner thigh and quickly whispered, "Okay."

His fingertips moved over her, spreading her slickness as he explored, exacerbating already sensitized nerve endings.

She felt his breath—and held her own.

"Already wet," he murmured while easing one finger just inside her, idly playing.

She needed more, and deliberately shifted.

He pressed his finger deeper. "Better?"

Without really meaning to, she clamped down on him.

"Let's try this." He kissed her thigh again—*so close*—then withdrew and worked in two fingers, gliding them in and out until she knew they were slick from her excitement.

Softly moaning, Honor opened her legs more, lifting one foot to the back of the couch and putting the other on the floor at the side.

"Nice and wide," he praised roughly. "So hot."

The way he spoke to her added to her growing tension. Toes curled, she squirmed—and he licked over her.

"*Oh god.*" Anchoring herself, she grabbed for the sofa cushions.

Keeping his fingers pressed inside her, he came back for another leisurely taste, his tongue moving over her sensitive flesh, stroking her clitoris until she gasped—and then drawing her into the heat of his mouth, sucking gently while still using his tongue…

Oh god, oh god, *oh god*. As if all that wasn't enough, he raised a hand and found her breast, his thumb brushing her taut nipple, and she lost it.

Groaning harshly, her hips lifting to his mouth to match the rhythm of his tongue and fingers, she climaxed. He stayed with her, eating at her as the pleasure pulsed, expanded, over and over until it gradually began to wane, until, finally spent, she dropped boneless into the cushions.

Body thrumming in all the right places, Honor drifted as she caught her breath, half-asleep, fully sated, blessedly numb from reality.

Only vaguely cognizant of Jason standing, she waited for him to move over her, but instead he lifted her in his arms, cradled her to his chest and carried her to her bedroom.

She supposed a man of his size needed more room than the

small couch provided. She put her arms around his neck and breathed, "That was amazing."

"You're amazing." He lowered her to sit on the mattress, finished stripping off her nightgown, then...tucked her in.

Panic immediately clawed to the surface. "What are you doing?"

"Taking off my shorts."

Oh. He wouldn't do that if he planned to leave. The darkness of the room made it difficult to see, but she heard him moving around and a second later the bed dipped as he got in with her.

Honor had the awful suspicion that he expected to go to sleep, so she crawled over atop him. "I want you," she said against his throat.

Always, his hands went to her backside. She was starting to think the man had a fetish.

"You just came," he reminded her.

"Mmm." Yes, she did. Thinking about it gave her another buzz, and she wiggled. "But you didn't."

"I'm fine."

Meaning...what? She cupped his face in her hands, kissed a cheekbone, his jaw and finally his mouth. "I want more." She licked his bottom lip, then lightly bit it. "I want *you*."

Sounding tortured, he asked, "You're sure?"

"I am so very, very sure."

As if he'd only been holding back out of some misplaced concern, he groaned and she quickly found herself on her back. His mouth, voracious now, ate at hers with a surprising hunger.

Where she'd been nearly insensate only moments before, his need spiked hers right back to the boiling point.

She loved feeling Jason between her legs, his weight pressing her down into the bed, his hair-roughened body teasing hers in all the right places. She ran a foot up his calf, opened her palms over his now-bunched biceps, and against her belly, she felt his erection throbbing.

His hands were everywhere.

So was his mouth.

Before she could catch her breath, he opened his mouth on her breasts, her belly—lower.

Against her damp, heated flesh, he growled, "I love how you taste," and proved it with single-minded attention.

She knew she was again close to losing it. "Now," she whispered. "Now, please. *Now.*"

Finally he moved away to get a condom.

It took him only seconds before he was back, kneeing her thighs apart, opening her with rough fingertips, and immediately sinking in with a harsh groan.

So perfect.

She locked her legs around the small of his back, holding him tight.

Balancing on his forearms over her did amazing things for the muscles in his chest and shoulders.

The way he rocked into her did amazing things to her.

Each thrust came harder and faster than the one before it, building the heat between them. The scent of sex permeated the air. Honor strained against him, reaching for release, needing it and the awesome oblivion it gave.

Readjusting, Jason slipped an arm beneath her hips and tilted her up so that each and every stroke went as deep as possible.

She cried out, but the cry turned into a throaty moan as the orgasm gripped her.

Taking her mouth, Jason let himself go, too, his entire body clenching with release…

It was the last thing Honor remembered.

11

NOT BEING AN IDIOT, Jason woke well before Honor this time, and he refused to go back to sleep. The sun was still crawling off the horizon when he got his heavy eyes open.

Honor remained curled trustingly against him, one of her slim, smooth legs between his, her head nestled on his shoulder, her small hands tucked against his chest.

He had his left hand opened over her ass.

That didn't surprise him. The lady had a soft, heart-shaped behind that naturally drew him. Careful not to wake her, he stroked the satiny skin of one plump cheek with his thumb.

She'd taken him by surprise last night. Sure, he'd wanted her to call. He'd wanted to be with her.

But he hadn't expected sex.

He hadn't expected her to need him like that.

Closing his eyes, he thought of how she'd tasted, the way she'd reacted, the wild way she'd come. Thinking about it was making him hard now, but he knew the morning would be vastly different from the night.

Today she had to once again deal with the ugly issues.

God, he wished for a way to shield her.

She'd crawled into his heart without even trying, and every day the ways that she affected him grew stronger.

With her face tucked under his chin and her tangled hair half hiding her, he couldn't see her. Using great care, he shifted her away, then brushed back her hair. She sighed and resettled herself again on her back.

She'd passed out after her last release and they were both still naked. Now that he'd displaced her, one pale breast peeked above the edge of the coverlet, exposing a soft nipple that he badly wanted to taste.

Honor had sensitive breasts, and if he didn't care so much for her, he could probably easily coax her into morning sex.

But he *did* care, and he'd never been a man ruled by his libido.

After last night, he felt closer to her, more involved, far more protective. Seeing her like this, so sweetly vulnerable, did insane things to him.

For another half an hour he watched her sleep, until the sun finally brightened the room enough to disturb her. She didn't ease awake. No, she came to with a jolt, her eyes flaring open, her body jerking.

"Hey," he murmured, soothing her with a stroke, giving in to the urge to kiss her.

She cleared her throat. "Hi." Her gaze traveled over him. "You're awake."

"Yes."

"And you're naked."

"You, too." He tugged the coverlet a little lower, until both breasts showed.

Pushing up to her elbows, Honor looked down at herself with surprise. "Um…"

Seeing her flushed cheeks, he asked, "Would you like coffee?"

"*Yes*. But I can make it," she said as she tugged up the coverlet. "If you'll just…" She looked at him expectantly.

He propped his head on a fist and asked, "What?" even though he knew exactly what she meant.

"I need to get up."

He was already up, but she definitely didn't want his lust right now. She was horrified enough by the situation, which reminded him that while Honor was open and honest about sex, she wasn't very experienced. *Two years.* He still had a hard time wrapping his brain around that. "I can make coffee."

"But—"

"It's not a hardship." Leaning over her, he put a warm, soft smooch on her parted lips, then tossed back the coverlet and stood.

Knowing she stared at his body, he stretched.

"You're hard."

So observant. Resisting a smile, he shrugged. "Yup. Happens in the morning, especially when I wake up next to a very sexy woman."

Her eyes narrowed. "Who?" When he grinned, she shook her head and said, "I mean, besides me." As soon as she thought about that she clarified, "Not that I think I'm sexy—"

Jason pulled on his boxers. "You're the sexiest, and no one before you matters right now." Let her take that however she wanted.

"Give me two minutes in the bathroom," he said, "then take whatever time you need. I'll be in the kitchen."

She took fifteen minutes. When she finally showed herself, she'd brushed her hair, was dressed in pajama pants and a big T-shirt and looked to be in an agony of embarrassment.

Jason, who'd since retrieved his shorts, pulled out a chair for her. As she sat he put a cup of coffee in front of her.

In a too careful, too precise way, she placed her cell phone on the table.

Thinking of her grandfather and the responsibilities she'd taken on, he figured she'd always had that phone on hand. Along the way, someone should have spelled her, given her an extended break—if not a whole vacation, at least a weekend.

Or hell, a day.

LORI FOSTER

Watching her, feeling her uneasiness, he said, "I already put in a little cream and sugar."

Avoiding his gaze, she used both hands and lifted the cup to sip. "Good. Thank you."

He could guess at the reason she looked so tortured, but he wasn't quite sure how to make her feel better. Pulling out his own chair, he sat. "I'm glad you called last night."

A cautious smile came and went on her soft mouth. "Me, too."

At least she admitted that much. "I'd like to stay again to-night."

Her gaze flashed to his.

Screw it, he thought, and set aside his coffee to take her hand. "You're rightfully sad. Any caring person would be. When my mother died, I thought I'd die right along with her. When Meg died, Colt looked like someone had ripped his world away. You're allowed to feel, honey. It's expected and it doesn't make you weak."

She looked down at the table. "What we did…what I wanted you to do to make me feel better—"

"What?" Damn it, he didn't want her to feel bad about it. "You feel guilty?"

Biting her lip, she nodded. "And a little ashamed."

Well, fuck. That almost pissed him off, especially since the night had seemed very special to him. Guilt and shame had no place in it.

"We all cope in whatever way works best for us." It wasn't the same, but… "When my mom died, I drove like a maniac down an old road, pedal to the floor, sort of daring fate to take me."

Her hand gripped his. *"Jason."*

"But I'm still here—and thank God I didn't end up hurting anyone else. It was a stupid, thoughtless thing to do."

She watched him with worry.

"I didn't hurt anyone with my driving, but I also jumped in the sack with half a dozen different girls."

Her eyes widened.

Realizing what she thought, he shook his head. "One at a time, Honor."

"Oh."

"Night after night. It wasn't nice of me, because the girls liked me and I knew I wasn't interested." He hated to admit it, but for Honor, he did. "I used them. In comparison, you taking a little comfort from a person who cares for you doesn't seem like such a bad idea to me."

He waited, hoping she'd admit she cared...but she didn't.

As if fighting off emotion, Honor's face pinched, then she pushed back her chair—and surprised him by climbing into his lap.

Hell yeah. Loving the feel of her gentle weight, her implicit trust, Jason cradled her to his heart. "Please don't ever feel guilty or ashamed for being with me."

She nodded, swallowed loudly and squeezed him tighter.

That made up his mind for him. "I'm sleeping here again tonight. Thought you should know that."

She made a sound somewhere between a laugh and a choking sob.

He rocked her, kissed her ear, her shoulder and hugged her tighter.

A few minutes later, a tentative tap sounded on the front door. Honor's head snapped up so fast she almost head-butted him.

"Take it easy."

Big eyes stared at him. "Whoever it is will know you stayed the night!"

"So?" She wasn't a prude, so why did she care? "We're adults, honey. We can do whatever we want." He bit her shoulder and whispered, "I want to do you."

Around a nervous laugh, Honor pressed him back. "People will assume things if they know you stayed over."

"They'll assume we had sex."

She glanced toward the front door worriedly. "I don't mean that."

Ah. So she was again concerned about him getting pressured? "They'll also assume you're off the market, rightfully so."

Her gaze shot back to his again. At this rate she'd give herself whiplash. "We're exclusive?"

"Far as I'm concerned, we are." He gave her a quick kiss. "I hope like hell you're not planning to see anyone else."

"I'm not," she said fast.

Jason started to say the same, but she was already scrambling away, smoothing her hair—and looking guilty again.

Biting back his frustration, he followed her to the front door. When she opened it, they found Hogan and Colt both standing there, and they had the dog—which immediately yanked away from Colt and lurched in, dragging his leash behind him.

Half laughing, Honor got out of his way as Diesel made a beeline for her couch, jumped up on it, circled twice and dropped with a doggy huff. Resting his head on his paws, he looked at her with big chocolate eyes.

Blank-faced, Colt stared at the dog. "I'm sorry. I wasn't expecting him to do that."

"He's fast," Honor said.

"Nathan had him at the station for a while and he got used to hanging out on their old beat-up couch, and now he sleeps on my bed with me, so—" Colt wedged in, too, going after Diesel.

"He's fine," Honor rushed to say. "Looks like he made himself comfortable, that's all." She strode over to the dog and sat beside him.

To her obvious consternation, Diesel crawled up and over her lap, draping himself across her legs, licking her face and thumping his tail. Since the dog was nearly as big as her, it was a sight to see.

They all made to reach for the dog, but stopped when Honor laughed, hugged him and started scratching his ears.

Grinning, Colt said, "Guess he likes you."

"Guess so."

Yeah, Jason thought, a dog wasn't a bad idea at all. Though Diesel didn't seem aggressive enough to be much protection, he owed Nathan for thinking of it. Already Honor seemed more relaxed just by petting him.

She glanced up. "You guys are here to see Jason?"

Hogan smiled at her. "Actually I wanted to see if you'd join us this weekend for the mud volleyball tournament."

Her brows lifted. "Mud volleyball?"

Hogan scrunched onto the couch next to her, toward the butt end of the stretched-out dog. "We play on a field back by the creek. Jason roped me into it when I first came here. Told me it'd be fun."

Jason grinned. "You enjoyed yourself."

"I ended up covered in mud from head to toe." Hogan's expression held a wealth of significance. "But it did give me something else to focus on for a while."

"As I recall," Jason said, "he focused on complaining."

"Only because my son abandoned me and sided up with Jason and Violet."

"Violet?" Honor asked. "From the diner?"

Hogan nodded. "If you've met her, you know what a competitor she is."

Puzzled, Honor lifted her shoulders. "I didn't realize."

"She's really good," Colt said. "And yeah, she's mean about winning."

"The three of them dominated, so even though the others on their team weren't that great, they still skunked my group," Hogan admitted.

"We get together a lot during the warmer weather," Jason explained. "From spring to fall, there's one activity or another. You should join us, Honor. You'll like it."

"I suck at sports."

"Wear a bikini top like Violet," Colt suggested with an impish grin. "It'll distract everyone enough that no one will notice if you can actually play or not."

Jason put him in a headlock and knuckled his head. "You're too young to be distracted."

"Yeah, right." He snorted as he freed himself. "A woman in a bikini? I've been noticing that since I was ten."

They all laughed—and that's when Jason noticed the dog had gone still and alert. "Hey, boy." He walked over, let Diesel sniff his hand, then slowly pet him. "We were just playing."

Expression watchful, Diesel looked at him, at Colt, then up at Honor.

Full of compassion, she reassured the dog, "It's okay, I promise."

And with that, Diesel dropped his head and closed his eyes to doze.

Interesting. They'd have to remember that the dog was, in fact, attuned to trouble. Had he seen abuse? Maybe suffered it?

Jason hated that thought, but he knew everyone else wondered the same thing.

Hogan picked up the conversation again. "I know you've got your hands full right now, but I'm thinking by this weekend you need to get around friends."

"I don't have any friends here."

Pretending affront, Hogan asked, "What am I?"

"And me?" Colt added.

"Sullivan and Nathan will be there, too, and Violet." All in all, Jason thought it was a terrific idea. "We can ask Lexie to join us. What do you think?"

Tempting her, Hogan said, "I'll be cooking ribs, and I don't mind saying they'll be the best ribs you've ever tasted, guaranteed. My ribs alone are worth joining us, but the others will have corn on the cob and salad and too many desserts to count."

"We tie a rope from one of the trees along the bank and

swing out into the creek to wash off the mud," Colt told her. "It's fun, I promise."

With an expression close to wonder, she looked around the room at each of them. "I could come along and help cook."

"And play mud volleyball."

"And swing out to the creek."

Jason laughed at the way his family twisted her arm. "You may as well say yes, honey. They can be relentless."

Keeping her attention on the dog, Honor said, "Relentless in a very nice way."

After glancing at Jason, Hogan let her off the hook—for now. "Promise me you'll think about it. Because seriously, Honor, the ribs are worth it."

"I'll think about it, thank you."

Jason saw the discomfort Hogan and Colt felt. Because Honor acted so stiff, almost formal, they weren't sure if they were intruding. Sometimes he wasn't sure, either.

"I'll work on her later." Because one way or another, he'd be close by in case she needed him. Also determined to help her accept their friendship, he added, "Since you're both already here, why don't I pour more coffee? We can sit on the porch."

Honor looked surprised, but not displeased by the idea. "I don't have any seats yet."

"Stairs work," Colt told her, and headed out.

Hogan went with him.

Honor remained on the couch with Diesel. Sitting beside her, Jason used two fingers to bring her face around to his. "What arrangements have been made?"

She looked away. Voice steady and rehearsed, she went through the details, naming the funeral home and grave site, both outside the neighborhood but still fairly close.

"Celeste insisted that the wake should be a little longer because Granddad had so many friends and business acquaintances.

Neil agreed that Granddad would want that. So the wake starts Wednesday, and we'll…we'll bury him Friday."

It was asking a lot to want her to join in on the fun the very next day—but he'd ask anyway. "Do you think your grandfather would want you to be so sad?"

She shook her head hard. "No. It always bothered him."

Meaning she'd been sad a lot? Outside, they heard Colt laugh at something Hogan said.

Wistful, Honor looked toward the door.

"They mean well."

"It's pretty wonderful, actually. Having neighbors visit, just… chatting."

Was that part of what she'd imagined when buying her own home? So many things were unfamiliar to her because of her upbringing and unnatural relatives. What others took for granted seemed to be gifts to Honor, and damn it, he wanted to give her everything.

Putting a hand on the dog's back, he asked, "What do you have planned today?"

"I have to run into the salon for a few hours."

That surprised him. "Seriously? They didn't give you any time off?"

"They offered me all the time I needed. But I have two regular clients with very special events coming up. One an engagement party, and another an important business trip. No one else has done their hair for years, and I don't want to disappoint them."

Unbelievable.

Honor shrugged. "Besides, I like to stay busy." She wrinkled her nose. "But I don't need to be anywhere for a few more hours at least."

He stood, took Diesel's leash and patted his thigh to get the dog moving, then took Honor's hand and pulled her to her feet.

"Outside with you, then. Visit. Relax. I'll be out with the coffee in a minute."

She glanced at the door with longing before giving in with a smile. "There's a tray on top of the fridge." She hesitated, stared up at him, and surprised him by going on tiptoe to give him a quick, soft kiss. "Thank you, Jason. For everything."

He wondered if her gratitude covered the sex. With Honor, he just never knew.

As usual, Honor insisted on going it alone. At this point, Lexie knew she was being a pest by calling, and offering, and worrying—not that Honor would ever say so.

In so many ways, Honor was like a sister, except that she so often got stubborn and refused to let Lexie help.

Knowing that Jason had been able to get closer to Honor both pleased Lexie and...damn it, it made her a little envious.

She wanted Honor happy, and as she'd told her, a sexy hunk could brighten any girl's day. But she wanted to be there for Honor, too.

And instead it felt like she'd been replaced.

Dumb. She would not complicate Honor's life more with petty jealousy.

Instead she decided she needed her own sexy hunk to give her a different focus. Never mind that Sullivan hadn't called, and that the last time she'd seen him, he made it clear he wasn't interested in a repeat.

Tough titty for him, because she wasn't done. And regardless of what he claimed to want, the way he'd kissed her...well, she thought she might have a chance of swaying him.

A very good chance, in fact.

Refusing to warn him, she mustered up her courage and, after calling to find out the details, showed up at his MMA school. The same pleasant, older woman she'd spoken to on the phone greeted her at a big front desk separated from the gym by floor-to-ceiling glass. Just beyond, she could see Sullivan talking to two kids while others of all ages jogged around the perimeter of the gym floor.

"You said adults could join this class?"

The receptionist smiled at her. "Some days are specific to age groups, but not tonight. It just happens that the oldest is only fifteen. If you'd like to come back for the adults-only—"

"No, it's fine." If she left now, she'd let her cowardice get the better of her and she might never return. "I like kids." At least if she totally blew it, she wouldn't have any adults witnessing her embarrassment.

"They're warming up right now. If you want to give me your information and make your first payment, I can introduce you to Mr. Dean and you can join them."

Heart beating too fast, Lexie had a difficult time pulling her attention off Sullivan. He stood barefoot, dressed in loose white pants with a white tunic tied at the waist. So gorgeous.

At least she'd dressed correctly, given what the kids wore— meaning T-shirts and shorts. Granted, hers were a little more stylish, and fit her body to perfection, but the idea was the same: comfort.

Sighing, she said, "Yes, of course." In for a penny…

Before she could change her mind, she signed up for a month, paid and put away her contract.

"Let me introduce you," the receptionist offered. But when her phone rang, Lexie shook her head.

"It's all right. I can handle it."

"If you're sure…?"

"Yup. Go ahead and take your call. I'll be fine." She hoped.

Grateful, the receptionist turned away and answered the phone with a cheery but professional greeting.

Well. Like it or not, Sullivan now owed her a month of nightly lessons. He wasn't cheap, but Lexie felt sure he'd be worth it.

She'd taken no more than two steps out to the gym floor before he noticed her. From across the room, his incendiary blue gaze locked on her. He ran through a gamut of expressions, starting with surprise, skipping over awareness and ending with narrow-eyed disbelief.

Without releasing her from his attention, he said something to the kids and started her way.

Uh-oh. He looked pissed.

Cocking up her chin, Lexie started toward him. She'd rather be proactive than stand there waiting for his censure.

"Hey, Sullivan." She gave a careless wave. "Hope you're ready to teach me some moves, because I wore my dazzle shoes."

He stopped in front of her, stared at her for a heart-stopping ten seconds, then slowly tracked down to her feet.

Resisting the urge to gulp, Lexie lifted the toe of one shoe. "Pretty, right?" She struck a pose. The sneakers were sparkly pink and added pizzazz to her outfit.

"No shoes on the mat."

That's what he said? Only that? She frowned at him, and forced a smile. "No problem." She pulled off the shoes, one at a time. "I have on my dazzle toenail polish, too. So I'm still good to go." She wiggled her toes to show him.

A huge breath expanded his chest, but he didn't implode. Instead he let it back out slowly.

Deliberately pushing his buttons, she asked, "You okay? Your ears are red."

A fight broke out behind him and in a split second, Sullivan was gone.

Cocking her head, Lexie watched how he handled the dispute between two boys who looked to be around twelve. He spoke calmly but with authority, and while he kept a hand on one of the boy's shoulders, the other did sit-ups. When he finished, they switched places.

LORI FOSTER

A girl heckled them, urging them on—and she quickly found herself doing sit-ups, as well.

Huh. Lexie liked that. No sexism involved.

She gave Sullivan room to do his thing, which included giving the first boy more sit-ups after he forgot to say "sir" when addressing him.

The kid didn't seem to mind, and in fact, it looked to Lexie as if he was out to impress the girl.

It'd be nice if just once Sullivan would try to impress her. Instead he kissed her, rejected her and now looked infuriated that she'd shown up.

Party pooper.

"Everyone who's warmed up, come sit up front." Sullivan looked at Lexie. "If you haven't warmed up, do at least twenty laps."

Ha. He thought to intimidate her? Not likely. She called out, "Yes, sir," in a crisp reply. Never let it be said she couldn't catch on. Keeping her pace even, she started to jog.

And every, oh, two seconds or so, she checked out Sullivan.

He'd divided the group of fourteen kids into three groups and, after demonstrating, had them doing different activities.

As she passed Sullivan this time, he said, "Five more."

She paused. "I only have two more."

"Make it seven."

Already a light sheen of sweat covered her chest, cheeks and forehead. But Lexie grinned at him and whispered, "Yes, sir," this time in a decidedly sexual way that made his nostrils flare.

If nothing else, she'd get in better shape.

Not that she minded running. With the way she liked to eat, it was either exercise or buy a new wardrobe.

When she finished, a little more winded and a lot more sweaty, she stepped up to the group he currently had kicking a heavy bag.

"Good, good," he said to the girl who'd gotten into trouble

earlier. "But remember, with the side kick, you keep your toes flexed, your heel protruding. Like this."

He kicked the bag to demonstrate, then brought the girl up again.

"You want to keep your heel higher than your toes. Do it with me." Together they went through the motions. "Rotate your hip, pivot on your support foot. Yeah, like that. Don't forget to keep your knee raised while recoiling." He patted her on the shoulder and instructed each kid to do five kicks.

Then he joined Lexie.

Without meeting her gaze, he took her arm and directed her to the first group. "You can start here. We're working on flexibility and agility. Follow along with the others. We'll rotate in fifteen minutes."

Lexie watched him go with a frown. Sure, she wanted more attention, but it still fascinated her to see him so calmly and patiently instructing the kids. She'd be here for a month; it wasn't like he could ignore her every minute. So she'd bide her time, make the most of the instruction and learn a little more about him in the process.

She turned to the boy next to her and whispered, "Are we allowed to talk?"

He grinned at her, showing a missing tooth. "Yes, ma'am. But we have to be respectful."

"Got it, thank you, sir." She tacked on the sir, since he'd called her ma'am, and earned another wide grin. "Are you allowed to tell me what's happening here?"

Puffing up with pride, he said, "Sure."

While she listened to the boy, she felt Sullivan checking her out. But she could play the same game and just ignored him, concentrating instead on what the kid told her so she'd get it right.

When it was her turn and she went to practice a ridiculous

kick into the air, she threw herself off balance, swung around and landed face-first on the mat.

The others in her group, all of them kids, cracked up.

So did Lexie.

Flopping over to her back, she said to them, "I hope you'll all be patient with me. And hey, I'm open to any pointers."

A giggling redheaded girl leaned over her. Lexie noticed she had a black eye. "You didn't snap it off."

Hiding her concern, Lexie sat up. "Oh, I snapped something." That set the girl into another round of giggles.

A big hand appeared in front of her. Sullivan. She looked up at him, all the way up his long, strong body, then delicately put her hand in his.

"Clair's right. You just kept going with the momentum. You need more control of the movement."

Oh, the fun ways she could twist those words. But with a whole bunch of kids watching on, she played nice. "Maybe Clair can show me the right way?"

Sullivan studied her, then gave one short nod. "Clair? Would you want to step to the side with Lexie and demonstrate the drill for her?"

"Yes, sir!"

The boy protested, "But, sir, I was showin' her."

"Since I'm new here," Lexie said fast, hoping to avoid another conflict, "maybe each of you could show me something. That is, if Mr. Dean doesn't mind?"

As if she'd pleased him—and he was surprised by it—Sullivan gave her another long look rife with curiosity and appreciation.

If the kids were as starved for positive attention as it seemed, she'd be more than happy to dole it out.

She sent him a cheeky smile. "What do you say…sir?"

His mouth twitched before he firmed it again. "I'm sure some of the students would enjoy that. Use that far corner of the rear mat. Spend no more than three minutes with each student who wants to show you a move, and then rejoin me."

"Yes, sir."

His eyes narrowed, but he only turned and walked away.

Lexie knew she was making headway. But toward what?

Every damn time he turned around, Lexie found a way to draw his attention.

She'd caught on far too quickly about his rules and not once had she given him a reason to reprimand her, much less deny her attendance.

She interacted with the kids in a terrific way, asking them to show her moves, bragging on them, showing them respect—all in all building up their self-esteem while not being the least put off by their mannerisms and attitudes.

Many of their own parents didn't show them that much consideration. The parents who were involved and doing their best were often at a loss as to how to deal with behavioral issues.

Not Lexie.

She wasn't trained in any way, but she never seemed rattled or discouraged when things went off course. Even when he had to intercede because of erupting verbal—and once physical—disagreements, she stayed cool.

No way did she miss Clair's black eye, but she'd commented only on her beautiful red hair. She'd ignored Jimmy's tattered, dirty clothes and instead raved on his great teaching ability after he showed her some positions.

In one way or another, she impacted each of the kids before the training session ended.

She seemed particularly alert as parents showed up to get their kids, scrutinizing each one and probably having the same concerns, about the same parents, that he had. After the class had emptied, they realized Lenny was still there.

Again, he'd been forgotten.

Sullivan remembered that feeling only too well from his own youth when he'd often been forgotten—although sometimes, being remembered was worse. He'd had no one back then and he'd lashed out by getting into trouble. He'd almost ruined his life, almost pushed things too far...until he'd tried crossing an MMA trainer.

In his gruff, no-nonsense way, that man had drawn him in, given him a focus, and without really trying he'd become a catch-all role model.

Sullivan badly wanted to do the same for these kids, but Lenny was a particular challenge, a tough nut to crack and a real heartbreaker.

He would have gone to Lenny now except that Lexie was already there, patience personified, chatting up the kid and giving Sullivan a chance to track down the dad. Finally, after nearly half an hour, he got an answer. Lenny's father was short-tempered and said he'd be by within the hour. Worse, he wanted the kid to wait on the curb out front.

Bastard.

Sullivan had two choices. Accept the man's edicts or not let the boy return. So really he had no choice at all.

All the kids in this particular class, as part of his outreach program, attended for token payments nowhere near what he usually charged. He wanted to make a difference in their lives, give them the same choices, the hope, that had been given to him...but he couldn't do that turning them away.

The boy attended because the mother wanted help with his angry outbursts, no doubt inspired by the dad. Unfortunately she worked all the hours and had to rely on her husband to help with getting Lenny to and from the MMA school.

As soon as Sullivan hung up, the sullen boy showed up at his side, a chip on his shoulder the size of a mountain.

"Guess he's late again?" he said with a sneer. "I'll wait out front. Later."

"Later, sir."

The kid pulled up short, glared at him, then grudgingly nodded. "Later, sir."

Structure, Sullivan knew, greatly helped kids to gain control. Consistency was also a contributor. Many of them yearned for boundaries, and that's what he gave—as well as an outlet for anger, and instructions on how to channel that inner turmoil.

There were times, like now, when it felt futile.

"Hey, Lenny, hold up." Hurrying to put on her shoes, Lexie said, "I'm ready to go, too. Mind if I wait with you?"

Lenny glared at her. "You don't have to worry about me. I'm not a baby."

She pretended affront. "I saw the way you followed Mr. Dean's instructions. You know to avoid trouble. But I'm new and I thought you could tell me what I've missed so far. I didn't mind being the entertainment today, but I'd like to catch up."

She was so convincing Sullivan almost believed her. "Would you mind, Lenny? I have a few things I have to do here, otherwise I'd instruct her myself."

He waited for some sexually charged gibe from Lexie, but it never came. She kept her attention on the boy, earning his appreciation yet again.

Suspicious gaze going back and forth between them, Lenny finally shrugged. "Sure. I guess I can tell her a few things."

"Great, thanks." With her shoelaces still untied, Lexie fell into step next to him. "Good night, sir. See you tomorrow."

On Lexie, the respect sounded more like subservience, tweaking his brain into thinking of sexual things where he instructed and she obeyed.

Not good.

"Good night, Lexie." He locked the door behind her and Lenny.

His receptionist had already left for the day, so Sullivan made quick work of returning equipment and mopping the mats. He put some paperwork in a folder to take home with him. Rather than shower at the gym as was his norm, he couldn't resist heading out to see if Lenny was still around.

The boy was just getting in his dad's car when Sullivan stepped outside. Lexie was at the passenger window saying something to the father—and getting eyeballed in return.

Sullivan had to admit she presented a sexy picture in the snug clothes, all warmed up and dewy.

But it was beyond rude for Lenny's dad to openly admire her. Bastard, Sullivan thought again, knowing it wouldn't be the last time that particular father strained his tolerance.

After waving to Lenny, Lexie stepped back, and the car drove away. She stood there staring after them, unaware of Sullivan, her expression pensive.

She was worried, the same as him, and damn it, that wasn't something he'd expected from her.

Remaining near the door, he folded his arms. "Hey."

Very slowly she turned to face him. Her short blond hair had lost its style and was now curlier from her sweat. Her T-shirt stuck to her in select, tantalizing places. Without kids around to gauge his every thought, he appreciated the sight of her legs in the close-fitting workout shorts.

And her shoes were still untied…because she'd hurried to go with Lenny.

From the start he'd pegged her as a party girl, focused on her own entertainment. Sure, she cared for Honor. But that was a world away from concerning herself over needy, unruly kids. Sullivan wasn't at all sure what he thought of her now, but his initial impressions were definitely off the mark.

"Are you staring at me for a reason?"

For many reasons, but he wouldn't go into them all now. "Thanks for waiting with him."

"No problem." Her golden eyes smoldered. "Mostly I was waiting for you."

12

SULLIVAN LOOKED GUARDED as she approached, probably with good reason.

Since they were both sweaty, maybe she could talk him into a joint shower. She tugged her shirt away from her breasts, letting in some air. "That was quite a workout."

Of course his gaze went to her boobs. "I'm surprised you hung in there so well."

"Well, sir," she teased, getting close enough to walk her fingers up his chest. "I didn't want to get in trouble."

He caught her wrist. "What are you doing here, Lexie?"

"Honestly?" She glanced around, but they were relatively alone on the quiet sidewalk. It was only eight-thirty or so, and a muggy heat hung in the early-evening air. "How much time do you have?"

"Not much."

So he wouldn't give an inch? Fine. "No sugarcoating it, then." She could give it to him blunt, no problem. "Honor is having a hard time of it. I badly want to help her out, but she's always been a very closed off person. Very much a loner. It's sort of…" She didn't want to be dramatic, but he had asked. Wincing, she admitted, "…killing me a little."

He still held her wrist, and now his thumb started a slow stroke over her pulse. "I thought the two of you were close."

"We are. But it took me a long time to get her there. It's not my history to share, so I'll only say that Honor had a few very tough breaks early in life." Much like the kids Sullivan worked with. "Because of it, she's afraid to lean on anyone. You've met her, so you have to know how resistant she is to help of any kind. I'd gotten her to loosen up some, but now she's reverted."

"Reverted how?"

"Her grandpa dying really hit her hard. It probably brought up a lot of feelings that, much as she tried, weren't buried all that deep. I want to help, but she's back to insisting she can do it all on her own." After a deep breath, she bared her soul. "Honor doesn't understand that I need her, too." God, that sounded pathetic.

Those bright blue eyes of his mellowed with sympathy. "Maybe she just needs a little time."

"That's what I'm hoping." She planted on a false smile. "But to make the waiting easier, I came here to use your gorgeous body as a distraction. I'm hoping you'll play along, because I'm seriously glum and need a pick-me-up."

"Sex?"

"You know a better pick-me-up than that?"

He hesitated. "You're here now. You've seen what I'm doing."

"Helping kids. Yeah, so?" She found it admirable, and actually pretty sexy, too. What could be hotter than a big, capable, trained guy who took time to help at-risk kids? Sullivan was the whole package, and she wanted to unwrap it...preferably in bed.

"I'm serious about this," he stressed. "The work I do can be time-consuming. It often overlaps my social life. It's not something I leave behind when I walk away from the gym."

"I think it's terrific." She wouldn't mind helping out now and then.

Skepticism kept him at a distance. "Anyone who gets involved would have to take it just as seriously as I do."

The way he watched her...finally, comprehension dawned.

"Ah." A slow simmering anger made her heart beat harder, and her chest feel tighter.

What was she? An ogre? He thought he had a patent on compassion? "I get it now. I mean, anyone with a heart and a brain could see that those kids need a little help and understanding. The one girl even had a black eye."

"She got that fighting on the playground."

If he thought to reassure her, he could stuff it. "She liked me. I think they all did. But I get your concern. I mean, I'm such a bad influence you wouldn't want them around the likes of me." The fact that she *had* teased him a little, calling him *"sir"* in a way meant to put thoughts in his head, left her feeling defensive. She didn't think the kids had noticed—but clearly Sullivan had and he disapproved.

Did he expect more of the same? Inappropriate teasing? Did he wonder how far she'd take it?

Even before he denied it, Lexie saw the truth in his eyes.

God, it crushed her. Sure, she gave off a carefree air, but she wasn't a person who would do anything—by word or action— to hurt a kid. Ever.

When she went to pull away, Sullivan held on. "Don't put words in my mouth."

"You didn't say it exactly, but you came pretty damn close, and since I'm not slow, I don't need it spelled out. You don't want me around them." Jerking away from his restraining hold, she pivoted to storm off.

Unfortunately she stepped on a shoelace and would have hit the pavement if Sullivan hadn't caught her arms, keeping her upright.

"I'm fine." Again she shrugged him away and bent to straighten her stupid shoe, tugging so hard on the laces she all but strangled her foot as she readied herself to go.

"Lexie…"

The lace knotted, frustrating her until she wanted to shout.

"Leave me alone." She'd known plenty of people, some who liked her, some who didn't. But never had anyone accused her of being unworthy.

Shoving back to her feet, she hiked her purse strap over her arm and concentrated on not looking as hurt as she felt. "Don't worry about me hanging around. Consider my monthlong contract a contribution to the cause."

She turned to go, but again he caught her arm. "Will you wait a minute?"

"You have more to say?" She kept her back to him. "Because honest to God, Sullivan, I know I'm a tough girl and all that, but I'm not impervious to insult. I already feel bad enough as it is."

"So honest," he said softly.

"What? You expected me to be a liar as well as a corrupter of innocents?"

He gave a low, muttered curse that she barely heard. A few seconds passed before he spoke. "Doesn't seem to matter what I expect, because you always surprise me."

Teasing? He *dared* to tease her? She whipped around to face him, prodding his rock-hard pec with a pointed finger. "You wanted me to sugarcoat things to make you feel better?" Another poke. "Forget it! You're being a dick and it hurts." Again trying to leave, she snapped, "Mission accomplished."

"Hold up." He stepped around in front of her, blocking her way. "Please."

Throwing up her hands, Lexie snarled, *"What?"*

He scrubbed a hand over his face, then released a tense breath. With a shrug, he said, "I don't want you to go like this."

That made her laugh, but there wasn't any humor in the sound. "You want me to leave happy? Fine." She managed a very mean smile. "I'm *happy.*"

"No, you're not." Oh so gently, he tucked back one wayward curl near her temple. "And truthfully neither am I."

For the longest time they stared at each other while a simmering heat expanded between them, sparked, caught flame. While searching her eyes, he murmured, low, "You were terrific with the kids today."

Lexie gave him a narrow-eyed look, confused by those words in the middle of the sexual tension. "Thank you?"

His mouth twitched at her uncertainty. "My concern was never how you'd influence them. Understand that, okay?"

Her chest tightened. "Then what?"

For the briefest moment, he looked away, but Sullivan wasn't a coward and immediately his gaze came back to lock with hers. "I used to be one of those kids. I know how they feel. I know the chaos of their thoughts, their emotional conflicts."

Imagining a badass like Sullivan as a needy kid made her knees tremble and softened a bit of her attitude. "I'm sorry."

He disregarded that. "The adults in their lives are either too busy, too burdened or too abusive to be as positively involved as they should be. That's why I'm here. I want them to know that they can count on me. Always."

"They need that," she agreed. Honor had been the same. It had taken a very long time for Lexie to convince her that she wouldn't turn her back on her. Time—and evidence. Only then had Honor begun to trust her. "It's admirable, but I still don't see why I'm a problem."

"You're a problem," he whispered, "because you confuse the hell out of me. How I react to you is different. I thought if you were just a self-absorbed party girl, we could play, then go our separate ways."

Lexie bit her lip, wounded all over again—even though she'd deliberately given that impression, and even that covered what she, too, had initially wanted. Stubborn to the core, she said, "I am a party girl."

"In some ways, sure." He drew in a slow breath. "You're also more than that."

Thank you for noticing. She didn't interrupt by voicing the sarcasm, but it did make her heart beat faster.

"You need to understand the time and energy I put into the classes and how determined I am to make the school work." Emphasizing that, Sullivan said, "Those kids are my priority."

Of course they were. Did he really think she'd missed that? "And now we're back to me being a jerk!"

"*Not* what I'm saying, Lexie." His gaze moved from her eyes to her mouth...and damn it, her entire body tingled. "I'm saying I don't always have a lot of free time, and I can't get serious with anyone."

"Gee, Sullivan," she quipped, letting the sarcasm out after all. "I think I can survive without your attention 24/7."

"Good." Cautiously he eased closer. "Because I'd like to spend my free time with you—and I'm free now."

"No," Lexie said. But her feet didn't move. "We need to talk about this."

He curved his hands over her shoulders and slowly drew her in. "Why? We both want the same things, right? That's why you're here."

"I said no." What did he want? At the moment she was more confused than ever.

His thumbs brushed the sides of her neck. "Will you consider saying yes?"

"No." But they both knew she already was.

He drifted his nose over her temple, and his warm breath teased her. "Sex between us was good," he whispered. "So fucking good."

Good? She'd have called it stupendous.

"If that's all either of us expects..."

She hoped for so much more, but God, she had no willpower.

Every breath filled her head with his rich scent and apparently, insulted or not, she wanted him. Didn't mean she'd give in easily. "So we'll get together whenever it's convenient for both of us, but neither of us will have any expectations beyond that?"

He paused, his brows together in consternation. "We could take it one day at a time."

Why she pushed him, Lexie couldn't say. But she still smarted from his impressions of her, and that prompted her to lift a brow. "You want to screw me tonight?"

Accustomed to dealing with bristly attitudes, Sullivan gave her a slight but heated smile. "How about I kiss you a lot, and you kiss me back? Then I touch you in all those places I've already learned you like?"

Quickly getting into it, Lexie asked, "And I touch you, too?"

"Yeah." He feathered kisses over the side of her neck, the rim of her ear, saying softly, "When you're good and wet, breathing deeper and wanting me bad, then we'll both come together."

Oh, wow. "Your version sounds better than screwing."

He tipped up her face. "Only because I was an ass and insulted you, so your version sounded very cold and detached. But neither of us would enjoy that."

"Oh, I don't know. I've enjoyed it before."

He put his forehead to hers and, full of confidence, whispered, "Not with me."

"No." He had her there, which was probably why she was currently chasing him down for a repeat—and more. "Not with you."

"Tell me you understand my dedication to the gym."

Giving in a little, she nodded. "I do, and I'll skip coming around, since it worries you."

"The kids enjoyed you, and they already know you signed up. If you don't show now, they'll wonder about it."

If they were anything like what Honor had been as a kid, they'd take it personally, like another rejection. Lexie couldn't bear the thought of adding to their hurt. Hopeful, she asked, "So it's okay if I keep attending?"

Appearing pleased that she wanted to, Sullivan smiled. "Better than okay. As long as we understand each other, it won't be a problem for me."

Well, bully for him, because for her it'd be all kinds of problems. Being an honest person, she knew she was already invested beyond the physical, but she'd take that to her grave before she'd humiliate herself. Giving a careless shrug, she said, "Sure. Then count me in."

"I'm glad that's settled." He tilted back to stare into her eyes, his gaze searching. "Now, about tonight...?"

"We're doing this?"

He answered by asking, "My place or yours?"

"Wow, I get a choice this time? Terrific." Lexie decided it might be a good time to advance her own private agenda by getting more familiar with his life. "I vote your place, since it's closer."

With no hesitation at all, he agreed. "My shower is big enough for two." Indicating she should precede him, he walked with her to the parking lot, and even opened her car door for her. "I'll follow you there."

Lexie's brain was still zeroed in on the idea of showering with him, so she only nodded.

Okay, so they had great sexual chemistry. She could work with that. And if he never decided to make room for her in his life...well, she'd just have to figure that out later. After all, he'd insisted they take it one day at a time.

And since he no longer objected to her being at his gym, she'd have a full month to work on him.

Over the next few days, it became routine for Jason to stay the night, and for Colt and Hogan to join them on the porch for coffee.

Honor loved it. It was such a friendly way to start her day, and honestly she felt less frazzled after the casual visit. Jason stayed so attentive to her it sometimes made her blush. And Diesel was so sweet she missed the dog when he wasn't around. He had a very calming effect on her.

What surprised her most though was the accumulation of porch furniture that accompanied the visits.

Hogan and Colt brought over two incredibly beautiful wooden rockers to sit on, but when they left they insisted they were a housewarming gift and absolutely refused to take them back.

The morning after that, Nathan came to visit, too, and he brought his own lawn chair—then left it behind. He claimed it was his "visiting" chair.

The day before the funeral, Lexie dropped by, and darned if she didn't have a big shopping bag with her.

Usually gifts made her uneasy, but she must have been getting used to it because this time it almost made Honor laugh. "Not you, too?"

"I've missed you," Lexie said, setting aside the bag and grabbing Honor for a very tight hug. Honor was aware of Hogan and Jason watching, indulgent smiles on their faces. This time Sullivan was there, too, sipping coffee and watching Lexie in a most intimate way.

Not that long ago, Honor would have felt like a spectacle under so much attention, but now…darn it, it just felt nice.

Lexie wasn't a morning person, especially when she didn't need to be at work for a few more hours. After a return squeeze, Honor held her back. "You're up and about early."

"I was in the neighborhood," she said with an exaggerated wink, which sent all curious gazes to Sullivan.

He looked to the skies as if praying for patience.

Practically advertising the fact that she'd been with Sullivan, Lexie said, "I saw the chairs on the porch and decided this would make a nice gift."

Honor accepted the bag but didn't open it. "You already gave me a housewarming present."

Lexie shrugged. "This one's from Sullivan."

Smiling at her, Sullivan said, "Lexie knows your taste better than me, so she helped with the selection."

"But…" She honestly had no idea what to say.

Jason squeezed her shoulder. "Don't keep us in suspense."

She peeked into the giant gift bag—and found seat cushions and throw pillows for all the chairs. The bright, sunny pattern was absolute perfection.

Slowly she sank to sit on a step. "They're beautiful."

Jason pulled one from the bag. "Nice."

Colt took it from his uncle and put it on a chair. "They look good."

Hogan sat down before Colt could, then proclaimed the cushions "Comfortable."

Covering her mouth with a hand, Honor laughed, sniffled and fought off emotional tears.

The mixed signals confused Diesel and he rushed to her, licking her face, snuffling against her neck until the only emotion she could feel was gratitude.

Little by little, the company waned.

Sullivan had an early class, so he hugged Honor, then kissed Lexie before going.

Oh boy. Honor couldn't wait to find out what was happening there. She realized that she'd been very self-absorbed the last few days and had clearly missed a few things.

After that, Hogan said he had an interview and needed to leave.

"Interview for what?" Lexie asked.

"A local accounting firm."

Arching a brow, Lexie said, "Seriously? Because even though you try, you're totally missing the corporate vibe."

"I was a damn successful accountant for years."

"I'm sure you'd be successful at whatever you do."

That stymied Hogan—until she added, "But were you happy? Rhetorical question, because I'm certain you weren't."

"You don't know what you're talking about."

Honor heard the edge in Hogan's tone and hoped Lexie would moderate her nosiness.

Instead her friend gave Hogan's biceps a firm squeeze. "I know you're built more like a bouncer. Or..." She considered him head to toe, making Hogan's eyes narrow. "I could see you doing something outdoorsy. Like landscaper maybe. What do you think?"

"I think you like being irritating."

Lexie sighed. "Fine. Resign yourself to a miserable fate. It's not my life." Without giving Hogan a chance for rebuttal, she hugged Honor again. "I have to get going, too. I'll see you tomorrow."

"I have the...the funeral tomorrow."

"I know." Lexie gave her a level, no-nonsense stare. "And I'll be there." When Honor started to speak, Lexie said, "No argument. It's what sisters do, and no matter what you say, I *am* your sister—in all the ways that count." She lifted a hand in careless farewell to the others and took off.

Honor stood there, bombarded by a dozen different emotional reactions. She wouldn't be facing the funeral alone. But it was so unfair to do that to Lexie. And what would the relatives think? For sure they'd butt heads with Lexie and—

"I'll be there for the visitation," Hogan said.

Her mouth fell open. "But—"

"And me," Colt added.

Eyes wide, Honor looked at each of them in turn. "You guys never knew my grandfather."

"They know *you*," Jason explained.

And they thought she was so weak they had to show up to a stranger's funeral to offer moral support?

In a move very similar to his brother's, Hogan cupped the side of her neck. "I have to roll or I'll be late. Thanks for the coffee, and the company." He kissed her forehead, leaving her flustered.

Colt looked at Jason, then Honor. "I'm taking Diesel for a walk." And he, too, kissed her, but on the cheek.

Totally flummoxed, Honor watched them go.

Then Jason's strong arms came around her from behind, his hands lacing over her stomach. "You probably already know that I'll be there, as well."

Her shoulders slumped.

She absolutely couldn't do that to him. "You met Gina, Janet and Terry. You know how they'll be. Even Celeste is tough to take on a good day. During a funeral, she'll be more autocratic than usual."

Rocking her a little, he said, "We'll ignore them."

If only it was ever that easy. "They'll think—"

Jason turned her so quickly it surprised her. Emphatic, he said, "Who cares what they think? I don't, and I wish you wouldn't, either."

That dangerous emotion of hope battled with uncertainty. Could it really be that easy?

"Think about it this way," he told her, ready to tip the scales. "If I'm there but *not* with you, then what will they think?"

Honor honestly didn't know, but she assumed it wouldn't be good.

They were still staring at each other when a car pulled into Jason's driveway, making him curse, low.

"Customer?" she asked.

"Yeah. He wants me to build a playhouse for his kids that coordinates with the design of their home."

"Like your garage and your house?"

"Same principle but much smaller scale." Somber, he reiterated, "I'm going with you tomorrow."

Having never been in a relationship like this one, Honor just wasn't sure what was the norm. She had a difficult enough time figuring out stuff with Lexie.

Feeling very tentative about it, she nodded. "Okay, thank you."

It was absurd that Jason looked so satisfied with her concession. The man would be attending a funeral.

With her relatives.

There was no way he actually wanted to do it. Heck, *she* didn't even want to do it.

"What do you have planned today?"

Honor had thought about it earlier, and decided staying busy was the way to go. "I'm going to get started scraping the paint off the house. It looked bad enough already, but now that I have those beautiful seats and cushions, I'm doubly motivated." She flattened her hands on his chest. "And no, I don't need your help. You have a customer waiting, so you need to go."

He glanced over to where the man stood outside his car, staring toward them. "Right." He tipped up her face. "I'll be back over later. And tonight we're grilling out, so you should join us." He started back-stepping toward his own property. "You're going to like dinner with friends as much as you like morning coffee visits."

For her, it was enough that he stayed over each night with her; she didn't need anything more. Lately, though, it felt like she fought him on everything—there was no reason to debate this, too. "Okay, thanks."

Surprise flashed over his face, then he grinned. "I call that progress, honey. We'll get there—one step at a time."

Progress toward what? Honor had no idea, and since he was already greeting the man who'd come to see him, she didn't ask. As she gathered up the coffee cups and started inside, her mind jumped ahead to the task at hand.

Anything was better than thinking about tomorrow, but she had to admit, having her own contingent of friends was going to make it much less desolate.

LORI FOSTER

★ ★ ★

It wasn't an easy thing for Jason, watching Honor work all day and not being invited to pitch in. He liked working with his hands, always had. Convincing her of that proved impossible, so he knew offering would be futile—or worse. She tended to take his offers as an insult, as if he thought she couldn't manage on her own.

He respected her tenacity too much to ever give that impression.

Shooting for subtlety, he did catch her before she really got started so he could show her the right way to wash the house first, using his pressure washer.

She listened intently, then got to it.

That was another nice thing about Honor—her willingness to learn.

In between his own jobs for the day, he moseyed over to check on her headway, and was pleased to see she'd let Colt lend a little elbow grease to the chore. His nephew was tall enough that he could hit a lot of spots without the ladder Honor used, and strong enough that he cleared away peeling paint twice as fast as she could.

By the time Jason finished up an ornate bookshelf, Honor and Colt were around back, working on the last section of the house.

He was headed their way when he heard Honor ask about Colt's girlfriend.

"She cut me loose."

Jason froze.

So did Honor—but not for long. "Is she *nuts?*"

Colt shrugged. "Guess she thought I was, for thinking she'd wait for me."

After chewing her bottom lip, Honor said, "I suppose it is difficult, keeping up a long-distance relationship."

"I guess." Colt pulled off his baseball cap, scratched the top of his head, then stuck the cap on again. "Definitely sucks."

"You really cared for her?"

"A lot," he said with emphasis. "At first I kept thinking Dad would get it together and we'd move back home. When he couldn't find work here, I thought for sure he'd pack it up. That's not happening, though, so I guess she's right. It doesn't make much sense to try to keep things going when we're in two different cities."

"I'm so sorry."

Colt blew out a breath. "I shouldn't be bothering you with this."

"You're not! I want you to feel free to talk with me anytime, about anything."

He slanted her a look. "The way you *don't* talk to anyone else?"

Wow. Score one for Colt. His maturity level amazed Jason.

"That's different."

"Nope," Colt said. "It isn't. But you're private. I get that. I'm just saying, if you ever do need to talk, you should understand that you have friends here now."

Honor set aside her scraper. "I'm catching on to that, I think." She tipped her head. "But what about you? You don't have friends here yet?"

"Since I didn't want to stay, I hadn't really been looking for any."

"You still dislike it here so much?"

Colt thought about that, then shook his head. "Not really, no. The people are nice. Uncle Jason's pretty awesome."

Jason smiled around his concern.

"But you miss your friends?" Honor asked.

"Sure." He sent her another long look. "Most of us like friends."

The dig was lost on Honor. Moving closer, she stared up at him. "I want you to think of me as a… I dunno. A doting aunt or something, okay?"

Jason wondered what she knew about doting aunts, given that hers were selfish nightmares.

Colt choked back a laugh. "Okay, sure."

"Great." She inhaled, then said, "You're a very gorgeous young man."

Even from where he stood, Jason could see Colt's ears go red.

Still singing his praises, Honor added, "You're also tall and athletic and as long as you're not still hung up on this other girl, you could easily get a new girlfriend."

"Thanks, but I'm not really interested in that just yet."

"So maybe date for a while without getting serious. Whatever you want. I'm just saying, it wouldn't be a problem for you."

Colt laughed. "Thanks, Aunt Honor."

She grinned with him. "You're not shy."

Like a devil, Colt said, "No, ma'am."

"And you're so smart but funny, too, and really sweet and—"

He laughed at her. "Clearly aunts are biased."

Hands on her slim hips, Honor said, "Stop helping me with junk like this and instead spend your free time checking out the neighborhood girls your own age."

"Maybe." He stepped back to survey his work. "But I like helping you, too, so don't try to get rid of me."

"Deal."

Deciding it was past time to announce himself, Jason strode toward them, saying, "Looks like you guys are just about done."

Colt and Honor both jumped.

Pretending he hadn't snooped, he checked out the job on the house. "Looks good. Do you have the paint picked out yet?"

"The colors," she said. "But I haven't bought it. I wasn't even sure how many cans I'd need, or if one brand is better than another." She shaded her eyes with a hand and looked up at him. "I was hoping you could help with that."

Such a simple thing, a request for advice. But Honor rarely made those moves and damn, it affected him. Looking only at her, he said, "Sure, be glad to. Why don't we go inside and talk about it?"

Snickering, Colt said, "Yeah, you two go on. I'll put away the ladder and tools."

"Colt Guthrie, we just talked about this."

Hoisting the ladder over one shoulder, Colt said, "Already got it half-done, Aunt Honor."

She frowned, but a grin snuck in on her anyway. "That boy is incorrigible."

"And smart and funny and *gorgeous*," Colt reminded her with smug humor.

She laughed—and that, too, primed Jason's need.

"Come along, Honor." Looping an arm around her shoulders, he propelled her forward around the side of the house. "You need a shower."

"I thought we were going to talk about paint."

"Sure." He got her up the porch steps. "We'll talk in the shower."

Honor almost tripped. "We?"

"I'm sweaty, too." He opened her front door and drew her in.

She finally caught on and even though they were alone in the house, she dropped her voice to a whisper. "We're going to have sex?"

"Yes." He got her into the bathroom and pushed back her shower curtain. It amused him that every inch of space was taken up by bottles of shampoo, conditioner, lotion, face wash, body oil and more things he couldn't identify. So much clutter in his own shower would have made him nuts, but Honor moved around it as if it didn't bother her at all. He turned on the water. "That's the plan."

"But…"

"But what?" Jason pulled her T-shirt off over her head. "You don't want me?"

"I pretty much always want you."

He paused. "Such a nice admission."

"It's true." Still looking scandalized, she whispered, "But Colt might still be outside."

"He's not a dummy. He's gathered up the rest of stuff and left by now."

Her eyes went comically wide. "Oh my god." Color crawled into her face. "You think he knew?"

Jason didn't have a doubt, but he only shrugged—and unhooked her front-closure bra. It still amazed him that a woman so honestly sexual could be so shy about it.

He stripped the bra away.

Hands to her cheeks, Honor looked around as if expecting someone to see her.

Crowding in close so that he could breathe her in and feel the heat of her small, soft body, Jason opened the snap to her shorts and dragged down the zipper. Sliding both hands into her panties, he pushed them and her shorts past her slim hips until they dropped to her feet.

Heart drumming fast and his dick already reacting, Jason said, "Step out."

Blinking fast, she did.

God, she was beautiful. And whether she realized it yet or not, she was his.

"One second." He adjusted the water temp to be tepid, and quickly shucked off his own shorts and boxers.

"This feels really decadent," Honor said as they stepped under the spray together.

He had an hour, tops, before Hogan would expect them to eat. He hadn't yet told Honor that Violet and Nathan would be joining them, too. He couldn't walk her into a group late, so he'd have to expedite things.

He smiled at her as he picked up her scented soap.

Watching him warily, she pushed wet hair out of her face. "Um…"

"Let me take care of you."

Thinking in the purely sexual sense, Honor agreed. "Okay."

She didn't understand that he wanted to take care of her in every way—physically, emotionally and yeah, sexually.

While watching her face, he lathered her head to toe, and all the sweet places between. Like a little hedonist, she gave in, sometimes leaning on him limply, other times gripping him tightly.

Honor was nearing the end of her control, so he turned her to face the spray, and while rinsing her, he ran his hands over her breasts, over her nipples, until she pressed back against him and moaned softly.

Near her ear, he asked, "Ever have shower sex?"

"You know I haven't."

The Neanderthal in him liked knowing she'd experience many firsts with him. Of course, before Honor, he hadn't shown any Neanderthal tendencies.

"Let me wash up real quick." He reversed their positions so that he was under the spray. He'd just finished soaking his hair when Honor's arms came around him, her small hands slick with soap.

With her breasts slippery against his back, she teased, "Let me take care of you."

Jason dropped his arms, wondering what she had in mind.

But a few minutes later, he started to wonder if it was pleasure or pure torture. Staying at his back, Honor kissed him in select places while working her soapy hands across his shoulders, down his spine, across his hips…then she knelt and began working on his thighs.

He locked his knees, feeling her breath on his ass seconds before she took a soft bite.

Remembering what she'd once told him, he said, "Nothing kinky," in a voice gravelly with lust.

Her laugh teased over him. "Turn around."

Hell yeah.

Still on her knees, she lathered her hands again, then washed his calves, up his thighs...oh God. Her small hands softly fondled his testicles until he had to brace a hand against the shower wall to stay upright.

"Don't move," she told him as she reached past him to rinse her hands, then wrapped them both around his erection.

"Jesus..."

"This is okay?" she whispered, working him in long, slick strokes.

"Yeah." Better than okay. Seeing Honor on her knees, her face a study in concentration, her eyes dark as she toyed with him, was more than he could take.

He pulled her to her feet.

"What's wrong?"

"I'm a stroke away from coming. Let me rinse before I lose it."

Looking hot and turned on with newfound power, she smiled. "I like teasing you."

"Anytime you have the urge." He caught her hands when she again reached for him. "Just not right now."

Her laughter echoed in the shower while he finished washing and rinsing...in under thirty seconds.

Hands shaking, he grabbed for the towels and, to Honor's amusement, did a cursory rush job on them both. They were still damp when he dropped into the bed with her.

Jason grabbed for a condom, rolled it on and finally pinned Honor down.

She smiled hugely. "Hi."

"Hi yourself." God, she was special, in too many ways to count. He kissed the smile off her lips, then wanted to go on kissing her for a lifetime. In so many ways she remained wounded from her youth, but she was also one of the strongest people he'd ever met, and definitely the most caring.

That she was also scorching hot just sealed the deal for him.

She took him by surprise when she pushed against his shoulders. "On your back please."

After a deep, bracing breath, Jason rolled to his back.

Honor immediately straddled him. "For once, I want to watch you come."

That almost did it for him right there. But with Honor sitting on him, stroking his body, her breasts there for him to fondle, he didn't want to miss a thing.

Resting his hands on her thighs, he whispered, "Lean forward."

"Why?"

He stared into her eyes. "Because I want to suck on your nipples."

A flush of heat stained her cheeks and she inhaled sharply. With a timid nod, her thighs tight around him, she slowly lowered herself to him.

Jason immediately drew her in, earning a harsh groan. Using both hands, he cupped that luscious little ass, rocking her against him.

He knew she was close when she knotted her hands in his hair. "Jason…"

"So sweet." He switched to her other nipple, circled with his tongue, gently nipped with his teeth, then tugged carefully.

"Jason," Honor breathed.

He sucked softly.

Whimpering in need, she breathed, "Now. *Right now,*" as she straightened away.

She had him, whether she realized it or not.

He was every bit as urgent as her. "Lift up a little." She flattened her hands on his chest and rose to her knees. To ensure she was ready for him, Jason fingered her damp sex, found her swollen and slick and positioned himself. "Ease down, honey."

Bottom lip caught in her teeth, she did as told. Jason watched as he penetrated, as his shaft slowly sank into her tender pink folds. So fucking hot. So wet and tight and *perfect*.

Nails biting into his chest, she paused.

"A little more," he urged, fighting the need to thrust up into her. This was her show and he didn't want to steal her thunder.

She took three big breaths and cautiously wiggled down onto him.

Feeling her squeeze every inch of him, Jason growled. "That's it."

At first a little awkward, she rocked against him, but in no time she'd found a rhythm she liked.

A rhythm he *loved*.

By sheer force of will he held back, waiting on her, watching the way her expression changed with the level of her excitement. When he knew she was there, he clasped her hips and helped push her over the edge.

Head back, thighs tensed, she came apart.

The second she mellowed, Jason turned her under him and with three hard thrusts, lost himself to release.

Impossible as it seemed, every time with Honor got better.

He knew it was because he loved her.

Soon he'd have to figure out how she felt.

13

WHEN THEY JOINED the others for dinner, there were a lot of telling looks. But with the funeral tomorrow, everyone treated her with extra care—making sure she knew she had friends without being obvious.

Violet raved over the grilled steaks and praised Hogan on his special stuffed potato recipe, which totally took Hogan off guard. He was used to Violent giving him more guff than Lexie often did. With his brother, Jason thought women either adored him or harassed him. There didn't seem to be a lot of middle ground. In his opinion, it was the savvier, more independent women who butted heads with Jason's Casanova brother.

Nathan supplied the beers—with colas for those who wanted them. Colt set up some music and the bonfire lit the yard.

It was always nice, but now, with Honor, it finally felt more like the home he remembered from his childhood.

But truthfully, having Hogan and Colt there helped add to that ambience. It was about family—and the people important to him.

After dinner, they all settled far enough from the fire not to be bothered by the heat. Crickets chirped everywhere, and the croaking of frogs in the creek carried in the breeze. The night was cooler, the sky studded with stars.

Unusually anxious, Diesel took turns going from one person to the next, occasionally curling his lip in a low snarl while staring into the darkness. Eventually he settled down between Honor and Violet, but he stayed on guard.

"Hey," Jason said to the dog. "You okay, buddy?"

Diesel whined, then sent his steely gaze back to the darkness.

Jason assumed he heard a critter of some sort, since he stared toward the back.

Beer in hand, Nathan studied the dog, glanced thoughtfully around the perimeter, then got up from his seat. "Colt, change chairs with me."

"Huh? Oh, sure." Looking pretty clueless as to why, Colt switched with Nathan, then went back to talking to the others, laughing as Violet and Hogan debated the right seasoning for ribs.

When Jason met Nathan's gaze, his friend gave a nearly imperceptible shake of his head.

What the hell?

He didn't want to alarm anyone else, but he realized Nathan had just positioned himself to face Honor's house. The urge to look over his shoulder, to see if anything was happening there, made the hairs on the back of his neck stand on end.

It didn't help when Diesel gave another low growl.

Casual as you please, Nathan stood. "Anyone else need anything while I'm up?"

Violet wanted another cola, but everyone else declined.

The thing Jason noticed was that Nathan bypassed the door at the back of his house and instead walked around the side yard— between his house and Honor's.

Pretending an interest in the fire, Jason strode to the far side and added more kindling. He could see Honor's house, so the second the security light blinked on at the far side, he stilled. Nathan checking on things? Or something else?

The light didn't go out.

With a feral growl, Diesel lunged to his feet.

Screw it. Saying, "Colt, stay here with Honor and Violet," Jason started around the back of the house.

Everyone else came to attention. Alarmed, Honor called his name. He didn't reply. He'd have to trust her to stay put.

"Kill the music," Hogan said, then jogged over to join Jason, no questions asked.

Before they'd reached the side of her house, pandemonium broke out. Shouts, curses, the sounds of a scuffle.

Jason broke into a run—and damn near collided with a rangy kid in his early twenties coming around to the back of the house. They stared at each other. The guy was dressed all in black and wore a black stocking cap.

Son of a bitch.

When the idiot made to run past him, Jason decked him.

One solid shot, right to the chin.

No way in hell would he let him anywhere near the women or Colt.

The guy reeled, went flat to his back, but he didn't stay there, so Jason was forced to put him down…and keep him down.

As pissed as he was, he almost enjoyed the fight, not that the brief scuffle could really be called that. He was bigger, stronger and more mature than the young man throwing ineffectual punches.

Once he had the guy facedown in the dew-wet grass, his knee digging into his back, Jason became aware of Hogan struggling to hold on to Diesel. The dog, snarling and barking, badly wanted a piece of the action.

"Diesel, down," Jason said, and showing that he did indeed have some training, Diesel obeyed.

"Jesus," Hogan said. "This dog is a beast and hard as hell to control. But I was afraid if I turned him loose, you'd get bit in the confusion."

"Thanks," Jason said. He didn't want to risk the dog getting hurt. Hell, he'd rather reward the animal. After all, it was Diesel who had alerted Nathan that something wasn't right.

That made Jason think of his friend and he lifted his head, searching the yard. "Nathan!"

"I'm fine." Disheveled, his hair mussed, a bruise on his cheek but with his gun still in the holster, Nathan appeared from the side of the house. In his right hand he gripped the back of the shirt on a second man. In his left he carried a tire iron and a knit hat. Clearly irate, he pushed the two men together and barked, "Sit."

Diesel plopped his butt down but kept his attention on the men.

Nathan did a double take, then shook his head with irony. "I didn't mean you, Diesel, but good dog."

Diesel thumped his tail, growled at the men again, then looked behind him.

Jason followed his gaze and found the wide-eyed concern of Violet, Colt and Honor. They were all still in his yard, Colt in front with the women held behind him.

Jason's heart swelled. The last thing Honor needed the night before the funeral was this kind of upset. But with any luck, the two yahoos they'd just nabbed were the same who'd broken into her house before, and later cut the cord on her floodlights.

Nathan roughly checked both men for weapons, made them lie on their stomachs, then put in a call.

Minutes later, a deputy showed up with blue lights flashing over the quiet street. Once Nathan had his backup, Jason left him to it.

Colt still stood in front of ladies. It was as if the three of them were frozen.

"Thank you," he told Colt.

Relaxing his broad, tensed shoulders, Colt said, "You need to talk to Honor."

"Oh?" Jason glanced at her and saw the paleness of her skin, the sheen in her eyes. "What did you do, honey?"

"He's younger." She wrung her hands together. "He shouldn't have been trying to shield us."

"I'm twice your size," Colt muttered meanly.

"And still underage." Voice softer, Honor said, "I care for you."

Exasperated, Colt threw up his arms. "You see?"

Yeah, Jason understood exactly what had happened—and knowing he loved them both, he almost smiled.

Colt turned on Honor. "Ditto that, lady." Thumb to his chest, he leaned into her space. "I care, too. Get used to it." Stomping, he headed off to join his father.

Since Honor looked dumbfounded, Jason decided to give her a minute to absorb all that. He smiled at Violet. "This is the quietest I've ever seen you."

"Color me stunned," she said in her heavy drawl. "You're a regular badass and I never knew it."

Jason snorted. "Because I took down a punk half my size?"

"You know, I think it was more about that killer look in your eyes and in-control posture." She shivered. "Delicious." In a ridiculous stage whisper, she told him, "Your lady was worried." With a wink she, too, went off to join the excitement.

When Jason finally looked at her, Honor swallowed. "You were worried?"

"Of course."

Still not touching her, he asked, "Are you my lady?"

Tremulous breaths made her voice unsteady. "I guess I'm closer to it than anyone else here tonight." Her worry scoured over him. "God, Jason, are you okay?"

"Sure." Needing to feel her, he stepped closer, caught her hips and pulled her in against his body. With his forehead to hers, he asked, "You?"

LORI FOSTER

One small hand fisted against his chest. "I'm not the one who was just in a fight."

"That wasn't a fight."

She gave him a disbelieving look. "What would you call it?"

"A bother?" Downplaying the whole thing, he kissed the end of her nose. "I think you insulted Colt's machismo."

"He's a kid."

"Who is almost a man. That's a touchy time for a guy."

"I didn't want to take a chance on him getting hurt."

Jason cupped her face. "Can't you accept that he feels the same? I see how important you've become to him." Jason smoothed back her tawny hair. "He lost his mom, he lost his home and everything familiar. But he's opened up to you. That much trust comes with some responsibilities."

"Meaning I have to let him do his thing?"

He liked how she put that. "Yeah. He's a protective guy trying to control what he can." He tipped up her face. "And he's right. He's twice your size."

Acceptance dropped her shoulders. "You're right. I'll apologize to him later."

"Thank you."

Leaning around him, Honor peered at the confusion.

Nathan and the deputy corralled the men toward the deputy's car.

"They were trying to get into my house."

"Seems so." It was an interesting thing, watching Honor brace herself. "I'm sorry."

"If it's over now, then it was worth it." She slipped her small hand into his and started over to the heart of the confusion. "Come on. I want to know why they kept targeting me."

That she clearly wanted him to go along with her felt like more progress. Not that long ago, she would have insisted on handling everything alone.

Drawn by the fanfare of the deputy's lights and sirens, neighbors crowded the streets. That was when Jason noticed Sullivan's door open—and both he and Lexie stepped out. Huh. So they were around but hadn't joined them for a visit?

Apparently they'd had better, more private things to do. Jason nudged Honor. "Did you notice?"

She followed his gaze, saw Lexie and Sullivan headed toward them and lifted her brows in surprise. "Lexie looks…rumpled."

Not the word he'd use, but he didn't want to point out that she'd clearly just had sex. Jason waved to them to draw their attention. Soon as Lexie saw them, she put a hand to her heart and quickened her pace to join them.

They all reached the deputy's car at just about the same time, but before anyone could explain to Lexie and Sullivan what had happened, one of the men panicked.

"What are you doing?" He fought against the deputy. "Where are you taking me?"

The deputy ruthlessly controlled his guy. Nathan just stared at the man he held, almost daring him to try something. When the guy remained still, Nathan turned to his accomplice.

"You're being arrested."

"For what? I didn't do anything!"

"That's a joke, right? Burglary of a house is a felony."

"We weren't stealing anything!" The deputy stuffed him into the car, but the idiot wasn't making it easy, resisting every inch while he continued to talk. "This is bullshit. It was *his* idea, and his money!"

The man with Nathan stiffened. "Shut up, Mike."

Jason said, "What money?"

"Let me handle this," Nathan insisted. But it was already too late.

"Darrow hid his own money in there. So it's not stealing, right? Besides, I wasn't even going in. I was just along as a lookout."

"And you fucking suck at it," the one called Darrow raged, "or we wouldn't be caught now!"

"I don't suck! They were all hanging out next door. Should've been the perfect time to sneak in and out, but you must've made a noise and they heard you, that's all."

"I didn't make any fucking noise."

"What money?" Jason asked again, ignoring Nathan's palpable frustration.

"Darrow hid his stash in the walls. The place was a pit, so he never figured on no one buying it. Now that stupid bitch moved in and apparently plastered over it! Darrow just wanted to get his cash, that's all."

Eyes mean, Darrow warned, "Shut. The fuck. Up."

Jason wanted to smash Mike for insulting Honor, but more than that, he wanted her to know what was going on.

Undeterred, Mike shot back, "Darrow's the one who sells weed! I only smoke it."

Sullivan asked, "Where in the house?"

"I don't know. Darrow never told me—'cause I'm *not* involved."

"I know," Honor said. "I remember patching the wall."

"Jesus, you're an idiot." Darrow started kicking, trying to reach his buddy, and as Nathan contained him, he yelled, "I'm going to kill you!"

"He's threatening me! You heard him!"

Fed up, Nathan shouted, "Both of you, *settle down*."

Like whipped dogs, the two idiots cringed and went silent.

Leaving Nathan to sort out the conflict, Jason started toward the house with Honor.

Over his shoulder, Nathan yelled, "Don't touch anything!"

Jason lifted a hand to let him know he heard, but kept going.

Lexie and Sullivan fell into step with them, and before they'd reached the front door, Jason had given them the bare bones of what had transpired.

Inside the house, shock plain on her face, Honor pointed to a wall. "It was there. Mostly behind the couch."

Jason quickly moved the enormous plant situated at the end of the sofa. Half behind it and the couch, he saw the obvious patch job Honor had done. It was about the size of a man's fist, close to the floor, and with the paint-over it wasn't as noticeable as it would have been higher on the wall.

Slowly Jason turned to face her.

It amazed him when Honor blushed. "Reading how to do it," she explained, "is totally different from actually trying it."

There was no reason for her to sound so defensive. "When did you patch it?"

"The same day I came here to clean."

The day none of them were home. For certain, he'd have remembered Honor if he'd ever seen her prior to that fateful day she actually moved in. He still remembered how poleaxed he'd felt at their first meeting.

Lexie propped her fists on her hips. "I remember that. You were super hyped up and hadn't even told me about the house yet."

"If I had," Honor said, "you'd have wanted to help me clean. And that type of cleaning isn't really your thing."

"Being friends with you is my thing, and damn right, I'd have helped. You shouldn't have had to do that alone."

"That's the crazy thing. I enjoyed it."

Lexie gave an indulgent shake of her head. "I remember coming over to the apartment to pick you up, but you were dirty head to toe, looking pretty beat and smiling ear to ear." Lexie glanced at Jason. "That's the first I heard of her buying her own place."

"There was so much garbage in here," she told them all. "The house had been empty for a while. I knew someone had used it, because there were old food wrappers and half-empty cups of cola from some different fast food places."

"Jesus," Jason muttered. If he'd known about the squatters, he'd have done something sooner to ensure that her house was secure.

"I changed out the locks first thing," Honor assured him; then she wrinkled her nose. "But there was graffiti on the walls and it was really trashed up. Before Lexie saw it, I at least wanted it cleared out, and I put flat paint over the worst of the...wall art." She cleared her throat.

"And you did some patching," Jason added.

"Yes." She waved a hand at the wall. "That was the biggest one."

"You didn't notice anything inside the wall?" Sullivan asked.

"No, but then, I wasn't looking. I was only hoping nothing came out of the hole, like a mouse or spider or anything." She shuddered. "It was pretty creepy being here alone without much light."

Tenderness bombarded Jason. Honor had done so much to prove she could make it without her grandfather's money—and now she'd inherit anyway. He pulled her close, looped his arms around her and held her.

She returned his hug, patted his back, then said in an aside to Sullivan and Lexie, "He was in a fight earlier," as if to explain why he was being emotional.

After a quickly stifled laugh, Sullivan asked, "Is that so?"

Jason grinned. "Yeah." Crazy Honor. Sweet, smart, capable and giving. She'd never again have to face being alone, because going forward, he'd be with her.

Nathan stepped in through the open doorway, looked at each of them and smiled. "Honor, honey, we need to bust up your wall."

They found five thousand dollars. Honor still couldn't believe it.

Jason had carefully cut away her not-so-great repair and exposed the roll of dusty money. It had been dropped into the wall and pushed to the side in an empty space. Even if she'd been looking, she wouldn't have seen it. It took Jason feeling around in there to reach it, and no way would she have done that.

After they uncovered it, Jason promised to show her the proper way to do a drywall repair.

Happiness, she decided, was having Jason around. He didn't insist on doing something for her, but instead offered his expertise. He accepted that she liked to do for herself, while also believing her competent and trusting her to learn.

His faith was a gift she'd never take for granted.

They were snuggled together in bed, not asleep but resting, when a phone rang.

Honor automatically went to jump from the bed, but Jason stayed her with a gentle hold. "It's mine." Reaching out one long arm, he snagged his cell from the nightstand.

Heart still punching, with regret as much as anything, Honor wilted against him.

How long would it take her heart and mind to accept that her grandfather was gone? She was so conditioned to relating late calls to her grandfather's need that she felt devastatingly bereft all over again.

Without saying a word, Jason drew her nearer to his chest in a gentle, comforting hug.

He was so aware of her and her thoughts, her reactions, that he made her feel special and cared for just by being near.

"I'm going to put you on speaker. Honor should hear this, too." He pushed a button, and said, "Go on."

"Sorry for calling so late, Honor."

Nathan. She hadn't expected that. "It's okay." She needed to sit up for this and regretfully disengaged from Jason's embrace. "Did you learn anything more?"

Jason, too, pushed up to rest against the headboard, his shoulder to hers.

"I did, in fact. The men are Mike Witty and Darrow Hedman," Nathan explained. "Mike, the squealer, has never been in much trouble before, but Darrow is a regular offender. I didn't know him because he was before my time."

Jason interjected softly, "Nathan's only been sheriff for a year."

"From what I'm told, after being busted for stealing a car, Darrow was still on probation when he was spotted dealing pot. He fled, taking officers on a chase—apparently with just enough of a head start to drop the money in Honor's wall and get out a back window, then halfway to the woods, before he was caught. He still had the dope on him, but no one found the money."

Because it was hidden in her house. Honor leaned into Jason; his presence grounded her and made it easier to face the unbelievable.

Jason put a hand on her knee, his thumb teasing over her skin. "How long ago was this?"

"The money's been in the wall for months, but Darrow got out of jail just days after Honor moved in. According to him, he'd only wanted to reclaim what was his."

"And my mailbox?" Honor asked, still plenty peeved about that.

"Darrow claims no connection to that, but given that it's a federal offense to tamper with a mailbox, I'm not sure he'd own up to that anyway. Could be he hoped to spook you enough to get you to leave so he could get in and get the money."

"Or maybe it was a distraction," Jason said. "While everyone was looking at the mailbox, he had a chance to go in and poke around her house."

Honor supposed that made as much sense as anything. "Jerk," she muttered.

"Might be the best explanation we're going to get," Nathan agreed. "Anyway, I just wanted to update you. I'll let you get back to your evening now."

She and Jason both thanked him.

That's when it hit her: Nathan knew Jason was spending the night. Unsure how she felt about that—or how Jason would feel about it—she turned to him with wide eyes. In so many ways, their relationship was still tenuous. There'd been many interruptions to what should have been a normal dating experience. She came with so much baggage, more than any woman should.

"You need to stop that." Too fast for her to react, Jason turned them both so that he pinned her down, his hands holding her face. "I don't care who knows I'm with you."

How did he read her so easily?

The press of his mouth to hers scattered her doubts.

"I *want* people to know." He met her gaze with piercing tenderness. "I plan to be with you a lot."

She wouldn't mind forever…no. She wouldn't think that. Losing her parents had been awful. Losing her grandfather was worse.

She couldn't lose anyone else.

She couldn't lose Jason, not when she'd just now realized she wanted him most of all.

His eyes were dark, watchful and waiting. Maybe for a commitment. Maybe for a reciprocal declaration. But how could she give either when so much of her life was in disorder?

She couldn't take sympathy-laden promises from him.

But she could take something else. "Jason?"

Those beautiful, thick lashes of his lowered in regret. "What is it, honey?"

"Are you tired?"

His eyes opened again. "I'm never too tired for you."

Hearing that, accepting the caring he gave, filled the emptiness with a much warmer, much sweeter emotion. "Then could we have sex again?" Feeling bold, she brought her open palms up and over his gorgeous, hairy, sexy chest. "I'd like that a lot if you're up for it."

"I'm in bed with you." Though a touch of disappointment remained in his dark eyes, he slowly grinned. "Trust me, I'm up."

14

JASON HOPED HIS presence made it easier for Honor to get through the funeral, but she was so stoic, he just didn't know. It wasn't that she remained unmoved, but more that she portrayed ever-enduring self-control.

Unlike her relatives, who tended toward loud, demonstrative displays of weeping and wailing, Honor kept herself contained to a few quiet tears.

During the funeral services, Honor started the eulogy, and hearing her speak about her grandfather emphasized how much she loved him.

Then she invited others to share their thoughts and memories. Her relatives declined, but Neil Mosely, as well as other friends, joined her up front. What they had to say emphasized how much Hugh had loved her.

Jason wished he'd had the opportunity to know her grandfather. He would have appreciated the chance to thank Hugh Mefford for taking a discarded young girl and giving her the love she so obviously deserved.

Much later, after all the condolences had been given, Neil proved himself a stalwart friend, solemn in his grief and insistent that Hugh's last lucid thought had included deep love and affection for his granddaughter. Honor promised Neil she would stay in touch.

Jason believed her. It was unfortunate, but Neil was her closest link to her grandfather—not her great-aunt, aunts or cousin.

On their drive home, Honor removed the pins from her hair, which had been up in a sedate but pretty twist.

"Headache?" Jason asked her.

"Just tired." Resting back against the seat, she turned her head toward him. "Thank you."

Jason kept one hand on the wheel, the other on her thigh. He needed the connection, even if she didn't. "For?"

"Being there with me." She covered his hand with her own. "I don't ever want you to feel obligated, but you need to know how much easier you made it."

He hadn't done anything except stand at her side. "There's nowhere I'd rather have been." *Just with you.*

Her poignant smile spoke volumes. "You are the most amazing man."

Because she thought loving her was so difficult? For Jason, it was the easiest thing in the world.

He considered a declaration, as ill-timed as it might be. Unfortunately, as they neared their houses, he saw a visitor waiting on Honor's porch. He looked to be in his early sixties, dressed in tan pants, a rumpled T-shirt, work boots and black-framed glasses. His head lifted as he spotted their car.

Jason was about to ask Honor if she'd been expecting anyone when he glanced her way and caught her tense dismay. Her face had gone white, her breath frozen. Her hands contracted into tight fists.

"Honor?" He quickly steered into his own driveway, then kept going until he had them both in the large barn. With alacrity, he shut off the truck and turned to her. "Honey, what is it?"

She swallowed hard, her eyes glassy and her expression appalled. "That man on my porch… I think that's my father."

Behind him, Hogan pulled in with Colt. He knew Sullivan and Lexie would be parking at Sullivan's house across the street.

Honor would have to do her reunion with a damn audience.

As she so often did, she drew in a fortifying breath, reached for the doorknob...and prepared to face the devastation alone.

"Not this time."

She blinked as if coming out of a daze.

Jason had no idea what the man could want at this late date, but if possible, he would have sent him away without any direct contact whatsoever with Honor.

But that would just be stalling the inevitable, and he knew her well enough to know she'd never take the easy way out.

"We'll greet him together." He shushed her automatic protest with implacable insistence. "*Together*, Honor."

Amazingly gratitude overshadowed her defiance. "You're sure you want to do this?"

Jason teased a fingertip over her downy cheek. "Positive." He got out and circled the truck to open her door.

The second they emerged from the barn, Hogan said, "Honor has company."

"My father."

Eyes going wide, then narrowing, Hogan predictably fell into step with them. Colt moved to Honor's other side. By the time they reached the side yard, Sullivan and Lexie were with them, too.

When they heard barking, they all turned to see Diesel, paws on the windowsill, looking out the same window Jason had often used to see Honor. The dog didn't like being left behind. Colt paused.

"It's okay," Honor said to him. "Diesel probably needs to visit the grass."

Hogan snorted at her delicate way of saying the dog had to use the bathroom.

Colt waffled, but after giving her a quick hug, he went to see to Diesel. The dog left the window, no doubt racing to the door to meet Colt there.

"Put him on his leash," Jason called after him. The last thing they needed was for Diesel to take offense at things and tear into the man.

Never mind that Jason was already of a similar mind.

As they reached the porch, her father stood, but neither he nor Honor moved to close the distance between them, a distance that felt far more than physical.

Finally Honor said, "Dad."

Pleasure brought a flickering smile to his mouth. "I wasn't sure you recognized me."

"I'm sure I've changed more than you have." Her hand in Jason's tightened. "I was only twelve when you left and now I'm almost thirty."

His gaze did a quick trip around at their group. "It has been a long time. Could we talk?"

"Sure." She made no move to give them privacy.

Damn, that pleased Jason.

After adjusting his glasses with a nervous hand, her father asked, "Alone?"

Assuming it'd be easier for her, Jason turned to the others. "Why don't you guys wait at my house? Honor and I will be over shortly."

"Very shortly," Honor added, her tone firm but not cruel.

There was some grumbling before everyone started to depart. Lexie stepped in front of Honor, her back to the house so Honor's father couldn't see. In a voice barely above a whisper, she said, "Remember that he doesn't deserve you. Do *not* let him hurt you. Not again. Promise me."

Honor smiled. "I can take care of myself." When Lexie scowled, she added, "I promise."

"We're sisters," Lexie told her. "Even if I was spared having him for a father. Don't ever forget that." With that parting shot, Lexie led the way as far as Jason's porch. From there, they all kept watch.

Taking his cues from Honor, Jason waited beside her until, after everyone had gone, she started toward the house. "We can talk here on the porch."

"You don't want to go inside?"

"No."

Giving up on that gambit, her father looked her over. "You're so grown up, Honor, and so pretty."

She took a seat without replying. Jason sat beside her.

"You look a lot like your mother."

"Granddad told me." She tilted her head, studying the man who'd fathered her. "He was buried today, you know."

The stark words made her father wince. "I know. That's why I'm here."

"Here," Honor said carefully, "instead of at the funeral?"

The man finally pulled up a chair. Ignoring that question, he asked one of his own. "Will you introduce me?"

While holding her father's gaze, Honor took her time deciding. Jason didn't push it; how she handled this was entirely up to her.

Apparently deciding it wouldn't hurt, she said, "Jason, meet my father. Dad, this is my neighbor, Jason Guthrie."

"Mr. Brown." Jason accepted the handshake.

Before either man could say more, Honor sat forward with impatience. "I don't see the point in this visit. You probably realize that today isn't the best day, so I'd prefer you just tell me what it is you want."

Bravo, Honor.

Managing to feign hurt, her father sat back, hands braced on the arms of the chair. "I'm sorry about Hugh."

"Thank you." Pretending she believed that the reason for his visit, Honor started to rise. "If that's all—"

"Celeste came to see me."

Taken off guard, Honor sank back into her seat. "When?"

"Two days ago."

Her mouth opened twice, but nothing came out.

Honor looked both betrayed and confused. Why would Celeste visit him? Whatever her reasons, it didn't matter.

Jason felt murderous. Staying silent wasn't possible. "As you probably already guessed, I'm more than a neighbor."

"I assumed," her father said.

"Then know this—in one more minute I'm taking Honor inside. If you have something to say, you damn well better spit it out. Now."

Honor stared at him as if he had two heads; then her mouth curled into a half smile. Turning to her father, she nodded. "What Jason said."

"Fine." Sitting forward, his elbows on his thighs, his fingers laced together, her father met her direct gaze. "Celeste told me that you'd inherited."

That conniving bitch. After acting concerned, she'd deliberately sabotaged Honor with her own unscrupulous father.

Realizing the same, Honor didn't even blink. "Celeste shouldn't have done that, but then she's done many things that she shouldn't."

"So it's true? You inherited Hugh's cash?"

Her eyes narrowed. "Yes, I did."

The ready reply stumped him. "She said it was substantial."

Honor shrugged. Reaching out, she covered her father's hands with one of her own. Very gently, she said, "Whatever the amount, it isn't your concern." Her father started to speak, but Honor didn't give him the chance. "I'm sorry that you came here for that—"

"And to see you."

"—because it was a waste of your time."

The words, spoken in a neutral way, still impacted like a slammed door. While Mr. Brown's breathing grew harsher, they stared at each other.

He lifted his chin. "You won't even hear me out?"

"I'm sorry, Dad. You and I don't have a relationship. That was your doing, not mine, and no amount of money now is going to change that."

"I was hurting over your mother!" He gripped her hand. "And I knew Hugh would take good care of you."

"I was hurting, too," she stated. "And yes, Granddad was wonderful." With an abrupt tug, she freed her hand and stood. "Now you need to go."

"Honor," Mr. Brown pleaded.

"There's nothing more for us to say." She turned her back on him, unlocked her front door and went inside.

Jason stared at the closed door, warmth filling him despite the way he hurt for her. Even while anguished, Honor was dignified and strong, and he was so damn proud of her grand exit.

Removing his glasses, Mr. Brown rubbed tired eyes. "That didn't go quite as I planned."

His plan had been to…what? Ingratiate himself now that he knew Honor had money? "Her life hasn't gone as planned. She's adjusted. I suggest you do the same."

He glared at Jason. "It's not like I meant to hurt her."

Weak excuses always rubbed Jason the wrong way. "You never cared enough to ensure that you didn't." Indicating the direction of the street, he said, "I'll walk you to your car." He wanted the man gone so he could rejoin Honor.

Mr. Brown got completely off the porch before he turned nasty. "Hugh gave her anything she wanted."

"Not parents."

Undeterred, her father muttered, "He gave her more than I ever could."

Jason glared at him. *Clueless bastard.* "Since you gave her nothing, I can't dispute that."

That took him aback, but not for long. He stopped in the middle of the yard, his voice rising. "You make it sound like I left her in the street. Hugh was wealthy! She had a pampered life with him!"

Fury amplified. "Even before you abandoned her, you didn't know your daughter at all, did you?" If he had, then he damn well would have understood that she was the type of person who gave instead of taking.

"Her mother left first. What the hell was I supposed to do?"

His voice pure gravel, Jason leaned in close, deliberately intimidating. "Back then? You could have loved her. That's all she really needed. Now? You can leave her in peace. She asked you to go, so you're going. End of story."

"I'm the only family she has left now."

"*Wrong.*" With Sullivan barely keeping up, Lexie stormed off the porch, across the yard and up to Mr. Brown. "*I'm* her family."

Colt joined her, saying, "And me."

"Me, too." Hogan contained Diesel on a short leash, stationing himself next to his son.

As Jason had suspected, the dog didn't like Brown much. Lips curling, he continually strained against Hogan's hold.

Jason was wondering if he should try to diffuse the growing animosity, but in the end it didn't matter.

Standing just outside the open door, Honor laughed. Not a fake laugh, or a dismissive laugh meant to show she didn't care, and not a laugh of irony.

She laughed as if tickled, and the sound stole a lot of his turbulence.

Changed into shorts and a T-shirt, her hair in a loose ponytail, Honor held her small tool kit in one hand. "Clearly," she said around an affectionate smile, "I have the most awesome family ever."

Jason took a step toward her, her father all but forgotten. The sight of her always affected him, but seeing her like this felt damn near like foreplay to his soul. "Planning to repair something, honey?"

"If you'll help, yes." She headed around the side of the house. "I figured it was past time I tackled that stupid side door."

Incredible. Every day she found a new way to amaze him. "I'll be right there." He glanced at her father, no longer wanting to tear the man apart. "I can't say it was nice to meet you."

Mr. Brown removed a card and flipped it at Jason. "When she changes her mind, tell her to give me a call."

The card landed on the grass.

Everyone ignored it.

Temper evident in every stomping footstep, her father finally went to his car, slammed the door, gunned the engine and sped away.

Jason picked up the card. He'd give it to Honor—after they got the door removed and planed.

Hogan stroked Diesel's neck. "Anyone hungry? I can throw on some burgers."

"I'm in," Sullivan said. "I'll bring the drinks."

Lexie gave a lot of attention to a fingernail.

Jason didn't know what was going on between Sullivan and Lexie, but far as he was concerned, she had an open invitation. "What about you, Lexie? Can you stick around?"

Shoring up the invite, Sullivan looped an arm around her.

"Sure. I'd love to."

Colt turned to his dad. "Okay if I lend a hand with the door?"

"I expected you would—after you change out of your suit."

Jason needed to do the same. But first…he went to Honor. She stood near the jammed side door, a fist to her heart, her eyes big and luminous as she watched the group disperse.

He had no idea what she was thinking, and it worried him. "Everyone's hanging out to eat. Okay?"

"It'll be great." She touched him once he got close, her small palm on his chest, stroking down the length of his tie. "It's crazy, but everything today showed me how lucky I really am."

Only Honor would see the upside of burying a beloved grandfather, then fending off the mercenary attention of an estranged father.

He didn't know how she did, but as usual she'd rolled with the punches.

She stood on the side door stoop, him in the grass, and it aligned them a little more evenly. She only had to lean up a little, her breasts brushing his chest, to lightly kiss his mouth.

Very softly, she said, "I'd like to take care of this door now. Okay?"

"Sounds good to me." Repairs were one way to help her cope.

He got that. There was something very satisfying about swinging a hammer, driving a nail. Being engaged both physically and mentally with a project. He often worked off frustration in the barn, building and repairing.

Since Honor had moved in, he'd found a much better way to expend energy.

Honor looked at the door, perplexed. "How do we get it out of there?"

"We're on the wrong side, for one thing." He kept her close with a hand on her slim hip. "The hinges are on the inside."

A wry smile twisted her mouth. "Guess I should have realized that."

"I'll show you." With any luck, he'd get a lifetime to teach her everything he knew about carpentry. "Let me change clothes and we'll get to it."

"Together."

She said that as if just understanding the possibility of such a thing. Her new acceptance further lightened Jason's mood while also sharpening his determination to get there sooner. "You and me," he agreed. "Together."

For the most part, Honor tried to ignore the fact of the money now sitting in her account. She knew it was there, felt the weight of the reality in her heart, but it still seemed surreal. When she thought of the financial boost, it was of what she'd lost, not of what she'd gained.

Pretending it wasn't there seemed the most expedient way to regain some normalcy.

Except that she no longer knew what "normal" looked like.

So much of her time had centered on taking care of her grand-dad that free time now felt like an additional burden. No matter how busy she stayed, and she tried to stay really busy, she still felt at loose ends. The second things got quiet, she found herself listening for the phone to ring, or subconsciously making plans to visit the facility. Once or twice she'd even considered reaching out to her random, slightly insane, always antagonistic relatives just to fill the emotional void. Unfortunately their feelings over the loss were so disparate she knew she wouldn't find any consolation there.

She also considered leaning on Lexie. But God love her, Lexie had already been there for her, in every way imaginable, through so much. This grief, this new adjustment, felt like something she had to battle on her own.

"You look lost in thought."

Honor smiled at Jason. "Maybe just a little." She finished washing the coffee carafe.

Behind her, Jason looped his arms around her and put small but heated kisses on the back of her neck. Near her ear, he asked softly, "Want to talk?"

For so many reasons, she cherished every minute with Jason, but mornings were extra special. His attention provided insulation against the bad thoughts and feelings. When he kissed her, especially when he touched her, all she felt was warmth and excitement.

"I'm fine," she lied, because dwelling on sadness definitely didn't help. Today they'd join the neighborhood by the creek for games and food and…fun. The concept felt so foreign that it made her hesitant. But she was determined to embrace the opportunity. Jason looked forward to it, so she wouldn't bring him down.

"You're sexy," he countered, his hands opening on her, one low on her stomach, the other just under her breast. "Unfortunately I can't do anything about it right now. Hogan's going to need a hand setting up the grills." His hands gently caressed but didn't wander. "I'll be back in an hour so we can head to the creek together."

"I'll be ready."

He turned her, slid both hands into her loose hair and turned up her face.

Jason never seemed to mind when she was morning-rumpled. In fact, he was his most affectionate in the mornings, as he showed her now by nuzzling her throat, teasing her ear and then putting his mouth softly over hers for a brief but stirring kiss.

His forehead to hers, he said, "If at any time you feel uncomfortable or overwhelmed, let me know and we'll leave."

She would never do that. "I'm looking forward to it." Another lie—and she could tell Jason knew it.

Gaze heated, brows angled in worry, he slid his thumb over her bottom lip and chose to let it go. "Wear something old, bring a towel and don't forget your sunscreen."

With one more kiss, he turned and left her.

Honor realized that her toes were curled, her heart raced... and she'd once again forgotten about her grief.

Jason could be the cure to melancholy. If she could bottle him she'd make a fortune.

She'd grown so fond of him, of his family. Colt had a permanent place in her heart, and Hogan would always have her respect.

When Hogan had asked her about joining them for a day of volleyball and picnicking, he surely hadn't realized what an aberration it would be for her.

That he'd been thinking of her, that he'd insisted on including her, meant so much. The entire day ahead would be consumed with volleyball and barbecuing, games and...friends. Real friends who cared for her. She knew that because she *felt* their caring in so many ways.

Things she once would have equated with pity she now recognized as understanding, commiseration, protectiveness and defense.

The same things she'd often tried to give to her grandfather. Because she loved him.

The morning sun spilled through every window as she packed a few supplies...or more like overpacked too many supplies. Her largest tote now overflowed.

As usual, when Jason returned, he tapped at the front door before opening it. From the kitchen table, Honor saw him lean in.

She loved that they'd moved past the formality of him being a guest. Although he hadn't quite moved in—that wouldn't make sense with his own house right next door—he did go back and forth with ease.

"Come on in," she said. "I'm almost ready." Finally she'd get to check out the creek. They didn't need to drive; they'd take the trail from the farthest part of Jason's backyard, making use of his wooden footbridge to get to the other side.

"Would you mind coming to my barn with me for a minute first?" His warm, lazy smile piqued her curiosity, especially when he added, "I want to show you something."

Intrigued, Honor tucked her sunglasses into the tote bag, smoothed a few wayward wisps of hair back into her ponytail and joined him.

He relieved her of the bag, then laced his fingers in hers, leading her from the porch.

"Did you build something new?" She loved seeing his various creations. Each piece was unique, always beautiful and extremely sturdy. From bookcases to benches, playground equipment to gazebos, Jason never failed to surprise her with his talent.

That he also repaired everything from toasters to trucks was truly amazing, and a testament to his skill.

As they crossed the recently mowed grass, he said, "Something new, but not anything complicated."

She breathed in the smells of clean air, dewy wet grass and... Jason. Fresh from a shower, his hair still damp, he smelled delicious.

But then, she loved his scent always. Mornings were now her favorite because she could snuggle against his chest and breathe in the warmth of his skin.

But then right after sex his scent was almost intoxicating. And while falling asleep, it soothed her better than any drug could.

She put her head against his shoulder and smiled.

Glancing down at her, Jason asked, "You're quiet again. What are you thinking?"

"How yummy you always smell."

Bemused, he grinned at her. "Yummy, huh?"

"Mmm. Always."

He stopped in the middle of the yard for another stirring kiss. She felt the sun warming her back, a gentle breeze moving her hair, and she felt Jason, big, strong, rock-steady and consuming.

He was shirtless—no surprise there—and she absorbed the heat of his skin, the softness of his chest hair.

And that scent...

"Ahem."

Honor jumped back and saw Colt, wearing a rascal's grin, walk past them with an enormous cooler. Diesel bounded behind him, contained on a leash.

Hands to her face, Honor groaned.

Unconcerned, Jason pulled down her hands and put them back on his shoulders. "He was only teasing, honey. No reason to turn so red."

"He saw us." Whenever she'd dared to dream about finding the right guy at the right time and getting involved, not once had she considered his family being so close by, or that she'd get busted so often. "You make me forget..." *Everything.* "...where I'm at."

"I'm glad." He pulled her to her tiptoes for one last smooch, making muscles flex and shift in his upper arms and shoulders. "Colt has seen worse on commercials, and he knows that I care for you, so don't worry about it."

Her heart tried to jump into her throat.

Still keeping her close, he added, "I'm the only one who hasn't given you a housewarming gift."

It took her brain a second to catch up to the topic switch. "You don't owe me a gift."

He shrugged those stunning shoulders. "It's not about owing. It's about wanting to share, though I think what I'm giving you is more of a welcoming present. I hope you like it."

Still in his arms, Honor whispered with complete sincerity, "You make me feel welcome every night."

His darkening gaze went to her mouth. "Keep thinking along those lines, and I'll be making you feel welcome this morning, too."

Oh, how he tempted her. But if they didn't go, her newfound friends would think she'd chickened out, that she was home being maudlin, and she didn't want that. Hugging him tight, Honor said, "You're so tough to resist, but I'm looking forward to the activities today, too."

"Huh." Jason held her back, his gaze searching hers. "That almost sounded like the truth."

"Because it is." *Now.* Jason had a knack for stealing her concerns, and giving her new focus. "I promise."

"Then let's get to it." He readjusted the tote and took her hand again.

Curious, Honor allowed him to lead her into the barn. Lined up in front of his truck, she saw sets of beautiful shutters. "Wow, did you do these? They're gorgeous."

"They aren't painted yet. I was waiting to see what colors you wanted."

She stopped midstep, speechless. *This* was his gift to her?

"I only did enough for the front windows because I wanted to see if you liked them first. If not, I can show you some different designs—"

"Oh, wow."

Stepping between her and the shutters, Jason tilted his head, his expression curiously intent. "Oh, wow, good or bad?"

With her heart so full, it wasn't easy to speak. She hugged herself, then breathed, "I *love* them."

Satisfaction eased his stance, and he went back to explaining. "Your type of house would normally have paneled shutters, like the ones that rotted away. These are just a step up with the cutout pattern in the top—"

"Just...*wow.*"

He stopped talking and instead a grin cut across his face. "You really like them?"

Dazed, she moved forward and knelt in front of the shutters. Emotional, nearly reverent, she touched the smooth design of the cutout. "They're like pieces of art. The wood is beautiful."

"I actually wondered about that. If you like the idea, we could stain and seal them instead of painting them. I think the natural wood would go great with the color you chose for the house."

She couldn't imagine anything more amazing. "Yes." That's what she wanted.

"Great. Now that I know you like them, I'll get started on making more for all the windows. Once I'm done we can pick out the stain."

It was dimmer, cooler in the barn. Honor looked around, her chest tight with emotions so out of the ordinary they almost frightened her. She twisted to see Jason. "Where's Hogan?"

"We went over earlier to set up two mammoth grills in the field. Hogan stayed to finish prepping his slow-cooked ribs. He got them mostly done here, but he'll add more barbecue sauce and by the time we eat, he says, they'll be perfect. You saw Colt leaving with Diesel." He watched her. "We're alone."

Only the songs of birds and the rustling of leaves intruded. Her quickened breaths inside the barn brought the smells of sawdust, oil and earth. For an outbuilding where he worked, he kept it incredibly clean and organized. Even with the trucks and a boat inside, he had plenty of room to move.

After she quickly scoped out the interior of the barn, the craftsmanship of the shutters recaptured her fascination. Jason had made these for her.

"It's so much work." Tiny details showed in not only the design, but the construction. Jason, she knew, was a perfectionist. She looked up at him. "I should refuse, but I just can't."

"No, you can't." He crouched beside her on the balls of his feet, his strong thighs open, forearms resting across his knees, his hands hanging loosely. "It would insult me if you did."

Lately it seemed the changes in her life came fast and furious, hitting her in ways she'd never expected.

She'd lost her grandfather, inherited a small fortune, made new friends...but Jason brought the biggest changes. For years now her granddad had been ill, slowly morphing into a stranger with only glimpses of recognition. She'd known his death was coming, and she'd prepared the best she could.

Never could she have prepared for Jason.

Before she'd even moved in, he strode into her life as if it were the most natural thing in the world. Each day was now as much about him as it was anything else, including her loss, her grief, her work or her house.

It was about him...with her.

And Jason hadn't come alone. He'd brought with him family and friends, and they'd all become so important to her. For years, she'd struggled just to open herself up to Lexie. It went against her instinct to protect herself at all costs. Because of her

LORI FOSTER

steamroller attitude in life, Lexie was easy. She insisted on taking part and there was no stopping her.

But Jason was different from anyone she'd ever known.

She knew Lexie was in it for the long haul. Lexie knew her faults, the details of her background. Heck, she'd lived some of that background with her—and she'd persevered.

Would Jason?

Her thoughts caught in a whirlwind, Honor ran her fingertips over the very smooth wood. "These are so beautiful I'd like to hug them. But that seems ridiculously dumb, so..." Instead she threw herself against Jason.

Taken by surprise, he couldn't brace for the impact and they both fell flat to the ground, Honor on his chest. She kissed his face everywhere, his brow, temple, nose and chin.

Laughing, Jason easily flipped her beneath him, protecting her head with one hand and closing the other over her hip. "We'll both be dirty even before we get to the mud."

"I don't care." She looped her arms around his neck and tried not to get turned on. "I don't even know what to say. How do I thank you for such an incredible gift?"

"You already thanked me when you plowed me over." Eyes warm and teasing, he readjusted to put one leg between hers. "Love your enthusiasm."

Her breath caught. Hearing that particular word while he looked at her in that mysterious way sent her emotions into hyperdrive.

He braced on his forearms over her. "I know you can afford to buy new—"

"No." She didn't want to talk about that money. "These *are* new. And custom-made by you. They're incredibly *perfect*."

As if judging her sincerity, he studied her face, then treated her to a small crooked smile. "I like seeing you happy." Slowly adjusting his hips to hers, he turned her thoughts carnal. "It makes me hot."

"You're always hot," she whispered back. "But I don't mind. In fact, I'm thinking maybe we should—"

"Guess we're interrupting," Sullivan said from the open garage doors.

Lexie bobbed her eyebrows. "Ignore us. We'll go on alone." They moved out of sight.

Good grief, how did she keep getting caught in these predicaments? But she already knew. Jason would never be far from those he cared about, which meant privacy would exist only behind a closed door.

After she'd spent so much of her life alone, interruptions by friends and family were kind of nice. Embarrassing, but nice.

Groaning, Jason dropped his head to her shoulder, but straightened again and called out to Sullivan, "Wait for us. We're ready."

Lexie called back, "Take your time. We're not in a hurry."

Jason smiled down at Honor. "I want you to enjoy yourself today, but tonight, you're all mine."

Honor liked that idea more than she should have, but just as she didn't allow herself to dwell on her inheritance, she didn't want to daydream about commitment with Jason.

She'd lost too many people whom she cared about. She couldn't lose him, too. So instead she'd concentrate on the immediate present—the fun, the camaraderie…and her oh-so-lovable neighbor.

15

SITTING IN THE shade of a huge tree, close enough to the creek to hear the gurgling of the water, Lexie watched as Honor lifted her arms and stretched.

"I've never had so much fun in my entire life."

That was actually pretty sad, but still Lexie smiled. For days it had felt like she'd lost a piece of herself. Honor was present, and she said the right things, but Lexie wasn't a dummy. She knew Honor too well for that.

She'd been shut out, and it had cut like a knife to the heart.

But today Honor had been more herself again. Lexie understood her struggle, maybe better than Honor herself did. "Tired?" They'd competed in games of mud volleyball, and now they were both covered.

"Maybe a little." Using a hand, Honor shaded her eyes. "But in a good way."

Unlike Lexie, who freely admitted to a wicked competitive streak, Honor had started out timid, trying to avoid the slick mud, only halfheartedly going after the ball. That wasn't unusual. Honor was, by nature, a reserved person.

But with Jason, Colt and Violet on her team, each of them going full force to win, and Lexie, Hogan, Nathan and Sullivan playing against them, equally fierce, Honor had finally gotten sucked into the excitement.

Others played with them, but they tended to rotate out and take many breaks. Their core group hung in there until they were tied two to two. Violet wanted a tie-breaker, but the guys decided they needed to cool off in the creek. Violet had joined them for that.

It bothered Lexie a little, but Honor was so unconcerned that she couldn't see saying anything. And honestly, from what she could tell, both Sullivan and Jason treated Violet like a mere friend.

Hogan, on the other hand…yeah, there was nothing platonic about the way he watched her.

"It was exciting, wasn't it?" Wrinkling her nose, Honor smiled. "Winning is a blast, and even losing isn't too awful."

"I love that you're getting into it." Lexie watched Sullivan swing out on a rope hung from a tree, then drop with a cannonball splash into the wide creek. He laughed, and her heart twisted. For so damn many reasons, she felt melancholy.

Shoving it aside, she turned to Honor. "And I love you."

Honor paused, comprehension blunting her smile. She dug out a wet wipe and offered it to Lexie. "I've been a terrible friend, haven't I?"

Lexie started to assure her otherwise, but Honor was so serious, so incredibly earnest, that this felt like a good time to reach her. "Not terrible, no." She used the wipe to clean mud off her arms. "Never in your entire life have you been terrible."

"But I hurt you."

Her insight surprised Lexie. "Honestly, when you wouldn't lean on me, it almost broke my heart."

Sad, Honor said, "That's because you're too used to propping me up."

Lexie frowned at her. "That's not true."

"Lex," Honor chided. "You've been my rock since we were kids."

"You've been *my* rock, too."

Taken aback by her vehemence, Honor stared at her.

In for a penny… "I know how you think, Honor. You figured it would be a bother or something silly like that. But I knew you needed me and there wasn't anything I could do." She swiped at the mud on her cheek. "I won't lie. That hurt."

Honor pulled out another wipe and, going to her knees, used it to further clean Lexie's face. Very softly, she said, "I'm sorry, Lex, but I didn't even know what to do. I guess I got so wrapped up in trying to figure it out, I didn't consider how it might be for you."

Feeling like an ass, Lexie let out a breath. "It wasn't about me. But you were so distant. So *deliberately* alone. It was like you didn't want me around."

"Never, ever that." Honor took her hands. "I don't want to say I'm a dummy, and I hate that it makes me sound so weak, but we both know I'm still learning to trust. That's not a good excuse because I've always trusted you."

Lexie wasn't sure if that was true or not, but hearing it helped. "You're not a dummy, hon, and you're definitely *not* weak."

Honor laughed. "Defending me, always."

Not for the first time, Lexie insisted, "Because we're sisters!"

"We definitely are."

Lexie's jaw loosened. Honor had never denied it, but neither had she verbally confirmed it—until now.

"You got me through so much, Lex. I know I'll never be able to repay you, but you are my family, and I figure we have the rest of our lives for me to try."

Tears pricked her eyes and Lexie grabbed her for a big hug. "You goof," she said in a choked complaint, squeezing tighter. "It means as much to me as it does to you."

Honor's hold was gentler, but just as heartfelt. "We're drawing attention."

"I don't care."

"From Jason and Sullivan."

"Oh." Knowing she had to get a grip, Lexie sat back and took a breath. With a frown, she glanced toward the creek and saw both Jason and Sullivan on alert. "They're so wonderful."

"Yes."

"I've been unfair, too." Since Lexie hadn't meant to blurt that out, she immediately winced.

Honor tipped her head. "How so?"

It was terrible timing, but the need to talk pushed her. "You always have to deal with the zoo, and losing your grandfather to that awful disease has been a constant worry for years now. I figured I shouldn't add to your troubles."

Her own frown starting, Honor searched her face. "There's something wrong?" Concern brought her closer. "Something you haven't told me?"

Working up her courage, Lexie nodded—and said it out loud. "I'm in love with Sullivan." When Honor said nothing, Lexie looked at her, then laughed. "Rendered you speechless, huh?"

"I never…that is, you're usually so…" Honor sank back to sit on her heels. "I was worried about you hurting him."

Ha! Talk about irony. "You consider me a ravager of innocents, huh?"

That made her snort. "He's not innocent. It's just that you're not usually one to get too involved."

"I know." Lexie picked at a blade of grass. "But Sullivan is different."

"How so?"

"You know about his MMA school? How he helps underprivileged and at-risk kids?"

"Jason told me."

"You should see him with them." She let out a long sigh. "Gawd, Honor, he's so incredibly warm and caring and he's exactly what they need. I've thought Sullivan was sexy from the moment I laid eyes on him, but when I see him with those kids…" She pressed a fist to her heart. "It really gets to me."

Honor smiled. "A big, badass guy with a heart of gold. No woman could be immune to that."

"Exactly." She peeked at Honor. "He's different in other ways, too."

"Like?"

"Well, for one thing, he's not all that into me."

"Oh, please." Honor gave her a small push that nearly toppled her. "Now you're just making up stuff. I've seen the way he looks at you. *Everyone* has seen the way he looks at you."

"Sure, Sullivan wants me. When it comes to sex, he's insatiable."

Biting her lip, Honor whispered, "That's pretty awesome, isn't it?"

Damn, but Lexie enjoyed seeing Honor glow. "Jason, too, huh?"

Dreamy-eyed, Honor nodded. "Yes."

When Lexie lifted her hand, palm out, Honor laughed and high-fived her. "We are lucky ladies."

"We are. But back to you and Sullivan." Gently Honor asked, "Have you told him how you feel?"

"Nope." *Because even though he wants me, he doesn't respect my character.* No, she wouldn't say that. She'd already unloaded enough. It was such a good day she didn't want to bring Honor down with her woes. "I'm not sure how he feels." *Such a lie.*

"I'm sure he's crazy about you. What guy wouldn't be?" With all the bias any doting sister would have, Honor began listing her attributes. "You're beautiful and hilarious and outgoing and fun."

Though Lexie smiled, she wished Honor had named some traits with more substance. But hey, she wasn't shy. "What about smart?"

"Brilliant," Honor confirmed.

"And caring?"

"Oh, Lex." Honor again took her hands. "You are, without a doubt, the most caring person I know."

Lexie glanced at Sullivan again. Maybe she just needed him to get better acquainted with her outside of bed. Maybe, during those times she visited him at the gym, she needed to stop tiptoeing around him and instead show him just how well she could relate to his pupils. "Come on." Lexie stood and pulled Honor to her feet.

"Where are we going?"

"To swim and remove the rest of this mud."

Digging in, Honor held back. "You go on. I'll watch from over here."

After giving her a look, Lexie cupped her hands to her mouth and shouted to Jason, "I need help getting Honor in the water."

Immediately both Jason and Colt started wading to the bank.

"There are snakes in there," Honor rushed to say.

Lexie rolled her eyes. "With that many people splashing around? No way."

Worried, Honor bit her lip. "The water is probably cold."

"Let's call it refreshing. Besides, Hogan is almost done cooking and you don't want to eat with that much mud still on you, do you?"

"Well…"

Startling her, Jason scooped her up from behind. He was wet, which probably meant cold skin given the way Honor gasped.

Lexie was laughing about that when Sullivan suddenly hefted her over his shoulder. "Hey!" Yes, very cold, wet skin.

Diesel, who'd been swimming with them, shook hard, sending water droplets everywhere.

Loving the show, Colt started to say something, but his attention snagged elsewhere. From their ignominious positions, both Honor and Lexie twisted to look…and saw a trio of girls in bikinis headed toward a shallower area of the creek.

Diesel looked at Colt, at the girls, and he took off in an easy lope in that direction.

"Smart dog," Colt said, and ambled after him.

Lexie's gaze met Honor's and they both burst out laughing.

Until the guys waded into the icy water, then their laughter turned into shrieks.

An hour later, feeling lazy from the outdoor play and exercise, Jason finger-combed his wet hair while keeping an eye on Honor. Since Lexie hadn't left her side, he watched them both.

God, he owed Lexie. More so every day, he realized she was exactly the type of friend Honor needed, and she'd always been there when needed most.

"Honor seems different."

Seeing that Sullivan was equally absorbed with the ladies, Jason nodded. "She's coming around. Today's been good for her."

Sullivan pondered that for far too long. "They're complete opposites. In a lot of ways, Lexie pushes her."

"In good ways," Jason agreed. "I was just thinking about that, in fact. You know they were kids when they met."

"Middle school, Lexie told me."

"Right. But even then, Lexie recognized what Honor was up against and she championed her. It's rare for family to be that loyal, but for a friend?"

"A kid." Sullivan fixed his possessive gaze on Lexie as she and Honor talked with Nathan and Hogan. "There's a lot more to Lexie than what you see at first glance."

"She's complicated," Jason agreed. "But she has a really good heart."

Still staring, Sullivan said, "Yeah." Just that, nothing more.

Jason noticed that Honor kept a watchful eye on Colt. Diesel was a hit with a girls, giving them all an excuse to stick close. When one of the girls hugged on to Colt's arm, Honor smiled with affection. The two of them might have joked about Honor being a pseudo-aunt, but if Jason had his way, she'd become one in reality.

Half under his breath, Sullivan muttered, "I think I under-estimated her."

"Honor?" She was so resilient he would never discount her success at anything she decided to do.

"No, I was talking about Lexie."

Interesting. "How so?"

Shoving his sunglasses to the top of his head, Sullivan scowled with stark confusion. "She's so damn sexy I might have missed other, more substantial things."

Jason gave Lexie a longer, more thorough look, scrutinizing her from head to toe. True, Honor's friend had a shapely, slender build. Add in the fluffy blond curls, the big hazel eyes, the seduc-tive attitude and smile, and most guys would be drawn to her.

But to him, when she stood next to Honor, there was only one woman to see.

"Guess I was always so focused on Honor I never paid that much attention."

Sullivan slanted him a look that clearly said: *Bullshit.* "You're not that obtuse."

"No, but from day one I've only seen Lexie as Honor's friend, so even if I did notice much about her, it was never personal for me."

"Probably a good thing," Sullivan said. He went back to de-vouring her with his attention.

Jason would have asked if they were getting serious, but Sul-livan was always serious, especially about his work and the kids he tried to help. It only made sense that he'd be serious about his relationship with Lexie, too. "Come on. Hogan's ready to serve and I don't want to be last in line."

Other neighbors helped man additional grills, but it was Vio-let who tended the second grill Hogan had set up. They worked side by side while other tables were loaded with a variety of do-nated side dishes.

Neighbors had spread out blankets and lawn chairs everywhere, especially in the shaded areas, as they claimed their favorite eating spots.

The local butcher who'd donated the meat got dibs on getting served first. He bypassed the hamburgers, hot dogs, brats and sausages, and instead snagged Hogan's ribs. Luckily the kids all seemed more interested in the other options.

Honor and Lexie met Sullivan and Jason at the grill in front of Hogan, who happily filled plates with ribs.

"For a man toiling in the sun," Lexie said, "you look mighty content."

While still serving, Hogan said, "That's because I finally nailed a job."

Surprised, Lexie widened her eyes. "No kidding? Good for you." She offered her fist and Hogan, after an eye roll, bumped it with his own.

Jason had found out about the job just that morning, but the others all took turns congratulating Hogan.

Violet, flushed from the heat of the grill, propped her hands on her hips. "We've been here cooking off and on all day, and you didn't mention it."

Hogan's attention strayed over her, then away. "It's not that big a deal."

Jason understood his brother's predicament. He and Violet had some heavy duty chemistry going on. Violet resisted, which probably made her more fascinating to Hogan. Under the circumstances, seeing no relief in sight, casual conversation wouldn't be conducive to Hogan's peace of mind.

Especially when other women were proving more accommodating.

Personally Jason considered it a losing battle for both of them.

After the mud volleyball, Violet had taken a dip, then somehow, somewhere, she'd changed from her bikini top into a floral halter that managed to be even sexier, especially with her cutoffs.

Her red hair was only half up, the ends curled from swimming, and she had a little too much sun on her nose and cheekbones.

The earthy look could inspire any red-blooded man; it definitely pushed Hogan's buttons, no matter how he tried to play it cool.

Jason whispered to Honor, "This ought to be entertaining."

Her fascinated gaze went back and forth from Violet to Hogan as if she'd never seen sexual sparks before.

Hogan rolled one shoulder. "It's boring stuff."

Arms crossed and hip cocked out, Violet asked, "What kind of stuff?" as if she had a very personal interest.

"Accounting."

Lexie tossed up her hands. "As I recall, you got peeved at me for pointing out how boring it is."

"It's not so boring," Sullivan said, "when the accountant saves you the headache of keeping impeccable records."

"Exactly." Hogan made an obvious effort not to look at Violet again.

"That might be true for some," Lexie conceded. "But it's clearly not Hogan's thing."

"I'm good at it," Hogan countered.

Violet gazed at him over her big sunglasses. "I'm bettin' you're good at all kinds of things."

"I am," he confirmed. "Want me to list them for you?"

Honor whispered, "Whoa," and Jason had to give her a one-armed hug. He wanted to eat, but it was clear Honor would rather wait to see how things worked out.

Hogan and Violet stared at each other, neither breaking eye contact.

"I'm curious," Lexie admitted. After a bite of meat, she said, "Mmm! Clearly barbecuing would be at the top of the list."

Releasing Violet from his stare, Hogan smirked at Lexie. "Unfortunately feeding the lot of you won't pay any bills." He

LORI FOSTER

slathered on more sauce. "The accounting job is local, the pay's decent and I'm anxious to get out of Jason's house."

"Hey," Jason said. "And here I thought I was a good host."

"The best. You've made Colt and me both feel welcome. But I prefer being on my own."

"I get that," Lexie said. "But this is like a calling or something."

Hogan shook his head and laughed.

Violet didn't. She looked thoughtful as she moved more corn on the cob onto a platter.

"If I get a vote," Jason said, "I like having you both around. When you are ready to leave, I hope you don't go too far."

Honor immediately chimed in. "I would miss you both horribly."

"We'll stay in the area," Hogan promised her, and then he put a serving of ribs on her plate.

Honor forked up a bite, and her eyes closed in pleasure. "Hogan, these are *amazing*."

He grinned. "You like to compliment people, honey."

"Only when it's true."

That got Violet moving. "Well, now I have to know." Setting aside her tongs and drying her hands on a dishcloth, she stepped over to Hogan's side and reached past him to grab a juicy chunk of meat right off Jason's plate.

"Hey," Jason complained.

"He's your brother," Violet told him. "He'll give you more." She popped it into her mouth, her expression analytical as she chewed. Then her eyes went heavy and she sighed. "Oh my god, that *is* good."

Hogan's neck muscles tightened in reaction.

"I need the recipe."

"No."

"Hogan," Violet warned. She smiled with evil intent. "You know I'm going to get it from you."

"Yeah," Lexie said, egging them on. "Give it to her."

Sullivan squeezed her for the innuendo, but he fought a smile.

"Not happening," Hogan said.

"Yes," Violet countered, her grill abandoned as she worked on him. "It's happening."

Leaving his brother to sort that one out on his own, Jason led Honor to the tableful of sides.

"That was intense," Honor whispered.

"Only because both of them are trying to deny the obvious."

She quirked a brow. "That they're interested?"

He shrugged. "At least in sex."

That had her frowning as she looked over the selection.

Others joined them, so she didn't mention Hogan again. Instead she chatted with the neighbors, her usual friendly self. But as Sullivan had said, she was different now. More...carefree.

With their plates filled, they headed to the blanket Honor and Lexie had spread out nearby. The sun had shifted and they no longer had as much shade.

Lexie stretched out her long bare legs and Honor turned her face up to the sun. It was peaceful, being here with Honor like this, sharing the moment with their friends.

As part of a local garage band, Nathan and his group fired up some music on a makeshift stage.

Stunned, Honor came to her knees to see. "Nathan plays the guitar?"

"And sings," Sullivan said.

He no sooner said it than Nathan began a fast-paced country song.

"Wow, he's really good!" Impressed, Honor moved so she could watch them while she ate. "I had no idea."

"Usually you'd hear them practicing on Tuesday evenings," Jason said, "since they mostly use Nathan's garage. But he was revamping the space to be better lit and more comfortable, so they've been going to Sam's basement instead."

"Do they have a name?" Lexie asked.

"Drunken Monkeys," Sullivan said.

Lexie loved it. "That's perfect!"

"The band's been around awhile, but when their lead singer retired and moved away, they were all ready to quit." Jason used one finger to ease a wayward lock of hair away from Honor's face. "Then Nathan moved in, and now the band has new life."

"I'm so impressed." She swayed to the music. "This town gets more interesting by the day."

Jason liked the sound of that.

In between serving others, Hogan and Violet sat with them, still debating whether Violet could have the recipe—and what she'd have to do for it.

Half an hour later their plates were empty and the music died as the band took a break so they could eat, too.

Honor heard a bark and searched the area for Colt. Surrounded by girls, Colt threw a ball and Diesel chased after it. The dog wallowed in the added attention.

Honor glanced at Hogan. "Shouldn't he come eat, too?"

Grinning, Hogan shook his head. "I'd say right now he has other things on his mind besides food."

Jason liked seeing Colt accepting the future as much as he enjoyed it with Honor. "He'll eat when he's hungry."

"He's far too much like his father and uncle," Violet said.

Hogan frowned at her. "Are you insulting my son?"

That made Violet and Lexie burst out laughing.

Honor smiled. "I believe she meant that Colt attracts women the same way."

Her smile mean, Violet said to Hogan, "But he's such a nice boy, I'm sure he's less of a reprobate than you."

"No doubt," Hogan replied with ironic pride.

Still insistent, Violet said, "Give me the recipe."

"Nope."

Groaning, Lexie tossed up her hands. "Know what I think?"

Hogan said, "Don't care," and he started to rise.

Grabbing for his arm, Lexie stated, "You should work for Violet."

He immediately choked.

Pretending to be helpful, Violet thwacked him on the back until he got away from her.

"It's not a bad idea," Violet said.

Hogan wheezed. "I just got a job as an accountant!"

"That's morning work, right?"

He glared. "Nine to five."

"So work for me on weekends." She stroked his shoulder. "You can be my official barbecue chef."

Eyes widening, Hogan looked at her hand with hot suspicion. "For what? Jollies?"

Lexie shoved him. "I'm trying to do you a solid here, you dolt. I watched you grill, I've eaten your food and seen your pride. You need to feed your passion."

"Will you two stop...*manhandling* me?"

Biting her lip, Lexie snickered. "Sorry."

Violet held up her hands. "Feed your passion, Hogan."

Harassed, Hogan growled, "I feed my passion on a regular basis."

Jason snorted over that. Sullivan pinched his mouth to keep from laughing. Lexie groaned.

Violet scooted closer. "Afraid of working for a woman?"

"Determined to make a living."

"I'll pay you well," she promised.

His smile taunted. "You know how I'd like to be paid."

Violet appeared ready to flatten him—until Honor snickered.

When everyone looked at her, she covered her mouth. "Sorry. Don't meant to interrupt. Carry on." But another strange, repressed giggling sound escaped. She tried biting her lips.

Lexie grinned at her. "It is pretty funny, isn't it?"

Nodding, Honor choked out another laugh, then completely

LORI FOSTER

lost it. She fell into Jason, laughing so hard she couldn't stay upright.

Jason caught her to him, his own smile flickering.

Robust friends surrounded her, bickering, teasing, harassing
and heckling each other. She'd spent so much time shut off from
the world, rejecting care and attention, and now she had it in
spades. He wanted her to accept him, to accept *them*—because
he didn't come alone. He was a package deal, all the chaos, in-
sanity and fun included.

Once Lexie joined in with Honor's amusement, the hilarity
proved infectious, and soon he was chuckling, too. Then Sullivan. Hogan shook his head, but he grinned ear to ear.

And finally Violet gave up and smiled. "Okay, what's so
funny?"

In a loud stage whisper, Hogan said, "I think we pushed her
over the edge."

Sullivan disagreed. "I think she knows you're both fighting
the inevitable."

"Possibly." Thrusting out her small hand to Hogan, Violet said, "Let's make a date to discuss a working arrangement."

Skepticism narrowed his eyes. "For my ribs?"

"To start with."

Not being a dummy, Hogan accepted her offer with alacrity.
"I get to pick the place."

She shrugged. "I get to pick the time."

They were all nuts, but it was days like this that Jason cherished. Family, friends, community…he wanted Honor to know
that she belonged.

With two fingers under her chin, Jason tipped up her face. Her
hair was caked with dried mud, her clothes limp and wrinkled
from her swim. She'd laughed so hard she had tears in her eyes.
And she was absolutely beautiful. "You done being hysterical?"

"I don't know." Another fit of giggles took her before she
sucked in a shaky breath and nodded. Looking around at each

of their friends crowded on the blanket with them, she said, "You're all pretty wonderful."

"At the very least," Hogan said, "we're entertaining."

"You're so much more than that. All of you." She grinned. "Thank you for showing me such a great time."

People often shared polite platitudes without really meaning them. Honor gave gratitude from the heart.

"Stick around." As he stood, Hogan squeezed her shoulder. "We'll have a repeat real soon."

"Next weekend at Screwy Louie's." Sullivan turned to Violet. "Nathan's playing, isn't he?"

"He is. We're making it a luau." She winked at Honor. "Bring your grass skirt."

"Fun!" Lexie floundered. "That is—"

Sullivan brushed his knuckles over her cheek. "I'm already looking forward to seeing your hula dance."

Buoyed by that, her smile returned. "You're on."

Sullivan brought her to her feet with him. "I'm going to get all the garbage together. Want to help?"

"Happy to."

Honor started to stand. "I'll lend a hand."

"Afraid not." Hogan stayed her with a pat on the shoulder. "No first-timers are allowed to do cleanup. Just relax."

"Next time," Violet promised her.

Together, debating the finer details of their deal, Hogan and Violet went off to close down the grills.

"Lexie is a first-timer, too."

"But Sullivan isn't, and he wants to keep her close." *Like I want to keep you close.*

Instead of arguing as Jason expected her to do, Honor went flat to her back, her arms folded behind her head. She looked up at the sky, her gaze wistful. "It was such a beautiful day."

So the heat and humidity hadn't fazed her?

By rights, given the life she'd led and her recent loss, the boisterous crowds should have thrown her off her axis. Instead she'd joined in the fun and activity wholeheartedly.

Stretching out on his side next to her, Jason propped up on an elbow. He wanted to kiss her. He flat-out *wanted* her. But that could wait until tonight.

He lightly tugged at a lock of her hair. "You're going to need a shower to get rid of the rest of the mud."

Her mouth lifted in a secret smile. "You, too."

His shower was bigger—but by silent agreement, they'd kept all intimate activities to her house. It wasn't that Hogan or Colt would judge, but Honor was private, Colt still a minor and Jason didn't mind adjusting a little to be with her.

The way she rested, her T-shirt had pulled up and he could see a smooth strip of flesh between the hem of the shirt and the waistband of her shorts. Using just his fingertips, he touched her.

"It's strange," she said in a thoughtful way, turning her head to see him. "Not having my phone on me, I mean."

She'd left it in a pocket of their soft-sided cooler. With her grandfather gone, there was no urgency, no reason to be constantly alert.

For years she'd gotten pulled into every conflict, every health issue, every family squabble, all while knowing one of those calls could be the one telling her that her grandfather had died. He couldn't imagine how awful that must have been, the stress it had carved into her everyday life.

"I hope, eventually, you'll be able to forget about your phone completely."

Sadness shaded her gaze, but she blinked it away and chose to tease him instead. "With you right next door, you never call, you just walk over. So forgetting the phone is possible."

Was that her way of telling him he was important to her? Jason hoped so.

Abruptly she turned to her side so that they faced each other. Wrapped up in her thoughts, her feelings, he still noticed the

don't tempt me

silhouette of her body, the dip of her waist, the flare of her hip, the shapely length of her thighs. Emotional and physical needs warred for attention.

Honor picked at a thread in the blanket. "I'd gotten into the habit of staying superbusy so I wouldn't dwell on it."

That helped explain the long hours she kept, except… "I don't think it worked." This was the first time he'd really seen her completely relaxed. Before her grandfather's death, she'd always been so subtly alert, almost vigilant. He hadn't understood…until now.

"He was fading away," she whispered. "It tormented me."

He laced his fingers with hers. Such small, soft hands, but also so incredibly capable. "When you care for people, they're never far from your thoughts, no matter what you do." He knew that, because Honor was always in the forefront of his brain.

He liked it that way.

All around them people talked, played, worked. The music from the band thrummed in his heart; he noticed Honor's foot moving to the tune. Little by little she learned to let go.

He wanted to help her with that.

She went flat to her back again, her fingers laced in his so that their hands rested over her midriff. "Today I realized that fun has the same distracting effect. Maybe even better than work."

Hoping to be further enlightened, Jason gave her a verbal nudge. "Yeah? How so?"

Lashes swept down to hide her eyes, but he knew it was in peace, not embarrassment, because the corners of her mouth tipped up. "At first I was worried about sucking at volleyball."

"In the mud? Everyone sucks. That's the point."

"Ha!" She swiveled her head toward him with teasing accusation. "You guys were rabid, sliding around, diving in to get the ball. Even Lexie. I worried about disappointing the rest of you. But then I got so into it I forgot everything except winning." Pride brightened her eyes, and her smile further warmed. "Winning was a huge adrenaline rush."

He felt her acceptance in his heart. "We've created a competitive monster."

"Maybe." Different emotions passed over her face, then eased into contentment. "Granddad always wanted me to get more involved. So many times he encouraged me to join a club or sign up for a sport at school. But I never even went to a dance."

Which was a testament to how her deadbeat parents had affected her. "I bet he's happy now, knowing you took part."

"Yes." She again closed her eyes. "I think he is."

They fell into a comfortable silence. Jason didn't mind because he realized that her being like this, totally at ease, unworried, spoke volumes, telling him more than words could.

Mired in thoughts of a future with Honor, he didn't notice Diesel running toward them, wet from the creek, his tail swinging with joy, until he leaped into the middle of the blanket with a happy bark.

Honor squealed and ducked, Jason rolled to the side and still Diesel got them both with sloppy wet kisses and muddy paws.

Laughing, Honor held his furry face, saying, "What in the world?"

As Jason caught his leash, he saw Colt jogging toward them. "Sorry! He got away from me."

Colt, too, was wet and shirtless. A pretty, dark-haired girl trailed him. Clearly they'd all just come from a swim.

Her gaze bouncing back and forth from Colt to the girl, Honor said, "We've got him now. Why don't you and your friend grab some food while you still can? They're putting things away right now."

Colt hesitated, but not for long. "You sure?"

More than ready to play Cupid, she nodded fast. "Positive."

When the girl reached his side, Colt brought her forward

with a hand at the small of her back. "This is Charish. She only lives a few blocks away."

Honor beamed at her.

Jason stood and offered his hand.

Anyone could see the girl was smitten, given the way she gazed adoringly at Colt. And since she wore only miniscule cutoffs with a bathing suit top, and had a real cute figure, Colt was more than appreciative of the attention.

After introductions, the young adults wandered off hand in hand, leaving Honor with an engaging grin.

Soon as they were far enough away, she grabbed Jason's arm. "Did you see her? She's so pretty!"

Pretty—and stacked. Jason patted the dog absently. "I believe Colt noticed that, as well."

"I'm so happy for him." She gazed toward a small group of high school kids now joining Colt and Charish in the line to steal the last of the food. "This could be the start of things."

"Don't marry him off yet, honey. He's got another year of high school."

Going bright red, Honor sputtered, caught his grin and gave him a light push. "You know what I meant. The start of friendship and fitting in and…and being happy here."

"I hope so." Jason wanted that for both of them. "Clearbrook is a nice town. Over time it's changed and grown, gotten bad and now better again." Much better with Honor around. Drawing her attention away from Colt, he tipped up her chin. "It's a great place to put down roots."

"Today has been so amazing." More mellow, she smiled. "I woke with you. Then you gave me those amazing shutters."

"I'm glad you like them."

"*Love* them," she corrected. "Then I not only played volleyball for the first time, I played in the mud—and our team won."

"Twice. But we also lost."

"Another wonderful first. Swimming in the creek was great, too."

"You didn't use the rope swing yet."

Eyes mischievous, she said, "Next time."

Meaning she planned to come back with him? He liked that plan. "Deal."

"I loved hearing Nathan play, and eating Hogan's ribs, and meeting some of the other neighbors and…" She hugged him. "I especially liked doing all those things with you."

Not kissing her was impossible, but Jason tried to keep it brief. "Me, too," he whispered.

"If Colt could find some happiness, that'd be the perfect ending to a most perfect day."

And speaking of endings… "You ready to head home?" He needed her. Now. But he made up other excuses to sway her. "Diesel could probably use a rest, and I'd rather he eat his dog food than all the scraps he keeps finding on the ground."

"I'm actually a little tuckered out, too." Covering her mouth with a hand, she yawned, then said sleepily, "But not *too* tired, just so you know."

He had to be the luckiest man around. Because she'd had a full day, he'd wait until tomorrow to tell her so—and hope she felt the same.

16

HAPPINESS, TRUE HAPPINESS, had always seemed such an elusive thing. Honor thought she'd known it, but until Jason, she hadn't even scratched the surface. He'd brought so much amazing depth to her life that now hope was easier, joy richer, passion so much hotter. Contentment, once so elusive, warmed her like a sunny day.

She needed to tell him how she felt. It was possible that for him, their relationship wasn't anything special. He might have shared the same with Violet or some other woman. Even many women. She wasn't experienced enough to know if, for him, it was only mutual respect, sexual attraction and…convenience.

An awful possibility, but she had to admit, having him right next door was beyond perfect.

If he wasn't as over-the-moon crazy for her as she was for him, she'd deal with it.

And she'd take what he offered all the same because it was more than she'd ever expected.

With so many things on her mind, all of them centered on Jason, it was no wonder she didn't at first notice her family had come to visit.

They were just circling to the front of the house when Diesel's sudden fit of furious barking brought her focus back to the here and now.

Looking very out of place, her aunt Celeste's shiny black Town Car and driver waited at the curb while Celeste stood staring at Honor's house with a slightly curled lip.

And not just Celeste. Janet, Gina and Terry had also accompanied her, though it appeared they'd driven separately, given the second sleek, new-model Mercedes.

Honor's stomach cramped with dread.

When her family looked at her, their disdain remained. Honor had the awful suspicion it had nothing to do with her muddy, wrinkled clothes.

Jason calmed Diesel, but it wasn't easy. The dog disliked them all on sight. She thought of all the people at the picnic whom Diesel had greeted with a wagging tail, but now he turned protective, just as he had when her father came to call.

The dog had amazing instincts.

"Shh." She put a hand on Diesel's scruff, and finally he settled. "It's okay."

He stationed himself beside her, still alert but now only giving a very low growl.

"That dog sounds vicious."

Doing her best to hide her unease, Honor stared at her Aunt Celeste. "He can be."

Near her ear, Jason whispered, "Remember, you're not alone."

But in this, with them, she'd rather be alone—and for once, she could admit why.

It shamed her to have family loathe her so openly. She used to think that spoke of her character.

Now she knew it only spoke of theirs.

"Have you been rolling in the mud?" Janet asked with disbelief.

"Yes."

That left them all in silence.

Sighing, Honor asked Celeste, "Why are you here?"

Never one to quibble, her great-aunt got right to the point

of her visit. "As I'm sure you know by now, I inherited Hugh's home."

"Yes, of course." Neil was privy to everything her grandfather had done, and he hadn't minded sharing. "You're his sister. It makes sense for you to have it."

After a brief scrutiny, Celeste sent a smug smile at the others.

Had they complained? No doubt. They were all mercenary in their hunger for her grandfather's wealth.

Celeste moved closer. "Though it wasn't specified in any documents, there are items there you might like to claim before I sell it."

That statement, given with so much disregard, took Honor back a step. "Sell it?"

Her aunt Janet snapped, "Of course she's selling. You're the only one who got cash, so what choice does she have."

After a visual rebuke at Janet, Celeste softened her rigid manner. "I know it has sentimental value for you, Honor, but I don't need a second home. Neither Gina nor Janet, and certainly not Terry, can afford to purchase it."

"Not that we would anyway," Gina said. "It's like a mausoleum, badly in need of updates."

For so many years, Granddad had been ill, too ill to worry about modernizing the decor. Everything remained in perfect working order, thanks to an estate manager, but updating style and color hadn't been a consideration. Thinking of the old-fashioned, well-worn flocked wallpaper in the study, the dark wooden paneling in the library, left her with a pang of regret. She could almost smell those rooms, feel the warmth of them, see how the sunlight filtered in past the heavy drapes.

Regardless of the incredible amount of cash she'd inherited, Honor knew it wasn't near enough to buy her grandfather's lavish home, much less maintain it.

As if he understood, Jason rested a hand on her shoulder.

"It's just a house," Celeste said with sharp impatience. "Selling it makes sense."

For Honor, it was so much more than that. It had been a refuge from the hurt of abandonment. Now, however, she had her own home—next door to Jason. She was no longer a lost, emotionally wounded kid. She had to remember that.

Loosening her shoulders, she nodded. "Yes, I understand."

"Because you lived there," Celeste said, earning a few grumbles from the other aunts who held back, "I'm offering to let you get your things—if you want them."

Janet snapped, "They're *not* her things! She came to him with *nothing*."

"And she's already gotten more than enough," Gina added. "Everything else should be sold."

"Be silent," Celeste snapped. "You weren't invited along for this visit."

"We couldn't let you come alone," Gina said with just as much heat. "Losing Hugh has made you as sentimental as he was with her. If we don't look out for you, you'll be giving her everything else."

"Like my father?" Honor asked. "Was that one of your gifts, Aunt Celeste?"

Silence fell around them. To Honor, it felt anticipatory, almost gleeful, at least from Janet, Gina and Terry.

Celeste, who'd always been more subtle in her possible dislike, merely shifted her stance. "So he did come to see you?"

"Yes." When she said nothing more, offering up no information, Celeste huffed her annoyance.

"There's no reason to be coy." Frowning, Celeste asked, "Did you reconcile?"

Honor lifted her chin. "I told him to go away and never come back."

It took a few seconds; then the smile slowly creased Celeste's papery cheeks. "Good for you."

That threw Honor, but only for a second. Her hands fisted and she leaned in. "Why would you do that to me?"

"To shake you out of your doldrums, of course."

Such careless disrespect for her feelings shouldn't have surprised her, but for some reason, this time it did. For once letting her aunt see her inner turmoil, Honor whispered, "It was incredibly cruel."

"It was a dose of reality." Unconcerned, Celeste lifted her chin. "You need to understand that your father was never worthy of your remorse."

Refreshing anger blunted some of the hurt. "Have you never heard of communication?"

The sharp tone lowered her great-aunt's brows, but Honor didn't care.

"You could have *talked* with me, Celeste. You could have shown an ounce of acceptance." *You could have cared...just a little.* "That's what civilized, caring people do."

"You had a much better life with my brother than you would have had with your father."

"I already knew that!"

Unruffled by her outburst, Celeste shook her head. "No, dear, you clung to the conviction that somehow you were to blame. Why else would you have not moved on?"

Honor automatically glanced at her other aunts, who throughout her youth had taken every opportunity to point out her circumstances. How could she have believed otherwise, when their every breath proclaimed her an interloper?

Celeste rolled her eyes. "If by now you don't understand how petty, small-minded and weak they are, then there's no hope for you at all."

While Honor stood there, completely overcome, the others started rapid-fire accusations, pointing out in a dozen different ways how it was Honor's fault, not theirs.

One commanding glare from Celeste silenced them. She'd always been a powerful force in the family, the only one to stand up to Hugh, and now with him gone, she'd taken the position as matriarch. Clearly the others understood that.

To Honor, it didn't matter. She'd been loyal to her grandfather out of love. Sadly the strongest emotion she'd had toward the rest of the family was guilt…and that was all but gone.

Celeste straightened the sleeves of her blouse, patted her hair and faced Honor again. "Now, back to Hugh's home, which *will* be sold. There's your bedroom suite, school papers of yours that Hugh saved and a few photos of the two of you together that I thought you might like to relocate—" Again she looked at Honor's house, and finally said with distaste, "Here."

Not knowing what else to do, Honor nodded. She didn't need the furniture, but she'd love to have the photos. "That would be wonderful, thank you. When would it be convenient for you?"

Ignoring that, Celeste flattened her mouth with revulsion. "This is ridiculous."

Behind her, Jason stiffened.

Honor girded herself, then asked, "What is?"

"You living here." She gestured at the house. "It's a hovel."

Ice crawled down her spine. "It's my *home*."

"I've done what I can in the ways that I know how. Apparently plain speaking is all that's left." She drew a sharp breath. "It's past time to give up this preposterous pride."

Her pride was *not* preposterous. For many years, it had been all she had. "I don't know what you're talking about."

Celeste leveled her censuring gaze. "Even you must realize that this miniscule shed is hardly suitable for Hugh Mefford's granddaughter, especially since he ensured that you can now buy something much, much nicer."

Jason's hand on her shoulder tightened. "Honor…"

She glanced at him over her shoulder. Both he and Diesel looked worried. *For her.*

Because they cared.

Her heart seemed to fill up her chest, warming her from the inside out, pushing away all the feelings of hurt and insecurity.

Smiling to reassure Jason, she said, "It's okay." *I'm* okay.

After quickly searching her face, he nodded.

Turning back to her relatives, she stated, "I love my house, every broken inch of it. I'm fixing it up, doing much of the work myself, and I *love* it." To keep Jason from getting involved, she stated it outright. "Under no circumstances am I selling it."

Terry laughed. "How can you even call that mess a house? You're angling for something more, aren't you? What else is it you want?"

Ignoring the continued insults, Honor declared, "It's my house and I'm keeping it."

For once, Celeste aligned herself with the others. "Fine. Perhaps you can get some rent from it. But surely—"

"You misunderstand." Honor moved closer to her aunt, doing what she could to protect Jason from the ugliness of her family. "I like my life here, Aunt Celeste. No, I *love* my life here. Clearbrook is home. I'm not moving."

"You stole his money," Gina accused.

Done with it, Honor snapped, "Then take the cash. I don't care."

Gina looked hopeful until Celeste intruded. "She's not giving it to you, Gina, so be quiet. My brother wanted her to have it, and by God, that's what will happen." Then to Honor, she added, "You can surely afford a real home now."

"This is a real home. *My* home."

Celeste narrowed her gaze first on Honor, then to Jason, and fashioned a look of cunning assumption. "It's not my business."

"No, it isn't."

"You've always done just as you please." Losing interest, she added, "Anytime this week before three would be fine to come gather a few mementos. My Realtor will be there to greet you."

Disappointed but resigned, Honor said, "Thank you."

Janet glared at her. "You think you're so noble, don't you?" Without giving Honor a chance to respond, she turned her cannon on Jason. "And you. Even Honor can't be naive enough to think you actually care. When did this courtship start anyway? I'm betting it was after she inherited."

Gina snickered, and Terry, unable to control herself, sneered, "He's *using* you, Honor. Open your eyes, already."

"They deserve each other," Terry said.

Bright fury stole her usual calm. *"You will all shut up!"*

At her commanding roar, everyone went still.

Jason stared at her in surprise, Diesel went still with uncertainty. Gina and Terry glanced around in worry.

Sucking in air, Honor reached for some measure of recognizable calm.

Then Janet stiffened. "The truth hurts, doesn't it?"

Renewed anger brought Honor charging forward. "You petty, mean-spirited idiot. That's enough out of you!"

"Honor," Jason said quietly. "It's fine."

"No, it is not fine." She encompassed Janet, Gina and Terry in her rage. "I've had just about enough of your combined stupidity. I've let you all have your say, nasty as it's been. But you will *not* come onto my property and insult my friends."

Janet started to speak.

Leaning into her, Honor whispered with menace, "Say it. I dare you."

Janet clamped her mouth shut.

Satisfied with that reaction, Honor looked at them each again. "Get out, all three of you, and don't ever come back."

Shaken, big tears welled in Janet's eyes and she spun away on a sob. Terry put an arm around her, quick to offer comfort, though she'd given no backup at all.

Gina stood there gaping in shock.

And into the tense silence, Celeste clapped. "Bravo."

Honor rounded on her, only to see her smile.

"I guess Hugh wasn't wrong about your inner fire. It just took a man to bring it out."

"No," Jason denied. "It was always there. It's one of the things I first admired about her."

After a lengthy pause, Celeste nodded approval. "I believe you." She turned back to Honor. "Let me know when you're coming by the house. I'll meet you. Perhaps we'll do lunch." Assuming Honor's compliance, Celeste put a hand on Gina to get her moving, and shortly Honor's unwanted visitors were gone.

As if the entire visit hadn't been momentous, Celeste waved as the driver drove off.

Depleted, Honor stiffened her legs to keep from stumbling. She felt like she'd been under siege and had just succeeded in fending off an enemy. Her stomach churned and her eyes burned. She struggled to calm her breathing.

With them now gone, the quiet neighborhood came alive with singing birds, a chirping squirrel and the rustle of leaves in the many trees.

Grateful that the others were still at the picnic and hadn't witnessed her loss of control, Honor kept her back to Jason.

When Diesel snuffled against her hand, she knew she had to say something. "I'm sorry. That was pretty awful."

"No," Jason said. "That was wonderful." Gently he turned her to face him, showing her a slight pleased smile. "I'm so damn proud of you."

Unbelievable. "*Proud?* My family despises me and I clearly can't deal with them." She covered her face. "I screamed like a maniac."

Jason tugged down her hands. "You should be sainted for how patiently you've dealt with them. No one could have done better."

"You really believe that?"

"Silly, Honor." He put his forehead to hers. "You're beautiful inside and out. If they don't see that, it's their fault, not yours."

LORI FOSTER

That made her both blush and sigh.

"Sometimes it's impossible to know what makes people the way they are. But that group is so petty and spiteful, I'm pretty sure they despise themselves the most."

She'd often wondered that herself, if maybe they were all so miserably unhappy because they couldn't find any inner peace. "Maybe."

Diesel leaned against her leg. She looked down at him, then knelt for a furry hug.

"He loves you," Jason said.

Honor nodded, but she knew Jason saw the truth. "He's fond of all of us, and he's especially protective of me. But you know he's Colt's dog, right?"

"Yeah, I know. Hogan just hasn't realized it yet."

Hogan still had a few things to settle, but he was overall a terrific dad. How else could Colt have turned out so amazing? "If he doesn't take Diesel with him when he moves, I'll keep him. But I hope that doesn't happen."

"Me, too." Jason pulled her back to her feet. "You're okay?"

She nodded, laced her hand in his and started toward his porch. The dog needed to eat, drink and rest after all his activity. "When I offered my inheritance to Janet—"

"It's yours to do with as you please."

"I know it wasn't a factor for you." She needed him to understand that.

"Whatever you want, honey. Okay? Keep it, give it away, burn it for all I care."

Such a remarkable man. She wasn't certain of much, but she knew Jason wasn't a man lured by money. "I wouldn't have really given it to Gina anyway. Aunt Celeste is right that Granddad wanted me to have it, and I'd already decided what to do with it."

"When was this?"

"At the picnic."

He opened his front door and unleashed Diesel, who ambled off for the kitchen and his bowls. "And?"

Honor stripped off her muddy shoes, then set them outside the door on the porch. "I want to finish fixing up my house."

One brow went up. He pulled off his shoes too, put them beside hers, then reached inside to hang the leash on the hook by the door. "You could easily rebuild it many times over with what he left you."

They stepped into the cooler interior. "But I don't want that."

"If your family made you uncomfortable about the house, it really does have potential—"

"I know, but it has nothing to do with them. When people look at the house, I want them to see what I see. It's a lot smaller than your home, but I think it can still be as beautiful." *And it's right next door to you.*

"Absolutely. It has loads of character. All it needs is some TLC."

God, she loved him. Getting excited, she shared her plans. "I want to completely remodel the kitchen and bathroom, but keep the look."

"Totally doable."

"And I need a new roof, landscaping, maybe windows—and I can't wait to hang those incredible shutters you made."

Jason touched her bottom lip. "Whatever you want, honey."

His mood confused her. He'd just seen the ugliness, but instead of being put off by it, he was warm and demonstrative. Maybe now was as good a time as any to discuss the other conclusions she'd reached at the picnic.

Taking a breath, she asked, "Will you help me with everything?"

His slow smile held a wealth of pleasure. "I'd love to."

She'd anticipated that reply, but still she burst with happiness. "Thank you."

"I've always enjoyed working with my hands. Working with you is especially satisfying."

"I can pay you—"

His thumb over her lips silenced her. "Don't go there."

Since she'd anticipated that, too, she smiled against his touch. "Okay."

"I love lending you a hand, Honor. I love being with you. You need to understand that."

Crazy hope blossomed, full and sweet, and this time it didn't scare her...much. He was so open, and he'd used that *L* word repeatedly.

"Do you..." Her courage flagged, but she rallied. "Do you maybe love me, too? Just a little?"

"I love you. Not a little, but a lot."

That husky declaration stole her breath. She stared at him for a few seconds before she could breathe, "Yes?"

Laughing, he looped his arms around her and lifted her off her feet. "I wouldn't mind hearing it back."

Honor squeezed him tight. "I really, really love you, too."

"I'm glad." He set her back and cradled her head in his palms. "You realize this leaves us with a conundrum."

Whatever it was, she knew it wouldn't matter. "What's that?"

"We'll have two houses when we only need one."

He just kept throwing her off balance. Pulse racing, she squeaked, "One?"

"I love you. You love me. After we get married, we'll live together, right?"

Her eyes rounded, her heart jumped into Mach speed, and she barely suppressed a squeal. *"Marriage?"*

"I want to spend the rest of my life with you."

Oh my God. Now she wished Lexie was here to share the moment with her. Soon as possible, though, she'd call her.

"Honor?"

"Yes. Yes, yes, *yes!*"

Jason caught her to him, his mouth on hers as he made his way to the couch.

"No!" She stiff-armed him. "We're both a mess. I don't want to hurt your furniture."

He thought about that, lifted her higher so she could wrap her legs around him, then pivoted around and went back to the front door. "We need that shower."

"And then I need you."

Still holding her, his big hands splayed over her bottom for support, he bounded across the yard to the side door that opened into her kitchen.

As he carried her inside, she said, "I can't sell it."

"Then don't. I don't care which house we live in."

His attitude was empowering. "I want to live in your house."

"Sounds good." He kissed her neck, her shoulder, as he headed to the bathroom.

Honor tunneled her fingers into his cool, thick hair. "I can't rent it to just anyone, either."

"So you'll wait until you find someone special. Someone who will love it every bit as much as you do." He set her in the bathroom and turned to start the shower. "Until then, we'll just enjoy remodeling it."

"If you're sure—"

He whisked her shirt off over her head. "I'm sure I love you and I want you. That's what matters."

Honor agreed.

It was a few hours more before everyone else closed up the picnic. By then, Jason and Honor were sitting out back, enjoying the star-filled evening sky. It was too hot for a fire, but they'd lit torches meant to keep the mosquitoes away.

Diesel slept nearby, secure, happy...much like Honor.

Sullivan and Lexie joined them first.

Unable to contain herself, Honor launched from her seat and ran to Lexie the second she emerged from the woods.

Slowly Jason stood, watching Honor as he, too, approached. He heard her talking a mile a minute, most of it jumbled praise for him.

Wide-eyed, Lexie listened with confusion. "Slow down. You're losing me."

Honor drew a breath.

"I love her," Jason said, anxious to get to the point. "We're getting married."

Lexie went blank, then she screeched and, together, she and Honor danced around in a way that made him smile crookedly.

Sullivan hugged Honor, then clapped Jason on the shoulder. "Congratulations."

Jason couldn't stop smiling. "Thanks."

Seconds later, Colt jogged into the yard, Hogan behind him.

They pulled up short when they spotted them casually talking, with Diesel back to sleep.

Confused, Colt said, "I heard a scream."

Honor laughed. "That was Lexie."

Cocking a brow, Hogan said, "And she screamed...why?"

Barely able to contain herself, Honor smiled up at him. "Jason and I are going to get married."

It was a toss-up who was more excited by that, Honor or Colt. Taking her by surprise, Colt lifted her in his arms and spun in a circle.

Hogan grinned ear to ear. "Looks like I found work just in the nick of time."

Honor froze. "Hogan, *no!*" She quickly disengaged from Colt. "I would never—"

"Of course you wouldn't." He took his own turn hugging her off her feet. "But since I was planning to move anyway, I'll just make sure I'm gone in time."

Honor didn't look at all happy with that idea. As she gazed at

Colt, she patted his shoulder. "It doesn't need to be right away. Jason and I are planning to finish remodeling my house, and then I have to find the right person to live there, and—"

Lexie raised a hand. "Can I put in dibs?"

Honor brightened again, but before she could get too excited over that, Sullivan spoke up.

"You'll be with me."

Lexie tipped her head at him. "With you?"

Put on the spot, Sullivan glanced around at their rapt faces, then took her hand. "Come on. We need to talk privately."

Lexie didn't budge. "About what?"

"About how I want you to move in."

She went still, both brows up as she drew in a breath. "You want me to move in with you?"

"Yes."

"Because…?"

He scooped her in for a kiss; then against her mouth, with the others looking on, he whispered, "Because I'm falling in love with you."

After the kiss, it took a second for it to sink in and then Lexie said with enthusiasm, "Oh!"

Sullivan kissed her again, fast and hard. "Tell me you feel the same."

"Heck yes."

"So you'll move in?"

"Living with you will be even better than living across the street from you."

Anxious to get her alone, Sullivan again started away.

Glancing back at Honor, Lexie said, "Don't make wedding plans without me! I just need twenty minutes."

"An hour," Sullivan corrected.

Lexie laughed. "Lucky me."

Squeezing her, Sullivan said, "I need the hour to explain how

LORI FOSTER

much I care, to apologize for being an ass and to tell you how amazing you are."

Beaming, Lexie said to Honor, "So give us an hour and twenty minutes, because I have a few needs, too."

Jason shook his head. Honor's friend was hilariously outrageous, and pretty damn wonderful. "It's late. Let's all talk in the morning."

Hand to her heart, Lexie said, "You are a fantastic man, Jason Guthrie. Congrats on grabbing a real prize." She blew Honor a kiss. "I'll see you bright and early." Then she took the lead and soon had Sullivan racing her for his front door.

Laughing, Jason hugged Honor close. "Guess Lexie won't be taking your house after all, but she'll still be close at hand."

"I'm thrilled for her," Honor said. "And even happier that she'll be nearby."

Hogan cleared his throat. "If it's okay, if you don't mind having me that close, I'd love to take your house. I can even help with the remodeling."

Turning with a renewed squeal, Honor launched herself at Hogan and started bouncing with him the same way she'd done with Lexie—only Hogan didn't reciprocate. He just laughed and tried to calm her.

Hands on her shoulders, he said, "You should know that means dog hair, because even though Colt pretended Diesel was for you, he'll be with us."

Colt grinned. "Seriously?"

"He's your dog," Hogan said. "I'm not obtuse."

Colt hugged his dad.

"I love Diesel!" Honor exclaimed, her eyes warm as she watched father and son embrace. "Of course he'll go wherever Colt goes."

As they separated, Hogan said, "It also means a ton of teenage mess, because on his best day Colt is seriously sloppier than Jason on his worst day."

"Uncle Jason is a neat freak," Colt accused around a grin. "I'm not that bad."

"You're *perfect*," Honor told him, tears welling in her eyes. She sniffed, her voice breaking. "And I would be *thrilled* for you both to take my house."

"Hey." Feeling indulgent, Jason turned her into his chest and rocked her. Both Hogan and Colt looked devastated, but he wasn't worried. "She's okay," he told them. "Just happy."

"So very, very happy," she agreed. She wiped her eyes and smiled tremulously.

"Because you'll have your family so close?" Colt guessed.

That he included himself as family had Honor welling up even more. She sniffled again, nodded hard and said, "Yes."

Jason smoothed back her hair. "That's as it always should be."

She agreed. "At least, when the family is this wonderful."

Hogan elbowed his son. "We'll have to be on our best behavior so we don't disillusion her."

"You couldn't," Honor swore. "I love Jason so much, but I love you both, too."

"Ditto." Colt mussed her hair. "And now you can really be Aunt Honor."

That so overwhelmed her the tears spilled over.

"Come on." Jason started her back toward her house. "You guys will kill the torches and take Diesel in?"

"Sure," Hogan said.

"Then we'll see you both in the morning."

"Good night, Aunt Honor."

She choked out, "Good night."

"Sleep well, hon."

She gave a wave to Hogan.

Grinning, Hogan and Colt headed in.

Her voice little more than a whisper, Honor asked, "Do you mind staying with me until we're married?"

"Long as we're together, it doesn't matter to me."

"Can we get married in the yard? Your yard is so beautiful."

He smiled. "Whatever you want."

"Do you think Nathan would play at the wedding?"

Jason had to laugh. "I'm sure the sheriff would be honored. But he only seems to know country music."

"It'll be so perfect."

Though she didn't realize it, *she* was perfect. Until Honor, he hadn't known anything was missing from his life. Now, having her with him, he didn't think it could get any better.

But just as they stepped inside, she said, "Jason?"

"Hmm?"

She peeked up at him, her eyes wet, her smile tender. "How do you feel about kids?"

Slowly, as the idea sank in, Jason smiled. "I've built some very cool playhouses and backyard gyms." Life with Honor would be about love—no matter how big their family grew. And that would always make it as perfect as perfect could be.

★ ★ ★ ★ ★

The Guthrie Brothers will return in
WORTH THE WAIT,
from Lori Foster and HQN Books!

Meanwhile, look for
UNDER PRESSURE,
the first in Lori's explosive new series.

For the men of the Body Armor agency,
the only thing more dangerous than the job they do
is the risk of losing their hearts.

Read on
for an exclusive sneak peek...

Lori Foster

EXCERPT FROM
Under Pressure

1

LEESE PHELPS STOOD in the cold early-evening air, his breath frosting in front of him, lights from the nearby bus station blinking in an annoying mismatched pattern.

Behind him, completely hidden in the shadows, his friend Justice complained, "My balls are freezing."

Still watching the surrounding area, Leese said, "You should try wearing underwear."

"The ladies would protest. They like me commando."

Leese started to smile—until a shadow shifted from the right side of an alley that bisected the station from a cheap hotel. He said, "Shh."

"This is it?" Justice whispered. "You see her?"

"Quiet." Leese pressed farther back into the darkness, his gaze alert, his senses zinging.

A woman, small in stature, emerged dragging an enormous suitcase with a broken wheel. As it tried to pull her sideways, she relentlessly forced it through slush and blackened snow. Her narrowed gaze scanned the area with nervous awareness.

Leese didn't move, but still her attention shot back in his direction. She stared, watchful and wary, until he stepped out.

Trying not to look threatening, Leese propped a shoulder on the brick facade of the vacated building. He glanced at her, then away, as if dismissing her.

She continued to stare.

Now what to do?

"What's happening?" Justice whispered.

"Nothing. Be quiet."

The girl wore jeans with snow boots, a puffy coat that covered her to her knees and a black stocking cap pulled down over her ears. Straight brown hair stuck out from the bottom.

When she finally looked away, it was to drop the suitcase and whip around, facing the way she'd come.

Two men stepped out, followed by a third.

The third smiled at her. "Going somewhere, Cat? Without saying goodbye?"

Suspicions confirmed, Leese watched Catalina Nicholson take a defiant stance. That didn't surprise him. As soon as he was given the assignment, he'd learned what he could of her.

She came from a wealthy family of lawyers and CEOs, people with far-reaching political and business connections. They were the movers and shakers of the world, influencing other powerful people effortlessly.

But Catalina had bucked convention by becoming an elementary school art teacher, something her family hadn't liked. She clearly enjoyed her luxuries but wanted to earn them herself. Some inheritances helped to pave the way on that, but from all reports, she'd proven herself to be headstrong and independent. Small in size but not in attitude.

Here, in the slums of Danbrook, Ohio, she was far away from her usual routine of dealing with middle-class families and their grade school children.

"That's right, Wayne," she said, her voice strong. "I'm leaving."

"I don't think so," the man called Wayne said, and his two cronies moved to surround her. "Not just yet. Not until you pay up on all those promises you made."

Strangely enough, Catalina looked back at Leese again, her expression a touch desperate.

Even from the distance, he felt her silent request for help.

"Stay put unless you see that I need you," Leese told Justice. He was pretty sure he could handle things—without drawing his gun—but there was always a chance he'd cause a ruckus and then, to protect her, they'd need to make a run for it. "Be ready with the car."

Justice grumbled, "I miss all the fun."

Stepping out, his boots crunching in the frozen snow, Leese headed toward her in a casual stride.

Relief took the starch out of her shoulders. If he could defuse things without violence, that'd be for the best. Right now the bus station was all but empty. But if a brawl broke out, for sure it'd draw attention from somewhere.

As he approached, the men all went still, attentive, before deciding he didn't matter.

Idiots.

Leese stepped up in front of her, blocking the pushiest guy, forcing him back a step.

"Hey!"

"Excuse me." Insinuating himself between her and the big goon, Leese insulated her from trouble, then turned to face her. Catalina was probably a foot shorter than him, and even in the thick coat she seemed slim all over. She tipped back her head and stared up at him with big blue eyes that were both wary and defiant.

By silent agreement, she trusted him, when that was the very last thing she should have done. No wonder he'd been sent to her.

Leese hefted her bag—which weighed a ton—and maintaining the casual vibe, said, "This way," indicating where he'd been standing watch.

Without bothering to look at the other men, she drew a careful breath, braced herself and nodded in agreement.

Insane. The woman had no self-protection mechanism. She didn't know him from Adam, but was prepared to willy-nilly saunter off with him.

When he was assigned this case, not once had he expected it to be this easy. On the contrary. Everything he'd been told had led him to believe it would be a total pain in the ass to keep her safe.

She took two steps.

The closest goon said, "This is bullshit."

Pausing, Leese huffed out a breath. "Let it go."

"The hell I will."

Hearing the elevated voice, he turned just in time to dodge a thick fist. Still holding her bag, Leese landed a knee to the man's midsection, then flattened him with an elbow to the chin.

The guy's eyes rolled back and he collapsed like a rag doll, one leg bent awkwardly beneath him, his jaw slack.

Eyeing the remaining two, Leese popped his neck and waited. "Anyone else?"

Being wiser than they looked, they declined further violence.

As the downed man came around with a groan, Leese backed up with Catalina. "Get your friend out of the slush, before hypothermia sets in." It was so bitter cold it wouldn't take long for the elements to affect a body, especially when drenched in wet snow.

While Wayne remained hostile, the other man rushed forward to help his friend back to his feet. Tottering, he made his way to a curb, where he slumped, still unsteady.

There were no more smiles when Wayne said, "She owes me."

"How much?" Paying off the guy would be easier than debating it on such a bitter night, and more expedient than refusing them with his fists.

Wayne's eyes narrowed. "Not money."

"Ah, well, I can't even up with you, then. Guess you're out of luck."

Jaw grinding, Wayne glared at him. "I gave her a place to stay. I fed her. Bought her those boots and coat—"

"And you figured on getting paid how?"

Throughout it all, Catalina stayed behind him.

Wayne growled, "She knows what I expected."

Leaning around, tone apologetic, Catalina whispered, "Yeah, about that... I never planned to sleep with you, Wayne. I'm sorry. I promise I will repay you, I just can't right now. But I do have your address, so—"

"Fuck you," Wayne snarled.

Growing impatient, Leese said, "Apparently that's not happening." He set down the suitcase and pushed aside his open coat, showing the Glock in a belt holster at his side.

The men stared uneasily. Catalina sucked in a startled breath.

Ignoring those reactions, Leese looked at her boots, then lifted the collar of the coat, examining it. While they were decent protection against the elements, they weren't high-end items. Probably bought at a discount department store.

Definitely not worth Catalina prostituting herself.

He withdrew his wallet and pulled out a few hundreds. "This will have to suffice." He folded the money, walked up to Wayne and held it out.

After a ripe hesitation, Wayne took the money.

With a dose of menace, Leese warned, "Don't come after her again."

Wayne nodded, said something low to the uninjured man and the three of them retreated behind the tall buildings.

Leese felt Catalina retreating, as well.

Out of patience and feeling stern, he faced her. "Don't run."

Eyes huge, her face pale except for the pink of her cold nose, she swallowed hard. "You were sent to bring me home, weren't you?"

Body Armor, the agency where he worked, had sent him…
but his job was to keep her safe, period. "You don't have to be
afraid."

With a shake of her head, she back-stepped.

Leese saw it in her eyes; she would run. "Don't."

She whirled to flee and plowed headlong into Justice. The
impact was solid enough that she bounced back, her feet slid
out from under her on the icy ground and she landed flat in the
frozen snow. Given the way she wheezed, she'd knocked the
wind out of herself.

Leese knelt beside her. "Shh." He cupped the back of her
head. "Hold still." To Justice he said, "You were supposed to
wait at the car."

"I saw it was clear and wanted to hurry you along."

Justice was still learning patience. He was here today with
Leese to get a handle on the job. So far, he'd failed with flying
colors. "Carry her bag to the car. We'll be right there. And, Justice, stay sharp, *and stay with the car.*"

On his way past, Justice said to her, "Sorry about that, honey.
Didn't mean to startle you." He carried the bag as if it weighed
nothing, but then, Justice was a six-foot-five former heavyweight
MMA fighter made of solid muscle.

Drawing her into a sitting position and raising her arms over
her head, Leese said, "Take it easy. You're all right."

She sucked in a strained breath, coughed and wheezed again.

"Running into Justice is like hitting the side of a mountain.
Did you hurt anything?"

She got her breath back with a vengeance. "Who *are* you
people?"

Her hat had come loose and silky brown tangled around her
face. With very cold hands, Leese brushed it back. Gloves would
have been nice.

But gloves skewed his accuracy whenever he needed to draw
his weapon.

　　　　　　　　　　　　　　　　　　　LORI FOSTER

He never discounted that possibility—so no gloves.

"I'm a bodyguard with the Body Armor Agency. I was hired to keep you safe."

"Oh God." Elbows on her knees, she dropped her head forward and rocked in agitation.

Sitting in the snow was not his idea of fun. "You're okay?" Instinct had him rubbing her back. She didn't seem to mind.

"Yes." She lifted her head and pinned him in her gaze. "You don't look like any bodyguard I've ever seen."

"Seen a few, have you?"

"Too many. They're pretty obvious, but not you. You don't fit the mold at all." She studied his face. "How did you find me?"

Leese was unaware of any mold, but he also knew Body Armor was vastly different from most other agencies. "I was told you were in this general area. It's a small town. Newcomers draw attention."

"I was two towns over the last time *bodyguards* found me."

So others had been sent to protect her, but she'd deliberately lost them, then tried hiding again? Leese wasn't sure what was going on, but he had an objective, and he'd see it through. "I showed your photo around and tracked you here."

Her eyes narrowed. "Since when do bodyguards track people?"

Since clients paid a small fortune to make it happen. Balanced on the balls of his feet, Leese let his wrists rest over his knees. "I learned a lot of neat tricks," he explained.

"Like?"

So she wanted to have this whole conversation while exposed to the elements? Appeared so. "Like how to locate people." He stood and pulled her to her feet.

She strained away. "What are you doing?"

Her unmistakable panic helped him to rein in his impatience. "Your seat is probably wet by now. The back of your coat, too. You need to get somewhere warm and dry."

"Where?"

"Let's go to the car and we'll talk about it."

She balked. "So you're taking me home?"

That sounded like an accusation. Leese tried to ignore the cold. "Is that where you want to go?"

Her brows lifted. "Not really, no."

"Okay, then, want to clue me in?" *His* balls were starting to freeze.

Puzzled, she narrowed her eyes on him. "You weren't told to take me anywhere?"

"I've only spoken to my boss, and she said to keep you safe, period." Why did he feel like he might be missing the big picture here? "That's the beginning, middle and end."

Incredulous, she asked, "For how long?"

He shrugged. "My understanding is that it's pretty open-ended at this point." Given her reactions so far, he could see why those who cared about her assumed she'd need protection.

But to be sure, at the first opportunity he'd give Sahara a call and have her fess up all the facts. Sahara Silver, the new owner of Body Armor, did like to do things her own way—and it was never conventional.

Catalina kept her gaze locked with his while working out something in her mind—and suddenly she stiffened. "Oh my God."

"Problem?"

Her hair whipped around as she searched the area again.

Who was she looking for? "Catalina—"

On a heartfelt groan of despair, she gripped the front of his coat. "You've probably led him to me."

Leese didn't know who she meant, but he saw honest fear in her expression. "Let's get out of the area, somewhere safe." He noticed that she limped a little as he led her quickly to where Justice waited with the car. "We'll talk more once I know you're secure."

Justice sat behind the wheel of the black Lexus SUV, the engine running so the car would be warm.

Catalina balked again at the sight of him, then squared her shoulders and hastened her pace.

"You don't have to worry about Justice." Leese reached the SUV ahead of her and opened the back passenger door. "Colorful as he might be."

She said, "He's fine."

Right. Height and a brick build were enough to make Justice intimidating, but he also had black-as-sin eyes, and a dark Mohawk and goatee badly in need of a trim. His earliest fighting days had left him with a crooked nose from too many breaks, and a right ear thickened from too many hits.

Overall, despite his massive size and capability, Justice was easygoing and considerate—especially to pretty girls.

"Let's lose the wet coat, okay? You'll be more comfortable."

She bit her lip, then quickly stripped it off. Leese took it from her as she climbed in.

She was so skittish that he didn't trust her to stay put and he definitely didn't want her trying to hop out of a moving car. Still holding the door open, he said, "Scoot."

"What?" Catalina pushed back her hair and blinked at him in question.

Rather than explain again, Leese took the expedient measure of getting in next to her, forcing her to make room for him. He watched her rump as she quickly crawled across the seat, moving as far from him as she could get.

As he draped the coat over her lap, he told Justice, "Go," and to Catalina, "Buckle up."

"Where to?" Justice.

"Head for the highway." Because she hadn't done it yet, Leese reached around Catalina and buckled her seat belt, then again tucked the coat around her. "We'll go south."

She pressed back in her seat. "Where's my suitcase?"

"In back," Justice said, taking several peeks at her in the rear-view mirror.

She confirmed that by twisting around to look in the cargo area. When she saw the battered suitcase, she dropped back into her seat and closed her eyes. "Thank you."

"Welcome." Then to Leese, he asked, "We expecting more trouble?"

"I don't know yet."

"Yes," Catalina said, opening her big blue eyes to stare at him. "Expect it, because it's definitely coming..."

LORI FOSTER